Romantic Suspense

Danger. Passion. Drama.

Undercover Escape
Valerie Hansen

Hunted For The Holidays
Deena Alexander

MILLS & BOON

DID YOU PURCHASE THIS BOOK WITHOUT A COVER?

If you did, you should be aware it is **stolen property** as it was reported 'unsold and destroyed' by a retailer.
Neither the author nor the publisher has received any payment for this book.

UNDERCOVER ESCAPE
© 2024 by Valerie Whisenand
Philippine Copyright 2024
Australian Copyright 2024
New Zealand Copyright 2024

First Published 2024
First Australian Paperback Edition 2024
ISBN 978 1 038 93530 4

HUNTED FOR THE HOLIDAYS
© 2024 by Deena Pysarchuk
Philippine Copyright 2024
Australian Copyright 2024
New Zealand Copyright 2024

First Published 2024
First Australian Paperback Edition 2024
ISBN 978 1 038 93530 4

® and ™ (apart from those relating to FSC®) are trademarks of Harlequin Enterprises (Australia) Pty Limited or its corporate affiliates. Trademarks indicated with® are registered in Australia, New Zealand and in other countries.
Contact admin_legal@Harlequin.ca for details.

Except for use in any review, the reproduction or utilisation of this work in whole or in part in any form by any electronic, mechanical or other means, now known or hereafter invented, including xerography, photocopying and recording, or in any information storage or retrieval system, is forbidden without the permission of the publisher, Harlequin Mills & Boon.

This book is sold subject to the condition that it shall not, by way of trade or otherwise, be lent, resold, hired out or otherwise circulated without the prior consent of the publisher in any form or binding or cover other than that in which it is published and without a similar condition including this condition being imposed on the subsequent purchaser.

All rights reserved including the right of reproduction in whole or in part in any form. This edition is published in arrangement with Harlequin Books S.A..

This is a work of fiction. Names, characters, places, and incidents are either the product of the author's imagination or are used fictitiously, and any resemblance to actual persons, living or dead, business establishments, events, or locales is entirely coincidental.

MIX
Paper | Supporting responsible forestry
FSC® C001695
www.fsc.org

Published by
Harlequin Mills & Boon
An imprint of Harlequin Enterprises (Australia) Pty Limited (ABN 47 001 180 918), a subsidiary of HarperCollins Publishers Australia Pty Limited
(ABN 36 009 913 517)
Level 19, 201 Elizabeth Street
SYDNEY NSW 2000 AUSTRALIA

Cover art used by arrangement with Harlequin Books S.A.. All rights reserved.

Printed and bound in Australia by McPherson's Printing Group

Undercover Escape

Valerie Hansen

MILLS & BOON

Valerie Hansen was thirty when she awoke to the presence of the Lord in her life and turned to Jesus. She now lives in a renovated farmhouse on the breathtakingly beautiful Ozark Plateau of Arkansas and is privileged to share her personal faith by telling the stories of her heart for Love Inspired. Life doesn't get much better than that!

Books by Valerie Hansen

Love Inspired Suspense

Undercover Escape

Mountain Country K-9 Unit

Chasing Justice

Pacific Northwest K-9 Unit

Scent of Truth

Rocky Mountain K-9 Unit

Ready to Protect

Emergency Responders

Fatal Threat
Marked for Revenge
On the Run
Christmas Vendetta
Serial Threat

Visit the Author Profile page at LoveInspired.com for more titles.

Make no friendship with an angry man;
and with a furious man thou shalt not go:
Lest thou learn his ways, and get a snare to thy soul.
—*Proverbs* 22:24–25

With love to all the relatives and friends who have supported my writing and shared their specialized knowledge to make my books as true to life as possible. I could not have done it without you, my sweet human *Google-ish* minds and hearts.

Chapter One

Rain pelted the van's windshield. Professional dog trainer Hannah Lassiter shivered. Her stomach knotted. Her hands perspired on the steering wheel and she flexed her fingers. This was the first time she'd actually feared volunteering at the maximum security prison in St. Louis and for good reason. Today it began. There was no way to rationalize the plan she was about to set in motion, not now and probably not ever, yet she had to do it. She had to help Deuce Fleming escape. Her grandmother's life literally depended upon it.

An excited yip from the back of her van reminded her how she'd gotten into this mess. Rehabbing criminals and saving misunderstood dogs had seemed like the ideal way to use her unique skills with canines to serve the Lord and her fellow man. For the last year it had been a pleasant addition to her regular dog training business. But no more. By the time this day was over she, too, would be a wanted fugitive. The thought brought tears to her eyes.

She pulled herself together and feigned calm as she eased to a stop at the gates and rolled her window down a few inches to greet the armed guard. The waning storm gave the air a crisp tang and drops of rain pattered, some breaching the narrow opening. "Morning, John."

"Good morning, Ms. Lassiter." He peered into the van as the canine cargo began a frenzy of barking in response to his voice. "Got a new crop for us?"

"Some likely candidates," Hannah said. She knew better than to try to hurry the amiable guard despite the fact her nerves were firing so fast she could barely control movement and her mouth was too dry to swallow.

"It's a fine thing you're doing," the guard said with a smile. "A fine thing."

Her muttered "Thank you" almost stuck in her throat. "You should get in out of the rain."

He saluted by touching the dripping brim of his cap and backed away.

Fine thing, indeed, Hannah thought. To save her beloved grandma she had no choice but to betray friends and colleagues who had trusted her and sacrifice her successful professional career at the same time. There was no other option, no way to win. In the best-case scenario she would succeed in smuggling a dangerous prisoner out of there without any innocent by-standers getting hurt, including herself. Once she was outside the prison walls and far away from any influence from Deuce Fleming, she prayed she'd find some way to make amends.

After closing the window she proceeded onto the grounds. It was hard to breathe, hard to keep from shaking all over. She was a law-abiding citizen, not the criminal they were trying to make her into. She wanted to help people, not hurt them, and by saving innocent dogs from kill shelters she'd been doing the animals good, too.

Nevertheless, here she was. Caught. Trapped as surely as the guilty men behind bars at the state prison in Lyell, Missouri. They were there for a reason and she was heartsick to have been coerced into helping one of them escape.

Having spent the previous night in prayer, Hannah was

positive God understood and would forgive her. It wasn't Him she was going to have to convince of her innocence; it was the new prison warden and the state police. If they failed to see the goodness of her heart and the necessity of today's actions, she was going to end up in big trouble.

"Providing I live through the actual jailbreak," she muttered to herself. By afternoon she would know if the bold plan worked.

Smothering in guilt she sniffled. "And everyone else will know what I've done, too."

Masquerading as convicted killer Rafe McDowell, state trooper Gavin Arthur stayed in character 24/7. This was the toughest undercover assignment he'd ever accepted but he couldn't turn it down. Not when his partner, trooper Andy Fellows, lay in the hospital, fighting for his life after a shootout, and the man's abducted teenage daughter was still missing. Because all clues had led to Deuce Fleming's gang being responsible, here he was, sharing space in prison in the hopes of learning enough to rescue the girl and even the score.

Gavin/Rafe had been briefed well enough to know that Fleming had contacts both inside and outside the prison. Part of his task was to get close to Deuce and learn their identities without revealing that he was the source of that information leak. It wasn't going to be easy. Nothing involving cagey criminals ever was, which explained the need to work undercover. Only two men knew who he really was; his own superintendent and the recently promoted prison warden. Computer files had been created to provide an impressive criminal past and he'd let his beard grow enough to present a scruffy edge. Add to that the tattoos and scars from combat as an army ranger and he appeared to be a damaged, world-worn man who perfectly fit the role.

At present he was sitting in a folding chair in a room with seven other men, Deuce included, waiting for the outsider who was scheduled to teach a dog handling class to selected inmates. While several of the others had brought dogs already being trained and were tending to them, he and Deuce lounged in the chairs as if they had no cares. That, alone, disturbed Rafe. He was aware that Fleming was known as a cool customer but judging by the way the man was behaving, he was more than merely pretending. He truly was at ease.

Rafe crossed one ankle on his knee and folded his arms, making sure his biceps and tattoos were prominently displayed. Fleming met the alpha male challenge in his gaze and returned it with a sneer. "What're you lookin' at?"

Shrugging, Rafe remained nonchalant. "Me? Nothing, man. Just chilling. You got a beef with that?" He saw his quarry open his mouth to reply, then stop when the door swung back. Little wonder. The attractive brunette woman entering the room was impossible to ignore. She was clad in plain denim, boots, and was accompanied by a prison guard escort pushing a cart dolly containing several large kennel boxes and one smaller one. Made of tan plastic, each box had a metal door that was fastened with a small padlock.

Before Rafe could react, Deuce Fleming was on his feet and joining the young woman. He saw her stop dead and flash a tension-riddled smile. The telling reaction was so brief Rafe might have missed it if he hadn't been keeping such a close eye on his quarry. Prison warden Hotchkiss had expressed concern that Fleming had been allowed to join the dog rehab program under his predecessor, but with no proof of dishonesty he'd chosen to let the man continue with the classes. The new warden's goal was to make as few changes as possible to keep from alerting the convict or any of his allies to the undercover officer in their midst. So far, nothing Rafe did or didn't do had seemed to make a difference in Fleming's daily routines or in the behavior of the guards who were suspected of aiding and abetting him.

Rafe leaned forward in his chair and studied the interplay

between Fleming and the dog trainer. Although she did her best to hide her feelings, he wasn't fooled. The woman was as nervous as a kitten surrounded by a pack of slavering coyotes. He supposed some of her unease might be due to the place where she was working, but that conclusion didn't fully satisfy. He'd seen enough of her class videos during briefings to know that Hannah Lassiter was normally calm and self-assured while guiding convicts and their assigned dogs through the training process. And she was good at her job. So why the change in demeanor today?

Getting slowly to his feet, Rafe sauntered over to where Fleming was speaking aside to Hannah and offered his right hand to her. "I'm Rafe McDowell. Your new student."

Pausing, poised to be greeted, he was disappointed when the trainer ignored his friendly gesture. Something was definitely wrong. He stepped back several paces to observe her interactions, particularly with Fleming. The con was practically smirking.

Rafe shoved his hands into the pockets of his orange jumpsuit, lounged against the edge of the only table in the room and heard Fleming snort derisively before laughing. The others in the room kept silent as if attempting to keep the peace. A brief glance at the young woman, however, spoke volumes. Her fair skin had paled, her eyes were brimming and there was a tremor in her graceful hands.

Whispering, she said, "I'm ready."

"Shut it," Deuce snapped.

Eyes downcast, Hannah sniffled and swiped at her damp cheeks. Her expression reminded Rafe of a prey animal facing certain capture or death. The poor woman was terrified.

Edging closer by pretending to peer into one of the kennel boxes, Rafe heard the hardened criminal say, "See that you remember your job, Red Riding Hood."

A tear trickled down Hannah's cheek as Rafe made the apparent connection. If Hannah Lassiter was Red Riding Hood,

Deuce Fleming was the personification of the Big Bad Wolf and nothing, no one, stood between the two of them but him.

Rafe's main disadvantage, as he saw it, was his place on the side of the criminal element while working undercover. There was no logical way to convince the frightened woman that he was one of the good guys when everything about his persona had been tailored to project the opposite.

Moreover, he reasoned, there was a slight chance the apparently innocent dog trainer was one of Fleming's people. In spite of her uneasiness it was possible she would choose the wrong side if given a chance. He huffed, remembering how close he'd come to making that mistake as a teen and how his friends had rebuffed him after he'd refused to take part in their idea of fun—rampant vandalism and physical violence. Most of them had gone to jail for their crimes.

That memory amused Rafe when he contrasted it to his current assignment. They should see him now.

Hannah could taste acrid remnants of the coffee and toast she'd eaten shortly before heading to class.

Nothing but the threat to someone she dearly loved would have made her agree to the plot she was involved in. The sweet face of her grandmother, Lucy, arose in her memory and nearly broke her. Fleming's cohorts on the outside had been stalking the only remaining member of Hannah's family and had sent her photos to prove it, while nondescript vehicles had been parking outside the house she shared with Gram and were following them everywhere, even to church.

This morning, Gram was safe in the church fellowship hall making lap quilts for a rest home with members of her sewing club, unaware of what might happen later. If Fleming wasn't delivered to a predetermined rendezvous site, his men were supposed to kidnap Gram and hold her until he was free. There was no alternative. No fail-safe plan. It was all or nothing, success or failure.

Silently, fervently, Hannah reached out to God. There were no flowery words to her prayer, no memorized verses, nothing. It was from her heart to the heart of her Savior and so powerful she couldn't help but be strengthened.

She squared her shoulders, pulled leashes from her tote and began to deliver her well-rehearsed opening speech. "Several of you are getting new assignments this morning. I'm going to demonstrate the proper way to handle a dog without hurting it before we work with the new animals I've brought. Think of them as your canine counterparts. They were jailed and facing execution for simply existing."

"Yeah, they're innocent, like us," Deuce commented, bringing laughter from all the others except Rafe.

"Only one of them has a history of biting and I've been working with him on my own. He was mostly frightened. Back a scared animal into a corner and if he can't run, he'll defend himself in any way he can."

"Humph. I get that, too."

As she bent to unlatch the first of the kennel boxes Hannah whispered, "Understood."

Across the room, Rafe raised his eyebrows and gave the outspoken convict a nod. His task was to get closer to Fleming, not alienate him, so he figured it was best to seem to agree. With the exception of Sam Peabody, an older prisoner who was already handling a smaller dog, everyone in the room deferred to Fleming. The older man, however, was giving him smug, knowing looks that bothered Rafe. It was as if Sam and Deuce were working together on something.

That put Sam in Rafe's suspect file. Several prison guards were already listed, including the one at the door right now, but other than a few minor incidents in the exercise yard, Deuce hadn't paid undue attention to anyone else. Oh, he had a group of followers. Most cons chose sides for their own protection.

But in Fleming's case the men who supported him by their presence weren't forceful types, they were lackeys.

Close observation revealed a tremor in the trainer's hands as she unlatched the largest cage, reached in to clip on a lead and coaxed a dog to step out. It was the largest German shepherd Rafe had ever seen, but its demeanor was that of a whipped cur.

The moment the trainer touched the coarse fur her own shaking ceased and she spoke gently. "It's okay, boy. You're okay. That's it. Take it easy."

Behind her, Deuce snorted derisively. "I hope you're not planning to give me that coward."

"If you will recall," Hannah said, "the pit bull you worked with the last time was cautious at first, too."

"Yeah, but you said he was just abused. He didn't turn into a sniveling mutt like that one is."

Rafe stepped forward. "I'll take him."

"I make those decisions, Mr..." She consulted the forms the guard had handed her. "Mr. McDowell. But I will keep your request in mind."

Hands spread wide, palms up, Rafe shrugged. "Fine. No sweat." As he observed the quaking canine it occurred to him that the behavior of this dog and the pretty trainer were similar and he wondered if their reasons for fear were also alike. Granted, some individuals were born with a shy nature. That was possible for the dog. But the woman was different. He'd studied videos of her previous classes and if he didn't know it was the same trainer he might wonder if she'd been replaced. Not only was her voice different, so was her body language.

His heart went out to her. Scowling, he watched Deuce posturing and bragging while the other cons stood back. One looked pleased, one frowned, and others did their best to fade into the background as though they were afraid to be noticed.

The trainer caught Rafe's glance and he allowed eye contact to continue for long seconds. Of course she'd be sizing him up because they hadn't met before. That made perfect sense. What was disquieting was the unspoken plea for help he thought he detected in her glance.

Then she bent over the paperwork, made a note in a margin and straightened with the shepherd on his leash at her side. "We will be approaching you, Mr. McDowell. I want you to stand still and avoid looking at Thor. Let him sniff you and don't back away but don't reach for him, either. This introduction has to be on his terms. Understand?"

Rafe nodded. "Yes, ma'am."

He did as Hannah had instructed, and more. It wasn't hard to feel empathy for the beautiful, shy animal. When he'd accepted this assignment he'd had no idea it would include a dog training class. Being there was the icing on the cake as far as he was concerned. Animals had made his troubled teen years bearable and he'd always had a special affinity for the downtrodden. Or in this case, the literal underdog.

As soon as he got the chance he intended to ask about Thor's history, assuming Hannah knew it. A large male like this one was unlikely to have been attacked by another canine. Chances were, Thor's fear was due to interactions with humans and Rafe intended to show him that not all men were bad.

Hannah had circled Rafe twice, slowly and purposefully, when she said, "You may sit in that chair over there now, Mr. McDowell. Hands in your lap. Still no eye contact."

Instead of turning toward the chair and therefore taking his eyes off Deuce, Rafe backed up. When his knees touched the edge of the seat he sat down. He didn't like the way the outspoken prisoner was leering at Hannah and he sure didn't like the way he was inching toward Thor. A man like Fleming was unpredictable and purposely cruel whenever he thought he could get away with it.

Air in the training room practically crackled with tension. Thor was panting but seemed a bit more relaxed and Hannah was concentrating so fully on the dog she seemed unaware of the increasing human threat. But Rafe knew. His instincts saw more than his eyes could. And he wasn't the only one. The guard at the door had rested the heel of his hand on his holstered gun and the other convicts, even Sam, were inching away.

Hannah and Thor passed in front of Rafe's chair and began to turn to the left. The moment her back was to him, Deuce lunged for her and the German shepherd.

Rafe rocketed off the chair, managed to block the attack with his shoulder and both men hit the floor. What he should have done, he realized belatedly, was provide a distraction rather than go head-to-head with Fleming. Instinct had taken over when he'd put himself between the other man and the apparently innocent woman, leaving him wondering how he was going to spin his actions to appear to be in Fleming's favor.

Strength-wise he knew he could flatten anybody in the room, including the apparently nervous guard if need be. Thoughts of his wounded partner and the man's missing daughter, Kristy, tempered his actions enough to cause him to pull his punches when what he wanted to do was hit hard enough to force a confession. Fleming and his group had already been proven guilty of weapons and drug smuggling. It was only a small step from that to the human trafficking they were now suspected of masterminding.

As far as Rafe was concerned, the only crime worse than that was cold-blooded murder. Nevertheless, he shouted, "Hey, cool it. We're both on the same side here."

Chapter Two

Jumping aside, Hannah barely evaded Fleming's grasp. Thor spun around so fast he tangled her legs in the leather leash and she almost ended up on the hard floor with the grappling convicts.

The remaining kenneled dog barked raucously, joined by the canines in the room, while men cheered the combatants. George, the guard, drew his gun, staying at the door and fumbling for the radio clipped to his shoulder.

Huddled against the farthest wall with Thor, Hannah could barely catch her breath. This was not what was supposed to happen. Not even close. So now what? How could she hope to restore order before more prison guards arrived to disperse her students and ruin any efforts to carry out the escape plan?

Close beside her Thor began to growl. Although Hannah could feel him shaking she had no doubt he was being protective because his posture had changed. His chest was thrust forward as he strained against his collar. A lip began to curl, revealing huge white canine teeth ready for battle.

She wrapped extra leash length around her hand, double grabbed and shouted, "Enough!"

At that moment, Thor barked twice. There was enough

menace in the resonating sound to draw everyone's attention, even that of the men wrestling on the floor. They froze. Time seemed to stand still. Hannah didn't relax her hold on the surprisingly protective shepherd, but she did nod to the class. "Chairs. Now. Everybody."

She'd thought about adding a threat to her command before she saw how unnecessary that was going to be. All eyes remained glued to the bristling, snarling German shepherd and the men were moving slowly, deliberately, to obey.

Because she was unaware of Thor's background or previous training, Hannah proceeded with caution. Saying "Good boy" quietly she eased up on the taut leash. The result was positive. Thor stopped snarling and relaxed a little, although his deep growl continued. That was fine with her, especially considering how close her whole class had been to jumping into the two-man melee.

"Fleming, over there," Hannah said, pointing by tilting her head since she still needed both hands on the leash, just in case. "McDowell, to my right. Now."

It was easy to tell the mood of Deuce Fleming. His face was red, nostrils flared, eyes narrowed. In short, he looked ready to tear the other man's head off. McDowell, on the other hand, seemed relieved. He edged in the direction she'd indicated while keeping a table between himself and Fleming. Smart move, she thought, stifling the urge to admire his strategy. An intelligent animal would act the same way because instinct would warn about keeping distance from an enemy.

Distance was exactly what she craved, Hannah reminded herself. But first she had to break the law. That idea was so foreign to her it was making her feel physically ill. Of all the difficult tasks she'd ever faced, this was the worst.

Heart and mind warring with each other, she slowly approached Rafe. There was something about him that instinctively reached out to her. The rest of the room faded into the background when she once again met his gaze.

Normally, Hannah took weeks to decide which dogs belonged with which prisoners, and some never did make the grade, humans or animals. In this instance, however, she sensed something in Rafe McDowell that was missing in the others. The quality that set him apart didn't have a name, nor did it need one. She simply knew he was the right man to work with Thor.

Stopping directly in front of him she laid a calming hand on the dog's broad head and spoke softly, gently. "It's okay, Thor. This one is okay. See?" She offered her right hand and Rafe shook it.

Although Thor was still trembling he stopped growling. Hannah kept hold of Rafe's hand and drew it closer to the dog's nose so he could sniff it. To her surprise, not only did the shepherd accept the introduction, Rafe began to smile. There was a slight sideways movement of Thor's tail, too.

Hannah sighed with relief. "I see I was right."

From across the room, Deuce snorted in derision. Hannah never took her eyes off Rafe, trusting the guard to continue to enforce order. She could see Thor begin to relax more as his new training partner reached forward on his own and made the first touch.

Thor did duck slightly, but he didn't give ground. Rafe sought Hannah's approval with an arch of his eyebrows.

"Yes," she said, "you can keep petting him. Just be ready to stop if he shows any sign of fear or aggression."

Deuce laughed, "Yeah, man. Go for it. We'd love to see him tear your arm off."

Instead of acknowledging the heckler, Hannah purposefully handed Rafe the leash right in front of the shepherd so there would be no doubt. "He's very intelligent," she said. "He sees that I'm giving him to you. Stand up and accept him, then shorten the slack in the lead to bring him to your left side and tell him to heel."

She didn't know why it surprised her to see Rafe handling

the big dog like a pro. Some people had a natural affinity for animals and some didn't. Commands could be taught. Instinct could not. Her greatest fear, besides the planned escape, was that she'd have to leave Thor behind with a stranger. Now that she'd chosen McDowell as his new trainer, a heavy weight lifted from her conscience.

A smaller terrier she'd also brought was soon assigned to a veteran prisoner who had worked with her dogs before, then one by one she let the prisoners demonstrate the commands they had taught their respective resident dogs since her last visit. And, one by one, they were excused to go back to their cells, as usual, until only she, Deuce, Rafe and the guard, were left.

Deuce's demeanor changed once the others were gone. "Get rid of him, too," the convict ordered, gesturing at Rafe as if he was of little concern.

Hannah resisted. "I need to set some ground rules first. He's too new to just be turned loose with Thor."

"What do you care?" Deuce said, sneering. "This is your last day."

Hannah cringed. Shot a quick glance at Rafe. Saw Thor react to the fear she felt and take a step forward. The shortened leash restricted him.

"I thought we were going to keep this just between us," she whispered hoarsely.

"Him?" Deuce laughed and pointedly eyed the prisoner. "I picture this guy getting shot trying to escape. And that useless mutt, too."

"No!" She was adamant. "You promised me nobody would get hurt."

"That was then. This is now. You're the one who let a stranger stick around after I told you to send him away. If anything bad happens it'll be your fault." He addressed the guard. "Are we all set, George?"

"Yeah, but we might need that guy's help lifting the box

into her van once you're inside it. That's the only way we'll get you out."

Hannah watched flickers of anger in the convict's expression. Thankfully, he opted to be sensible.

"Fine. We bring him along as far as the loading dock. After that, he's your problem. Got it?"

"It'll be my pleasure to shoot an escaping con," the guard said, smiling. "Now climb into that dog crate and let's get this over with."

As Hannah fastened the lock behind Deuce Fleming and made sure the wire grid of the door was hidden behind the smaller crate; she didn't look at Rafe or Thor. All she could hope for at this point was that he would protect himself and somehow help the innocent dog, too.

It wasn't fair. None of this was fair. She was about to sacrifice her career and maybe her own life because she loved her grandmother, and had been able to see no other way out of the trap Fleming had set for her. She'd made the mistake of mentioning a few personal details in class and the criminals associated with him on the outside were using that information to force her to break the law.

More than once she'd tried to approach the new warden for a private meeting and had been rebuffed. The only conclusion she could come to was that Hotchkiss, too, was part of the broad criminal organization that was working with Fleming. Therefore, she had no choice but to proceed.

Here she was. About to take an irreversible step toward her own destruction. It was like stepping onto railroad tracks, hearing the warning bells and knowing a speeding train was approaching, yet being unable to lift her feet and step aside in time. She was a fatal accident in the making and there was no feasible escape.

Rafe tagged along without being told. He found it difficult to believe Hannah Lassiter was aiding and abetting a criminal even though that was how things looked. If she had shown the slightest affection for Fleming, maybe he could understand it, but she'd seemed to loathe him as well as fear him. So why was she about to smuggle him out of Lyell?

Thor paced Rafe's strides perfectly, never taking his focus off the cart with the plastic kennel boxes and the young woman helping to push from behind it. A second guard offered to help and was rejected, meaning that he was probably one of the honest ones. So far, Rafe's list of insiders was short and until he could get a message to the warden there was nothing he could do to stop the escape other than start shouting about it. Chances were, if he tried that, he'd be the one who was shot and Deuce would still get away in the confusion.

They finally reached a warehouse-looking area and the guard who had guided them there signaled for a cohort to open a garage door. Motors whirred. The door rose revealing the top of a white van level with the floor of the loading dock. Light rain was still falling but it looked as if the deluge was past.

Hannah gasped. "That's no good. Why did you bring it back here? Look at it. We can't load it like that."

Rafe considered making a run for it while the others were distracted, but that would have meant abandoning the woman and letting Fleming get away. The way he saw the situation, his only viable choice was to try to talk his way into the van with the others.

"I can move it," Rafe said. "Or the woman can, if you're not afraid she'll drive off without you."

Fleming made a grumbling noise from inside the box. His orders were muffled but clear enough. "All right. George, keep her with you and let him take care of the van. If he tries anything funny, shoot *her*."

Rafe took the chance of meeting Hannah's gaze as he said, "I'll just park it off to the side, okay?"

A muttered, "Yeah," came from the box.

At the last instant, Rafe decided to keep Thor with him.

He couldn't abandon the dog in the warehouse. If he wasn't presumed dangerous and shot on the spot he'd be hauled off to a shelter somewhere and probably euthanized because there would be no Hannah Lassiter to rescue him. Before the guard could object he was down the concrete stairs, splashing through puddles and climbing into the van with Thor. If the dog had refused to get in, he would have had to force him, but that wasn't a problem. Thor beat him to the seat and moved over to make room as if he'd done it hundreds of times.

Rafe checked the mirrors, inched the van out, backed it into position for ease of loading from the ground and stopped it, engine idling.

By the time he climbed out, George and Hannah were opening the rear doors. They loaded the smaller box without him.

"All right, McDowell," the guard called. "Get over here and give us a hand. We ain't got all day."

"Yeah, yeah." As he rounded the van he prayed that the woman wouldn't notice he'd left Thor in the front seat or say something that might alert the guard. Right now, all he wanted to do was get the crate containing Fleming loaded and secured.

The guard was on the right, Rafe on the left, and Hannah in the rear directing placement. When she was satisfied all was well, she closed the rear doors, then headed for the driver's seat.

Rafe waited, feigning calm while every muscle in his body was screaming for action.

The instant he heard the driver's door slam he tackled the crooked guard hard enough to knock him down, leaped over the prone body and sprinted for the passenger side.

He was half in, half out, when Hannah said, "You're not supposed to be here. Get out!"

"No. Go, go, go," Rafe shouted, gesturing ahead wildly.

Thor gave his face a slurp and moved over to sit on the center console and make room. Momentum of the accelerating van finished slamming the door.

In the side mirror Rafe saw the crooked guard getting to his feet. "Keep going and act natural when we get to the gate," he shouted at Hannah. "George won't dare report my escape. That would stop Fleming, too." He donned a black jacket and ball cap she'd brought along, presumably to disguise Deuce Fleming, then fastened his seatbelt.

She stared at him, incredulous. "You can't do this."

"Looks like I am doing it."

"You're ruining everything. Please, please jump out before we get to the gate."

"Not happening, lady. You heard what they planned to do to me once you were gone."

"They meant it?"

Rafe huffed. "You've got a lot to learn about criminals, Hannah, especially hardcore ones like you're helping to escape. They don't make threats unless they're ready to carry them out."

As he watched, her eyes filled, tears threatening to spill out. She blinked rapidly, then nodded. "That's what I'm afraid of."

Chapter Three

Hannah's fears of what she'd say when they stopped at the prison gate were for nothing. The friendly guard waved her through instead of questioning why she'd managed to pick up a passenger. She felt like screaming. How had this horrible day become so much worse? Even if she was able to explain the coercion behind her initial involvement, there was no way she could hope to excuse helping the second prisoner.

It had occurred to her to find her grandmother, make sure she was safe, then drive to the nearest police station. The trouble was, since Fleming had so many friends inside the prison, what was to say he wasn't just as involved with the local cops on the outside?

Plus, she now had another escapee on her hands. "I'll stop at the next corner and let you out," she told him. The man beside her didn't comment. She slowed, then stopped. "Okay. Get out. Go. Run for it."

"Nope."

"You aren't even supposed to *be* here." Her tone rose. "Get out of my van."

"Not happening," Rafe said. Not only was he refusing to listen to her, he was actually starting to smile.

"I won't be responsible for what Fleming's buddies do to you when they see you messing with their boss."

"You're not actually planning to deliver him to his gang, are you? It's hard for me to believe somebody like you would help a known felon break out of jail."

Hannah set her jaw, her hands fisting the wheel, her neck and shoulders so tense her head was pounding.

"Look, mister, this is not funny. I have to take him to them as promised or…"

"Or what?"

She chewed on her lower lip. "None of your business. Just go away. I won't tell the authorities where I dropped you or which way you went. I promise."

"Suppose I stick around instead, me and my pal, Thor. It looks to us like you need some backup."

"Hah! The dog, maybe. A convict like you, not so much. What was your crime, anyway?"

"Being in the wrong place at the wrong time," Rafe said.

Hannah leaned past Thor and made a face at him. "Listen, you're making a bad situation much worse for me. The best way to help is to vanish." It amazed her when he chuckled so she added, "I'm being serious here."

"I'm sure you are, but you're in way over your head, lady."

A voice from the rear of the van echoed. "Hey, you locked me in. Get back here and open this door."

Hannah saw Rafe arch his eyebrows. Her response was a silent nod of her head.

Rattling and banging and muttered cursing echoed inside the van as Deuce battered the metal grid door of the kennel box. Hannah knew he might spring it open if he continued so she sought to calm him. "Take it easy, Fleming. I told you I'd get you out and I have. Patience, okay?"

"You…"

"Yeah, yeah. You don't impress me with foul language. I've heard all that before."

Thor had begun to growl, obviously sensing her unrest and the mood of the man trapped inside the kennel box. Hannah didn't try to stop the shepherd when he turned a tight circle and made his way to the rear cargo area. While she was driving she could only watch in her rearview mirror but that was enough to see the big dog zero in on the largest crate and put his face close to the metal grid. The effect was immediate silence.

Rafe smiled over at her. "See? I told you we'd be useful."

"And I told you the dog was all I needed. That's still true."

The spread of the man's grin wasn't menacing the way Hannah had assumed it would be. Could he be the answer to her prayers to be rescued from this dilemma? That notion was difficult to accept, yet it was beginning to look like the only possibility around.

She sighed deeply. Gram would sense whether that was true and, remembering past experience, would probably give Rafe the benefit of the doubt. Hannah wasn't ready to be so accepting. Not nearly.

Continuing to drive away from the prison she asked, "What's your story? You never said."

"No, I didn't."

Hannah waited. The only reply she got came from the locked box in the rear of the van. "He's in for murder."

That was not quite the way Rafe would have presented his backstory, but it followed the false criminal record his superiors had set up so he had to go with it. Up to a point.

"I was framed."

Deuce laughed until Thor's single bark silenced him.

"Like the majority of the prison population claims. Care to enlighten me?"

"No, but if I don't I suppose your other passenger will. It all started when I got involved with the wrong people."

"And?"

"And there was a killing nearby. My so-called buddies pinned it on me."

"Ri-i-i-ght." She drew the word out.

Rafe chuckled. "Now you sound like the prosecutor."

"Well, you were convicted."

Crossing his arms he struck a macho pose. "Rotten lawyer."

Her brief chuckle seemed out of place so he studied her. Was she acting or was she actually this functional in the company of one real murderer and a man she believed was also guilty, namely him? Despite his law enforcement training Rafe wasn't sure. It was clear that the pretty dog trainer was nervous. Anybody except a sociopath would be shaken by this untenable situation.

He changed the subject. "Where are we going?"

"A drop-off point. I suggest you leave us before we arrive if you know what's good for you."

"Like I said, I tend to make bad choices. Maybe you're one of them."

"Thanks heaps."

"You're welcome. What happens to you after you turn our passenger over to his friends? Have you given that any thought?"

"Of course."

"So?"

He saw her try to suppress a shiver. "So, it's none of your business."

But it was, wasn't it? Rafe didn't believe for a second that he'd wound up involved in this jailbreak by accident. His desire—his prayer—was always to be given the chance to right wrongs, to be in the right place to benefit someone in need. As far as he could see, this woman needed his help, and more. Unfortunately, as long as she continued to aid and abet Deuce Fleming there was no way he dared reveal his true identity. Therefore, he'd bide his time and roll with the punches, so to speak, although he had high hopes he wouldn't have to risk his life more than he already was.

Yes, he wanted to be a hero. No, he did not want posthumous medals. That was the tightrope he found himself walking. It wasn't a good sign that he found the dog trainer attractive. Poisonous snakes were also beautiful.

Hannah was fighting herself. No matter how much she resisted liking Rafe McDowell, she found her reactions to him warming. There was an unidentifiable quality about him that kept insisting he was a good man. Was it possible that he actually was innocent?

Past experience said, *no.* Her feelings, however, contradicted sensible conclusions. *Am I losing it?* she asked herself. How was it possible to actually begin to like a convicted murderer? Yes, the Bible told believers to forgive everyone, but that didn't mean a person should trust everybody. Discernment had to figure in there somewhere. Statistically, somebody who had taken a life once was more likely to do it again.

Which brought her thoughts right back to Fleming and his friends on the outside. There was no doubt that that man was dangerous. He'd proved it by his past actions and his cohorts had added plenty of emphasis when they'd sent her the jail-break instructions and those candid photos of her grandmother Lucy's home and habits. They knew exactly who Gram was and how much she meant to Hannah. And they knew how to get what they wanted. She didn't doubt for a second that they would do exactly what they'd threatened if she didn't play along.

Hannah startled when Rafe leaned closer, but since she was driving there was no way to get away from him. When he began to whisper she had to strain to hear his words.

"What happens when he doesn't need you anymore?"

"What?" Her brow furrowed.

"Think about it. You're taking him to his men, right?"

"Yes." Her jaw clenched.

"They won't want anybody to know who they are or where contact was made. What's the easiest way to guarantee that?"

Trying to swallow she found it almost impossible. Her palms were wet, her throat dry and every nerve in her body firing wildly. So much of her concern had focused on Gram she hadn't stopped to consider threats to herself. Would they? Could they? The answer was a flat "*yes*."

Blinking back tears of frustration she glanced at Rafe. His smile was gone, his dark eyes piercing, his expression grave. Once more he whispered to her. "Why did you let yourself be dragged into this in the first place?"

"It's complicated."

"It would have to be." Easing back into his seat he paused before he asked, "Tell me about your family. Parents? Siblings? A husband, maybe?"

"Just—just my grandmother. She's all I have."

"I see." He crossed his arms again and seemed to be thinking.

Hannah made an abrupt turn and heard cursing from the rear of the van. Deuce Fleming was not a happy camper. But what could she do? How could she save herself and Gram, and while she was at it, an innocent dog and a strangely considerate convict?

"Is your grandmother well?" Rafe asked in a low voice.

"Yes. At least I hope so." Admitting that was akin to a confession and although Hannah regretted saying too much, she was also relieved. Carrying the burden of being the only one aware of the threat had weighed heavily.

"Understood," he said.

Did he really understand? Or was he playing her for a fool, too, same as Fleming had? That was more likely than not. Too bad she wasn't in a position to be picky about allies.

"Suppose we unloaded early?"

Hannah shook her head. "We can't. I told you it was complicated."

From the rear, Deuce made his displeasure evident again. "Hey. Pull over and unlock this stupid crate. I'm gettin' cramps in my legs."

A quick glance showed the arch of Rafe's eyebrows. "You could drop off your cargo early."

She shook her head. "No. Not happening. I gave him my word. I never lie."

"Humph. What makes you think everybody is as truthful as you are?"

"What choice do I have?" She pressed her lips into a thin line. "And while we're at it, when are you bailing out? I can't have you with me when my delivery is made or they'll think I double-crossed them."

"Who you double-crossing?" Deuce shouted. He began to rock the plastic crate from side to side. Hoping to distract him, Hannah took the next corner fast.

The crate slid across the van, then bumped into the side wall and landed on its side. Thor returned to the front, frightened, and tried to squeeze between Hannah and Rafe. Deuce shouted. "Hey, watch it."

When she looked over to see that Rafe was all right she noticed him concentrating on the side mirror. He turned to her with concern. "Faster. Now."

"Why? What…?"

"We're being followed."

"Are you sure?" Even as she asked it, she knew the answer. The expression on the man's face left no doubt. "Is it the police?"

"I wish." Rafe undid his seatbelt and pushed past Thor to enter the rear of the careening van.

Hannah was frantic. She didn't want anybody to get hurt,

not even the cruel man who had threatened her tiny family. Driving erratically was bound to cause injury, perhaps to innocent people. However, if she stopped, whoever was following them could get the upper hand.

"I'm almost to the rendezvous point," she shouted at Rafe.

He had one hand braced on the side of the van, the other reaching toward the huge crate. As she watched, he pushed off the wall and landed atop the crate as if grappling with it.

"What are you doing?" Hannah yelled. "Don't let him out."

"Too late. The door sprang when the crate rolled."

Before she could comment she saw the shadow of a second large male body rising from the floor. Fleming was loose. She'd lost her only advantage.

One of them swung a punch, she couldn't tell which. It connected with a sickening cracking sound. The second man grabbed for the aggressor and they went down again, out of Hannah's sight.

Next to her, Thor had assumed the passenger seat and was watching the fight without making any effort to participate. Hannah supposed that was for the best, given the careening van and the shepherd's lack of professional training.

Wet fallen leaves were piled along the curbs. Hannah wasn't about to slow down enough to give either convict the chance to overpower her so she made the last turn into the parking lot of a strip mall on two wheels, sliding on the leaves and slightly missing the actual entrance. Two of her tires bounced over a curb. The rear doors banged open. One of the combatants was slammed into a side wall and barely missed being ejected.

Hannah saw him make a grab for the other man and miss. She braked hard, hoping momentum would keep either from falling out. It worked for her ally in the black jacket and ball cap. Deuce disappeared through the opening.

Following closely, an SUV swerved to miss the prone body, then slowed to a stop behind her van. Men jumped out both sides and began to gather around Fleming. She could tell they were concerned for him because they ignored the idling van for a few brief moments.

Crawling toward her on the floor, Rafe shouted, "Keep going."

"We didn't kill him, did we?"

"He's still moving, if that's what you mean. Now, drive."

"No. I have to tell them it was an accident. He was fighting and fell out."

"Best thing that could have happened," Rafe countered. He regained the passenger seat, shoving Thor aside to make room.

"Was that Fleming's gang? I need to explain."

"Really?" Rafe ducked as loud booms echoed and glass in the passenger side window shattered.

They were being shot at! She slammed her foot down on the accelerator. Tires screamed seeking traction. Fishtailing, the van slid sideways just in time to head into the drive for the exit and smoothly merge with passing traffic as if she actually knew how to drive defensively.

Seething with anger and trembling all the way to her core, she covered the next two blocks before she chanced speaking to Rafe. "You've ruined *everything*."

"Hey, I got rid of Fleming for you."

Her fists whitened on the wheel and she could barely breathe when she said, "You may have just killed my Gram."

Chapter Four

Reaching across, Rafe grabbed for the steering wheel. "Stop the van. We need to talk."

Hannah resisted, going so far as to pound his fingers with her fist. "Let go. You'll wreck us."

Surprised by her resistance he backed off, rubbing his hand. "Okay, okay." Because he'd been watching the road behind he was certain they'd escaped whoever had been following. "Look, I'm just trying to help you out here. Pull yourself together and tell me what's really going on."

"Why should I do that? Why should I trust you?"

That was an excellent question. All he had to do was tell her the truth and she'd know she could trust him, assuming she believed his wild story. Yeah, assuming he also bought hers, he added to himself.

"I could ask you the same thing," Rafe drawled, working to appear calmer than he felt. "You just aided and abetted a prison escape. You're in big trouble."

"Don't I know it."

"Then tell me why." He paused a few beats before adding, "I'm not like Fleming. You know I'm not."

"If I've learned one thing by volunteering at Lyell it's what good liars people can be." She scowled at him for an instant. "Even the ones in uniform."

"Most of the guards are honest."

"And you know that how?"

"Instinct," he explained. "I'm a fair judge of people."

"I wish I could say the same," Hannah countered. She eased the van to the curb and left the engine running. Something in her expression told Rafe that she was close to capitulating so he waited, feigning patience.

When she just sat there staring at him he chanced a slight smile before he said, "Look, you're going to be hunted down by the authorities as soon as they realize Fleming is gone. If I knew more details, I could be a witness that you acted under duress. Get you off with probation, maybe. What have you got to lose?"

"Why would you help me?"

He shrugged. "To even the odds against you? To get back at a lowlife like Fleming? To stick up for a woman who loves dogs and rescues them the way you do? Take your pick."

Hannah's lower lip began to tremble. "I do need help. I just…"

"You just didn't expect to get it from somebody like me, right? Don't make the mistake of waiting for the motorboat when God sends a canoe. They both float."

"God?"

"Sure. You don't think He can show up in a prison? Look at the apostle Paul."

A lopsided grin lifted one corner of her mouth. "You do a good imitation of a believer."

"Who says I'm faking? Don't you know you're not supposed to judge?"

By this time Hannah was slowly shaking her head, obviously mulling over the apparent change in his persona. Finally, she sagged back in the driver's seat. "Okay. I'm not saying I trust you, but I do need help."

"I'm listening."

"The people who wanted Fleming to escape have been following and photographing my grandmother. They know our every move. I saw the pictures. If I don't show up at the rendezvous point with him when I'm supposed to, they'll kidnap Gram."

"They don't already have her?"

Hannah paled. "I don't think so. I hope not. I mean, she was going to a meeting of her quilting group at church this morning. I phoned her after she got there to make sure she was safe and to tell her I wouldn't be home at the usual time. I didn't want her to go looking for me if I was late. She tends to be overly protective."

"Sounds like you need protecting." Rafe glanced at the clock on the dashboard display. "Would she still be there?"

"Yes. If we hurry. They usually share a potluck lunch after they quilt."

"Okay," Rafe said. "Close the cargo doors and we'll head for the church."

"You could do that for me."

He grinned over at her. "If you're afraid I'll steal your van, pull the keys. I'm not getting out so you can drive away without me. Remember, you're going to need me if kidnappers are waiting for your granny."

"Trust goes both ways," Hannah told him.

Chuckling, Rafe was nodding. "Oh, I trust you, lady. I just know what I might do if I were you. Go secure those back doors and let's get this show on the road."

It didn't surprise him one bit when Hannah fisted the car keys before climbing out. In her shoes he'd have done exactly the same thing.

The sanctuary of the community church had been built of native stone, then added to as different denominations came and went. Sunday School rooms extended one arm of a T and a fellowship hall filled the other with a kitchen at the ell.

The front parking area was deserted, giving Hannah a brief start until she remembered that the ladies usually parked in the rear for ease of access.

"Nobody here?" Rafe asked, leaning forward to peer out.

"In the back, I hope," Hannah replied, proceeding. "Some of them bring portable sewing machines and don't want to have to carry them far."

"Gotcha. Want to stop and let me out here so I can sneak around?"

"And have you desert me when I need you?"

"Hey, that hurts. I told you I'd help."

"Fleming made promises, too. He seemed so nice until he had enough information about my family to threaten us."

"Okay, okay, so you have trust issues. I guess I can see that. How do you intend to explain me to your grandmother?"

"One thing at a time. First, you help me make sure she's safe, then we'll talk about what comes next." She eyed him, hoping he'd be willing to turn himself in when the time came. After all, he hadn't planned to escape any more than she'd meant to include him. Perhaps, told together, their stories would make enough sense to help them both.

The van eased around the corner of the fellowship hall. Few cars remained in the parking lot. A familiar, nondescript green sedan sat at the farthest end of the area. The trunk lid was raised. A slight woman with short sandy-colored hair stood beside it, facing two burly men. Hannah gasped.

"Is that her?"

"Yes!"

Rafe had his seatbelt off and was braced to jump out as soon as the van screeched to a halt. Thor followed in a blur.

Hannah was right behind them. She screamed "Gram" at the top of her lungs.

Before she could come between her grandmother and the

men, Rafe's outstretched arm stopped her. Momentarily distracted, she tried to push him aside. When she looked back at Grandma Lucy, the sixty-one-year-old had slammed the trunk lid on the arm of one of the men and was swinging her heavy sewing machine by the handle of its carrying case. It collided with the second man's midsection, doubling him over.

Hannah struggled to free herself from Rafe's grasp while Thor bristled and barked at everybody. "Let me go."

"Hang on," he rasped. "She's got this."

"You have to be…" Wide-eyed, Hannah realized he was right. Lucy was braced like a warrior. She dropped the sewing machine and gave the hunched-over man a karate chop to the back of his neck, whirled and pushed the trunk lid down for the second time, making the first thug howl in pain.

She acknowledged Hannah with a warning look before she grabbed the groaning man by his shirt collar, shoved him toward his partner, then watched as they fled, supporting each other.

A second woman from the church group, elderly but stalwart, waved a cell phone. "I called the police, dear."

Hannah knew that was the right thing to do in almost every circumstance. This time, however, she wanted time to consult with her worldly wise grandmother and work out the best way to surrender to the authorities. If the police arrived before they had time to talk there was every chance they'd be separated and perhaps forever denied the chance to speak privately.

Lucy joined her with a thankful embrace, then set her away to look into her face. "What are you doing here?"

"I—we—came to rescue you."

"What's going on. And who's *he*?"

"It's a long story. I'm in trouble, Gram. Big trouble."

"Looks like it." She eyed Rafe who was still supporting Hannah by grasping her elbow. "Why's he wearing a prison jumpsuit under that jacket?"

Rafe replied. "Like she said, it's a long story. How about we go someplace quiet to fill you in?"

"Might be worth hearing," Lucy said. "You didn't happen to get a license number of the car those two idiots drove off in, did you?"

Hannah shook her head and blinked back tears, thankful her gram was unhurt but terribly worried about their tenuous situation. Lucy took control, beginning by pointing at the woman with the cell phone. "Go back inside where it's safe, Norma, and keep everybody there until the police arrive." She turned to Hannah. "You two, get in my car and we'll go somewhere quiet to talk this through."

"But, Gram..." Hesitant and more than a little frightened, Hannah eyed Rafe, then Thor.

It was Rafe who complied first, putting Thor into the back seat and holding the front passenger door for Hannah. As soon as she was seated he closed her door and joined the dog.

To Hannah's amazement, Lucy slid behind the wheel as if they were merely friends going for a pleasant Sunday drive. She'd seen her grandmother stand up for herself before but never physically. And never in such apparently overwhelming circumstances. Now, as Hannah's trembling fingers fumbled the catch to fasten her seatbelt, Gram was acting so calm it was even more unsettling.

If it hadn't been for the escaped convict in the seat behind them Hannah might have questioned Lucy about her hidden expertise. She'd lived with Gram since her teens, but she'd never seen anything like the encounter in the church parking lot. It was as if she'd glimpsed a part of her sweet grandmother she'd never imagined existed.

Boy, was *that* true. The safety belt clicked. Hannah straightened, staring at Lucy. The older woman was smiling.

"Um, Gram?"

Lucy laughed. "I know, I know. You're surprised I was able to defend myself."

"Yeah, a little."

Pointedly glancing in the rearview mirror, Lucy eyed Rafe. "Bear in mind that I'm capable of much more than you just saw," she warned. "So don't even think about trying to overpower me to steal my car. Keep your hands to yourself and mind that dog or you'll find yourself cuffed and back in prison so fast it'll make your head swim."

Hannah didn't know what surprised her more, Gram's threat or Rafe's immediate "Yes, ma'am."

She swiveled to look at him and her jaw gaped. He was grinning almost as widely as Lucy was.

Chapter Five

Rafe felt as if he'd parachuted into a fractured fairy tale.

Hannah's grandmother was nothing like he'd imagined she'd be, and he was both curious and fascinated. No wonder the pretty dog trainer had been so brave in the face of Fleming's threats. She came from strong stock and a family that functioned well in difficult circumstances. That strength of will was a gift, a trait many people coveted but few possessed. When it was used for good, as in policing or firefighting or other forms of lifesaving, it was a valuable asset. Used the way men like Fleming did, however, it was dangerous.

He decided to plead his case before Hannah explained her part in the escape. "Your granddaughter had been threatened by a guy in the training class. She was told harm would come to you if she didn't help him escape." Seeing the older woman's gray eyes narrowing he raised both hands and quickly added, "No, not me."

"Who?"

"Deuce Fleming. He's…"

"I know who he is. I didn't like it when Hannah told me he was in the class."

"She really didn't have a choice."

"There's always a choice," Lucy countered. "She could have found a way."

"Hey!" Hannah raised her voice. "I'm sitting right here." She made a dour face. "If I'd had the slightest notion you were a martial arts expert I might have resisted more."

Lucy snorted wryly. "Yeah, well, you didn't need to know everything."

"I do now. Where did you learn those moves you used back at the church?"

Sighing, Lucy paused, then explained. "Years ago your grandpa Rob worked for the government. He was worried about being gone on long covert assignments so he taught me some simple self-defense moves. It's been a long time since I practiced but thankfully it all came back to me when I needed it."

Rafe chanced leaning forward slightly to make the conversation more personal. "He'd be proud of you."

"He always told me he was."

The approach of a police car from the opposite direction caused Rafe to duck. When it had passed he resumed his position behind Lucy's right shoulder. "Your family never suspected what your husband did for a living?"

"My daughter and son-in-law, Hannah's parents, knew. They were government agents, too."

A gasp from Hannah was enough to make Lucy reach for her hand. Rafe paused to give them time for silent communication. "What happened to them?" he finally asked.

Before Lucy could answer, Hannah said, "They were killed in an airplane accident when I was sixteen. I've lived with Gram ever since."

The older woman cleared her throat, apparently fighting emotions, before adding her own explanation. "Actually, my daughter was taken—kidnapped—and was being flown out of the country. Her husband lost his life trying to rescue her. Rob blamed himself, of course. I did, too, at first. He'd been trying to break up a human trafficking ring and they'd targeted our daughter in retribution. That brought everything to a head and the brains behind the ring were arrested. The rest died trying to escape with their victims. All aboard were killed when their plane went down in the Rockies."

"Hannah's mother, too?"

"Yes. Missing and presumed dead with the others after the crash," Lucy said sadly.

Hannah stared, eyes wide, lips parted. "You told me Mom and Dad both died in a plane crash, but you never said anything about kidnapping or spies."

"It was the kindest way."

"Kindest?" She withdrew, leaning against the car door as if trying to escape. "How could you keep me in the dark like that?"

"I didn't do it to lie to you—I did it to keep you safe," Lucy insisted. "And speaking of safe, what in the world possessed you to help in a jailbreak? I raised you better than that."

"I did it to keep *you* safe," Hannah shot back. "How was I to know you were some kind of retired spy?"

"My Rob was the actual operative," Lucy countered. "I may have picked up a few tricks along the way, but basically I was just along for the ride." She sobered. "And it cost me my family. You're all I have left. I wanted—I want—to protect you. That's why we have to make this right."

"You just told me everybody I love has lied to me my whole life. Why should I go along with anything you say?"

Rafe decided it was time to chime in. "She may have been less than specific, but she did tell you how they died. My concern is how many guards at Lyell and how many others on the outside are in Fleming's pocket. Going to the police right away will be fine as long as all of them are honest. Throw one bad one into the mix and anything can happen."

His glance connected with Lucy's in the mirror. She was nodding. "And you know this how?"

"Word gets around. Nothing is secret in a place like Lyell. I was in there long enough to learn who to trust."

"Is that why you hitchhiked in my granddaughter's van?"

"That was spur-of-the-moment." To his relief, Hannah provided details of his being framed for murder, and his narrow escape from being shot by the crooked guard.

"So, he tricked them?" Lucy asked.

"Yes. I was sure we'd be stopped at the gate but we sailed right on through."

"Did you? Hmm. Maybe that guard was in on it, too, and thought you were sneaking Fleming out. Did you consider that?"

"No."

"Meaning he might tell tales about how you managed to smuggle Deuce past him, probably blame you instead of admitting he was complicit," Lucy ventured.

Hannah's voice cracked. "I can't win."

Rafe and Lucy spoke in near unison. "Yes, you can."

"We'll work this out. Together," Lucy vowed.

Rafe silently agreed. His goal had always been to uncover the people who were backing Fleming's operations, in and out of prison. Putting himself back inside Lyell when his target was free would accomplish nothing. The only drawback to staying with Hannah and her grandmother was that that could put them in jeopardy when and if he caught up with the escaped prisoner.

"You'll need to back off and leave Fleming to me," Rafe said flatly. "Whether the men who picked him up were on his side or not, he's going to blame you for not carrying out his plan to the letter. You need to leave town. Make yourselves scarce until the manhunt is over."

"They'll be after you, too," Hannah said.

He didn't argue. "Forget about me. You two need to stay out of this, period."

The car was slowing as Lucy pulled into the parking lot of a strip mall with a big-box store. "This guy threatened my granddaughter and me. He's also trying to frame her for a felony and ruin the life I swore to guard with every fiber of my being after her parents were killed." She parked and turned off the engine. "What's your stake in all this, mister?"

"Okay." Rafe didn't have to pretend to be disheartened as his shoulders sagged. "Fleming is responsible for the kidnapping of the daughter of a friend of mine."

"Oh, no. Is she still missing?" Hannah swiveled to face him, clearly empathetic.

"Yes. He was shot trying to get her back. It was touch and go for a while. I promised him I'd do everything I could to make things right, even if joining Fleming's gang was what it took."

The closed expression on the older woman's face lent an air of suspicion to her next comment. "So how did you manage to get thrown into the same prison?"

"Friends in high places," Rafe said.

"Convenient. Care to mention names?"

A barely noticeable shake of his head brought an arch to Lucy's eyebrows. She was acting as if she'd guessed which side of the law he was really on while Hannah was still in the dark. Well, fine. Whatever it took to get her to agree to step back was fine with him.

"So," he said, leaning back and giving Thor's head a pat. "It's settled. You understand."

The two women had locked eyes and appeared to be communicating silently. Finally, Lucy nodded and began to smile. "Yes. It's settled. We owe Fleming for what he's put our family through. We're with you a hundred percent."

"Wait, I didn't mean…"

Lucy fisted the car keys and started to get out. Pausing at the door she reached into the center console and took out a small automatic pistol which she passed to Hannah. "I'm going to go buy our new friend some street clothes. If he makes a move, shoot him."

Assuming she was kidding, Rafe started to smile. Then

he looked at Hannah's face. The joke was on him. Both the women he'd inadvertently allied himself with had a lot more courage than he'd imagined.

With his back against the rear seat and Thor draped half across his lap, Rafe raised both hands, palms toward Hannah. "Thirty-four long. Shirt XL."

"Shoes?" Lucy asked.

"Elevens. I prefer running shoes." The joke had been inadvertent, but he took advantage of it by adding, "Pun intended."

Hannah wasn't used to holding someone at gunpoint and quickly decided it would be best if she didn't actually point the pistol at Rafe so she lowered it to her lap, aiming away. Instinct told her she was in no danger from this man despite his imposing appearance and evident criminal history. Some of the tattoos on his well-muscled arms had looked more patriotic than menacing and he could have gotten the scar on his cheek and over one eyebrow in an accident rather than during illegal activities. His bearing was different from most convicts, too. Stiff and almost military. Still, she supposed he could have been involved in other activities during his career in lawbreaking.

Sun shone through the window on Hannah's side of the car, warming her shoulders and helping her relax a little. So many questions were whirling in her mind that it was hard to pinpoint what she wanted to ask. Finally, she decided to begin with personal information and made eye contact as an opening gambit.

"You can lower your hands. I don't intend to shoot you. At least not right away."

Rafe gave her a lopsided smile and began to stroke Thor's thick coat. "Thanks. My arms were getting tired."

"Were you telling the truth? Is your friend's daughter still missing?"

He sobered. "Yes. After he was shot, the kidnappers disappeared with the girl."

"How long ago?"

Rafe shrugged and Hannah could see his jaw muscles clenching before he answered. "Seventeen days. We think she's being prepared to be shipped overseas. Since Andy intervened and got himself shot it's been just over two weeks."

"Then she may be long gone."

"Yes. Unfortunately."

"What do the police think?" There was, of course, an underlying reason for asking this question. If Rafe answered the way she hoped he would, she might then be able to unmask his true identity. Assuming he wasn't an actual murderer, she added, hopeful. When he said, "How would I know?" her hopes were dashed.

"I just figured, since you seemed to be connected enough to worm your way into the same prison ward as Deuce Fleming, you must have an inside track."

"It's complicated."

Scowling, she stared at him, trying to peer inside his brain and find the truth. "I don't doubt it. Can't you see it would help if Gram and I knew the details?"

"Help who?"

"Whom," Hannah said, smiling as she delivered the grammar tip.

"Whatever," Rafe countered. "You already know the story of my friend and his daughter. Fleming's people were behind the disappearance. I was there to get closer to him. That's all."

"It's a good thing for you that the former warden was replaced then. He'd have outed you for sure. Hotchkiss actually may be honest, in which case your story might hold water. I'm reserving judgment."

"Have it your way."

"There is one way you could prove it to me."

"How?" Leaning back against the seat, Rafe crossed his arms.

Even beneath the sleeves of the black jacket Hannah couldn't miss noticing how muscular he was. She fingered the gun in her lap, then forced herself to feign calm. "I could go visit Andy at the hospital and hear the story in his own words."

"Not happening."

"Why not? What are you afraid of?"

"He's still recovering. It might be too much for him to have to relive the trauma."

She humphed. "Or, he might tell me a totally different story."

"Chances are he wouldn't talk to you at all."

"He would if you were with me."

The arch of one of Rafe's eyebrows gave him an intriguing expression. So did the partial smile he seemed to be fighting to subdue. "You actually expect me to take you to my friend's hospital room?"

"Not exactly," Hannah countered, keeping close watch on his face in the hope of catching a clue, however fleeting. "I expect you to take me and Gram."

"Impossible."

"Uh-huh. That's what I thought you'd say, especially if you were lying."

"What I told you about him and his daughter is the truth."

Hannah was enjoying having the upper hand so much she allowed herself to grin. "We'll soon see."

Chapter Six

As Rafe pondered his current dilemma, it was easier to see ways out than it was to envision sticking to the job he knew was his duty. In order to get a handle on the missing teen, he had to locate and interrogate Deuce Fleming, or at least some of his closest cohorts. At present he also felt beholden to Hannah and her grandmother. Once Fleming and his gang got organized enough to plan their next move it was highly likely some or all of them would pursue the women who had thwarted them. Retribution didn't have to make sense when it came to a vendetta. Fleming would be furious, and a man in that state was unpredictable.

An additional reason for keeping Hannah and Lucy close was for their sakes. Yes, they would be a hindrance. No, he couldn't simply abandon them. Not with Fleming on the loose. If Deuce didn't attempt to get even with them, he'd lose face in front of his gang so he'd have to act. Soon.

Rafe was ready with a plan by the time Lucy returned with clothing for him. To her credit she hadn't shopped for new garments. What he pulled out of the plastic grocery bags was clean but gently worn. The older woman was beyond clever and that was unsettling.

"I'll drive around back of a gas station and you can duck into their restroom to change." She looked pointedly at Rafe. "No tricks. You helped get my granddaughter into this mess and you're going to help me get her out of it."

"No argument from me," Rafe said. "Hannah wants to go to the hospital where my wounded friend is recuperating. I think that may be a good idea. Since his daughter's kidnapping is also tied to Fleming we may be able to learn something that will help us track him down now that he's on the loose."

"Do we need him to prove Hannah is innocent when we have your testimony?"

"Maybe not," Rafe countered. "But if we can take part in putting Deuce back in jail it will count in our favor. As a plus, we might actually get a lead on the missing girl."

"Best-case scenario," Lucy said, pulling into traffic. "It's a bit much to hope for, but nothing is impossible."

Hannah piped up. "I thought you were going to say that nothing is impossible for God."

"Let's leave Him out of this until we see where we stand," Lucy said flatly. "You and I are not exactly dealing with normal people."

Chuckling softly, Rafe sorted through the clothes, amazed at how well the older woman had assembled a casual wardrobe. He smiled. "I'm getting the feeling I haven't joined up with run-of-the-mill folks, either."

A quick glance at Lucy's face in the mirror told him how very right he was. There was a crafty, almost feral look in her gray eyes and they were narrowed at the outer corners as if she was a nanosecond away from a wink. He wasn't going to press her, not right now, but he was getting a strong impression that her late husband, daughter and son-in-law were not the only ones formerly affiliated with a government agency. If sweet old Lucy had not been a covert operator in her younger years, she'd missed a golden opportunity. Everything about her was perfect for the job, including her intelligence and martial arts expertise. She had to have been a master at spy craft to keep her past from Hannah for this long.

And what about Hannah? Rafe asked himself. How deeply was she involved with Fleming. Yes, she looked innocent but that didn't excuse her decision to smuggle him out of the prison. There were other avenues she could have taken instead of breaking the law. Most of the prison staff was honest and he knew from experience that the new warden was beyond reproach. She should have said something to somebody instead of just assuming Fleming was in control.

Lucy pulled to the rear of an older style gas station and stopped, engine idling. "This way you won't have to go through the minimarket part of the store," she said. "Hurry it up. We don't know how much time we have before those yahoos from the church report back with a description of my car."

Wide-eyed, Hannah stared. "Do you think they hung around the neighborhood long enough to watch us leave?"

"I would have," Rafe answered. "If they didn't, they'll know we ditched the van when somebody spots it at the church."

"It's going to create quite a fuss all full of bullet holes like that." Hannah sighed. "I'd just made the last payment."

Checking their surroundings before getting out of the back seat, Rafe jogged to the restroom, relieved to find it unlocked. At least one thing had gone right this morning, he mused. One out of many challenges, unfortunately. Once he was changed and had trashed his orange prison jumpsuit he'd be able to contact his boss without attracting attention. He needed to report in, to try to explain why he'd gone along with Fleming's plan instead of trying to stop him.

A lot of those choices had been dependent upon injury to himself or others in the line of fire, particularly the pretty dog trainer. Ideally, he'd have been able to leave her behind except getting through the prison gates would have been impossible without her and her van. Besides, if he had driven off with Fleming there had been a chance that one of the crooked guards would have blamed Hannah and shot her to save his own skin, just as they'd threatened to do to him and Thor.

No, Rafe decided. To live through the incident they had to be together. Stay together. Work together. It wasn't to his liking or even that sensible, but he couldn't see a way out other than the capture of Deuce Fleming. If he could get himself thrown into the same holding cell maybe he'd be able to worm into the criminal's good graces and complete his original assignment; namely locating the missing teenager.

And in the meantime, he'd keep an eye on a couple of unpredictable and hopefully innocent bystanders. Buckling the belt Lucy had given him, Rafe checked his reflection in the small mirror, put the original cap and black jacket back on and peeked out the exit door. It was only a couple of long strides from there to the corner of the building. If he could slip away long enough to make a call it would sure help his nerves.

He saw Hannah in the car. She was turned around to pet Thor in the back seat. There was no sign of Lucy. Encouraged, Rafe ducked around the corner. No pay phone. He should have known. Common use of cell phones had pretty much done away with the old-fashioned booths.

Almost to the glass doors fronting the service station minimarket, Rafe was caught short, managing to stop just in time to keep from crashing into Lucy.

She grinned at him. "Going someplace?"

"Looking for a snack."

"Uh-huh. I figured. You got money?"

"No."

"I didn't think so. How were you planning to get snacks? Steal them?"

"No. Of course not."

"Keep lying and you'll dig yourself a bigger hole," she warned, gesturing with one hand slipped inside her purse as if she now had the gun. "Get a move on. Back to my car."

"Yes, ma'am."

"And can the politeness, mister. I know you're not what you've told us you are. I just haven't figured out who you really are and which side you're on."

"Ditto," Rafe said solemnly.

Although he'd turned away and started down the sidewalk he heard Lucy mutter, "Good."

As far as Hannah was concerned, everyone was getting along pretty well. She already loved Thor and with Gram in her corner she felt much more hopeful. Rafe, on the other hand, was still an unknown. The more she learned about him the less confident she became. When they'd parked behind the gas station she'd hoped to have a quiet, intimate conversation with her grandmother and perhaps figure something out. Unfortunately, Gram had bailed out and disappeared around the building as soon as Rafe had closed the door to the men's room.

Seeing them returning to the car together was doubly puzzling and she started asking questions the minute Lucy was behind the wheel. "Will somebody please tell me what's going on?"

"Your buddy here was trying to escape," Lucy offered.

Rafe immediately countered. "I was not. I just wanted a snack, that's all."

"Uh-huh."

There was enough sarcasm in the older woman's tone to tell Hannah she wasn't buying his explanation. She did, however, see his point. "If we're going to drive all over town we probably should stock the car with a few survival items."

Lucy was nodding. "Agreed. We'll stop back at the house and load up."

"The house?" Hannah was scowling over at her. "Fleming's people already know where we live. They've been watching us. We can't go there."

"I have my reasons," Lucy countered.

Worried, Hannah pressed her point. "That's the first place they'll look. We can just stop at a grocery store or something."

Her grandmother's laugh was tinged with enough irony and sarcasm to give Hannah pause. "What? What's so funny?"

"You are. I'm not talking about a bag of chips or a couple of sodas. I'm talking about real survival gear. We can't go into battle empty-handed."

"Hold on. That's not what we're doing." Seeing Gram make eye contact with Rafe in the rearview mirror, Hannah was certain she saw unspoken communication. Talk about unsettling!

Frustrated, she folded her arms and stared straight ahead. "Fine. Have your secrets or whatever. Considering everything I've learned so far this morning, you'll have a hard time surprising me more."

Again, Lucy made eye contact with Rafe, then reached across to pat Hannah's arm. "I doubt that, honey. I really do. I just don't want you to worry."

"Me? Worry? Why in the world would I worry? Huh? I've been shot at and lied to, and I'm currently riding in a car with an escaped convict and a grandmother who's acting like a geriatric James Bond. How would that give me extra concerns?"

"I don't mind being compared to a legendary spy," Lucy said with a smirk. "But I'm hardly over the hill. I thought I'd proved my skills back at the church."

Chastened, Hannah softened and sighed. "Okay, okay. Those were impressive martial arts moves. I—we—were impressed. What I don't like is the way you two keep looking at each other as if you're sharing some big, dark secret. Like it or not, we're in this together. At least tell me enough to give me the tools to help." Surprised at a welling of tears she blinked them back.

"You'll get the gist once I've picked up my gear," Lucy said. "I'm just trying to decide how to explain everything."

"The truth would be a nice start," Hannah said flatly.

"Ah, the truth. So subjective. And so elusive sometimes."
Lucy again shot a glance in the mirror. "Right, son?"

Son? Good grief. Now Gram was acting as if Rafe McDowell had been adopted into their family. That was the last straw.

Hannah reached for the steering wheel and clamped a fist around it. "Pull over. Now."

To her surprise, Lucy's resistance was minimal. As the car steered parallel with the curb and came to a stop in the quiet residential neighborhood, she was nodding. To Hannah, she seemed almost relieved.

"Where to start," Lucy murmured.

Although Hannah wanted to answer, she chose silence and let the older woman take her time. Finally, Lucy said, "Okay, honey. Hang on to your hat. You and I are the last survivors of a family of government agents that goes back generations to, long before Roosevelt created the CIA. Their lives weren't as glamorous as the stories about Mata Hari, but they did have their moments."

"Including you?" Rafe asked from the back seat.

"Something tells me you've already figured that out," Lucy said. "I retired long ago but some things can never be forgotten."

"Like hand-to-hand combat?" Hannah asked.

Lucy was shaking her head and pursing her lips. "I was thinking more of the way we lost your mom and dad. That particular human smuggling ring was wiped out, but I can't help feeling as if this situation is giving me a chance to save others from the same horrible fate my own daughter faced."

Gaping at her, Hannah could barely think let alone speak. Rafe, however, did not seem to have that problem. "You'll help me? Really?"

"I just said so, didn't I?"

Beginning to comprehend the connection between Gram's story and Rafe's, Hannah was anything but comforted and she said so. "Count me out. I'm just a civilian with a clean slate.

We need to go to the police and turn ourselves in. Closed-cir-cuit cameras at Lyell will prove we were forced to aid Flem-ing's escape."

Rafe gave a cynical chuckle. "Remind me how you resisted. Did he have a gun on you? Were you accosted on camera?"

"Of course I was."

"Are you sure? Think back. The way I remember it, we worked together to get him into the van and you drove through the guarded gate as if everything was business as usual."

As the escape scenario replayed in her mind, Hannah grew more and more despondent. She had to admit how easy it would be for an impartial judge to view her as guilty. And if some of the law officers who were involved chose to impli-cate her, she had no proof to the contrary. It was foolish to hope Deuce Fleming or his cohorts would back up her story even if he was recaptured. Still, it would be wrong to break the law again just because she'd been forced to break it before.

"Look," Hannah said flatly, "this is a no-win situation for me."

"Not exactly," Rafe said. "All I ask is that you hold off con-tacting the police until I've had a chance to reconnect with Deuce and find out where my partner's daughter, Kristy, is being held."

"That's the second or third time you've referred to some-body as your partner. What kind of partnership are you talk-ing about?" Hannah asked.

Above Lucy's laughter in the background, Hannah heard him say, "You'll find out once you meet him so I guess I'd better confess." Of all the things she'd expected he might re-veal, the least likely was what he actually said.

"Andy Fellows and I worked together as state troopers."

Chapter Seven

Rafe figured he could convince Hannah that he was no longer in law enforcement despite his confession so he decided to tell her enough to placate her. The entire truth was not only unnecessary, he knew they'd all be safer in the long run if she didn't expect him to behave like a cop. That was one of the hardest elements of undercover work; bending the law for the right reasons. Someone like Hannah Lassiter, who viewed the world in black-and-white, was bound to have trouble with gray areas. He did, too. Constantly. Keeping focused on the ultimate goal was the only way he was able to keep functioning in such trying circumstances.

Judging by the set of Hannah's jaw and her scowl, she was not on board the way her grandmother was. That figured for the very reason she'd cited—she was an untrained civilian while he and Lucy understood both sides of the dilemma. It would have suited him better to be proceeding without the pretty dog trainer, but the way he saw it, there was no way to safeguard her unless she stayed close. Undoubtedly, Lucy felt the same.

Rafe leaned over the seat backs to speak to the women in

the front, hoping to change the subject. "The best way into the hospital without being noticed is probably through the ER."

"You know what room this guy is in?" Hannah asked.

"I know where he was a week ago so unless they've moved him, yes."

He saw Hannah eye Thor before saying, "I wish I'd thought to grab a *Working Dog in Training* vest out of my van. It's easier to gain access to closed areas when I have a K-9 that's identified that way."

Lucy piped up. "I intend to make that stop at the house first. You can pick up a spare then."

"No." Rafe was adamant. "That's unsafe."

"For once I do agree with him," Hannah said. "I know for a fact that some of the pictures the Fleming gang showed me were taken there. A couple were snapped through a window. They were that close to us and we had no idea."

"Right now they'll be busy reconnecting with their boss," Lucy countered. "I can't think of a better time to catch them by surprise, get what we need and get away."

Frustrated and upset, Rafe smacked the backs of the front seats with his open hands. "Aargh! You're impossible, lady."

"So my late husband often told me." She was smiling over her shoulder at him. "It never did him much good."

"I gathered. I'm not going to talk you out of this, am I?"

"Not likely. A workman without the right tools is at a disadvantage before he starts."

"Can't argue with that." Rafe was nodding slowly, mentally expanding and altering his plans. Since the escape everything had been in flux anyway so he'd have to remain flexible, even if it meant listening to this civilian.

"Hey!" Hannah interjected. "Don't I get a vote?"

Rafe's "No" was echoed by the older woman.

"This is not a democracy," Lucy added. "I'm calling the shots."

Rafe almost laughed aloud when Hannah made a face and

said, "I suppose it's too late to vote you out of office or arrange a coup."

Chuckling quietly, Lucy said, "Honey, it was too late the minute you came to live with me. I promised God I'd always look after you and I intend to keep that promise. Period."

Hannah huffed. "You sure have a funny way of showing it."

"Not at all," Rafe said, looking to Lucy to be certain she understood what he was trying to tell Hannah. "Calm down and think this through. Your Gram and I have experience and skills that you don't. It's nothing against you, it's simply a fact. If you're half as smart as I think you are, you'll listen to us and let us make the important decisions."

"Put my life in the hands of two people who are such great liars that I was totally fooled? That doesn't sound like a good idea to me."

Sobering, he pushed away and sank back into the rear seat. "Good or not, that's how it is."

Fuming and struggling to accept the night-and-day difference in her grandmother, Hannah barely took notice of their surroundings until Gram missed the turn into their familiar driveway. Hannah's head whipped around, her gaze pinned on their house as they pulled farther and farther away. "Hey. I thought we were going home."

"We are."

"But you just passed…"

Lucy's hands were fisted on the steering wheel, her concentration as much to the rear as forward. "Something was off. I don't know what it was, but my instincts have always been good. We'll go around the block and get a fresh look."

Hannah flinched as Rafe leaned forward again and asked, "What am I looking for? What did you notice?"

"I'm not sure. Call it a subconscious warning. I know better than to ignore it."

"Terrific." Hannah straightened in the bucket seat and faced forward, trying to process the nightmare her life had become in the space of a few hours. She supposed it was normal for her to resist accepting such a drastic change in Gram but this was bordering on lunacy.

Finally, she formed coherent enough thoughts to express them. "Look, you guys, we've lived in that house for years. I know what it looks like and I didn't see anything odd when we drove by, okay? Let's just grab whatever we need and get out of this neighborhood before Fleming's men figure out we're here."

Instead of arguing with her, Gram gave a slight nod and kept driving. "The black SUV down that side street. Did you see it?"

"Who, me?" Hannah asked.

"No," Lucy said, "I was talking to our friend in the back seat."

"Yes," Rafe replied. "And the old pickup in a driveway right behind it, too. Could be either, or both."

Listening, Hannah felt so left out she was ready to scream, or cry, perhaps in unison. "Stop it. Just stop it. You're scaring me."

As if he, too, was anxious, Thor laid his big head on her shoulder. She could feel the canine trembling and felt responsible for some of his angst. Sensitive animals picked up on human emotions as well as those of their own species, and she'd probably been sending out waves of fear despite the outward calm she was trying so desperately to project.

Hannah laid her cheek against the side of Thor's muzzle, cupped his face and consciously slowed her breathing. She might not understand people as well as she liked, but it was easy for her to connect with the spirits of animals. Maybe that was because words weren't necessary, although a softly spoken "good boy" could have a beneficial effect on almost any canine.

As a child she'd missed her parents when they'd had to be away for work, which finally made sense now that she knew their secret occupations. Before they had been killed in the plane crash, they'd relocated the family every couple of years and Hannah had repeatedly been the outcast, the new kid in school, so she'd made friends with animals, particularly dogs, to fill the void. In retrospect, she could see the plus side of that choice and it comforted her slightly.

Glancing over at Gram, Hannah felt a deep sense of loss, not of her actual grandmother but of the person she'd thought her grandma was; the safe homebody who had taken her in as a teen and finally given her stability and security. The one who had loved and accepted her wholly, without reservation.

And the one who had lied to her from the beginning, she added, blinking back tears. She could understand the subterfuge when she'd been an impressionable teen but she was a mature adult now. If these complicated circumstances had not warranted a confession, would Gram ever have told her the truth?

What else was she still holding back? Hannah wondered. Finding out that she'd been raised in a family that was all pretense had been bad enough. Was there more? Was Lucy continuing to pretend or was what Hannah was seeing now her real persona? Did someone who had lived a double life have the capacity to revert to the kind of unvarnished truth normal people took for granted?

Hannah would have asked that question aloud if Lucy hadn't abruptly pulled into a long, narrow dirt driveway and stopped at the end. "Where are we? What are you doing?"

"Remember when you were little and used to come visit me and Grandpa? We let you play in the wooded lot behind the house, but the old cabin back there was always padlocked."

"Right."

"Well, there was a good reason." Lucy climbed out. "This is it. Follow me."

"What about Thor?" Not knowing what lay ahead or how

long they'd be away from the car, Hannah was concerned for the dog.

"Leash him and bring him. We won't be coming back."

"What? I thought we were here to pick up supplies."

"We are," Lucy said. "And to ditch my car."

Although she was proceeding to let the big dog out, Hannah felt trapped in a bad dream, one that kept getting creepier and creepier. Reality had morphed into a hazy scenario that melded childhood memories with the solid reality of a nondescript little wooden building that had sat, undisturbed, in the wooded plot for as long as Hannah could remember. Surely, that couldn't be where Gram had stored survival equipment. It didn't look big enough for more than a couple of backpacks and maybe a folding cot.

Keeping Thor on a short leash was not only sensible under the circumstances, his proximity gave Hannah a feeling of security and boy, did she need it. One of her companions was her beloved grandmother who was not the benevolent person she'd been pretending to be. The other was either a hardened criminal she'd met in the prison or an undercover cop who did such an amazing job of faking his anti-social persona he'd been able to convince prisoners and guards alike. So which was he? And what was she going to do with the older woman who had been playing the part of a normal run-of-the-mill senior citizen?

Hannah was more than confused, she was disappointed and disheartened. Nothing was as she'd thought and nothing would ever be the same again, not now that she knew the truth about her family. Part of her wanted to be proud of their patriotism. A more personal take on the situation had her feeling so bereft she didn't want anything to do with anybody, particularly the two people she presently found herself stuck with.

Halting abruptly as they approached the small cabin, Hannah kept Thor close at heel. Lucy, in the lead, didn't seem to notice the change but Rafe did. He approached closer and reached out. His hand almost touched her shoulder when the dog began to growl and bare his teeth.

Rafe froze, speaking quietly. "Lucy. We have a situation."

The spry, older woman paused and looked back. "What's wrong?"

"I suspect your granddaughter is about to rebel."

"I wondered what took her so long." She smiled. "Hannah, honey, I know this is a lot to take in but you need to trust me. We can get out of this in one piece if we work together, and that means following my lead."

"I don't even know who you are anymore." Her narrowed gaze shifted to Rafe. "And you. You're probably as bad as Deuce Fleming. Maybe worse, since you're apparently playing both sides against each other."

"I told you, I'm one of the good guys."

"Right." Hannah's voice was rising. "And Gram told me she was a regular grandmother living out her golden years after retiring from her job as a county clerk. I don't know who to believe but one thing I am sure of—I'm not getting in any deeper than I am already. I don't have to protect Gram anymore and I sure don't have to defend you." She set her jaw and tried to keep from sounding hysterical. "I quit. Here and now. I know where I am. You two can go off on whatever idiotic mission you think is necessary. I'm going to walk out of these woods with my dog, turn myself in to the police and explain everything."

"No, you are not," Rafe said. The underlying menace in his tone gave Hannah the shivers. She looked to Lucy, expecting moral support, and was shocked to see her shaking her head.

"Gram?"

"You need to do this our way to have the greatest chance of survival," Lucy said. "I don't trust your friend here any farther than I could throw him, but we need him as backup and to give us a connection to Fleming, providing we're able to locate him under amiable circumstances."

"Why go looking for trouble?" Hannah was starting to show panic.

"Because an organization like Fleming's isn't going to just leave us alone after what's happened. They'll have to punish you to save face and believe me, it won't be a slap on the wrist. If you were anybody else's granddaughter I'd recommend witness protection but even that isn't foolproof. No matter how careful the US Marshals Service is, a good percentage of people with new identities are eventually located and eliminated. This isn't a kid's game we're playing, Hannah. This is life and death. There are no do-overs. The minute you agreed to take part in the jailbreak, you were permanently committed."

"They said they were going to kidnap and kill you if I didn't cooperate."

Lucy pulled Hannah into a motherly embrace and gently patted her back. "That's partly my fault for not telling you the truth long ago. If you'd known my real history, you might have come to me with your problems instead of getting sucked in by a clever crook."

"He had pictures of you," Hannah reiterated. "Lots of them. He showed them to me on a phone somebody had smuggled into prison."

"Meaning he had people on the inside, like your friend here claimed," Lucy reminded her. "That's another reason we have to give this guy the benefit of the doubt."

A branch broke in the distance. Thor growled. Hannah jumped. Lucy thrust her away and deftly inserted a key into the padlock that secured the cabin door. She stepped back out of the way and gestured. "Everybody inside. Now."

"But…"

Hannah found herself being swept up and half carried through the open doorway by Rafe. Lucy was right behind them while Thor circled at the end of his leash.

A shout echoed. Another answered. Hannah was struck speechless by confusion and raw fear. What she still wanted to do was turn herself in, but it was looking as though that was no longer an option. Whoever was outside the cabin was approaching, and judging by the noise they were making they weren't very concerned about being spotted or reported.

That made sense. Nobody else would know where they were unless Gram used her cell phone to call for help and chances of that happening were slim.

Thoughts whirling, Hannah belatedly realized she'd left her own purse behind in the van when they'd switched cars. She didn't have her phone and had no identification with her. The only defense she had left was the novice K-9. And her own wits.

Rafe turned to slide a heavy timber across the weak-looking door to bar it. Hannah stood motionless in the center of the fifteen by fifteen cabin, unsure what, if anything, she could do to help Lucy.

That question was answered in seconds. Lucy lifted a tarp, levered open a trap door and pointed. "Go."

"I can't. We can't." Hannah pulled Thor closer. "He hasn't learned to climb ladders."

"I'm not leaving you behind," Lucy said, clearly determined.

Rafe stepped up. "Help me sling him over my shoulders. I'll carry him down."

Hannah's loud "*No*" blended with her grandmother's. Voices outside were growing louder. Something solid hit the cabin door so hard it jarred the whole building and knocked dust from the low rafters.

The men outside attacked the wooden door again and again until the air inside the cabin was clouded with swirling particles of dirt. Hannah coughed.

Rafe stripped off his jacket and thrust it at her. "A sling. Make the dog a sling. And hurry!"

Her hands were shaking so badly he had to help her tie the arms together behind the dog's shoulders. "Keep tension on the leash," he shouted. "Here we go."

Chapter Eight

Lying prone, Rafe fisted the knotted arms of the jacket and began to lower the dog through the trap door. At this point he half expected the frightened animal to snap at him but Thor made the short drop easily. Lucy was at the bottom to catch him and Hannah scrambled down next.

"Pull that door in after you," Lucy ordered Rafe. "Make sure it latches in place and push that rod through the U-bolts."

As he did as he was told, he wondered what possible advantage there was to locking themselves in a subterranean chamber with potential assassins waiting for them above. It didn't take long for him to realize he'd been underestimating the older woman. Not only was she opening the door to an underground passage, she looked pleased with herself.

He huffed. "I don't believe it."

That made Lucy smile. "Believe it, mister." She started down the dark narrow corridor, patting the walls as she went. "Keep up and I'll have us out of this in a jiffy."

"This is why you didn't want me to play in the shack?" Hannah asked softly.

"Among other things. It needed to look unused. Derelict. We didn't want anybody else messing with it, either. It took forever to set this up ."

"Where does this passageway lead?" Rafe asked.

"My house. Once we enter the basement, stealth will be crucial. I assume all of Fleming's men followed us into the woods, but they may have been smart enough to leave someone behind. If that's the case, we can't take a chance on him sounding an alarm."

Rafe knew what she was implying and hoped it didn't come to a confrontation under these circumstances. As far as Deuce Fleming knew, Rafe was a fellow escapee. To catch him in the company of Hannah and her grandmother would cast him in a different light, particularly if he couldn't convince the gang that he was keeping the women with him as hostages.

He reached out to tap Lucy's shoulder. "I have a proposal for you."

"No time for making deals, mister," she said.

A keypad lit up under her touch and she punched in a series of numbers. Rafe tried to see them over her shoulder and failed, not that there was any proof he'd need the combination to that lock again, anyway.

Lucy began to ease open the door into the cellar. A musty odor assailed him. Hannah seemed to be more at ease now that she was about to enter familiar space and, consequently, Thor was more settled, too. To Rafe's relief the ambient light from high windows showed a normal staircase as an exit.

The only audible breathing came from the panting canine. Hannah had him on a short leash and was tiptoeing along behind her grandmother. There were no sounds from the house above and apparently nobody close by outside, either.

Falling back, Rafe gave them plenty of space while he cast around for a makeshift weapon. The retired secret agent was undoubtedly armed with the gun from her car and Hannah had the dog to protect her, meaning he was the only one walking into who-knows-what empty-handed. That hindrance he intended to remedy ASAP.

He was reaching for a heavy wrench atop a tool bench when

Lucy glanced back. Rafe froze. Was she going to ditch him here and now because she didn't want him armed? He raised both hands, palms facing toward her. "I just want to be able to defend myself."

"Second drawer down, far left," Lucy said in a hoarse whisper, "and keep it quiet."

Cautiously, Rafe followed her instructions. The drawer contained a tangle of fishing line, old lures and floats and plastic packets of snelled hooks. He pushed them aside and spotted a long narrow sheath. A fish filleting knife.

He picked it up and displayed it, waiting for Lucy's acknowledgement. At her nod he threaded the leather sheath through his belt. Any worry he'd had about whether or not she trusted him was negated.

The shocked expression on Hannah's face, however, gave him pause. She looked as if she was trying to decide if she should conk him with the nearest shovel or scream and make a run for it. To her credit, she did neither.

The three humans and one dog gathered at the top of the interior stairs. Lucy eased open the door and peered out. Rafe held his breath. Then she was through and moving quickly past the kitchen and down a hallway with Hannah right behind her.

The women and Thor turned into a bedroom. Rafe decided to post himself at the door as their rear guard. His back was to the wall, his palm resting on the hilt of the knife. Every sense was heightened.

Braced to repel an attack, he waited.

Hannah wished she had a chance to sit down and mull over everything that had occurred since breakfast. Not that she wasn't capable of thinking on her feet. Until today she'd congratulated herself on her decisiveness and quick thinking, and now it occurred to her that much of that pride was misplaced. Then again, she'd never have imagined finding herself in a situation like the one she was experiencing. People were proving that her reserved personality was one of her best traits because the more interaction she had with her companions, not to mention the thugs pursuing them, the more she yearned to withdraw, to nurture the shy, reclusive person she was before and to make everybody else vanish along with her troubles.

That, of course, was not going to happen, at least not until something else changed. Sadly, she remembered little about her parents other than the fact that they were away often and she'd stayed with her grandparents during those times.

Trying to picture her mother and failing to produce a clear memory, Hannah gave up and looked to Lucy. Not only had the older woman disappeared into the bedroom closet, she was tossing things out onto the carpeted floor.

One black backpack landed with a clunking sound. Lucy straightened and pointed at it. "Pad that with extra clothing so it doesn't rattle."

"Mine or yours?"

"Go get some of yours from your room," Lucy said. "Warm clothes and shirts you can layer if the weather changes. I can handle this by myself. And take your dog with you."

What Hannah really wanted to do was pitch a temper tantrum and refuse to aid anything illegal. That reasoning almost made her laugh aloud. Since her actions at the prison had started all this, she figured she owed the others at least a modicum of cooperation, particularly with erstwhile assassins prowling around the premises.

Startled to find a man standing like a statue right outside the bedroom door, Hannah started to swing the heavy pack at him, then recognized Rafe just in time to stop. Her heart was threatening to burst out of her chest. At her side, Thor panted happily, tail wagging.

She faced Rafe. "What are you trying to do, scare me to death?"

"Nope. Watching your backs."

"Did Gram tell you to do that?"

"No, my training did. We need to operate as if there is danger around every corner, which may very well be true. I suggest you save your indignation for a better time and start thinking the way your grandmother and I do. It'll keep you alive longer."

"God gave me life and He will look after me, especially if I keep His commandments."

"I agree, to a point," Rafe said. "He also allows us to make our own mistakes and with those errors in judgment come consequences. Being a Christian doesn't mean we'll never have trials, never be disappointed. It means we won't have to face them alone."

"Right now," Hannah said, making a face at him, "I'd settle for all the alone time I could get."

"Away from people, maybe. Don't turn your back on your faith. Please."

"What makes you think I'd ever do that?"

"It happens, okay. I almost made that mistake when Andy's daughter was kidnapped and he was shot. I asked plenty of questions, but in the end I chose to trust the Lord enough to agree to go undercover at Lyell."

"That whole story is true? For real?"

"For real."

Reading unspoken confirmation in his dark eyes, Hannah was finally able to believe him. Relief flowed through her as if she'd been locked in a prison of her mind and had suddenly been released.

She sighed noisily. "Okay. One thing at a time." She held up the pack. "Gram wants me to pad this with some of my clothes so it doesn't make noise."

"Where are they?"

Hannah pointed. "Over there. We only have two bedrooms."

"Do you always close the doors when you leave?"

"No, I…" Scowling, Hannah did a double take. "No. We usually leave the interior doors open." Before she finished her sentence, Rafe had withdrawn the filet knife, pushed her aside and was approaching the closed bedroom.

"Thor would have alerted me if there was anybody in there," she said.

"Humor me."

Moments before, she would have argued. Something had changed. It was subtle enough to miss had she not been so tuned in to the situation. To him. Viewing him through new eyes she let herself appreciate his courage as well as the way he looked with that dark, wavy hair and expressive brown eyes.

The first time she'd met him, in the prison, she'd made a personal assessment that was now being expanded at light speed. Rafe McDowell had been ruggedly handsome in the training class, yet she'd refused to admire him as a man, choosing to classify him on the level of her arch nemesis, Deuce Fleming. Now she was seeing a handsome, concerned, wildly brave hero who was risking his life to save others, including her. That viewpoint made all the difference.

A blush warmed her cheeks. Thor had been way ahead of her in assessing Rafe's character, hadn't he? The enormous shepherd had sensed the good man beneath the hardened persona and had accepted him within minutes of their meeting. As a professional dog trainer she knew she should have heeded the animal's instincts then and there. Perhaps in the deep recesses of her brain she had, at least enough to bring him to meet Gram.

Was that why she'd given in and had taken him with her to the church? Hannah wondered. Had she been fooling herself about Rafe to keep from liking him even a little?

Watching him ease open the door and step through, Hannah felt a surge of warmth, of concern, that merely added to her appreciation of the man.

Aloud, she whispered, "Be careful." In her mind she prayed, "Jesus, help us all."

Rafe moved out of sight. There was a crack, then a thud.

The door swung in and a shadowy figure emerged, fleeing.

Thor broke away from Hannah and barreled down the hallway chasing someone dressed all in black. Out of sight, a door slammed so hard it shook the window panes.

Hannah entered the bedroom in time to see Rafe levering himself up off the floor. When he stood, however, he was clearly lacking balance.

"I took a swipe at him. Might have caught his arm. I'm not sure." Staggering, he lunged toward the doorway and caught himself with one hand on the jamb. "Which way did he go?"

"Thor chased him off." Hannah proceeded to grab clothing and stuff it into the pack.

"We have to stop him before he alerts the others."

"Too late for that," Hannah said, relieved to see the K-9 returning, tail wagging, tongue lolling. "Looks like the guy got away." She dropped to one knee and hugged the big dog's thick neck ruff, checking for hidden injuries as she said, "You were wonderful."

Rafe's "Just doing my job" struck her as terribly funny, and although she tried to keep from giggling, she failed. Once she started it was impossible to stop. Soon, she was laughing so hysterically it drew Lucy over at a run.

She knelt beside Hannah and Thor. "What is it? What happened?"

Wiping away tears and struggling to catch her breath, Hannah finally gestured toward Rafe and managed to explain, "When I said 'you were wonderful,' I was talking to the dog."

Chapter Nine

Rafe insisted, "I knew that," but both women were enjoying laughing at his expense so much that neither seemed to hear. Rather than belabor the point he checked his head, feeling the rising lump, and was relieved there was no bleeding.

"If either of you care, one of the gang conked me, but I'm okay," he said.

Lucy regained her composure first, sniffling and wiping her face with her hands. "Good to hear."

"That guy ran off, thanks to the dog. I think we'd better get a move on."

"When you're right, you're right," Lucy said. She pointed at Hannah who was still chortling and brushing away tears. "Let's get this show on the road."

"How? We left your car in the woods."

"We left one car in the woods. Who says that's all I have?"

Rafe slipped his arm around Hannah's shoulders to guide her through the door and also to temporarily prop himself up. His head was clearing quickly but he didn't want to slow their escape. At the last second he remembered the backpack and grabbed it by one of the shoulder straps.

"You hid a whole car for an emergency?" he asked.

"Of course not. That would be overkill. I just never sold my late husband's wheels. There's a pristine Dodge Charger under a tarp in the garage."

Picturing the sporty car, Rafe arched a brow, discovered that it made his head injury hurt more and schooled his features. "I assume it will hold three."

"Four," Hannah said, ducking out from under Rafe's arm and tugging on Thor's leash to keep him close.

If the older woman hadn't been grinning when she turned to look at him he would have worried when she said, "If we're short on room, we can stuff the felon in the trunk."

"As long as you don't try to put Thor in there," Hannah quipped back, also smiling.

Rafe was starting to wonder what kind of unstable family he'd gotten himself involved with until he recalled the common stress relief habit of many first responders after a particularly difficult assignment. They called it gallows humor, the darkly funny comments that not only helped them release tension but also distracted their wounded minds from the reality they dealt with on an almost daily basis. He wasn't particularly surprised to hear Lucy resorting to such wry humor, but he was a bit unsettled when Hannah joined in so effortlessly.

"I'll hold the beast on my lap if I need to," Rafe said, joining the spirit of the conversation. "At least *he* likes me."

Ahead, Lucy held up a hand, signaling a stop before easing open the side exit off the kitchen. Rafe saw her listening intently, as was he. The house and garage seemed deserted except for their little party. Nevertheless, he saw Lucy draw her gun, signal once more, then step down into the darkness.

The irrational urge to accompany her hit Rafe. He knew the woman was a pro and on her own turf so she'd be safer than anywhere else, yet he still wanted to cover her back. That was part of his training, of course, and the reason why partners were so important. They could be the difference between life and death.

Thoughts of poor Andy and his missing teenage daughter dumped Rafe's mood lower than the cellar they'd used to escape. It wasn't just a job for him. Not anymore. It was penance. A calling beyond anything else. He'd failed Andy and his daughter, Kristy, and he intended to make things right again, one way or another.

His problem now was the added responsibility for two civilians who were anything but normal, and who had ended up swimming in the same pool of hungry sharks where he was trapped. In retrospect he couldn't see any way he could have changed previous circumstances to avoid the mess they were in, yet he kept thinking, wondering, imagining a different scenario.

If he'd been positive the women would be safe in police custody he'd have told them to turn themselves in. Unfortunately, he wasn't convinced that that was the best course of action. Truth to tell, he didn't know what was.

Lucy reappeared out of the dimness, startling Hannah enough to make her jump and leading Rafe to grasp her shoulders. When she didn't object he kept hold for extra seconds before releasing her.

"You," Lucy said, pointing to him, "Go back to the room I was in and bring the two duffle bags I left on the floor. I'll have the trunk open for you to stow them."

"Then what?"

"Then you get in as fast as you can. Drag your feet and we'll leave you behind. Got that?"

"Affirmative," Rafe said, slipping into official jargon. He wanted to ask for her assurance she wasn't planning to ditch him regardless but thought better of it. She could have chosen plenty of other ways to get rid of him if she'd wanted to, yet she'd not only kept him with them, she'd provided a weapon.

He moved swiftly and stealthily through the silent home, located the bags she'd readied and returned with them. A shiny black Charger sat in the rear of the garage, waiting. An overhead door began to rise. Rafe expected the car's powerful motor to roar as soon as he'd loaded the trunk and slammed the lid. Instead, he heard the starter turning over repeatedly, as if the battery was not quite powerful enough to start the engine.

Holding his breath as he dove through the door into the rear seat he sent up a silent prayer for success. Once the car was running its generator would recharge the battery. The key was that first cough, that first catch after being left idle for so long.

Lucy tried again, rested a moment, then turned the key once more. The car sputtered, then roared. She raced the engine. Black smoke billowed from the rear.

Looking back over the trunk lid, Rafe saw movement. People? Yes! "Goose it!" he shouted, realizing that Lucy was already doing just that. Tires squealed as they spun and slipped on the cement floor.

As the Charger fishtailed out of the garage and straightened in the long driveway, the rear window shattered into a thousand tiny shards.

Rafe grabbed Thor without thinking and pushed him down in the seat to protect them both.

Even a low growl was not enough to cause him to let go.

From the front he heard Hannah shout, "Down," and felt the K-9 drop below him. Before he had a chance to thank her she was climbing over the center console into the back seat with him and the dog.

"I'll take care of him," Hannah shouted. "Get up front with Gram where you can help her."

It occurred to Rafe to ask how he could hope to help while they were fleeing in a speeding car. Instead, he obeyed. His long legs gave him trouble but he managed to finally get squared away and slide down into the bucket seat.

There was no doubt that Lucy was a master at defensive driving. He was thankful for that since they seemed to have eluded the assassins.

"How can I help?" Rafe was nearly yelling.

"Center console," Lucy shot back. "In the bottom."

Lifting the lid and reaching deep, Rafe felt the hard, cold metal of another gun. "You want me to...?"

"Yes. I can't very well drive and shoot at the same time." Inclining her head she indicated the rear seat. "Hannah is a crack shot, but I'm not sure she's up to firing at a human target."

"And you think I am?"

"I know you are," the older woman said. "I saw it in your eyes before you said a word to me back at the church."

He saw no reason to argue. She was right. As much as he loathed the idea of harming anyone he was trained to make that decision when he must. It was nothing to be proud of. It was simply a fact. Sometimes even those sworn to uphold the law had to employ deadly force in the course of their duties.

After removing the firearm from the console he examined it, extracted the clip to make sure it was fully loaded, then reassembled the gun and cocked it. "Ready."

"I figured you would be," Lucy said, grimacing. "You're not my first choice for a partner but you'll have to do."

Remembering his mistaken reply to Hannah back at the house, Rafe smiled wryly. "I should be your first choice. Don't forget. Hannah says I'm wonderful."

From the back seat came a loud, clear, "Hah!"

As far as Hannah was concerned it was no longer necessary to visit the wounded state trooper in the hospital to prove Rafe's backstory. However, since Gram was driving and had practically deputized him by giving him a gun, she figured she might as well go with the flow, so to speak.

Once they had reached busier streets in downtown St. Louis Lucy had begun to drive more normally. Hannah's nerves insisted she keep watching the traffic behind them, to no avail. They weren't being followed. Best of all, whoever had been on their tail would have no idea where they were headed or when they'd surface next so they couldn't be setting up an ambush.

Thoughts like those reminded Hannah of the predictable plots of old Western movies. Too bad she couldn't rewind reality the way you could a video recording.

Intent on soothing the frightened shepherd, she stroked his fur while staring out the car windows. Cold air was whooshing in through the broken rear glass, making her glad she'd grabbed a hoodie as part of her getaway wardrobe. As soon as they stopped she planned to fish it out of the pack. In the meantime, she warmed herself by cuddling Thor.

In the front seat, Rafe was pivoting to keep scanning their surroundings. Hannah met his gaze when it landed on her. "What?"

"Nothing." Smiling, he turned away. "I'm just glad your furry pal didn't bite me when I shoved him down to keep him from getting shot."

"I think he's decided you're one of the good guys."

"What about you?" Rafe asked. "Have you decided that, too."

"The jury's still out, but I have to say you've been consistent. And if Gram trusts you, I guess I do, too."

"You don't make up your own mind about things like that?"

"I used to," Hannah said, "before I made a big mistake and got too friendly with the men in my prison class."

"Not everybody is like Deuce Fleming," Rafe reminded her.

Lucy had been staying out of their conversation until then. "Enough are to make me leery. In this case, however, I'm glad it's all turning out this way. I've waited years to even the score for my family."

"Vengeance is Mine, I will repay," Hannah quoted from scripture referring to God's promises.

Lucy snorted a wry chuckle. "True, true. I do believe the Good Lord evens the score eventually. The thing is, what's to say He isn't doing it through us this time?"

That seemed right and wrong at the same time. Hannah held her peace until Rafe piped up with a heartfelt "Amen."

Then she shook her head and said, "I think you're both wrong. I think this is happening as a result of what I've done."

"Plenty of guilt to go around," Lucy said wisely.

Catching Rafe's eye in the side mirror Hannah was convinced she saw signs of his sorrowful agreement. Perhaps this was a good time to quiz him regarding his former law enforcement partner.

"Tell me more about this man we're going to see at the hospital," Hannah urged. "I don't want to say the wrong thing and make him worry more. What set this whole thing off, anyway? An assignment or pure chance?"

Noting the squaring of his shoulders she didn't ask more. As he finally began to explain she was glad she hadn't. The situation was worse than she'd imagined, meaning Rafe and Gram had been right taking the unfolding of events so seriously.

"Andy and I were part of a task force looking into the disappearances of high school– and college-aged young people. We were getting close to unmasking the gang behind the kidnappings when Deuce Fleming was arrested for parole violations and sent back to prison. He was incarcerated when Andy's daughter, Kristy, was taken so it was evident he was running the whole show from behind bars."

"Okay. That explains why you were undercover, but how did Andy get hurt?"

"He thought he had a hot tip about a warehouse that might be Kristy's location. We requested backup before going in but his fatherly urges were too strong to wait. I should have stopped him from making entry. Instead, I went with him."

"And he was shot."

"Yes. We never saw the sniper. Clearly, we'd been set up and fell for the oldest trick in the book."

"No Kristy?"

"No Kristy or any other teens, either. The place had been used as a halfway station at one time, but there was no current activity and very few clues."

"What's the connection between what happened and Fleming? I'm not seeing that clearly." Hannah paused. "I mean, how can you be sure *that* gang is the one that took Andy's girl?"

Rafe cleared his throat as if there was a huge lump in it before he explained further. "Because they taunted our team. We had word Kristy Fellows was missing hours before she was reported gone from school. They not only took her, they were proud of doing it."

"So you went to prison."

"Yes. It was the least I could do under the circumstances."

"It was dangerous."

Rafe huffed. "Everything I do on the job is life-threatening. Being in prison was just one more way to die. Like you said before, if it isn't my time it isn't my time."

"Except that God allows us to make mistakes, as we all know. There can be extenuating circumstances."

"Agreed," Rafe said. "All I can do, all any of us can do, is our best in any given situation."

"You've got that right," Lucy chimed in. She was slowing for a turn into the hospital parking lot so Hannah sat back.

Had she ruined Rafe's chances of rescuing the teenager? Hannah asked herself. *Please, Lord, no.* The unspoken plea was followed by a more specific prayer. *Father, let me make this right and not mess it up again. Please, please.*

There was no booming voice from heaven, no flash of divine lightning to let her know she'd been heard, yet she was sure she had. Courage and trust in her faith would play a big part in her future actions, of course, and there was always Thor to rely on, even if no people stayed by her side through this trial.

Yes, she wished she'd had more time in which to assess and train him. He'd clearly had some lessons in walking on a leash and defending his handler against attack because she'd seen that in action. Reliably calling him off was another story.

Nevertheless, Hannah thought as she slipped an arm over the

shepherd's shoulders and gave him a pat, he was large and formidable-looking enough to make an actual command for pursuit and takedown unnecessary. She hoped. Smiling slightly, Hannah corrected that thought. It was more than hope, it was assurance. Her actions for the greater good would be blessed. They had to be. The alternative was simply unacceptable.

Chapter Ten

"I think Hannah should stay in the car," Rafe told Lucy as
she parked.

As expected, the dog trainer had other ideas. "No way."

He shook his head. "Your grandmother and I can do this
without you and the dog. You can't leave him locked in the car
alone. He'll get scared. You should stay with him."

"I intend to stay with him," Hannah shot back. "All the way
to Andy's room and back."

"Security won't let him in." At least Rafe hoped not.

"They will once I put a training vest on him. Gram, pop
the trunk and let me grab my hoodie and the special harness."

"I take it I'm outnumbered," he muttered as he straightened
beside the car to tuck the gun into the back of his belt.

Lucy huffed and smiled while Hannah dressed herself and
Thor, then faced Rafe, hands on her hips. "You betcha."

"That's what I was afraid of." Turning, he led the way toward the side entrance portico. Unless someone in the hospital
intervened and stopped them he was going to have to put up
with his unwanted entourage. Well, so be it. He'd dealt with
plenty of uncomfortable situations in the past. Compared to
most of them, this was not so bad. What bothered him most

was providing adequate protection for them all while they were out in public. Risking his own life was one thing. Letting civilians do the same was entirely different.

Except for signs warning of contagion and portable sanitation stations, the small lobby leading to the emergency room was essentially empty. Someone pushing a patient in a wheelchair passed them as they entered the double swinging doors, and he could see nurses ducking in and out of Emergency room cubicles but that was all.

"Third floor, rear," he said, ushering the others to an elevator and pushing the call button. Panting, Thor was seated politely on Hannah's left. Lucy flanked her on the right. The older woman was obviously well trained and aware of the chances they were all taking. That helped Rafe relax a bit. So did the obedience of the K-9. He'd liked that dog the minute he'd laid eyes on him and nothing had happened since to change his mind.

Crossing the threshold into the elevator was new to Thor. He cringed and stopped. Hannah's gentle encouragement brought him through and once inside he seemed calmer, although Rafe could see him trembling.

"I told you to leave him in the car," he said.

"He'll be fine," she countered. "This would be part of his regular orientation, anyway."

"I guess getting shot at would be too, right?"

"I hope you mean like what happened when we were in the car. You haven't seen any threats here, have you?"

"I'd have told you if I had."

Lucy agreed. "So would I."

Everyone fell back behind Rafe as he led the way onto the third floor and headed for Andy's room. The so-called patient in the second bed was actually an armed officer. The task force had chosen to protect their injured member that way to avoid making a guard evident. In truth, the powers that be were using Andy as bait, hoping Fleming's gang would try to finish the job and leave themselves open to capture in the process. Secrecy was paramount, meaning Rafe was not about to inform his present companions. Not unless he absolutely had to.

He pushed open the door. Andy was sitting up in bed, eating with the hand not hampered by a sling. The second bed had privacy curtains drawn around it.

Grinning, Rafe greeted him. "Good to see you looking so well, buddy." As he spoke he cast a telling glance toward the other bed, wondering why the officer sent to guard Andy hadn't stopped them. "Everything okay?"

Andy pushed away the tray table and scowled at Rafe, then looked past him at the women and dog. "Yeah, yeah. What's going on? Why did you abandon your assignment?"

"I didn't." Approaching the bed he gestured. "This is Hannah Lassiter, the dog trainer from Lyell. Fleming coerced her into helping him escape. I went along to keep an eye on him."

"So, where is he?"

Shrugging, Rafe shook his head. "We don't know. We believe that members of his gang have him and are taking his orders because they've been trying to get even with us for botching his escape. We should be able to get a line on him soon." He paused. "Providing they don't kill us first."

"That's a comforting plan. Is that the best you can do?"

"For the present," Rafe said. "Hannah and Lucy, her grandmother here, have a target on their backs so we're sticking together in this. I brought them to see you to prove I'm on the up-and-up. We've all had to do things we didn't like and it's my goal to get back in Fleming's good graces as soon as possible."

"By hanging out with them?" There was barely disguised anger in the wounded man's words.

Rafe understood. "It just worked out this way, buddy. Once they were involved I couldn't abandon them. Deuce would have killed them in a heartbeat."

"What about Kristy?" Andy was almost shouting. "What about my daughter?"

"I'm not giving up," Rafe promised. "Lucy has experience with human trafficking operations and may actually be of help to us."

"And the dog lady?"

"She's the reason Deuce escaped, yes, but she wants to make amends, and Thor has already been useful."

"I take it Thor is the dog and you're not hiding a Viking bodybuilder out in the hall."

"Right." He chanced a smile. "We will do this. I promise we will. I'm not sure why I ended up saddled with this posse but here we are."

From behind him Rafe heard Hannah's indignant "Hey…" before Lucy silenced her with "Hush."

Seated between the women, Thor stood and began to growl. Rafe tensed. Looked to Hannah. "What's wrong with him?"

"The mood in this room is probably affecting him." She laid a hand on the shepherd's broad head. His whole body had started to shake worse than it had in the elevator.

Rafe drew the gun Lucy had given him and stood with his back to Andy's bed. Thor was still growling and staring at the closed-off area containing the second bed.

"Give him some slack," Rafe told her. "Just enough to tell us what he senses."

Andy piped up. "It's probably the guy in the other bed. He's okay."

"Do you know his name?"

"Brad, something."

"Okay, Brad," Rafe said. "Hands in the air and open the curtains."

Long seconds passed. Rafe tensed more when he saw Lucy draw her own gun and push Hannah to the side. Thor resisted, remaining focused on who or what was behind the heavy privacy curtains.

A shot echoed in the small room, skimmed over Andy's bed and left a round hole in the window.

Hannah shrieked and ducked to protect her K-9. Lucy took a two-handed shooter's stance. Rafe jerked back the curtain. "Freeze. Police."

A black-clad figure bolted out the opposite side and through the exit.

"Are you all okay?" Rafe shouted, hesitating momentarily to check for himself.

Satisfied at the answers, he yelled, "Hold the dog," ran for the door and burst into the hallway, aiming at the ceiling for safety. Except for a nurse standing there, frozen in shock, it was empty.

Gripping Thor's leash with both hands Hannah was barely able to keep him from giving chase. Control by the handler was essential, of course, particularly since neither she nor Rafe knew what the dog might do inside a busy hospital. Moreover, if Thor was triggered by the sight of a running man, he might go after Rafe, himself, instead of the man he was chasing.

She watched her grandmother begin to relax, then move to check on Andy as soon as Rafe reentered the room. Instead of going to his former partner, however, he swept back the curtains to reveal the empty bed. Correction. It wasn't empty. There was a young-looking man lying in it, moaning.

"Is that Brad?" she asked, hardly needing an answer.

Andy confirmed it with a nod. "Is he okay?"

"I think so." Rafe pushed a call button to summon a nurse, although Hannah figured they'd have plenty of company in the room soon, thanks to the gunshot.

"Did the shooter get away?" Again, an unnecessary question. Making eye contact with Rafe Hannah said, "We can probably use Thor to track him if we hurry. Otherwise, we'll be stuck here explaining to Security who we are and why we came."

Wheeling, he grabbed her elbow and called to Lucy. "She's right. Let's go."

There was no way for Hannah to command Thor to track since she hadn't trained him yet so she simply let him lead her out of the room and down the hallway. He stopped at the elevator they'd used to get there. Whether that meant the shooter had left that way or the dog was merely retracing his own steps was anybody's guess.

The door slid open immediately. Thor leaped over the threshold and Hannah followed.

"Is this how he got away?" Rafe asked her.

"It may be. Or the dog may just want to leave. It's impossible to tell until we get back to the lobby or parking lot and see which way he goes from there."

"Better than nothing," Lucy said flatly, pushing the door close control, then ground floor. "I wasn't looking forward to explaining how we got these guns into the hospital and why we need to keep them."

"Yeah."

Hannah could tell Rafe was upset, probably more at himself than anyone else, although she supposed there was enough disappointment to go around. He'd made a tactical error by not checking the other bed space himself rather than just taking Andy's word for it. Desire to be in and out of the hospital as quickly as possible did explain it, although she figured poor Rafe had to be beating himself up over the lapse in judgment.

Thor pushed his way past Lucy and Rafe to lead Hannah out of the elevator. Because he immediately turned toward the main exit she assumed he was merely taking her back to the parking lot.

She ordered him to stop at the curb outside by giving the leash an abrupt tug. "Sit."

Rafe joined her on the side opposite the canine while Lucy flanked her on the other. Sirens in the distance were getting louder fast. Feeling his hand at her elbow again Hannah looked up at him. "You could leave me and Gram here and take her car."

"Not unless you have a death wish," he countered. "Whoever was up there with Andy now knows for sure that we're working together. That blows my chances to convince Deuce I was acting on his behalf when I went with you."

"I hadn't thought of that." Hannah peered over at Lucy. "Is he right?"

"We'd have to make a lot of assumptions to be sure. Probably."

"So, now what?"

"We find a safe place to talk it over and regroup," Rafe said.

Letting the leash slacken, Hannah was surprised to have Thor pull to the side. "Hold on. Our car is over there." She pointed. "He wants to go the other way. Maybe he is actually tracking and doesn't know how to tell us."

"Okay," Rafe said. "As long as we get away from the building we should be okay for a few more minutes. They'll have us on camera and once they check their videos we'll be IDed."

"How long?" Hannah asked.

"If they're efficient, maybe ten minutes. We can't count on any longer."

"All right." Hannah stepped off the curb and began to follow Thor's lead. He put his nose to the ground a few times, apparently relying mostly on airborne scents. There was no wavering, no hesitation to his mission and she was beyond thrilled. This K-9 was even more special than she'd thought when she'd pulled him from the shelter in spite of a sign on the kennel door warning that he was vicious. Maybe he had snapped at somebody in the past. Frightened animals with no other recourse or a viable escape route often used their teeth and claws for defense. That didn't make them bad, it merely meant they had been mishandled.

At the end of a row of parked cars, Thor paused, then began to pick up the pace. Hannah kept up by giving him more lead when she fell behind. She could sense the others following her and the thrill of the chase was making her heart pound.

Things were about to turn around for them. Thor was going to help apprehend an armed thug and solve Rafe's problems without anybody else being harmed.

Thor strained against his harness. Elated, she started to follow him across the street to an auxiliary parking lot.

An engine roared. Tires squealed. Hannah was jerked backwards in the nick of time to avoid being run over by a speeding SUV.

The leash came out of her grip. She screamed. "Thor!"

Rafe held her tightly by one arm, Lucy by the other.

A sob choked her. She covered her face, afraid to look. Afraid to imagine. "Thor?"

Chapter Eleven

Because Hannah had buried her face in her hands and Lucy had immediately begun to comfort her, Rafe was the first to see what had actually happened. He was elated. "Look!"

"I can't." Hannah shook her head.

"No. Look." Rafe clasped her shoulders and physically turned her. "See? He's okay."

The big German shepherd cowered barely ten feet away. Rafe crossed the street with the women, still partially supporting Hannah because she seemed unsteady, then released her as she fell to her knees at the curb to embrace her brave dog.

He turned to make eye contact with Lucy. "Did you get a plate number."

"No. Did you?"

Disgusted with himself, he shook his head. "No. I was busy."

"Yes. Thanks. For everything," the older woman said. "If I hadn't seen it I wouldn't believe it. How in the world did that car miss the dog?"

"It had to be by a hair," Rafe said soberly. "If Hannah had been able to hold on he would have been hit for sure."

Teary-eyed, she looked up at him. "I was trying to pull him

back." She choked back a sob. "If I had, he'd have been killed."
Again, she buried her face in Thor's ruff and hugged him.

To his embarrassment, Rafe found his own eyes growing
moist with empathy. Was there a lesson in this? Were his best
efforts not being rewarded because there was a better way to
proceed? If there was, he sure wasn't seeing it. The would-
be assassins escaping in that SUV were undoubtedly on their
way to inform Deuce which side of the law he was on, thanks
to his casual conversation with Andy. All that effort, all those
days spent in prison, all the background created to support his
story had been for nothing. Except for a few crooked guards
he'd managed to ID while incarcerated, his undercover mission had been a washout.

Bending to take Hannah's arm and urge her to stand he
spoke kindly yet firmly. "I hear sirens. We should go."

Lucy agreed. "You two stay here. I'll bring the car."

"No, Gram," Hannah said. "I'm okay and so is Thor. It'll
be faster if we go with you."

If Rafe hadn't been in full cop mode he would have told her
how proud he was of her bravery and rapid recovery. For a civilian, Hannah Lassiter was behaving with amazing courage
under fire, so to speak. Her only flaw, that he'd seen so far,
was being too tenderhearted.

Rafe joined Lucy and spoke aside. "She's really something,
isn't she?"

The older woman smiled. "You're just now figuring that
out?"

"Guess I'm a little slow."

Lucy chuckled. "I'd say so." She took a few more steps before she asked, "How do you think they located your partner?"

"I don't know, but if we hadn't shown up when we did he'd
probably be a goner."

"Yeah. That's what I think. So, there's a leak inside your de-
partment, too? I mean, you said there was trouble at the prison.
I suppose it's logical to assume others outside are involved."

"I don't like to believe it but you're probably right."

"Thought that's what you'd say." Lucy put out an arm to block him and called to Hannah. "Stop. Now."

"Why?"

"My car," Lucy said, pointing. "The trunk is open. And look at the tires."

Rafe immediately went into a defensive posture and turned with his back to the others. No threats were evident. However, considering the state of their getaway car they were in deep trouble. All four tires had been flattened. There was no way they were going anywhere in that vehicle.

Scowling, Lucy looked at him. "Well, *that's* not good."

"You have a gift for understatement," he said. "Give me your phone and I'll call my superintendent for backup."

"How long will that take?"

"I don't have a clue," Rafe admitted, "but we can't just stand here in the open waiting for the police to shut down the whole hospital."

"True," Hannah said, starting away. "Follow us."

His line of sight took him to her solution and he almost laughed in spite of the seriousness of their plight. The clever dog trainer was on her way to one of the volunteer-run trams the hospital provided to assist patients or visitors who had trouble walking back to their cars.

By the time he and Lucy joined Hannah she had already loaded Thor into the second seat and was waiting for them. An elderly driver wearing a bright yellow vest with the hospital logo was smiling. "Where to, folks?"

While Lucy joined her granddaughter, Rafe sighed and briefly displayed his gun. "Sorry, man. I'm afraid I have to insist that you get out and let me drive."

The man paled and waved his hands in the air as he stepped aside. "Don't shoot. Don't shoot."

"I'll take your vest, too."

"Sure, sure." He shed it quickly.

Rather than reassure him, Rafe chose to simply don the vest over his jacket, slide behind the wheel and press the accelerator. The tram was electric and its top speed was probably ten or fifteen miles an hour. Still, it was better than standing in the midst of the parking lot waiting to be spotted.

"Is this as fast as it goes?" Lucy asked, sounding miffed.

"Yup. Sit back and enjoy the ride."

Hearing Hannah giggle, even a tiny bit, lifted Rafe's spirits. Not much had changed to lessen the danger they faced, yet she had begun to return to her normal self. Once again he was favorably impressed. Someone who had been orphaned and raised by grandparents, regardless of the elders' hidden occupations, should have been less self-assured, less brave, less able to think clearly during stressful periods. Come to think of it, most people would fall apart under constant threat no matter what their backgrounds.

Unfamiliar with the parking lot, Rafe made a turn that took him back toward the door where several patients waited in wheel chairs pushed by more volunteers.

Bypassing them he waved. "Sorry. Full. Catch you next time."

Behind him he heard Hannah laugh again. "You are a chameleon. If I didn't know better I'd have insisted you were the real driver."

"I'll keep that in mind if I ever need to change jobs." Proceeding to a secluded spot at the rear of the sprawling hospital, Rafe stopped the tram and turned to Lucy with his hand out. "Phone."

"Not until I've had a chance to call in a few favors," she said. "Now that Hannah here knows the truth about our family, I figure I may as well take advantage of my connections."

"I thought you were retired," Rafe said.

Lucy paused to pat Hannah's hand and smile before she said, "Some jobs end at retirement, some don't. I like to keep communication open." With that, she stepped spryly out of the tram and walked away, phone pressed to her ear.

When Rafe looked at Hannah's face he glimpsed the concern he'd expected to see before. Yes, she was brave and, yes, she could handle herself well in difficult situations, the same as her beloved grandmother could. Part of that was likely good acting. Hannah was smart enough to realize how desperate their predicament was, yet strong enough to cope with it calmly.

He finally decided to compliment her. "You're doing very well, considering our circumstances."

"Hah!" Shaking her head she grinned at him. "The fun just keeps coming, doesn't it?"

If he hadn't seen the slight trembling of her lower lip he might have been fooled into thinking she was carefree. Of course she was scared. Anyone would be. Even Lucy was probably worried despite her secret agent persona. After all, Hannah was her only close relative and she obviously loved her immensely.

Without pausing to think first, he reached over the back of the driver's seat and touched her hand.

To his surprise she not only didn't pull away, she turned her hand over and laced her fingers through his.

That level of trust and acceptance floored him. Instead of breaking contact he closed his grip and gave her hand a squeeze, unsure whether he was doing it for her or for his own benefit.

Truth to tell, Rafe thought, he'd prefer to enjoy the moment of contact instead of trying to analyze it. Giving comfort had been his intent. Receiving it back in equal proportion was totally unexpected. And nice. Very nice. Then he looked into her eyes and their shared touch became far more personal.

Hannah didn't want to release Rafe's hand. Ever. Something about the way he was holding her hand was making her feel strangely comforted in spite of their short history. Only the return of her grandmother was enough to make her let go.

Lucy waved her cell phone. "Everybody out of this race car," she quipped. "They'll be looking for it by now and we have real wheels on the way."

Relief flooded Hannah. Keeping her cool and behaving rationally under the present circumstances had taken a lot of effort and she was looking forward to truly relaxing, assuming they would ever be through running.

She'd realized earlier that the only way to survive and prosper again was to eliminate the Fleming gang. As a bonus, when they did that, they would be in position to rescue not only Andy's daughter but hopefully many other victims of human trafficking. Recent news reports and even TV documentaries and movies had made the public aware of the worldwide problem. It was going to feel very good to take part in thwarting the horrible crime. She just wished she could save every child who had been taken.

Looking to Lucy, she asked, "Can they tell you anything about where Kristy might be?"

When Gram shook her head, Hannah looked to Rafe. "What about you? Didn't you say there was some kind of task force involved?"

"They're how I managed to get sent to Lyell," he said, shedding the vest and leaving it in the tram. "We know Fleming was running the operation from prison. Now that he's out and can do it in person, it's going to be much harder to break up the ring."

That reality had been lurking in the recesses of Hannah's mind. Hearing it voiced caused her actual physical pain. She sighed. "I am so, so sorry. I tried to reach the new warden ahead of time, but I never managed to get through to him. Somebody always put me off."

"That's interesting to hear," Rafe said. "Did you happen to get a name?"

"No. I assumed it was his secretary. It was a woman."

"I'll pass that on to my superintendent." Once again he reached a hand toward Lucy. "Your phone, please?"

Although she hesitated, she did finally hand it over. "You need—we need—a couple of burner phones. Pay as you go can't be easily traced, if at all, particularly if we destroy them after one or two uses."

"Agreed," Rafe said. "Is this one encrypted?"

"How did you guess?"

In the background, Hannah huffed. "Because you're a spy, silly. You're probably loaded with secret weapons."

"Don't I wish," Lucy said wryly. "I'm afraid I'm all out of exploding pens and cyanide capsules."

"Well, that's a relief."

Leaving the others, Rafe stepped away to make private contact with his superintendent. The call went directly to voice mail. Two subsequent tries had the same result so he gave the phone back to its owner. "No answer. Thanks anyway."

"So, now what?" Hannah asked, looking from one of her companions to the other. "You guys are the pros. Thor and I are just along for the ride." Shaking her head she made a sound of derision. "I must admit it's not nearly as much fun as it looks like on TV or sounds like in books."

"Reality can be unpleasant," Rafe replied. "It can also be awesome when the good guys win."

"Are we?" she asked. "Are we really the good guys when we've had to break the law over and over. I have real trouble rationalizing what we've—what I've—been doing."

"I get it," he said. "I do. The thing is, sometimes it's necessary to step over a line because that's where evil is hiding. Keep thinking about Kristy and all the scared, suffering kids like her and you won't have nearly as much trouble doing whatever is necessary. Fleming and his gang need to be taken down and for some reason we're in a position to do that."

"Are we really?" Hannah was far from convinced. "You've

lost your in with Deuce and Gram and I are apparently on a hit list. How is that a good thing?"

"A connection is a connection," Rafe said. "The more they come after us, the greater our chances of catching one or more who will cave under pressure and tell us what we need to know."

"You mean about where Kristy is?"

"Her, and others." He paused. "The more time that passes, the greater the probability she will be flown out of the country. She's a pretty girl and Fleming has bragged that he intends to break up the task force, one way or another."

"Doesn't he realize that the more he hurts people, the greater their desire will be to stop him?"

"He's a sadist. He gets thrills from causing pain in others. At this point I wish I could say he's merely defending his illicit businesses, but I think this has turned into a personal vendetta."

"Against us?"

"Us and the whole task force," Rafe told her. "We have guards on our families and some have even been moved to secret locations."

"What about you?" Hannah asked. "Do you have a family?"

"No," he said, sounding sad.

"Parents? Siblings?"

As he shook his head and made eye contact with her, Hannah realized that he was even more alone in the world than she was. At least she had Gram. Poor Rafe had no one.

"I'm sorry," she said.

"I'm not. Especially in situations like this," he said. "If there is nobody special in my life, they can't hurt me as badly."

"You care about Andy and Kristy, though."

"Yes, I do. I've known her since she was little. That's another reason why we have to rescue her. It's personal for me, too."

Chapter Twelve

If Rafe had had his way, they would have stayed together. Instead, Lucy insisted that she and Hannah separate from him. He might not like the idea but he did see the older woman's logic.

Thor was the giveaway to any observer. Even an untrained eye could tell the big German shepherd was special and his presence painted a bulls-eye on Hannah's back. That was undoubtedly why Lucy had led her off and found them a hidey hole in shrubbery several hundred yards away while he took up a position behind a trash collection array to wait for backup.

He would have been a lot happier if he'd had his own cell phone so he could keep trying the superintendent's private line. There had to be information of some kind filtering into the station. The more he knew, the better his chances of success—and survival—would be.

A golf cart with two uniformed security guards in it rounded the corner and approached. Rafe ducked back out of sight and peeked between large trash containers.

The driver stopped the cart. He and his partner got out, drew their guns and approached the abandoned tram. They were so intent on repossessing the stolen transport they only briefly scanned their surroundings then ignored them to inspect the tram. He expected them to leave it parked there and call a forensics team but they didn't. One of the guards slid behind the wheel while the other returned to the golf cart and they drove off together.

Luck? No. He didn't believe in luck. He did, however, give credit where it was due so he sent a quick glance into the clouds and smiled. "Thanks."

If he had been running an investigation into the gunshot on the third floor he would have sent someone back to canvas the area surrounding the recovered tram ASAP. With all the police officers now inside the hospital he figured it was only a matter of time before they did just that. Besides, he wanted, needed, to be near Hannah and her grandmother when their replacement car arrived. They weren't going to get rid of him. Not now. Not yet. And certainly not after they had been observed in Andy's room. Fleming already knew who Hannah was and where she and Lucy lived. Deuce was far from stupid. He'd see the connection to law enforcement, put two and two together and find even more incentive to come after them.

Ducking into the shrubbery where he'd last seen the women he expected one of them to answer when he called. "Hannah? Lucy?"

Nothing. Nobody. The old growth was brittle and small pieces had been broken off the hedge. Rafe tried to follow without leaving more signs of passage. Once he was inside the clump of vegetation he could see that it wasn't as dense as it had looked.

He emerged onto a side street, dusted himself off and checked the nearby area. A small strip mall sat across the street while other medical offices filled in the rest of the space. If he was choosing where to go with Hannah and Thor there would be no question.

Checking for oncoming traffic he stepped off the curb.

* * *

Rather than call attention to themselves, Hannah had waited outside while Lucy entered the drugstore to buy supplies. There was no hope of replacing everything they'd lost when the car had been robbed, but at least she'd be able to get the extra phones they needed and perhaps energy bars and something to drink. Hannah's mouth was dry and she imagined Thor was thirsty, too.

It seemed kind of silly to be worrying about food when their lives were in danger. Then again, there was nothing like eating a little chocolate to make a person feel better.

Thor had been sitting at her side while she stood behind an array of spring flowers displayed on a tall rack. Suddenly she felt him tense, then stand, bristling.

"What is it, boy? What's wrong?"

The dog took a step in slow motion, as if creeping up on an enemy.

Hannah held him back. Away from Gram and Rafe, with only Thor to defend her, she was very vulnerable.

"This is why wild animals freeze in place when they sense danger," she muttered, letting her own voice soothe her while she watched the K-9 closely for signs of what their next move should be.

Standing hackles on the shepherd's neck and shoulders made him look even larger than he was, and he was plenty big. She glanced between the door to the store and open space on the other side of the flower display. Cars were passing slowly, each one bringing a possible enemy closer. Prior encounters with Fleming's gang led her to believe they would be driving black cars or SUVs. Logic insisted otherwise. Every encounter could be deadly. Every passing car could hold evil personified.

Thor shifted his focus to the left. Hannah's gaze followed. Was that...? It sure looked like Rafe. Nevertheless, she stayed hidden. When Gram was with them she had a lot less trouble relaxing in the company of the supposed convict. His story gibed with Andy's and there were plenty of other reasons to believe him, of course. It wasn't just that. The closest she could describe it was an inner survival instinct. She wanted to trust Rafe completely, really she did.

"Who are you trying to convince?" Hannah whispered to herself. Thor responded by giving her a quick glance before zeroing in on the approaching man and beginning to wag his tail.

Intense relief washed over Hannah like a warm, tropical wave and thanksgiving rippled along her nerves. It was Rafe. And, to her great surprise, she was genuinely happy to see him. So what had become of her caution, her hesitancy? She didn't know and she didn't care.

She heard him call, "Lucy? Hannah?" as she brought Thor to heel and stepped into view.

The instant Rafe spotted her his countenance bloomed into joy, complete with a silly grin. He pivoted then jogged toward her.

There was no way Hannah was going to avoid the kind of fond greeting she expected from him. On the contrary, she was so filled with relief and her own happiness she opened her arms to him and accepted his embrace as if they were long-lost friends.

All he said at first was her name. That was enough, particularly since his tone was so gentle. Their hug was easy, too. Although it didn't last nearly as long as Hannah had hoped, the emotion they shared was clear.

Finally, he set her away, hands on her shoulders. "Hannah. I was afraid I'd lost you."

Blinking back happy tears she tilted her head toward the store entrance. "Gram saw this place and figured they'd have some of the things she wanted so we came over. We were going to go back for you. I know we were."

"I hope so."

"What happened? Did they find the tram?"

"Yes. Some security personnel showed up and took it away."

To her delight Rafe stayed very close, their shoulders almost touching. Hannah agreed with his obvious desire for proximity. She kept Thor on a short lead while she spoke quietly. "I'll be happier once Gram's contacts bring us wheels but I have no idea where we'll go from here, do you?"

Rafe was shaking his head. He slipped one arm around her. "Not a clue. I'm hoping I can get through to my superintendent soon. We're flying blind until we get better intel."

"And word about Andy's daughter," Hannah added. "That has to be everybody's first priority because elapsed time increases the danger to her."

"True." He gave her shoulders a squeeze. "In one way I'm sorry you're involved, but if you stop and think about it, we do make a pretty good team."

"You and Gram do," Hannah said flatly. She leaned into him, feeling intrinsically connected and drawing strength from him in spite of her earlier misgivings. "I'm not that important."

"Yes, you are. If you and I hadn't gotten involved in the first place, you could have been eliminated as soon as Deuce was free and we wouldn't have federal help, either."

"Surely, the government has its own anti-trafficking forces. Citizens are being transported across state lines and even overseas."

"They do. And we're in contact with them, at least my superiors are. The thing is, you and I and Lucy are boots on the ground, so to speak. Because we're in the thick of things we have different opportunities to break up this particular smuggling ring. It won't end everything. Nothing short of Armageddon can do that. The way I see it, every bite we take out of the system is a victory."

"I can't imagine how scared those young people like Kristy Fellows must be. It's mind-boggling."

"Yes, it is."

Sensing his deepening concern and frustration, Hannah didn't know what to say, how to soothe him. He was right about the unspeakable horrors of the crime they were fighting. It was so vast, so organized, their job seemed insurmountable. Which it was. That wasn't the point, was it?

"So, one Deuce Fleming at a time, right? And then another and another. That's a good thing."

"Humph. Yeah. Let's get the first one behind bars before we celebrate, shall we?"

"Of course."

"Will you be okay if I go inside and look for Lucy? There are a few things I want her to buy for me and she's the one with the money."

Hannah risked a slight smile. "So, what you're saying is that you're going to dump me for a wealthy cougar?"

"Something like that." His mouth twitched as if he was repressing a grin of his own.

"Okay. I'll let you go this time. Just don't forget to come back for me."

"Never," Rafe said soberly, giving her a poignant parting glance. "You're unforgettable in many ways, Hannah Lassiter."

Glad he'd left her without saying more or waiting for her to comment, she watched him walk away. A casual observer wouldn't see anything unusual about him. He was that good at pretending to be carefree and therefore anonymous. She'd called him a chameleon before for good reason. And there lay the conundrum.

Who was he really? Inside all the pretense, what kind of man was Rafe McDowell. For that matter, what was his real name? She doubted it was Rafe. Yes, he was an officer of the law. And, yes, he had been on a covert assignment inside Lyell. That she could accept. The worrisome details now encompassed her personal involvement. As he had said, they needed each other if they hoped to put an end to Fleming's operations, particularly his human trafficking. She was totally on board for that.

When this assignment ended, however, what would become

of him? He'd go on to the next job and then the next, wherever he was sent, meaning his presence in and around St. Louis was temporary, at best. Which meant...?

"Do not fall for him," Hannah muttered, knowing she was absolutely right and suspecting it was already too late.

She shook her head and made a face before adding a cynical, "Yeah, right."

Locating Lucy in the store wasn't as easy as Rafe had assumed it would be. Not only was she fairly short, her clothing was nondescript enough for her to blend in with every other regular shopper.

When he finally did spot her he approached quietly. "It would help if you had white hair."

"Take that up with my DNA," she said, frowning at him. "Why are you in here?"

"Hospital security picked up the tram. I figured it was better to join you again instead of waiting to be discovered hiding near the hospital. Why? Were you planning to ditch me?"

"Not at all." Lucy gestured at the shopping cart she was pushing. "I got us some hoodies, new phones and energy bars, flashlights and extra batteries, bottled water and soda pop. What else?"

"Weapons?"

"In a drugstore?"

Rafe nodded. "You could trade those cans for half liters of soda so we'll have the bottles. Go buy matches. And something flammable to use for wicks."

"Not very good for defense," she said.

"Unless we're stuck somewhere. We need gloves, too."

"I have latex ones in the cart."

"Work gloves, too. Hannah's...our hands may need protecting."

"I did think of her needs. They don't have much of a grocery selection in here. No dog food. I already checked."

"We need to hit a couple of ATMs, too. It's not sensible for you to be the only one carrying cash."

"Already thought of that. The car they're sending us will have new, untraceable credit cards and IDs for all three of us."

"You included me? How?"

That brought a wry chuckle. "You're forgetting who I worked for. Big Brother knows everything about everybody."

"I can't say that's too comforting but in this case it's handy. What else have you done while I was dumpster diving and watching your backs?"

The older woman eyed him up and down. "Not actually diving, I hope. Which reminds me. We need hand sanitizer and wipes."

"And a first aid kit," Rafe added. "A big one."

"The car should be well equipped with things like that," Lucy said. "I'll pick up the rest of the stuff and meet you outside. Go protect Hannah."

"With my life," Rafe said quietly.

Eyes narrowing and jaw clenching, Lucy nodded and said, "I'm counting on it."

Chapter Thirteen

Seeing Rafe returning without Gram worried Hannah until he explained.

"Okay, fine," she said, resting one hand on Thor's head and wiggling her fingers to scratch behind his ears. "How are we supposed to recognize the good guys or the new car they're bringing? I mean, they're not supposed to look like Secret Service agents in black suits and aviator glasses with listening wires sticking out of their ears, are they?"

Rafe chuckled. "Probably not."

She inched farther behind the rack of spring plants, wishing there was a better hiding place available. "I don't like standing out here like this. One of the St. Louis patrol cars drove through this parking lot a few minutes ago. I didn't realize what the white car was until I saw the blue lettering and picture of the arch on the side."

"Widening the search. I was afraid of that," Rafe said.

"If he comes back he may spot us. You need to go warn Gram and tell her to hurry."

"We could move to a more secure location."

Hannah huffed in frustration. "Oh? Where? I don't see anything except open space." Continuing to monitor the parking lot as she spoke she kept imagining potential enemies. Every vehicle that rolled slowly past sent her pulse racing, even the ones with geriatric drivers, mothers with small children or groups of teens whooping it up.

"School must be out," Hannah remarked, indicating a passing car with the bass of its radio so loud it rattled windows.

Rafe looked at his left wrist out of habit, then shook his head. "I keep forgetting I'm still in prison mode. No watch."

"I've been thinking about that," Hannah said. "What's to keep the police from shooting you as an escaped convict? The news about us and Fleming must be all over the TV and radio." She shivered. "Come to think of it, they're probably hunting me and Thor, too."

"Hopefully, Warden Hotchkiss has taken charge of press releases and we're safe for the present."

"You don't know that he's on our side. And what about the shooting in Andy's room? They probably think we did that, too, in spite of whatever the warden may say. He can't tell them everything without taking a chance on Fleming finding out and tracing us."

"I'm pretty sure that ship has sailed," Rafe said. "From now on we need to look for chances to go on the offensive. Otherwise we'll be running until we make a mistake and he catches up to us."

"That's not very comforting."

"It's not intended to be."

Lucy's return was a relief for Hannah and presumably for Rafe, too. She pushed a loaded shopping cart toward the flower display rack, then ducked behind with the others.

Hannah gave her a hug. "I thought you'd *never* come back."

"I told you I would."

Eager to do something, anything, Hannah grasped her grandmother's arm. "What now?"

"Find someplace away from people where we can safely

activate a couple of these phones," Lucy said, gesturing at the plastic shopping bags. "I need to coordinate with my people."

"I thought you already did that," Hannah said, confused. "Aren't we waiting for a car?"

"Such things aren't necessarily easy to provide," she countered, "which is why I bought us all black hoodies. Even in a big city it can take hours to put together a delivery like the one I requested. We don't have spy supply stores on every corner, you know."

As Hannah made a face she was sure she heard Rafe stifling a chuckle. Well, so what? How was she to know how these things worked? Obviously the portrayals on TV and in movies were exaggerated.

"There's no need for the two of you to make fun of me," Hannah said flatly, looking from one to the other. Sadly, neither of her companions argued their innocence, leaving her convinced she was the odd man out. It was as if all the other players in this deadly game knew the rules while she was the one blindfolded and groping in the dark. She might as well have been, she reasoned, given her lack of law enforcement training.

Starting away, pushing the cart, Lucy circled the building. Hannah followed with Thor, assuming that Rafe was behind her. When Lucy halted in the delivery area of the stores Hannah discovered that he was not. Panicky, she searched the distance for him. "Gram?"

Lucy patted the air to wave her quiet. "Hush."

Time seemed to slow to a snail's pace. Finally, Hannah spotted a familiar figure ahead of them. He was gesturing and pointing at a loading dock. Clearly, Gram and the pretend convict had worked out a form of silent communication that she, Hannah, was not privy to. Well, fine. Let them cut her out if they didn't think she was smart enough or capable enough to be included in their subversive actions. As long as they all survived this waking nightmare, she'd swallow her pride and go along with whatever they had in mind. She might not like being excluded, but she'd manage to tolerate it. For now.

Lucy started moving faster, almost jogging behind the rattling shopping cart. Hannah kept pace with Thor trotting obediently at her side. Portions of the pavement were still damp and there were puddles in low spots.

"All right," Lucy said when she was inside the raised concrete sides of the dock. "Good choice." Rummaging in a bag she handed everyone a new hoodie to put on, donned hers, then pulled out two cell phones and gave one to Rafe. "Activate it and call your superintendent."

As Hannah watched, her grandmother opened a second package and began to work with another phone.

"I know how to do that, too," Hannah said. For a few seconds she thought no one had heard her. Then, Rafe reached into the plastic bag and brought out a third phone. Without asking, he passed it to Hannah with a slight smile. "Knock yourself out."

Out of the corner of her eye, Hannah saw Lucy frown at him, but she didn't try to take the phone back. That was a plus. Hannah wanted, needed, to feel useful and valued. Yes, it was a bit selfish. She knew that. It was also a sign that at least one of her companions valued her presence as more than just the human on the end of the leash handling a smart K-9. Properly trained, her dogs filled jobs people couldn't do, of course, such as tracking and intelligent defense. Some had even been used to locate victims buried by disasters or children lost in the wilderness.

The usefulness of the animals wasn't in question. The usefulness of their trainer and handler was. Hannah knew she had an important job to do regarding the dogs' training. What she needed now was to feel just as useful in and of herself.

She smiled at Rafe as she removed the phone's packaging. It was a basic unit which needed a Wi-Fi connection in order to be activated. The others were obviously connecting to nearby sources, probably in the store where Lucy had shopped. Hannah let her device do a search, then chose the strongest signal. Completing the installation and activation slightly ahead of the others gave her ego a tiny boost and brought a grin.

She held up the phone. "Ta-da!"

Gram acted less than impressed while Rafe gave her a thumbs-up and leaned closer to share his screen. "Here's my number. Put it into your phone and give me yours so we can talk if we get separated."

Complying, it occurred to Hannah that separation was a possibility no matter how hard they tried to stay together. The thought of being on her own when assassins were on their trail sent a shiver down her spine. The day had been fraught with danger already and it wasn't over yet. Considering what might take place on the next day and the next was terrifying. It also helped ground her by increasing focus.

"All right," Hannah said when she also had her grandmother's new number. "Somebody please tell me what to expect now. Are we going to stay here or what?"

Pressing the phone to her ear, Lucy turned away to speak more privately. Rafe, on the other hand, put his phone on speaker and let Hannah listen in as he tried once again to contact his superintendent. Her heart hitched when she heard him succeed.

"Yes, Colonel," Rafe said. "Circumstances developed that caused me to join Fleming's escape. It's complicated. I visited Andy and…"

Hannah saw Rafe clenching his jaw and gripping the phone tightly at the muffled sound of an angry tirade. She didn't have to clearly hear each word to know the superintendent was not happy.

"Yes, sir, I am with others at present. No, sir, they're not part of Fleming's gang. I'm afraid that bridge burned when we were overheard at the hospital."

Again, Rafe paused, this time pressing the phone to his ear. Hannah was watching his face and saw his expression changing. Finally, he shook his head and said, "Impossible. With all due respect, Colonel Wellington, I can't."

Hesitating, listening to the cell phone, Rafe said, "Let me rephrase that. I will *not* abandon these people. They are involved through no fault of their own and have helped me as much as I've helped them. We can use this situation to our advantage. I know we can. Fleming is furious at all of us. He's already sent minions to eliminate me and the women. Together, we may survive. Alone, it's less likely."

After a few more moments of listening, Rafe held the phone away and spoke to Hannah. "He wants you and your grandmother to come in so we can protect you."

"What about you?"

"I'll try to complete my mission."

"Without us?" Hannah scowled. Leaning toward his upheld phone, she began a loud protest. "Fleming is mad at me. He's mad at Gram, too. With Rafe we triple the reason he keeps coming back. Taking us out of the picture will cut your chances by two-thirds. That's ridiculous."

Rafe pressed the phone to his ear again, ending her tirade. "She didn't say anything I wasn't thinking. Yes, sir. I know she's a civilian, but the older woman isn't. She's former CIA."

Pulling the phone from his ear as if it hurt, Rafe said, "Whoa! No sir. I'm not joking. She really is."

Hannah looked over at her grandmother and saw that she had been listening to the exchange.

Lucy held up one finger as she continued to speak into her own phone. "Yes. I understand. Unsanctioned. That's fine with me. It's looking like you'll need to contact the head of the Missouri State Troopers and confirm my credentials. Yes, his name is…"

Rafe provided it. "Wellington. Colonel Roger Wellington. His private number is…" He displayed it for Lucy.

"All right," the older woman said. "Tell him to expect a call from DC. It's about time we coordinated this operation, anyway."

"It's about time all right," Hannah said. "I'm not happy being the bait on the end of a line that's being played out with nobody ready to reel it in if the big fish takes the hook."

Next to the drugstore was a nail salon and past that a health food store. The third business was a chain pet shop. When Rafe spotted it his first reaction was relief. He pointed at its rear door. "See if you can get in that way," he told Hannah. "If not, we'll spot for you and tell you when it's safe to walk around front."

"Why?"

"Because you need food for your furry partner and there wasn't any in the store where Lucy got the other supplies," he said. "It's the perfect cover for you and the dog. If the police start canvassing these businesses you can duck into the dog-washing cubicle and pretend to give him a bath."

"I'm surprised they haven't already done it," Lucy said. "I saw a couple of units cruising the parking lot while I was waiting to rejoin you."

"So did Hannah. It's probably a matter of manpower. The hospital will be their first priority and it will take a while to clear all the floors."

"Okay. We'll go," Hannah said, scowling, "but only because I think it's for the best. If the two of you try to ditch me you'll be sorry."

Lucy gave her a sober look. "Nobody is ditching anybody, is that clear? My handlers know we are working together and so does the state. Parting company now is not in anyone's best interests."

Rafe had led the way to the rear of the pet supply store and was trying the door. "It's locked, as I'd suspected. Besides, Hannah and Thor will look more normal if they use the public entrance." Without waiting for consensus he started off, satisfied when he heard the rattle of the shopping cart on the pitted pavement.

It was closer to retrace their steps from the drugstore so he went that direction. Lack of sirens wasn't necessarily a good sign because all it meant was that the patrol cars had resumed normal activities such as cruising past nearby stores and offices. Even with his superintendent's input he was certain the three of them were still being sought, definitely by Fleming's men and probably by the local police as well. Neither could be allowed to capture them. Not until they were in a position to act to bring down the trafficking ring. How he and his unusual partners were going to do that was beyond Rafe to the extent that he felt the need to rely on divine intervention as well as human aid.

God is in the details, he mused, praying he'd be alert enough, wise enough, to recognize a viable plan when he saw it. One thing was certain. He had been joined to the most unlikely pair of partners imaginable, not counting the addition of a dog, and it was up to him to make sense of their extraordinary team and put it to use.

Peering around the corner he watched passing traffic until enough cars had gone by to assure him the coast was clear. "Now," he called back, gesturing. "Go now."

Hood up, Hannah quickly walked past him then slowed her pace to normal and ambled toward the pet shop.

With Lucy at his side, Rafe continued to scan the traffic. She elbowed him. "Your ten o'clock."

He squinted. "I don't think so."

"Not taking a chance," she said, maneuvering the cart past him and pushing it to the flat red-painted curb that led to the parking lot.

She paused at the edge.

Rafe kept his eye on the dark-colored car that had worried

her as it turned down a side aisle and cruised closer. By this time Hannah had almost reached sanctuary in the pet store.

The driver of the car slowed even more as if looking for a place to park—or for the elusive dog trainer.

In the blink of an eye, Lucy shoved her loaded shopping cart into traffic, let go and screamed.

The vehicle in question came to a halt when its front bumper collided with the cart. Lucy was gesturing wildly and tugging to free the bent cart.

Rafe fully expected the driver to stop and get out to check for damage. Instead, as soon as Lucy pulled the cart back he revved the engine and drove away, not slowing until he had reached the busy street and merged with traffic.

Pausing to watch him go, Lucy turned to Rafe. "She's safely inside?"

He swiveled to check. "Yes. They weren't police so they could have been some of Fleming's men"

"I think it's likely. They didn't recognize me under this hood so I'm sure they missed seeing Hannah, too."

"They or others like them won't give up."

"I know." The older woman seemed to age right in front of Rafe as her countenance reflected despair. "You'd better go inside with Hannah and get the dog food while I wait for our car. No sense both of us standing out here, especially since you're a wanted man in the eyes of local cops."

Rafe sighed. "You're right. I just hate to leave you, especially after your suicide maneuver with our supplies."

"I have your phone number. I'll lay low and keep you apprised of the situation out here." Lucy managed a wan smile. "Go protect our innocent civilian."

"She won't be so innocent by the time we're done," Rafe said, pocketing the money. "She's learning fast."

Shrugging, Lucy sighed audibly. "Yeah, that's what I'm afraid of. A little knowledge can be worse than none in a life-and-death scenario."

Chapter Fourteen

"Aww, what a sweet puppy," a patron of the pet supply store said. When the friendly woman reached toward Thor, however, Hannah stopped her.

"Please don't touch him while he's working."

"I'm sorry. I didn't know."

"You can always tell by the vest a dog is wearing. Some will tell you they're in training and others will say what job they're currently doing. See? Service Dog in Training."

"How long does it take?"

Good question. "Right now I'm mostly assessing his skills and temperament. I haven't had him long."

"What do you do if he washes out? I mean, some dogs must not make the grade."

"You're right," Hannah said sadly. She laid a hand atop Thor's broad head. "I have high hopes for this guy, though."

A flash in her peripheral vision caught Hannah's attention and made her jump. Thor picked up on it and backed around her, trembling and staying tight against her legs.

The shopper reacted, too, inching away as if suddenly wary of the power the K-9 possessed. By the time Hannah had soothed him and his hackles had relaxed, they had been joined by Rafe.

"You scared us," Hannah told him.

"I did? Are you sure? He's never acted afraid of me before."

The truth of his words was unsettling. "You're right. I was standing here, talking to a friendly woman, when he acted startled. Funny thing is, I got the same vibes. I suppose I could have been reacting to his fear."

"Or sensed danger without spotting the source," Rafe said.

"Possibly." It was her fondest wish he'd never have to use the gun Gram had given him, but it was a comfort to note the bump the weapon made resting at the small of his back.

"Let's move to the dry dog food section," Rafe suggested. "We need dinner for Thor and putting one of those big sacks on my shoulder will help hide my face."

Instinctively, Hannah tugged her black hood closer. She would never have thought of disguising herself if Gram hadn't taken charge.

"Know what my problem is?" Hannah asked as they followed Rafe. "I still think like an innocent bystander. You and Gram are more devious."

Rafe gave a soft chuckle. "That's one way of putting it. Personally, I prefer *trained professional*."

Pensive, Hannah trusted him enough to voice her thoughts. "I wonder if I might have chosen a career in law enforcement if Gram had told me the truth when I was younger." Seeing him shaking his head she asked, "What?"

"I don't picture you as a cop."

"Why? Because I'm not smart enough?"

"No, no." As he hesitated, Hannah started to get upset. It was only when he said, "You're too tenderhearted," that she mellowed.

"Who says a person has to be tough to be a good cop? I could train K-9s for the police. Maybe even partner with one. Look at how Thor and I are bonding."

"It's not a question of bonding," Rafe explained. "You've seen dogs that were too stubborn to be taught or too timid."

His gaze rested on Thor. "It has more to do with intrinsic strengths and weaknesses."

"And you're saying I'm weak?"

"That's not what I meant, either."

She didn't buy his excuse any more than she believed her grandmother's story about why she'd never revealed the family's background. Neither of her human companions gave her enough credit. In her heart Hannah knew she was courageous and intelligent. She could and would match them in whatever tasks they took on, even the deadly ones. If she had thought for an instant that she was fooling herself she'd have backed off, but she was not about to let herself or her temporary partners—or God—down. Not for a second.

Gram and Rafe had been ordering her around as though she was a clueless child. Well, that was over. She was a member of this strange team and she was going to start acting like it. God would not have included her if He hadn't had a job for her, would He? Of course not. Believers might not always understand divine plans but it was up to them to follow as best they could. She was no different.

Facing Rafe she stood tall, chin up, and demonstrated her decisiveness. "I'm going to wait back here while you buy the food. Get the one in the red and white bag, high-protein, adult mix. Take it out to Gram so we have all our supplies together when our ride gets here."

"I'm sticking to you."

"Then put the food in her cart and come back in. I don't want to be caught without the proper supplies for Thor."

Although Rafe arched an eyebrow and tilted his head like a curious pup listening to commands he didn't quite understand, he did back away. Hannah saw him approach the brand of dry dog food she wanted and point to it, waiting for her response.

Mouthing *Yes*, she nodded. He slung one of the medium-size sacks over his shoulder and headed for the checkout counter.

Watching him go, Hannah had a brief flash of regret that

was quickly replaced by a sense of purpose. She had asserted herself and he had listened instead of arguing. It felt good to be in charge for a change. Very good.

One aisle behind her there were broad windows, a glass-topped door and signs explaining the dog-washing station. Drains in the floor took care of the overflow and soap dispensers stood on a shelf above a raised tub. No one was using the facility at the moment, but there was enough soggy dog hair on the floor to prove it was a popular feature.

She checked her surroundings, saw no other potential bath customers and entered the small room with Thor. He didn't need a bath, but it would be a good time to teach him a few simple commands. Shutting the door behind her kept him in while allowing her to also view the majority of the store.

Nose down, the shepherd investigated the room, checking corners and equipment as if on a mission. Hannah unclipped the leash and let him explore at will to begin with. Then she patted the steps leading to the tub and called his name.

"Thor. Here. Up."

He looked rather confused but interested in what she was doing.

"Up here, Thor. Come on. You can do it." One hand on his collar was enough incentive for him to place his front paws on the bottom step. Hannah didn't rush him.

"That's it. Good boy."

He took one more step then stopped, shivering.

Hannah decided to show him the water spray so she turned it on to hot, waiting for it to warm up, and checked the temperature with her other hand.

Results were almost instantaneous. "Ouch. Hot." She reached toward the cold tap. Thor jumped off the steps and circled her, facing the closed door. His hackles were up and his teeth bared in a snarl. A low growl rose above the sound of the running water.

Hannah whirled.

The man standing in the now open doorway was sneering. "Well, well, what have we here. My old friends."

She was face-to-face with Deuce Fleming!

Thor placed himself at her side, obviously ready to attack. Fleming took little notice. His bulk blocked the doorway. Hannah couldn't tell if there were others with him or if Rafe was on his way back yet. All she knew was that she'd sent her human protector away to bolster her own pride and might be about to pay for her hubris.

Her grip on the shower hose had slackened from surprise, reducing the water to a trickle. *Hot* water. Shouting "No!" she aimed the spray at her antagonist's face and squeezed the handle, sending a scalding stream toward his eyes.

Deuce grabbed his face and doubled over. Hannah slammed into him with her shoulder, managed to pass and saw Thor jumping his prone body in one leap.

She scrambled for the exit. A darkly clad figure made a grab for her as she passed, presenting his wrist as the perfect target for the K-9's canines. One quick nip was all it took to give Hannah a clear path to the front door.

She straight-armed the exit and ran straight into Rafe's arms. He shoved her aside and stood as a human roadblock while she and Thor joined Lucy at the open door of a black SUV that was idling, waiting for them.

Thor didn't have to be told to get in. He beat Hannah and scrambled across the rear seat. Gram gave her a push from behind then slammed the door. "It's Fleming!" Hannah managed to gasp out. "He's in there. We have to get him."

Rafe was way ahead of her. He'd already entered the store, gun drawn. In seconds he was back, panting and scowling. "Lost him. Drive around back."

Lucy accelerated so fast she almost threw Rafe out before he managed to close the passenger door behind him.

Hannah hugged Thor and leaned down to keep them out of the line of fire. Deuce Fleming was mad at her before. Now, bested and shamed in front of some of his men, he was bound to be even more furious. That was good only if it made him careless.

The big SUV slid on a corner, tires screeching. Hannah wanted to know what was happening so badly she chanced a peek. Rafe was braced with one hand on the dashboard, one arm out the open window, ready to fire at Fleming and his fleeing men.

Lucy muttered under her breath.

Hannah pulled herself up more to see why.

The alley was empty. And sirens were wailing in the distance.

Rafe pulled his arm inside and lowered the gun. "I can't believe this. We lost them."

One look at Hannah's face told him she was crestfallen. Her words affirmed it. "It's my fault."

"Pinning blame is useless," Lucy said. "Now that we know he's still in the city, we can inform law enforcement. Who knows. Maybe they'll spot him for us."

"It would help if we knew what they're driving," Rafe said. "It must be fast."

"Don't let this car fool you," Lucy said. "There's plenty under the hood if we need it, just no sense racing around and calling attention to ourselves if we don't have good reason."

In the back seat Hannah sniffled. Rafe sent her a smile. "Don't worry about it. We'll get him. What happened in there, anyway?"

When she related the story of the hot water, he chuckled. "Serves Deuce right. He should know better than to underestimate you. I wish I could have seen you scald him."

"I wish the water had been a lot hotter," she said honestly before recanting. "Sorry. I shouldn't have said that."

"Why not?"

"Because it's mean. I don't want to sound vindictive."

"See what I was trying to tell you?" Rafe said with a hint of tenderness. "You don't have the right temperament to be a cop."

"I defended myself when it counted."

"Yes, but then you wished you hadn't."

"Uh-uh. I never meant that exactly. I wasn't sorry I acted, I was just sorry I enjoyed it so much."

That brought laughter from Lucy. "Might be best if you didn't try to analyze yourself too much until this is over," she said, grinning. "We do what we do for many reasons, some of them not the best. Never beat yourself up for survival instincts. Those come with humanity. You wouldn't be normal if you didn't choose sides in this war."

"War?" Hannah asked.

Rafe agreed. "Yes. A war against evil. It's been going on forever. We have to keep trying, keep fighting, even if the enemy seems to be winning. Every battle counts. That's what I meant before."

"I get it," Hannah said. "I do. I just feel so outnumbered."

"Which we are," Lucy said, sobering. "I'm going to put some distance between us and this last episode so we don't get pulled over and arrested because of the altercation and brandishing a gun. I want to finish what we started and I think my friends in high places may be able to help."

"By tapping into the closed-circuit cameras at the strip mall?" Rafe asked, expecting to be correct.

"Hah! That's kid stuff." As she steered into passing traffic, Lucy floored him by saying, "Satellite observation. I can give my people the proper coordinates, tell them what times to look, and have a clear enough picture of Fleming's getaway car to read the letters on the license plate."

"Whoa. Are you kidding?"

She laughed, made eye contact with her granddaughter in the back seat and winked. "I would never joke about something like that. The idea of an eye in the sky may not be comforting to regular people but it's invaluable to folks like us."

"Once they ID him, do you think they'll be able to find him in this sea of cars?" Hannah asked.

Rafe answered. "In this case, that is my fondest hope."

"It was mine, too, until I was face-to-face with him," Hannah admitted. "Right now I'd rather the police picked him up and I never had to see him again."

"As long as they can get him to reveal where he sent Kristy," Rafe reminded her. "Time is running out for her."

Chapter Fifteen

Once out of downtown and on the highway, Hannah got her bearings from the famous Gateway Arch that rose 630 feet above the banks of the Mississippi River. Night had fallen and with it came much cooler temperatures.

She shivered and hugged Thor to share warmth. It helped that he had chosen to drape himself across her lap and had finally relaxed enough to doze. Truth to tell, her own eyelids felt so heavy she had to fight sleep.

"I'm going to pull into a parking garage so we can all get some rest," Lucy said.

Hannah met her gaze in the rearview mirror. "Sorry. I can't seem to keep my eyes open."

"You expended a ton of energy today," Rafe said. "We all did. Resting, even for a few hours, will help us stay at the top of our game. We can't afford to let ourselves function at less than our best."

"It feels like it's been weeks since the prison break," Hannah said, yawning.

Lucy huffed. "You've got that right. We've been through enough to wear out a marathon runner." She took the next off-ramp. "First we'll pick up some hot food and then I'll find us a place to lay low."

"I'll need to feed and walk Thor, too," Hannah said. The mention of his name caused the big shepherd to lift his head and look at her. She quieted him with a gentle pat and he closed his eyes again.

"I need to advise my boss, too," Rafe said, "and find out if Andy's okay. That hospital fiasco has to have taken a lot out of him."

"It's nothing that finding his kidnapped daughter won't fix," Lucy offered. She looked at Hannah again. "How are you doing? Truly, not what you think we want to hear."

"I'm tired, of course." She managed a genuine smile as she pondered her state of mind. "It's kind of scary how being afraid and then winning a battle against the bad guys is starting to appeal to me. That's counter intuitive, right? I mean, why should I be thinking about facing Deuce Fleming again when I already said that was the last thing I wanted?"

"Because you're beginning to believe we can beat him," Rafe said. "That bothers me."

"Why?"

"Promise you won't get mad again?"

"Promise," Hannah told him.

"Okay. It's unsettling because it means you may act too brave when your previous escapes weren't due to skill. Face it, Hannah, you were fortunate to survive. More than once. Please don't count on yourself to bring him down. It's going to take a team effort and outside aid to end his reign of terror for good. We thought we'd done that before and he managed to run his operation from inside Lyell."

"I understand what you're saying. Really I do. It's just, I don't know...exciting?"

Lucy tut-tutted and looked over at Rafe. "We should have figured out a way to leave her behind."

"Well, it's too late now," he replied. "Fleming has to be out of his mind about the scalding she gave him. There's no way he'll give up until he's in custody."

"And maybe not then," Hannah added. "I know. Just remember who made the first mistake that started all this."

No one rebutted that statement, nor had she expected them to. Fleming had so successfully coerced her that she'd gone against her sense of right and wrong and broken the law. That was how she and Gram had gotten sucked into this mess. Only Rafe was involved on purpose and that for a good cause, meaning none of the blame rested on him.

Conversation ebbed until they had ordered and picked up their food to go. The enticing aromas roused Thor. He and Hannah ducked instinctively when the SUV entered a dimly lit parking structure. The spot Lucy chose for their respite was at the very top in a far corner. Hannah didn't realize she'd been barely breathing until they stopped.

Thor was antsy so she leashed him and immediately got out of the car, prepared to clean up after him, while the others divvied up the meals. It was good to be away from the reality of the vehicle, even for a few short minutes. Part of her wanted to be an active participant in the manhunt and rescue of Kristy, while another part of her wished she could just walk off into the night and be done with everything. She couldn't, of course. It didn't take an expert theologian to imagine the reasons why. And it didn't take a cop or a former spy to convince her of the danger. She knew. She'd always known, deep down inside.

Looking back, Hannah could see how her choice to minister to convicts via the dog rehab program had set the stage for this current drama. The initial error lay in who had gotten permission to participate, not in the idea, itself. Other prisons supported similar outside aid with great success. Hers had been wonderful for the first couple of years.

Suddenly truth hit her. Rafe had been right. She was as much a victim of Deuce Fleming and his cohorts as poor Andy was. Their lives had been affected beyond reason when Fleming had become involved. He was the catalyst. They had to take him out, one way or another, or his list of victims would grow.

Hannah closed her eyes and prayed. "Father, thank You for putting the three of us together this way. Please help us, help me to be who You want me to be and do what You put me here to do. Stay with us, Jesus. We trust in You." And she did. With all her strength.

She looked back at the parked black SUV and her heart swelled with emotion. With thanksgiving. The two people she was with were perfect for the job they all faced. Therefore, she could count herself as capable, too. They would do this, whatever it cost. Go wherever the tasks took them. Win.

Fortified, changed and reassured, a new Hannah stood tall and started back toward the car.

Rafe had rolled down his window to listen and watch over Hannah and Thor from his vantage point in the front seat. If she had strayed too far away he would have gone after her, of course. That went without saying. The only reason he hadn't insisted in the first place was because he'd sensed her need to be alone and think.

In the interim, Lucy had received a report from her insiders. Fleming had chartered a private plane and made plans to leave the country, ostensibly with a group of young women who had volunteered for charity work abroad. Consensus was that many of these women had been either kidnapped or coerced. Everyone's hope was that Kristy was among them and therefore still in the States.

He handed Hannah a fresh alcohol wipe to clean her hands before passing her the paper sack containing her burger and fries. "Water or soda?" he asked her.

"Water, please. And one of those empty plastic boxes so I can let Thor drink, too." She put it on the floor for him, smiling when he splashed her foot. "My back seat buddy is a messy drinker."

"Just make sure you don't accidentally lose your burger to him," Rafe warned lightly. "He's looking at it like a hungry wolf."

"Distant ancestor," she quipped. "I'll be careful. Dogs can't have onions. They're really bad for them."

"I didn't know that." Facing forward he took pains to remove any trace from a bite of his own meal before holding it out for the K-9. "Is this okay?"

Hannah nodded. "Yes. Okay, Thor. It's okay."

The dog's whole mouth closed over the ends of Rafe's fingers with an audible snap. "Whoa! Easy boy. I need that hand."

"Next time you want to feed him, give it to me and I'll work on his manners."

"Good idea," Rafe said as he cleaned his hand with another of the sanitary wipes. "He's all yours."

Laughing, she ate more before breaking off a piece of bun. This, she offered in a closed fist so Thor had to be gentle to nose it out. By the third bite he looked as if he'd learned.

Rafe waited until she'd finished eating before he began to fill her in on the latest details. "Our friends with the spy in the sky located the vehicle that got away from us and traced it to an old hotel outside town."

"Really? Are we going there?"

"Not right away," Lucy said. "We need to give our people time to get into position before anybody approaches."

"We can't wait, Gram. What about Fleming? What if he escapes or hurts Kristy?"

"We're counting on the fact that she's too valuable an asset to lose," Lucy said with conviction. "He's planning to fly abroad the day after tomorrow. According to reliable intel he's waiting for the arrival of another batch of victims so they can all go together."

"He must be awfully sure of himself."

Rafe agreed. "He is. Always has been. My people are watching the airfield. He won't get by them even if he changes plans and tries to leave early."

"What if he drives?"

"We have that covered, too," Lucy said. "What we need to do now is to get some sleep so we're ready for tomorrow."

Frowning, Rafe caught her attention and gave a slight shake of his head to keep her from explaining further. There was more to the infiltration strategy the two agencies had been discussing and if they stuck with the notions they'd already presented, rest for Lucy and for him was imperative. So was keeping the details from Hannah until just before executing the risky plan. He had no doubt she was going to object in the strongest of terms and he wanted to save arguments for last.

Sighing, he leaned his head back against the seat and pictured Hannah the moment she learned that a female law enforcement officer was going to take her place in the assault on the hotel. She was bound to go ballistic and he was not looking forward to trying to talk her down.

Sleep eluded Hannah—for about five minutes after she finished eating. Warm food and the plush seats soothed and calmed her.

Thor curled up beside her and she rested one hand on his shoulders knowing that any disturbance would rouse him instantly. Reassured by that knowledge she sank into a deep sleep beyond dreams and awoke to see the sun rising outside the parking structure.

Yawning, she stretched and looked around. Lucy and Rafe stood at a concrete railing. Because they were facing the eastern sky they were surrounded by haloes of warm light as if caressed by the morning. Their body language, however, did not carry the same image of peace. Lucy was leaning toward him, acting intent on making a point. He was shaking his head.

Hannah snapped the leash on Thor and climbed out. The change in her companions when they saw her was unquestionable. They not only stepped apart, both were acting nonchalant, *acting* being the key word. She smiled. "Good morning. What's up?"

"We were just waiting for you," Rafe said.

Lucy agreed. "Right. There's a public restroom on the ground floor." She pointed. "Elevator's over there. Want me to hold the dog for you?"

"No. Thanks. Thor needs to be walked anyway. We'll be back in a jiffy."

"I'll go with you," Rafe said. "Lucy can drive down and pick us up at street level. Then we can go grab breakfast."

His forced casual attitude gave Hannah the shivers. "Has there been any word on Fleming?"

"Not since last night," Rafe said.

She didn't quite believe him so she raised an eyebrow. "Really? Neither one of you even asked?"

"I did check in," Lucy offered. "There wasn't much to report. No activity at the airfield."

"What about that hotel they were watching?"

Rafe took her elbow and urged her toward the elevator. "I'll fill you in while we ride down."

With a parting glance at her grandmother, Hannah complied. It was clear something was up although neither of her companions seemed as nervous as she figured they'd be if danger was imminent. Instead, they were acting reluctant to engage with her, as if there was some secret between them that was being kept from her, in particular.

She stepped onto the elevator with Thor, pleased that his hesitation at the threshold was brief. The door slid closed. She turned to Rafe. "Okay. Let's have it. What's going on?"

"I don't know what you're talking about."

"I don't believe you. And I don't believe Gram, either. You two are up to something behind my back. Now what is it?"

Unfortunately, the elevator reached the ground floor and

the doors opened before she got an answer so she stopped him as soon as they'd stepped clear. "Well?"

"It's not carved in stone. It's just…" He made a face. "Listen, it's not something we sanctioned, okay? The feds and state people are basically running this op now."

"And?"

Shrugging, Rafe stuffed his hands into the pockets of his jacket. "And, they've decided to use only trained personnel for the infiltration."

"So?" She didn't like the feeling she was getting or the ideas flying through her head. Were they cutting her out? After everything she'd done and the way she'd stood up to Fleming on her own, were they actually going to force her to step away?

"So, we'll be met at the Randolph Bend of the Missouri River by members of the primary assault team. One of them will be a policewoman who resembles you as closely as possible. She'll take over with Thor and stand in for you if it turns out we're needed. They figure, with the dog involved, Fleming's men won't question the handler's identity."

"This substitute is a K-9 officer?"

"Um, I don't know. I guess so. I mean, I've never met her."

"That's what I figured." Facing Rafe she spoke her mind. "People tend to underestimate somebody like me. Because I make the job look easy they think anybody can step into my shoes and do things just as well as I do. Well, they can't. You and Gram should know that. You've seen proof."

"It wasn't our idea."

"Doesn't matter. Did you protest? Did you try to explain that I have certain skills worth considering? "

"We weren't invited to discuss it," Rafe countered. "We were just told about the plan and thankful to be allowed to be present." He paused, apparently choosing his words carefully. "They could have cut us out completely."

"You mean like they're cutting *me* out?"

Hannah could tell it cost him dearly to say, "Yes."

Chapter Sixteen

Tension inside the unmarked SUV was so high Rafe was surprised the air wasn't actually vibrating. His senses were heightened by what they were about to do and he could tell that Lucy felt the same. As for Hannah, well, she was harder to read. Not that she was a good actress, he concluded. It was more a case of her emotions being on a roller coaster ride. At the topmost portion of the tracks she could be elated. Anybody could. It was when the coaster carried her to the bottom of the loops and turns that she seemed withdrawn and he hadn't decided whether that meant anger or depression.

In many ways, Rafe would have preferred that Hannah showed she was mad at their group's plans even if that meant she was also furious with him and Lucy. Anger tended to heighten a person's awareness while being down in the dumps had the opposite effect.

Outlying portions of St. Louis had swallowed up a small historic settlement on Gabaret Island, one mile south of the confluence of the Missouri and Mississippi Rivers, yet it had somehow managed to retain its name and a spot on the map. Explorers Lewis and Clark would undoubtedly be shocked at the way their campsite had changed after more than two hundred years.

"My GPS indicates we can drive across if we go north and use the bridge to Chouteau," Lucy said.

"Where is our first rendezvous taking place?" Rafe asked her.

"Off Highway 70, a little way from the arch, where we won't be so likely to draw attention," the older woman answered. "Once we're on the island there's only thirteen hundred acres to hide in."

"Where are you supposed to be dumping me?" Hannah asked, sounding beyond miffed.

Lucy frowned at Rafe. "You should never have told her."

"It was only fair," he countered. "She's been with us from the beginning. She *was* the beginning."

"Yes, well, I can't say I'm unhappy about taking on a substitute human target for the Fleming gang to shoot at," Lucy said. Hannah met and held her gaze in the rearview mirror but didn't comment.

Rafe could tell she was upset without becoming irrational. That was a definite plus. Convincing her to step away at this last crucial juncture might not be as hard as he'd anticipated. One of the reasons he'd told her details of the plan ahead of time was to give her a chance to think things through and accept the inevitable. Fortunately, it was beginning to look as if that was exactly what she'd done.

Swiveling in his seat as far as possible without removing his seatbelt, Rafe looked back at Hannah. Her features were as pretty as ever but there was a disquieting glint in her eyes. "I really am sorry about this. You know I'd have included you if it was possible. After all you've been through you deserve to be in on the capture."

"I'm glad somebody realizes that." He saw her gaze dart to the back of her grandmother's head for an instant. "I'm not the orphaned Lassiter kid anymore. I don't need coddling."

"Loving and protecting you is *not* coddling," Lucy shot back. "You will always be my precious grandbaby."

"I'm not a baby," Hannah said. "Not anymore."

Rafe decided it was time to interrupt. "Okay, ladies, let's talk about where we're going and what's expected of us when we get there."

Hannah huffed. "Why tell me?"

He ignored the gibe. "Members of law enforcement attempted to infiltrate the hotel staff and failed. None of Fleming's people could be bribed or coerced so they don't have anyone inside who can pass them the information they need for the final takedown."

"Why not just storm the place?" Hannah asked. "They know where Deuce is and where the victims are, don't they?"

"That's part of the problem." Rafe looked to Lucy, wanting her okay to proceed. When she merely gripped the steering wheel and stared at the road ahead he continued anyway.

"We believe that the people we want to rescue, including Kristy, are being held somewhere else. They're supposed to be brought to the hotel and then leave with the Fleming gang."

"You're sure?" Hannah asked.

Shrugging, Rafe said, "As sure as we can be. Listening devices on the outside have picked up most of what we know. It looks like Fleming's pride is going to be his downfall. He wants to be able to personally march those prisoners aboard the plane so they'll all know who's the boss. If he'd shipped them off in smaller bunches we might have already missed saving some."

"I don't get why he chose to rendezvous on Gabaret. I'd think he'd be safer in a much more crowded area the way you're planning on meeting the strike team."

"Overconfidence, I think," Rafe said. "After everything he's gotten away with, in and out of prison, I suspect he's feeling invincible."

"I suppose it's possible. He never struck me as foolish, though. I mean, look how he manipulated me."

"That success undoubtedly bolstered his ego which is another element in our favor."

"And a very good reason why the takedown should include me," Hannah argued.

Studying her expression as he commiserated, Rafe was certain she had come to terms with the inevitable change about to take place. One side of him wanted to continue to work beside Hannah. A more practical side insisted it was wiser to leave her behind and substitute an armed, trained professional. Assuming his goal was to protect Hannah, and it was, he had to choose leaving her behind. The problem was how to justify that conclusion without revealing how fond of her he'd grown in the short time they'd spent together. It was bad enough that he, himself, knew.

If they hadn't been currently confined to the car he'd have taken her hand again and led her aside to privately explain his dilemma. He could do that later. He *would* do it. In the meantime he stared through the windshield and wondered how such a clear, beautiful morning could be so fraught with danger, with the very real threat of death.

"Not Hannah," Rafe prayed in a whisper that was muted by the roar of the powerful engine. He blinked to clear his vision. "Please Lord, watch over Hannah."

That prayer was still echoing in his mind when Lucy pulled off the highway and into a spacious, busy truck stop.

Rafe kept checking and assessing their surroundings until he spotted a handful of white patrol cars and a mobile command center van with a satellite dish mounted on its roof.

If he had been positive there were no double-minded officers in this group he might have actually been able to let down his guard enough to relax.

Watching her grandmother and Rafe greeting the officers at the command center vehicle, Hannah took a deep breath and sighed once before leashing Thor. "Okay big boy, you behave now, you hear?"

Panting, he seemed to smile up at her.

"That's a good boy. Let's go."

In no hurry to relinquish control of the basically untrained K-9, she stepped out of the SUV. Thor was behaving as though he had accepted her authority. What he might do if they were physically separated was another story. Besides, she reasoned, Deuce Fleming knew what she looked like. He'd been in her training classes at Lyell. How any substitute expected to fool him was beyond her.

Nevertheless, she did respect the police and the tough job they were tasked with doing. Under her breath she murmured a surrender prayer and approached the people Gram and Rafe were speaking with.

A man wearing a black protective vest over totally nondescript black clothing nodded to acknowledge her and went on addressing the others. "We're waiting for news from our spotters on the arrival of the victims. They're being delivered in small batches, which is why we didn't move in sooner. Once Fleming knows we're on to him and his operation he'll stop everything and we might lose any who haven't already arrived."

"You don't have info on all branches of his organization?"

"We know a lot. Trouble is, we can't be sure we're not missing anybody."

That made sense to Hannah. Sort of. If she had been in charge she knew she'd have wanted to storm the hotel ASAP and clearly that was not for the best. *Which is why they're running things and I'm not,* she told herself. In the background she noticed a young woman whose build and hair color were similar to hers. Although this woman wore the same kind of protective vest the other team members did, she wasn't in uniform.

Hannah tightened her hold on Thor's leash. Sensing her nervousness the dog pressed his shoulder to the side of her leg and leaned in. She rested her free hand atop his broad head to comfort him and spoke softly. "It's okay, boy. It's okay."

But it wasn't, was it? The dog might not know they were

about to be separated, but he'd sensed tension in the atmosphere around the group of vehicles.

The agent in charge motioned to her. "Bring the dog."

"Thor, heel," was all Hannah said, starting forward. She was met halfway by the woman officer she'd noticed.

"My name is Layla," the policewoman said, taking off aviator sunglasses, then offering her hand.

Hannah shook it reluctantly. "This is Thor. Please understand. He's new and hasn't had a lot of training. He understands basic commands, just don't make the mistake of counting on him the way you would a fully vetted working K-9."

Scowling, Layla turned to her superior. "I thought you said the dog was a pro."

"We thought he was." Stepping aside he spoke into his radio, then returned. "We'll use him anyway."

Layla held out her open hand. It was all Hannah could do to force herself to pass the leash. Once the officer had assumed command she gave a tug. "C'mon, dog."

Thor sat on his haunches and refused to leave Hannah's side.

"Tell him to come with me," Layla ordered.

"Even if I do that and he obeys here and now, what's to say he'll act normal later when you need him? Deuce not only knows my face, he's seen me handling Thor. No matter how good your disguise is, you can't fool the dog and that means you won't fool Fleming and his men, either."

When Layla wrapped a length of Thor's leash around her hand and dragged his paws across the asphalt, Hannah had had enough. "Stop that. You'll hurt him."

"Then do something about him," the female officer said in a raised voice that was attracting the attention of her fellow officers as well as passersby.

"Give me that." Hannah jerked the leash from her hand and resumed command of the frightened shepherd. Together they approached and faced the agent in charge. "The dog stays with me."

"We want to use him as part of this operation. If I'd known he wasn't properly trained I'd have had another German shepherd standing by."

"Well, you don't. You have Thor and you have me. I've worked one-on-one with Deuce Fleming, and even with those sunglasses on, your substitute won't pass for me. We both know it. Otherwise, why would you insist on using Thor to convince him?"

Up to now, she had been ignoring Rafe and Gram. Now, she looked to both of them. "Tell him. Make him understand how right I am for this job."

Seeing them look at each other for long, silent moments Hannah was afraid they wouldn't back her up. Then, in unison, they said, "She's right."

Hannah was far too nervous to continue pleading her case so she simply stood there under the scrutiny of the top agent and tried to appear unruffled.

Finally, he motioned to Layla. "Give her your vest and earbud."

"But, sir…"

"We have to take a chance." He pointed to Rafe and Lucy. "These two are experienced enough for all three of them. We're closer to breaking up this trafficking ring than we've ever been and I'm not about to let a four-legged problem mess things up. Lassiter goes with the dog."

Hannah's heart cheered and she grinned so broadly her cheeks hurt. They were going to let her help avenge her murdered parents and make up for all the sacrifices Gram had made raising her. Moreover, she was going to get the chance to help Rafe rescue his partner's daughter. Having met Andy, she knew how desperately Rafe needed to accomplish that, to be directly involved in not only solving the kidnapping but to also make amends for Andy's on-the-job injury while they were working together.

A sudden shiver snaked up her spine and prickled the hair

at the nape of her neck. She had just talked her way back into imminent danger and it was dawning on her that she was about to walk smack into the presence of the man who hated her most in all the world. Plus, there was Thor to think of.

"*That's* why I need to go," she muttered to herself, following Gram and Rafe back to their SUV. "The others are here to rescue people. I'm here to look after this loyal dog."

That conclusion made perfect sense. It also made her tremble all the way to her core and left her mouth so dry she could barely swallow.

What she didn't expect when she climbed into the vehicle with Thor was a barrage of intense chastisement from the very people she was there to help.

Chapter Seventeen

Lucy led the tirade so well Rafe didn't feel the need to do anything but agree. "What did you think you were doing back there, huh? Don't you realize that taking care of you will put the rest of us in jeopardy?"

"I've done all right so far," Hannah reminded her grandmother.

"Hah! You may be a crack shot but paper targets are a lot different than human ones."

"I could give her a crash course in tactics while you drive," Rafe offered.

"And accidentally shoot me through the seat back? No thank you."

The more he thought about it, the better he liked his idea. "No bullets. I'll make sure the gun is empty. I just want to see how she handles it in case of emergency."

"Gram was right, I could never shoot anybody," Hannah said.

"You could hold someone at bay who didn't know you were so softhearted."

It surprised him when she joked, "At least you didn't say softheaded or wimpy."

"There is nothing wimpy about you," Rafe assured her with

a slight smile. "If anything, you're too brave. Put that vest on under your hoodie so they can't tell you're protected."

Pausing as she complied, Rafe did the same with his. Lucy had already hidden her protective clothing like the old pro she was.

"Okay," Hannah said, smoothing the soft black fabric over the top of the bulky vest. "I just have one question."

"Shoot."

She snorted a chuckle. "Lousy choice of words. What I want to know is what happens if they don't shoot me in the middle of my body where this thing protects me? Huh? What then?"

Rafe answered, "You get hurt. Badly. So I suggest you plan to duck as often as possible. Best-case scenario, if we get captured, would be getting thrown into the holding cell with the prisoners so we could tell them they were about to be rescued and try to confirm that they're all there."

"Terrific. What makes you think they'd let us keep our cell phones to report to the strike team?"

He produced a tiny black object and held it out to her. "They won't. That's what this is for. It clips onto fabric and transmits up to a mile under ideal circumstances." He fitted a pliable receiver into his ear and handed one to Lucy. "These will pick up what's being said without any action on your part."

"Any crook worth his pay will find it on me."

"I agree," Rafe said soberly. "That's why you're going to pin it on the inside of Thor's harness. Only a fool would try to frisk a dog."

Seeing the sparkle in her eyes and the lopsided smile she was obviously trying to subdue endeared her to him. This was no normal woman. Hannah was so special he had no words to adequately describe her. She had adapted so well to their situation, it was akin to working with a fellow officer. Tenderhearted or not, she had what it took to do this job and do it well. She was intelligent, brave and quick-witted.

And adorable, his mind added. No argument there.

Tempted to voice his thoughts he spoke to Lucy, instead. "Pull over for a sec so I can trade seats with Thor and teach Hannah how to safely handle an automatic."

"The Glock I gave you?"

"Yes."

She produced a smaller pistol and also handed that to him. "Use this one. It's easier to work the slide. I had to switch to a smaller caliber when arthritis weakened my grip."

He accepted the extra gun, got out and waited until Hannah had sent Thor over the center console into the front passenger seat before he joined her. Judging by the way she was frowning, she was not thrilled with the lesson he was about to give while Lucy continued driving toward Gabaret.

Rafe emptied both guns and checked to make sure there was no ammo left in the chambers after he dropped the clips. "First rule, never point a gun at anything unless you plan to shoot it."

"Well, duh. I know that. So, how am I supposed to hold anybody at bay if I don't aim at them?" Hannah made such a ridiculous face he almost laughed. Instead, he said, "Okay. One exception. Just keep your finger off the trigger and lay it beside the trigger guard like this. See? It never touches the trigger unless you're ready to fire."

As he handed it to her, empty, he felt her tremble as his fingers brushed against hers. Truth to tell, he wasn't feeling all that steady about it either. To help distract himself, he concentrated on watching her hands and continuing the lesson. "Here's the safety on this gun. It's almost the same as the other weapon. You can disengage it with your thumb."

It pleased him that Hannah was able to follow his orders and had the grip strength to pull back the slide and chamber a round in the larger Glock 9mm. With his encouragement she handled both guns appropriately—until he reloaded them. Then, she acted as if she was holding a live rattlesnake. "I thought you were used to firearms."

"I am," she countered. "It's just different when I think about harming somebody."

Rafe reclaimed the guns, checked the clips before replacing them, then passed Lucy's to her over the back of the seat. "Lesson finished. Too bad this isn't the time or place to do some live firing so I can check her accuracy."

Snorting, the older woman tucked the gun into her belt. "Trust me. She's got good aim. The question is whether or not she's got the guts."

"Don't be so cynical," he warned, hoping the disparaging remark didn't undermine Hannah's confidence. He had no way of knowing what they were about to face or whether she'd need to actually use the gun to defend herself, but he hoped she'd never be tested under fire.

"I won't chicken out," Hannah chimed in. "I promise. But shooting at somebody is going to be a last resort." The wisp of a smile she gave Rafe grew broader when she added, "I'd much prefer swinging a frying pan or a baseball bat if I have to fight back."

"Let's hope and pray this assignment is nothing like that," Rafe said, almost ready to smile in spite of the circumstances.

When Hannah added, "Or steaming hot water from a doggie spa," he broke into a grin. "You are really something, you know that?"

From the driver's seat he heard Lucy muttering. "We all need our heads examined."

Sobered, Rafe stowed his Glock, reached for Hannah's hands and clasped them in both of his. "What we're about to do is very dangerous. You do realize that, don't you?"

"Meaning we could die? I get that. I also don't think it's my time to go."

"Nobody ever does." Her grip on his fingers tightened as if she meant to comfort so he held fast, too. Unshed tears glistened in her eyes, making his own begin to water in spite of the macho image he carefully maintained. This woman got under his skin the way no one else ever had and he sensed a shared empathy that unnerved him. She understood how important it was to him to rescue Kristy and how Lucy had waited half a lifetime for the chance to avenge Hannah's parents, but that wasn't all. Somehow, Hannah had tapped into his heart and made herself at home there.

Rafe was loathe to accept his feelings for her, yet there they were. Undeniable. Unfathomable. And, God help him, unacceptable. Once this current danger was past and their reasons for being together ended, he'd go his way and Hannah would go hers. Parting was inevitable. So was a cooling of the emotional attachment they had formed due to this assignment. He'd seen it happen before. He'd even taken part in psychological debriefings to help him come down from the highs created by danger. To put it into layman's terms, cops and firefighters could get addicted to adrenaline the same way skydivers and race car drivers did.

And when it was over, it was over, he reminded himself. Thinking about the future in the midst of what could be a deadly assignment was a futile exercise. Truthfully, they had only this moment in time and no more.

Without taking time to rationalize his actions, Rafe lifted their joined hands between them and kissed the backs of Hannah's fingers.

She touched his forehead with her own and they sat that way, head to head, for longer than Rafe had intended. It was a beautiful moment, one he would have maintained longer if Hannah had not leaned her head on his shoulder and sighed.

He was lost. Overwhelmed. Releasing her hands he slipped one arm around her shoulders and pulled her into a tender embrace regardless of the sounds of derision coming from the retired government agent behind the wheel.

Hannah's heart was racing, her breathing ragged—and all she was doing was sitting there beside Rafe. If she was already this agitated, how in the world was she going to cope when the operation actually got underway?

Traffic was at a standstill approaching the bridge north of their destination. Everything seemed normal until she saw Lucy slam a fist into the steering wheel. Worse, Gram seemed to be unduly concerned about something behind them.

Rafe leaned forward. "What is it? What do you see?"

"Not sure." Her glance kept shifting between vehicles behind her and the reason for the blocked roadway ahead. "I'd like to know if this tie-up is thanks to our people or for some other reason. I don't like being trapped."

"Looks like actual construction to me," Rafe said. "The state has been doing a lot of infrastructure repair lately."

When Hannah saw Lucy tilt her head as if questioning, she shivered. If Gram was worried then she was worried, too. Still, anything that delayed their progress should also hamper Fleming's plans so it couldn't be all bad. Or could it?

The line of cars was moving slowly. Men with signs and walkie-talkies took turns letting a few vehicles through. Hannah studied the faces of the workers, looking for anything off-putting or familiar. Nothing seemed amiss.

"They look legit to me," she murmured, surprised when Rafe said he agreed.

"I'll call it in just the same," he added. "Can't be too careful."

Watching and listening, Hannah was so nervous her stomach was upset and she was perspiring despite the cool weather. If there hadn't been so much construction noise outside she would have rolled down a window to get some fresh air. One thing about all that racket, she reasoned, fake workers wouldn't have bothered bringing in so much heavy equipment.

Finally, they were motioned to proceed via a temporary detour. One short section of the road was so narrow Hannah held her breath and marveled at her grandmother's driving prowess.

She glanced back. Two more passenger cars had made it

through. The semitruck behind them, however, seemed to be teetering.

"Oh, no. Is he...?"

Rafe whipped around. Lucy checked her mirrors. They both made unintelligible noises.

As their SUV put more distance between it and the detour, Hannah saw the semi slow, then stop. Something was definitely wrong.

"Is he off the road?" Lucy asked.

Hannah got on her knees to peer out the rear window. "I can't tell from here. Looks like it."

Still on the phone with the strike team leader, Rafe filled him in. "That's right. Looks like the bridge is going to be impassable until they manage to tow that eighteen-wheeler out of the way."

He paused, listening to the phone. All Hannah could hear was the thumping of her own heart in her ears.

"Yes, we're across," Rafe reported. He listened again, then looked at Lucy. Hannah didn't have to see his face to know he was concerned when he said, "No, it looked like a real accident," then added, "How long will that take?"

Finishing the call, Rafe explained. "There was roadwork scheduled for that bridge this week. I don't know if the accident was planned but seems too convenient to suit me. The rest of the strike team will either have to drive a hundred miles around or be brought to Gabaret by boat or chopper. All that takes time. They'll also attract attention if they approach by air."

Hannah's mind was racing, filled with endless questions and possible answers, none of which satisfied. "Wait. If they can't get onto the island, then Fleming won't be able to get off, right?"

Judging by the quick exchange of looks between Rafe and Lucy, they didn't see it her way so Hannah asked, "What?"

"If they're the ones who blocked the bridge then it stands to reason they've prepared an alternate escape route."

"It won't matter as long as he can't get the victims out of the country. Police are watching the airfields, right?"

"At least the one his private plane always uses," Rafe said. "I hope it's not a decoy."

Hannah struggled to process the notion of all the innocent young people whose futures would be ruined if they weren't rescued. She looked to her companions. "Gram, Rafe, what are we going to do? We can't let this happen. We have to stop him."

Neither offered answers. Nor did Hannah have any. There were too many unknowns, too many ways the assault on the old hotel could go wrong. Too many ways even the cleverest plans could fail, she admitted with regret and more than a little fear. It was no good acting the part of a Trojan horse during a siege if there were no troops waiting to surprise the enemy and turn the tide of battle. Only a fool would walk into Deuce Fleming's hideout with no way to survive, let alone escape. She had intended to assist law enforcement, not replace it.

"This island hasn't been mapped for GPS," Lucy said. "Aerial views show a small settlement close to the southern tip. That's where we're heading."

"The whole place looks deserted."

"Not totally," Rafe warned, his voice raspy. His cell phone vibrated. He answered.

Hannah wasn't able to make out what was being said to him. However, his stricken expression told her he was receiving dire news. "Yes, sir. I understand."

He lowered the phone but didn't speak so Hannah did. "What? What's wrong?"

"Plenty," Rafe said.

"Well?"

"Our people on the east side of the river have reported unusual criminal activity. They're assembling another assault force over there but they won't be ready to move in on the hotel for at least three more hours."

Puzzled, she recalled the information they'd been given

earlier. "That's still okay. Fleming isn't going to leave until tomorrow, right?"

Rafe was shaking his head. "No." He pocketed the phone, reached for his gun and rechecked the ammunition, chambering a live round the way he'd shown Hannah. "I was just told he's changed his plans at the last minute. They're set to fly out tonight as soon as it gets dark."

"How can you be sure this new information is correct?"

It was not a bit comforting to hear Rafe admit, "I can't."

Chapter Eighteen

Ramshackle farm buildings sat grouped beside fallow fields as if their caretakers had been gone for generations. Roads were pitted and covered with fine, sandy dirt making them appear unpaved. If it had not recently rained to dampen the dust Rafe knew they'd be announcing their approach with every revolution of the tires. Not that it looked as if anyone would be able to sneak up on the old hotel no matter which direction they came from or what conveyance they chose to use.

"Fleming wasn't as dumb as I'd thought when he chose to stage here," Rafe said, assessing the landscape. "He's bound to spot us and anyone else long before we arrive."

"It'll take too long to park and walk in," Lucy said. She handed him an aerial view printed on copy paper. "I propose we drive to the built-up area you can see here and let Hannah out so she has a place to hide until backup finally shows."

Rafe knew what Hannah's reaction was going to be before she spoke and he wasn't disappointed. "I'm not hiding, okay? We're in this together."

"We were, before everything fell apart." Lucy slowed and pulled off the road, letting the SUV idle. "Things have changed."

"For the worse," Rafe added. "Your grandmother is right. You need to sit this one out."

Hannah made a face showing her disapproval. "Not happening."

"Too bad I didn't bring handcuffs," Lucy muttered.

"I can't believe you'd even consider cuffing me when I may need to defend myself." As she spoke, Hannah was rolling her eyes. "I'd be a sitting duck."

"You think you won't be if you try to approach the hotel with us?" He hated using such a derogatory tone but saw it as the lesser of two evils. The best thing Hannah could do for him and Lucy was back off so they didn't have to worry about her safety. Unfortunately, it didn't look as if she intended to comply.

"Let me get this straight," Hannah said. "You two plan to drive up to this derelict hotel where we know the Fleming gang is hanging out and just march into the lobby in the hope you can do something to keep him there until reinforcements arrive? That sounds way riskier than anything I might do."

"I suppose you have a better idea?"

"Not yet, but I have high hopes." She patted Lucy's shoulder. "Let's get going while we still have daylight. If Deuce really does plan to hit the road after sunset today we don't have much time left."

"I don't want to do something to set him off and make him start eliminating witnesses," Rafe warned. "We need to be very cautious."

"Assuming we can get close without being seen," Lucy said. "I have a bad feeling that won't be easy."

"Well, three people and one dog can't successfully storm the place, that's for sure," Hannah countered. "Until backup arrives there's no way we can cut them off or keep them from loading the victims and taking off with them. If there were a dozen of us, we'd probably still be outgunned."

Cautious and loathe to encourage her, Rafe tilted his head to one side. "What do *you* think we should do to stall his leaving?"

"I prefer to show you rather than tell you," Hannah said.

Hair on the nape of Rafe's neck prickled and he suppressed a shiver. He didn't know what Hannah was up to. He didn't have to know. What he must do, however, was stop her from getting hurt or putting herself into an untenable position in regard to Fleming himself. They already knew the man had a score to settle with her.

"As long as it doesn't include you getting yourself shot," Rafe gibed, hoping to lift the somber, confrontational mood with irony.

"Back atcha, mister," Hannah said. "It's my fondest wish that we all get to go home."

"Together," he said just above a whisper, not surprised when both women echoed, "Amen."

The grounds of the stone-built, turn-of-the-twentieth-century hotel were overgrown with wild vegetation and weeds. If Hannah had not known Deuce and his gang were inside she would never have guessed that anyone was, which was undoubtedly his plan when he chose the old building as his temporary headquarters.

Hannah lagged back after Lucy parked behind the remains of an old carriage house and everyone climbed out. Their black clothing would be a help once night fell, but right now it was unfortunately quite noticeable against the pale gray landscape. Only Thor blended in and even he had too much black accenting his brownish coat.

From her vantage point Hannah could see portions of the roof of the three-story hotel building. It didn't take binoculars to spot the armed sentries. Their silhouettes stood out against the cloudy sky.

Gram waved a signal for her to stay put while she and Rafe separated to approach from opposite directions. Hannah could already tell that the guards on the roof knew they were there because several of them were on the move, ostensibly to provide better protection against a ground assault.

Hannah saw only one way to stop the riflemen from firing on her companions. She needed Fleming's people to know who was there so they'd underestimate the threat. Underestimate her, specifically, just as Deuce had done during the prison escape.

Memories of movies where foolish heroines walked unarmed into dark houses or alleys flashed into her mind and almost made her smile. Many times she'd seen that happen and had judged those woman as beyond foolish. Now she could identify with them enough to start to understand.

Saying, "Thor, heel," she raised her hands above her head and stepped out where the sentries could see her.

When no one shot at her, she began to walk steadily toward the front doors of the hotel.

In the distance someone shouted, "No!"

Hannah kept going.

A lobby door swung open. She and Thor passed through. There was no going back now.

Running along behind the carriage house, Rafe rejoined Lucy. "Did you see that?"

"Yes." The older woman looked stricken. "I thought she had better sense."

"So did I or I would have tied her up."

"She'd have escaped anyway," Lucy said. "At least they didn't shoot at her when she showed herself."

"Small favors." Rafe was beside himself. He pulled out his phone, saw only one tiny bar of connection and used it anyway. Thankfully, he got through to the task force leader and was able to report the latest developments.

"Gutsy of her," the agent replied. "She's wearing the wire?"

"No," Rafe said. "We put it on the dog."

"Smart." He paused. "All right. Keep listening and relay anything pertinent ASAP."

"How is the accident on the bridge coming along?"

"A wrecker's on scene but there's so little room to maneuver on the detour he's having trouble clearing the road."

"Are your units ready to roll?"

"As soon as we can."

"Copy that." Rafe heard an odd thumping sound and looked to Lucy. She was pointing at the sky so he asked, "Did you send a chopper?"

"No. Why?"

"Because we see one circling to land in a field behind the hotel. I have a feeling our escaped felon is about to try to make his move."

"Do whatever you need to to stop him," the supervisor ordered. "Don't let him get away."

"Copy that," Rafe replied. He ended the call and focused on Lucy. "Any ideas?"

"Yes," she said. "I'm going to cause a diversion and you're going to get inside that hotel to rescue my granddaughter."

It occurred to Rafe that his chances of success were slim to none, yet he nodded agreement. Not only were there kidnap victims to free, he now had an unbelievably brave dog trainer to save, too. By himself.

He grabbed Lucy's arm to stop her and get her attention. "Tell me the plan."

Pointing, she explained. "As soon as that helicopter touches down and I hear the rotors slowing I'm going to drive this SUV right at it. If I time it right I'll be able to disable the chopper so Fleming can't use it. The trick will be to wait long enough that the pilot can't lift off and dodge but not so long that gang members are in place to provide covering fire."

"That might work."

"It has to," Lucy replied. "I'll try to give you time to circle around and come in from the opposite side, but I won't wait too long. We'll only have one shot at this."

Rafe knew she was right. He also knew she was risking her life. They all were. Hannah was inside, Lucy was about to ram a helicopter with her armored SUV and he was charged with gaining covert access to a well-guarded fortress when no trooper in his right mind would try it.

Perhaps that was why the plan might work, he reasoned. Anything so off-the-wall would be unexpected.

The helicopter hovered, then slowly settled to the ground.

Lucy revved the engine and broke cover.

Rafe heard shouting and saw guards on the roof running east toward the wall facing the landing site.

A Jeep on the ground appeared out of nowhere and headed in the same direction, clearly racing to cut off the SUV attack.

Chancing an open run toward the front door Hannah had used, Rafe took the stone steps two at a time and burst into the lobby, gun drawn and ready to fire.

It was deserted.

Deuce Fleming's grin gave Hannah chills the moment she was delivered into his presence. Standing tall, she faced him with Thor at her side.

"What a nice surprise," he drawled. "Welcome."

"You won't escape this time," she said, thankful to note there was no tremor in her voice.

"We'll see." He motioned to one of his armed men. "Get rid of the dog."

"No!" She wrapped both arms around Thor's shoulders, using her body to block a potential bullet.

Fleming seemed amused. Laughing, he rescinded the order. "All right. Let her keep the cur for the present. We'll use him for target practice later when everybody can watch."

Hatred rose within Hannah to the point she was speechless. The commandment to love her enemies was impossible to keep when faced with the personification of evil that was Deuce Fleming.

Someone grabbed her arm and started to pull her away from Thor. Hannah screamed, resisting, and saw the loyal K-9 snap at the hand holding her.

"I'll come with you," she shouted. "Just don't hurt him. Please."

"Check her for a wire and lock them in with the others," Fleming ordered. "I'll personally deal with her later."

More than willing to submit to a search then follow one of the armed thugs down a hallway while a second trailed behind, Hannah kept Thor close and prayed he wouldn't try to bite unless she wanted him to. This was why he'd needed more training, more controlled practice, she thought, wishing there had been time to work with him. Having a basically untrained dog with the strength and protective instincts Thor possessed could be dangerous to everyone, even to her if he chose to cause trouble and she wasn't able to call him off.

The leader paused at wide polished oak doors and used a large key to unlock one of them. As it swung open, Hannah saw a stirring of individuals huddled in chairs and on blankets spread on the floor. As near as she could tell there were at least two dozen women, all young and all frightened.

No one spoke until the door shut behind her and its lock clicked. Then Hannah began to talk for the benefit of the listening device on Thor's harness. "This looks like a banquet or ballroom. Ground floor. There are lots of people here, maybe twenty-five or thirty."

Keeping her dog on a short leash she scanned the crowd. "Is one of you named Kristy Fellows?"

A hand was raised cautiously. "Me."

"Your father is a state trooper?"

Kristy quickly put down her hand and shook her head.

"It's okay," Hannah assured her. "I've met Andy. He's still in the hospital but recovering."

The teen remained visibly leery so Hannah changed her focus. "I want you all to know that the authorities are aware of your presence and are making plans for a rescue. We need to stay calm and wait."

"How long?" someone in the dim background asked. "Some of us have been prisoners here for weeks."

"That's better than the alternative," Hannah said. "Once you're shipped out of the country, it'll be too late."

"What are you doing in here with us?" another asked.

"Have you ever read the story of the Trojan horse?" Most of the women shook their heads. "Well, never mind. Just think of me as your guide to getting rescued, okay."

Crossing the room she began to investigate the tall windows hidden behind heavy drapes. There were, unfortunately, iron grids on the outside preventing escape.

"They're all like that," Kristy said, joining her.

"I take it the doors are pretty solid, too."

"Like a fortress," the slim young woman said. "Did you really see my dad?"

"Yes. His former partner took me."

"Gavin?"

"No," Hannah said before realizing that might be Rafe's real name. "Rafe McDowell."

Kristy made a face. "Never heard of him."

"Doesn't matter. I know it was your father I spoke with. He's on the mend and praying for you. Lots of people are."

"Yeah, well, I already tried that and I'm still here."

"Ah, but help is coming," Hannah reminded her. "That's a direct answer to a lot of prayers."

"Only if it happens," Kristy grumbled, eyeing the nervous German shepherd and Hannah. "So far I'm not real impressed."

"Give us time," Hannah countered. She smiled at Thor and spoke close to his harness to make sure her message was received. "As soon as my friends hear we're being held in a big room on the first floor with fancy iron bars over the tall windows, they'll know just how to break us out."

Kristy snorted in derision. "Right. And that dog is going to make like Lassie and go tell them."

"In a manner of speaking," Hannah said.

She led Thor to the center of the room and climbed up on a chair to be seen and heard by all. "I know you're scared. Me, too. But we have to be ready to move when help arrives. I can't tell you exactly how or when that will happen. All I know for sure is that there are lots of brave police officers and government agents working together to get us out of here."

A low murmur among the prisoners told her they were discussing the news and deciding whether or not to believe her. Mistrust was normal. After all, they'd been kidnapped and moved around for who knows how long. They were bound to be skeptical.

"Remember," Hannah told them, "I chose to walk into this place and join you. I believe we're all going to survive."

Which was true, as far as it went. The more she thought about what she'd done, however, the more she likened herself to one of those movie heroines who walked boldly into untenable situations. Her problem was that this was not a script with a guaranteed happy ending. This was real life.

Chapter Nineteen

Once inside the hotel, Rafe kept to the periphery of the lobby, hugging the walls and darting from hiding place to hiding place as much as was possible. A tarnished, dusty chandelier hung from the high ceiling and yellowing sheets draped the upholstered furniture. Myriad footprints had disturbed the layer of dirt on the marble floor. To his relief, Thor's paws had also left their marks.

Rafe was about to break cover and circle the base of the spiral staircase to look for the room Hannah had described via the radio Thor carried. A rumble of voices stopped him. Crouching behind a settee he listened intently.

Someone muttered a curse. "He has to be out of his mind."

Another man answered. "Who cares as long as we're on his good side. Just don't make a mistake and you'll be fine."

"Mistakes? Deuce is the one making those. I can't believe he didn't shoot that woman and her dog the minute he saw them."

A shiver snaked up Rafe's spine and made the hair at the nape of his neck prickle. Any mention of a woman with a dog had to be Hannah and Thor. *They're still alive!*

"Didn't you hear what the boss said? He's saving them for later. There's nothin' like watchin' somebody get shot to make all the others behave better."

"Yeah, yeah, I know. It just seems dumb to put her in with our cargo, if you get my drift."

"She wasn't armed. She can't cause any trouble that we can't handle."

"What about the chopper. Somebody took that out."

"No sweat. The boss has another one coming. Boats, too. We'll be heading for warm, sandy beaches and palm trees by tonight. You'll see."

"Yeah, well, in the meantime, what're we supposed to do with the driver who messed up our getaway bird?"

"That was just some old lady. They're bringin' her in. Nothin' to worry about."

Every muscle in Rafe's body was taut, his heart racing, his stomach clenching almost as tightly as his fists. They had captured Lucy, which sounded good only because it meant she was also alive and presumably mobile. He waited, ready to intervene if necessary and praying he wouldn't have to show himself until he was in a better position to gain control.

Two other thugs appeared at the door, supporting the older woman between them. She was acting groggy and disoriented but Rafe suspected a ruse on her part. The gang had already written her off as being no threat. Continuing to act that way was definitely a ploy the former spy would use.

Assessing Lucy's condition as the trio passed, Rafe saw her eyes open briefly and scan the lobby. That was enough to reassure him she was faking. Chances were she hadn't made it out of the SUV with her gun, but at least he now had a second ally inside the hotel. Hopefully, she had relayed the information they'd heard over the radio to the main task force. When they finally arrived they'd need to know where the hostages were being kept and how big a force was needed to free them.

Deuce Fleming appeared at the top of the staircase and started down. He laughed. "Well, well, well, if it isn't Granny, herself. She's got more guts than I thought."

One of the men supporting her asked, "What you want we should do with her?"

"Throw her in with the others. It'll be a lesson to them."

Rafe could not have made a more advantageous choice if Fleming had consulted him. Putting Lucy and Hannah together was akin to mixing gasoline and matches. He was positive they would do whatever they could to delay the departure of the human trafficking victims until backup arrived. Lucy had begun active interference when she'd eliminated the first helicopter. No matter what came next, those two extraordinary women would hinder Fleming. Once the gang's escape plans were carried out and they were airborne, stopping them would be next to impossible.

Wild notions of Hannah and Lucy trying to hijack Fleming's plane gave Rafe the shivers. This operation must never be allowed to get that far. Not if he expected to save all those kidnap victims as well as the spunky former spy and the woman he... Rafe held his breath. The woman he what? Admired? Yes, and more...

Unwelcome feelings of both joy and dread filled him. Circumstances had apparently acted as a catalyst and had influenced him beyond belief. Like it or not, he was definitely falling in love with Hannah Lassiter. What a disaster.

Hannah had herded the others away from the doors and into a back corner of the ballroom, stationing herself and Thor between the victims and the door she had entered. When it opened again and someone shoved a small figure through, she knew at a glance who it was. The others, however, did not so they shrank back as the door slammed shut again. Some were weeping. Some acted so depressed Hannah wasn't sure she could motivate them enough to engineer a mass exodus.

"Gram!" Thor followed her as she ran to Lucy, fell to her knees and embraced her.

The older woman barely moved until she'd scanned the

room. Then she took a shaky breath and pressed a hand to her ribs. "Help me up."

Leaning on Hannah's arm she gave a muffled groan, dusted off her dark clothing and cautiously stretched sore muscles before cracking a smile. "Feels worse than it looks."

"But you're okay?" Hannah asked.

"I will be. Don't worry. I relayed your info to the task force just before I took out the chopper."

"Good. I was hoping the bug was working. Now what?"

"Now, we wait."

Hannah scowled. "I'm not convinced we'll have enough time to get away if we're too passive."

"Why? What else have you heard?"

"Plenty. The plans to move out keep changing." She gestured at the group behind her. "They tell me the kidnappers have gotten so used to having them around they've started talking freely in front of them. Fleming plans to gather everyone at a private airfield where he has a chartered plane waiting. Exactly where that is keeps changing so they can't agree on that detail."

"What about timing? You say it's changing?" Lucy asked.

"Yes. We all thought he was going to leave tomorrow. Now, it's supposed to happen today."

"I take it the chopper was part of his escape plan."

"Yes." Hannah smiled. "He was so steamed about what you did, they could hear him hollering through the walls."

"Good." She grinned briefly before sobering. "I worry that you're not taking this whole thing seriously enough. I've seen agents with too much confidence pay the ultimate price for that kind of blasé attitude. Don't make that mistake, Hannah. Life doesn't get more dangerous than this."

"I know that, in an academic way. Without the experience you and Rafe have had, it's really hard to believe any of this is actually happening to us." Gesturing at the prisoners, she shook her head pensively. "I mean, look at all of them. It's so sad to think about how many families are grieving."

"Did you locate Kristy?"

"Yes." Hannah pointed out a slim brunette standing off to the side and comforting a weeping blond teen. "That's her."

"She looks pretty levelheaded. Think we can count on her not falling apart in a crisis?"

"I do."

"What about you?" Lucy asked, eyebrows raised. "How are you feeling? Steady? Strong?"

"I thought you wanted me to be worried," Hannah said, half teasing, half serious. "Do you think Rafe is okay?"

"I do. These guys would be bragging if they'd taken him out."

"I guess that's comforting." She stroked Thor's broad forehead to help calm herself. Thinking about Rafe, worrying about his safety minute to minute, was bound to distract her and that wasn't good. Not good at all. Gram was right, though. If they had harmed Rafe they'd be celebrating the defeat of an enemy whether they knew he was a cop or not.

She considered warning Kristy to keep that information to herself, then recalled the gang member who had tried to shoot poor Andy in his hospital room. Fleming was smart. He must have figured out which side Rafe was on long ago. Truth to tell, there probably wasn't a lot that the clever criminal didn't know. What he chose to do with that info, how he might use it, was the only real unknown.

That, and how she and Gram were going to shepherd this sad bunch of victims to safety without setting off World War III. If she let herself look at the big picture and take everything into account, she'd have to admit their chances were poor. Except, the good guys in the white hats were supposed to win, weren't they? Wasn't that how such stories ended?

Trying to calm her turbulent thoughts and clear her head of unnecessary concerns, Hannah took a deep breath and released it slowly, then another. And another. By that time she had concluded that God would not have put her into such an untenable situation if He didn't intend to get her out of it.

"If His will is really how I got here," she murmured, recalling the poor decisions that had led to the jailbreak in the first place. Believers had free will. They could make all the mistakes they wanted in spite of prior commitments to their faith. Surrendering to Him didn't mean they would never face hardships. It did, however, promise that they would never have to do so alone. Forgiveness waited for anyone who asked for it, for anyone who realized they had done wrong and admitted it. *Even Deuce Fleming*, her heart suddenly insisted.

Hannah refused to listen. Surely there were some sins, some crimes, which were beyond forgiveness. Look at all the terrible suffering that man had caused and was still causing.

She was not about to forgive a man who had harmed so many innocents, ruined so many lives, and left hope shredded and trampled in his wake.

If evil had a face it was Deuce Fleming's.

Rafe was essentially trapped in the lobby. Fleming had gone back upstairs but his men kept coming and going, even posting an armed guard just outside the front door. He shifted as he crouched to keep up circulation in his legs. Ambient noise as the gang prepared to travel was to his advantage. Knowing how close they were to leaving, however, was more than unsettling. It was terrifying.

He'd overheard plans vital to an effective capture and would gladly have relayed them to the task force if he'd been alone. Stuck in the cavernous lobby he didn't dare make any noise, let alone carry on a phone or radio conversation.

Seeing the door guard turn his back and pace away, Rafe decided to take a chance on changing positions. Nobody was currently on the stairs and he didn't see other gang members loitering around the lobby at the moment so he slowly straightened, bracing himself on the back of the settee. He listened. There was muted conversation in the distance but nothing sounded close by.

Moving toward the rear of the room he ducked beneath the sweeping staircase. Beams of pink and orange sunlight filled with swirling dust particles cut across his path, reminding him of how little time he had left before night came.

Thanks to Lucy's capture, he knew the prisoners were confined behind the double doors to his right. To his left lay an open corridor. He chose the latter, hoping and praying it would give him enough cover to safely report to the strike team by phone. Once he had done that and had learned how long it might be before backup arrived, he'd decide what to do about freeing the prisoners. About rescuing Hannah and the rest.

An acrid smell gave him pause. *Gasoline?* Yes, Rafe concluded. There was no reason for that to be kept inside, yet there was no doubt about the odor.

Following the fumes he opened a door marked Janitor, intending to duck out of sight and make his phone call. The smell became overwhelming. He looked down. Rows of gasoline-filled bottles had been rigged with wicks sticking out their necks, ready to be lit and thrown as weapons. He frowned. These men had plenty of armament. They didn't need Molotov cocktails to defend themselves. So what were they planning to do with them? The only conclusion he could come to was to anticipate the total destruction of the old hotel by fire.

Coughing from the fumes in the closet he pulled out his phone, made the connection and began to report. "Yes, Colonel. That's right. It looks as though they intend to set fire to this place when they leave. How long before you get here?"

"The bridge is clearing as we speak. Some of my people started the drive around so I don't have a full team but we're also pulling units from the Illinois side of the river."

"What's your ETA?"

"I should arrive within the next ninety minutes. We'll stage away from the hotel until we have enough firepower to take the place by overwhelming force."

Rafe felt sick. "A siege isn't going to protect the hostages. If anything, it'll get them killed."

"I'll try to talk Fleming down first. We've already cut off escape by land and I'm working on blockading the river."

"There's still the air to think about," Rafe warned. "I told you what happened to the first chopper they brought in. I've since heard that they've got more than one. With all the flat fields around here they won't have trouble finding a new place to land."

"We'll use drones to reconnoiter once we're in position. Do what you can on your end to keep them from being shot down."

"Copy." He coughed more, smothering the sound with his sleeve. "I'll try to check in again if I can find a secluded spot to call from. If you don't hear from me, that won't mean I'm out of commission, okay? According to what I've been hearing, the women and the dog are locked up with the other prisoners. I'm going to do my best to get them out of here before it's too late."

"Just don't get yourself killed, Gavin."

It seemed odd to hear his real name spoken when he'd been called Rafe for so long. Nevertheless, it was strangely comforting to hear his boss refer to him that way.

"From your lips to God's ears," he said, repeating a saying he'd heard Hannah use as he ended the conversation. That led him to add, "Please, Father. Help me help her and all of them."

Resolved, he opened the closet door, checked the hallway and started out.

He'd barely gone ten paces when he turned back, reentered the closet and tipped every bottle on its side. It wasn't much but who knew? It might actually help.

Chapter Twenty

As far as Hannah was concerned, as long as the heavy doors stayed closed they protected as much as hindered. Since Gram had arrived so unceremoniously, she'd kept insisting she felt fine. Hannah was not so sure. She didn't like the older woman's pale color or the perspiration glistening on her forehead when the room was anything but hot.

"Just let me catch my breath for a few seconds," Lucy said. "Then we'll figure out how to escape."

"We could wait for rescue," Hannah told her. "The bridge must be clear by now."

"Right, I…" Lucy's voice faded to nothing. She closed her eyes and slumped in the chair.

Hannah caught her before she could slip to the floor. Kristy helped her lower the older woman onto a blanket on the floor. "What's wrong with her?" the teen asked.

"I don't know. It could be anything. She drove our SUV into the helicopter. I thought she was faking being out of it when they brought her in, but maybe she really was injured."

"I'm so sorry," Kristy said. "How can I help?"

Normally, Hannah would have deferred to her grandmother. Now that wasn't an option. She checked Lucy's pulse and found it strong, watched her breathing and judged it even enough for now. If she hadn't seen Gram faint moments ago, she'd have thought she was merely sleeping. She knew enough about human medicine to alleviate serious worry, at least for the present, although broken ribs were a worrisome possibility.

"Okay," Hannah said. "Here's what I know and what I don't. I came here with Gram and one other person, the man who calls himself Rafe McDowell. He said he was your dad's state trooper partner and he's been helping us track Fleming ever since the jailbreak."

"I heard them talking about that," Kristy said in a near whisper. "That was you with the dog?"

"Yes. Thor," Hannah replied, causing the K-9 to lean against her even more.

Kristy fell to her knees next to the German shepherd and hugged him as if he were a big stuffed toy. That Thor let her do so was something of a surprise to Hannah. Soothing the dog with a "Good boy," she touched the girl's slim shoulder through her shirt. "You should never hug a strange dog like that."

"He's a sweetie. I can tell."

"Sometimes," Hannah said. "He's been known to bite the bad guys."

"Smart, too, huh?"

That made Hannah smile. "Yes, but untrained. Always keep that in mind. He's protective but not predictable."

Seeing Thor duck out of the girl's embrace and turn to the blanket where Lucy lay, Hannah was relieved to see her grandmother had regained consciousness so she knelt next to her. "How are you feeling?"

"Good enough to get out of here." Lucy raised on one elbow and grimaced. "Ouch."

"Stay down and rest a bit more," Hannah said. "Kristy and I are going to scout around for an escape route."

Lucy glanced at the heavy brocade drapes. "Can't we break a window?"

"They're barred," the girl said.

"Then we'll find some other way," Hannah said flatly. She touched the older woman's shoulder. "You stay put and just use your brain to figure things out. We'll walk around and investigate."

"I can come with you."

"And keep me from concentrating on my job because I'm too worried about your health? I don't think so." This was the first time in recent memory she had overtly disagreed with her wise grandmother and refused to consider doing everything her way. In Hannah's mind it was less a matter of independence than it was of respect. As long as Lucy was at her best Hannah was perfectly willing to defer to her opinions. Now, however, things were different.

The expression on Lucy's face was a combination of surprise and disagreement so Hannah restated her decision. "You know I love you, Gram. I do. But I'm right this time and you know it."

"Okay, okay." Lowering herself all the way, Lucy tucked part of the blanket beneath her head as a makeshift pillow. "Go explore without me. Just don't do anything rash."

Relieved to be able to carry on a lucid conversation with the sweet lady who had practically raised her, Hannah managed a smile. "What, like helping felons escape from prison, you mean?"

"Yeah, something like that." Lucy returned the smile.

Standing beside Hannah, Kristy grabbed her arm. "Wait a second. You got Fleming out of jail?"

"It's a long story," Hannah told her. "One for another time. Right now, you and I need to check this room for some way out."

"There isn't any. We looked." She gestured at her fellow kidnap victims. "All of us did."

"I'm sure you did. Now we'll see what the dog can tell us."

In reality, Hannah wasn't expecting much. She already

knew the heavy doors were locked and the windows barred. Still, as she'd just told Kristy, it wouldn't hurt to look again.

Leading the shepherd to the wall on her left, she walked slowly along it, came to the rear corner and made a turn. The walls looked solid. Impenetrable. When Fleming had chosen to lock his victims in the ballroom, or whatever it had originally been, he'd chosen wisely.

There was one thing she was thankful for, the view through the tall windows. Checking each one as she passed, she noted the wrecked SUV embedded in the lower part of the helicopter tail section. No way was that bird going to fly anytime soon.

A dusty, camo-painted Jeep was slowly circling the building. She ducked behind the curtain to keep the driver from noticing her. If Rafe could steal that and wrap a chain around the grid on one of the windows he might be able to pull it off and let them escape that way, except what would they do about Fleming's armed men? she asked herself. And what good would it be to get out of the hotel with nowhere to go, no place to hide?

Most of all, Hannah wished she knew how much longer it was going to be before the force she'd seen preparing to attack actually got there. Not knowing that crucial detail meant they didn't dare leave the hotel. They'd be sitting ducks out in those flat, treeless fields.

It occurred to her that escape from that room was only the beginning. Once she'd gotten all the kidnap victims out, what was she going to do with them? And how much cooperation could she expect if and when they were free?

Pulled from her whirling thoughts by Thor's tug on the leash, Hannah frowned. He was pawing at the base of an ornately carved credenza. She signaled Kristy. "Come help me push this."

Although the teen asked why, she nevertheless put her shoulder to the heavy piece of furniture and shoved.

Dust swirled. A mouse darted out. Thor ignored it, continuing to dig at the narrow space between the cabinet and the wall.

It wasn't necessary to completely displace the furniture in order to see the waist-high, built-in pass-through. It had obviously been closed off long ago.

Hannah dropped the leash, worked her fingertips into a gap between the small door and jamb, then yanked. It took her three tries before it budged. By this time, some of the other victims had joined her.

"Back off. Everybody. Give me room."

Eager hands pushed and pulled the credenza until the small access to the opening was clear. Hannah paused, waved both hands and shushed them. "Quiet down before somebody hears you and comes to see why you're so excited."

She opened the door to the passage and saw a similar one barring the way on the other side. If there was another piece of heavy furniture barring that door, they'd never manage to push hard enough to move it.

Turning to address the prisoners, she waited for complete quiet. "Listen carefully. I have no way of knowing who or what is on the other side of this hole. I did see a diagram of the hotel when we met with members of your rescue team and I think there's a kitchen through there. If so, there may be a bunch of men using it right now."

A murmur went through the group.

"It might make noise when I try to open it and that may bring guards to check on us." She had an idea. "Get a couple of those blankets and drape them over me to muffle the sound, just in case."

As soon as her plans were in place she gave the door a push. Nothing happened.

"Okay, it's really stuck. A few of you stand close and support me so I can lean back and try to kick it open."

Ranks closed behind Hannah. She rested against helpful hands and arms to literally walk her feet up the wall, planted the left one and kicked with the right. The jamb splintered. The little door swung open so hard it hammered the wall then vibrated to a stop.

Hannah jumped down to peer through. As she had hoped and prayed there was an empty room on the opposite side. They had a way out!

The blankets fell away. Someone cheered softly while some wept and hugged each other. Only Hannah seemed to realize they weren't in the clear. Far from it. Once she had moved all the prisoners out of their temporary prison they still had nowhere safe to go. Not until the task force arrived.

Joy mixed with trepidation brought unshed tears to her eyes, too. Seeing her grandmother at the rear of the group, silently clapping her hands, was enough to make the tears fall. She dashed them away and climbed up on a chair to stand where they could all see and hear her.

"This is just the beginning," Hannah said. "If we run outside we're bound to be recaptured. We have to be smart. Smarter than the gang that put us here."

A low rumble filled the room, causing Hannah to pause her instructions. "Listen. Listen."

Eager faces were upturned, watching her intently. "Here's what we need to do. This is a big hotel and I doubt they've opened many guest rooms because they don't need them. It will be up to us to find those empty spaces and hide ourselves until we hear the police arriving. They are coming, I'm just not sure how soon. Above all, we need to keep from being transported somewhere else. That's the key to survival and rescue. Understand?"

She saw nods spreading through the group. "All right. Who's first?"

From the rear, Lucy's voice rose over the ambient noise. "Send the dog and then you follow him to defend us when we get there."

That made Hannah smile. So did Kristy's comment. "I see who you inherited your brains from."

"Right," Hannah said. She lifted Thor's head and shoulders to face the opening. Kristy boosted from the rear. As soon as he landed and Hannah saw he was waiting for her, she stood on tiptoe and wriggled through.

"I recommend coming feet first," she called quietly back to the others. "Unless you want to land on your heads."

As she stepped back, arms out and ready to assist the next young woman to pass through, it occurred to her that she might have just put them all in worse jeopardy so she began to pray.

"Thank You, Father, for providing this chance. Please continue to protect and guide us. Guide me."

Hannah had to believe God was on her side and had placed her with the prisoners in order to help them, because if she was wrong about divine guidance she could very well be making a grievous error.

That thought made her tremble. If they were caught again it was possible Deuce Fleming would keep his promise to shoot Thor and probably her, too.

The urge to turn and flee, to run from the duty she had accepted regarding everyone else, was so strong it made her weak-kneed. It also brought unfounded guilt for merely considering abandoning them. Of course she was staying. There was no doubt of it.

Considering her past life in comparison to an unsure future, she had only one regret. That she hadn't spoken up when she'd had the chance and told Rafe McDowell how fond of him she had grown. Now he was out there somewhere, risking his own life for all of them.

"Please, Lord, let me see him again," Hannah added to her ongoing prayers, promising herself she'd confess everything she felt for him. The only question left to ask was, why had she grown to care so deeply for that man when she didn't even know his real name.

Chapter Twenty-One

Working his way through the hotel on the main floor, Rafe managed to keep from being spotted. The last he'd seen of Fleming he'd been climbing the staircase, meaning he was likely still upstairs.

It occurred to Rafe that if he could actually capture the leader, the gang might surrender. Then again, they might not. Plus, he had Hannah and Lucy to worry about besides the original hostages. One man with one gun, namely himself, was not going to be able to control everybody. Period. He might be good, actually he was very good, but that didn't make him omnipotent. Only God was that and judging by their present predicament, Rafe wasn't convinced He was paying enough attention.

Looking back on the trials he and Hannah had shared, he did have to admit something awesome was happening. When she'd broadcast Kristy's name over and over, as if they were already friends, he'd felt an enormous relief. A burden had accompanied that, of course. Now he knew for sure that Andy's daughter was among the prisoners, meaning there was no margin for error. Truth to tell, there never was when he was on the job, even if a few mistakes did sneak past him from time to time.

The key to being fearless in the face of danger was total self-confidence. Doubting himself even a little was not a good sign. Not good at all. And doubting the sovereignty of God? *Worse.* Way worse. Rafe closed his eyes and sent up a silent prayer for forgiveness. For strength of body and character. And for the innocent victims he and those in his profession had not been able to save in the past. Their numbers had to be staggering.

He had earlier muted the Bluetooth-like radio receiver stuck in his ear. Now that he was away from anyone else and able to listen without risk of being detected he reactivated the sound. Instead of the conversation he'd heard before there was shuffling and grunting and panting. Whispers were distorted by background noise. Oh, how he wished the connection was two-way so he could ask what was going on.

Breaking cover, he headed for the core of the hotel, the central ballroom. That was where Hannah had reported being held with the kidnap victims and that was where he'd seen them put Lucy. Since he had not heard or seen any mass movement of gang members or prisoners, they had to still be in there. What he'd do when and if he reached them was an unanswered question.

As he peered around a corner into a section of the lobby he noticed two armed men; a bulky one with a military buzz cut and another, shorter and slimmer, with a head of brown curls. They each had an ear pressed to massive oak doors and were arguing.

"I tell ya, I heard something," Curls said.

"Yeah, yeah. You're always hearing stuff that ain't there."

"We need to have a look."

"Well, I'm not unlockin' this door. If you want to do it and the boss blows a gasket, it's all on you."

Rafe watched Buzz Cut hand an ornate large antique key to his partner and back away. Curly holstered his gun then bent over the lock, apparently having trouble inserting the key.

"If I'd known you were gonna shake so bad I'd of done that myself," the larger man said. "Hurry it up, will ya?"

Yes, please, Rafe thought. As soon as they opened that door he would know Hannah and Lucy and the others were all right and could proceed to locate Deuce so he'd be in position to detain him when the strike team was about to arrive. Forcing him to call off his men wasn't the best plan Rafe had ever had, but given the situation he saw no alternatives.

Cursing, the short-haired thug shoved his own sidearm into its holster and wrested the key away. Unlocking the door he gave it a hard push, shouted to the slimmer man and they both disappeared through the doorway.

Rafe paused only a millisecond before sprinting across the lobby to the same door. Neither gang member noticed his entry. They were too busy fighting over which one was going to crawl through a small opening in a far wall.

The enormous room was empty except for the three of them.

"Hands in the air," Rafe shouted. "Now."

Buzz Cut started to go for his gun, then froze when he turned and saw Rafe pointing the Glock at him. Curls raised his hands first.

"On the floor," Rafe ordered. "Both of you. Face down." Crossing quickly he disarmed both men then used the handcuffs they were carrying to lock them in place, back-to-back. "You have the choice to keep quiet on your own or be knocked out." He displayed the grip of one of the guns he'd taken off them. "Which will it be?"

"I'm not sayin' a word," Curly immediately offered.

His companion agreed with a grimace and a nod. "Yeah, yeah."

"Okay. I'll come back and see that neither of you ever talks again if you break your promise. Got that?"

"I said so, didn't I? The boss is liable to do it for you if he thinks we let his merchandise get away."

"That's your problem," Rafe said. "I'll send somebody back

for you once everything is under control." He took a moment to look through the hole in the wall, saw nothing but a white-painted board blocking the other side, and tried to push it open. Since it didn't budge he figured it was locked and left it as he'd found it.

"Who are you, anyway?" one of the men asked.

"Your worst enemy," Rafe told him.

"Naw," Buzz Cut argued. "Our worst enemy is Deuce Fleming."

Enjoying his unexpected success Rafe cracked a smile. "Funny you should say that. He's mine, too."

Leaving them prostrate on the bare floor, Rafe gathered up their guns and started away.

"Hey. Where are you going?"

"Don't worry, boys. I'll lock you in and keep the key so you'll be safe enough until this is all over."

And just like that there were two less adversaries to worry about when the siege began, he mused, locking the room and pocketing the heavy brass key.

Stepping into a small alcove for privacy he opened his cell phone to check the schematics of the hotel that they'd been given. A kitchen and prep area lay on the other side of the opening he'd seen. Clearly, Hannah had found a way out and taken the other captives with her. For once he wished she hadn't been clever enough to secure the second little door after passing through.

Then again, nothing indicated that she'd stayed where she'd landed. She was too smart for that. No, she'd have led the victims to someplace she felt was safe, meaning it was highly unlikely they were still gathered in the kitchen.

Nevertheless, he circled to one of the rear accesses and checked. Dust coated every surface except one section of stainless steel counter. That area showed overlapping foot and hand prints with places where bodies had landed and slid off. Rafe was elated. Hannah had done it. She'd freed the others just as he'd hoped and led them away. Good for her.

He was turning to leave to search for them when he decided to pause long enough to disturb the dust in other places and use a dry mop to obliterate any footprints on the dusty floor. If he could tell which way the group had gone, then so could Fleming's cohorts.

By the time Rafe was finished, he'd left false trails to both outside exits and had swept the interior hallway. Then he backed away, dragging the dry mop behind him so whoever discovered his tracks wouldn't be able to tell if he was coming or going.

Satisfied, he stuffed the mop into the janitor's closet with the spilled gasoline and went looking for the victims. Pride in Hannah made him smile in spite of the tenuous situation. Intel had shown that the kidnapped women had been held at the hotel for days, yet it took Hannah Lassiter to find a way for them to escape. What an amazing person she was. When all this was over he was going to make sure she was recognized for her heroism.

Fond thoughts carried him further and he imagined being the one chosen to pin a medal on her or hand her a certificate for exceptional valor. His heart swelled with pride and affection. Awareness grew. If she had merely been lovely, as she certainly was, she would have been appealing. Knowing how brave and clever she was had taken his admiration to another level. He'd met and even dated pretty women in the past, yet none of them had impressed him this much. None had made his head spin and his heart race the way thinking of Hannah did.

Rafe paused, listening to his earpiece and wondering why everything seemed quiet. The next words he heard were so softly spoken he had to strain to make them out.

"Gram? Gram, can you make it?"

Whatever the answer was, the tiny radio pinned on Thor

didn't pick it up. Thankfully, he could hear Hannah say, "Come on. We'll help you." Then a pause and, "Hurry."

Where were they? Had they left the building? Were they still inside, and if so, where?

The schematics on his cell phone showed the main staircase where he'd last seen Deuce. Looking carefully at details of the kitchen area he noted a narrow, closed-off stairway meant for staff use. If he was Hannah, that's how he'd have left the kitchen. The problem was, once she and the others reached the upper floors they were likely to run into Fleming and the men in his closest circle.

Rafe reentered the kitchen and easily located the simple stairs behind a door. He wasn't picking up sounds of movement ahead, but the disturbed dust on the worn, wooden steps was a strong clue. Not only were there shoe prints, the paws of a large canine had left clear marks along one edge. They were up there. And, if they weren't careful, they'd stumble onto their captors.

Moving as silently as possible, Rafe was about to start his climb when he thought he heard something in the distance. *Sirens.* He pulled out his cell phone and tried to call his superintendent. *No service.*

At his wit's end, Rafe took the stairs two at a time, paused at the door at the top to draw his gun, then eased it open and peered out.

There was no sign of Hannah, but armed men were running past. In the background, Fleming was shouting orders that sounded as though he was dispersing troops to defend a fort.

Anxious to find Hannah and the other prisoners, Rafe held himself back until the hallways emptied. Then he slowly counted to ten and eased the door open for a better look. All was quiet. He couldn't have cleared the second floor more efficiently if he'd tried.

"Speaking of answered prayer..." He cast his eyes upward. "Thank You, Father. Now where are the women?"

Lacking a clear answer he turned right, away from the stairs, and made his way to the corner at the far end of the hallway. More closed rooms lay ahead. What he wanted to do was bang on each door in turn until Hannah showed herself. He would have if caution hadn't been called for. Suppose all of Fleming's men had not descended to the lobby. It would only take one sounding an alarm to spoil any chances Rafe had of getting to the prisoners and guiding them to safety.

His cell phone vibrated in his pocket. "Hello?"

"Situation report," his supervisor said without wasting time on polite conversation.

"The hostages have escaped and are at large in the hotel," Rafe reported. "Fleming may not know they're gone yet. Right now he's acting more worried about how many of our units are closing in. I know he's posted snipers on the roof and probably other places, too. Tell our people to assume everyone is armed and dangerous."

"Copy that. Where are you?"

"At the moment, on the second floor. If I don't locate the victims here, I'll go on up to three."

"Advise when you have them and we'll give you cover as best we can."

"I think we should hold off trying to move anybody until you have the gang disarmed. We'll have casualties if we don't."

"Copy."

Rafe heard him broadcasting to the cars making their approach. Sirens wailed louder, closer. He opened one of the first rooms he came to and hurried to the window. The glass was barely clean enough to see through but flashing red and blue lights helped him tell what was transpiring in the twilight below.

Someone fired the first shot. A volley of gunfire ensued. Rafe ducked just in case a stray bullet came his way. Men on the floor below were shouting and cursing. Deuce Fleming's voice rose over the din. "Go get the women. We'll use them as human shields."

Rafe held his breath. As soon as they discovered their prisoners had escaped they'd begin a frantic search. There would be no place to hide. Not with a dozen armed thugs searching for them.

He fisted his phone again. "They're about to find out the victims aren't locked up where they left them. I'll make a stand at the top of the main staircase but I don't know how long I can hold them off."

"Do your best," his superintendent said. "We'll make entry ASAP, but I can't guarantee how soon that will be."

There was nothing more to say. Rafe took up a defensive position at the corner facing the top of the stairs, laid out the extra guns he'd taken from the men he'd overpowered in the ballroom and waited, knowing he might be living his last moments on earth.

The urge to pray was strong but he had no words, no sensible pleas, not even a remembered verse from his childhood. *That doesn't matter*, he thought soberly. It didn't take flowery words or complicated prayers to reach out to God. A simple, heartfelt "Jesus," was more than enough. So that's exactly what he whispered. Over and over.

for them.

Chapter Twenty-Two

Hannah had shepherded her group as far as they could go without actually stepping out onto the roof. She knew there had been snipers up there before and likely still were so she chose a room at the farthest point away from that access. The plan wasn't foolproof. Nothing could be under such desperate circumstances. But anything was better than staying locked in that ballroom and waiting for their captors to come for them.

It had occurred to her more than once that she could have remained outside when they'd arrived at the hotel. Maybe it was foolish to have offered herself as another victim, but she still couldn't see any other feasible way to contact these poor girls and let them know help was on the way. Plus, she and Thor had managed to free them from that room where they'd been held, providing an added buffer against the explosive temper of Deuce Fleming. If he acted impulsively as he had before and decided to shoot them or use them to facilitate his own escape, he'd have to find them first. And that would take time, time he might not have once the police assault on his hideout began in earnest.

The hotel room smelled musty and was even dirtier than the common areas. Several of the women chose to sit on the edge of the bare mattress, but many preferred to stand. Lucy stood at one of the windows peering out through slits in the vertical blinds.

"What do you see?" Hannah asked.

"A full-on assault," her grandmother answered. "The command van we saw before just pulled behind the carriage house where I parked. Police cars are driving around this building. I can't see them all but it reminds me of a siege. It looks like Fleming is trapped."

"Perfect."

"I'll feel better once they've made entry and taken the gang into custody."

"It shouldn't take long. Deuce is going to be furious when he opens the ballroom and discovers we've escaped. I have high hopes that that will unhinge him enough to give the police an added advantage."

"Works for me." Sighing, she leaned her shoulder against the edge of the window. "Chances are good that most of their potential escape routes are covered. I suppose he could bring in a second chopper, but that takes time."

"Very true." Hannah patted Kristy on the shoulder. "As far as you know, are all the latest victims here with us?"

"Yes." The teen smiled slightly. "I can't believe anybody found us. I thought for sure we were goners."

"I know what you mean," Hannah said. "The more I learn about how so many people came together for your rescue, the more impossible it all seems."

"I just wish I could tell my dad," the teen said.

Hannah gestured at Thor. "I'm pretty sure Andy knows by now." A smile blossomed in spite of the still tenuous situation. "My dog is wired."

Hearing that, many of the victims gave a subdued cheer and gathered closer to pet the brave K-9. Hannah warned them off. "Easy. Thor isn't as socialized as most dogs. I haven't had him long enough to be sure he won't get scared and bite."

"This big teddy bear?" Kristy asked, embracing the shepherd with her arms around his shoulders. In response, Thor gave her chin a slurp.

"Maybe I've been underestimating him," Hannah said, amused. "He was picked up as a stray so I can't tell what hang-ups he may have. I do know he's very protective."

"And smart," Lucy added. "We'd never have thought to look behind that heavy cabinet if he hadn't alerted us."

"True." Gazing at the dog with affection, Hannah saw him tilt his head to one side, then rise slowly and take a step toward the closed door to the hallway. "Uh-oh."

"Maybe the cops are already inside and coming for us," Lucy said.

"And maybe not." She pressed her index finger to her lips. "Everybody hush."

In a heartbeat, the only disturbance inside the room was the sound of humans breathing and Thor panting. He put his nose to the carpet and returned to the exit.

Hannah followed. Pressed her ear against the door. Listened. Didn't hear a thing and peered through the tiny peephole.

There was nobody out there. Not a soul. Yet the dog had reacted to something, hadn't he? Her fingers closed around the knob. Did she dare open the door to take a better look?

Before she could decide, Lucy called to her. "Something's up. Something has changed. Look."

Hannah left Thor sniffing at the base of the closed door and returned to the window. Gram was right. Not only had the string of police cars stopped moving, five of them had gathered directly in front of the hotel with their headlights pointing toward the entrance. Uniformed officers were climbing out and donning riot gear as if they expected to encounter violent resistance. Sadly, they were probably right.

Peeking from his vantage point at the top of the ornate staircase, Rafe could see a lot of what was happening below. He didn't get to watch when Deuce unlocked the ballroom and discovered that the young women were missing but his verbal response was loud enough to echo through the whole hotel.

"Where *are* they?!"

Rafe heard a scuffle, more shouts and curses, then two shots in rapid succession. He hadn't intended for the men he'd captured to be killed, but that couldn't be helped at this point. He'd given them a chance when he'd left them both alive and able-bodied. Momentary guilt assailed him until he reminded himself that he'd acted for the good of innocent victims.

"You and you," Deuce yelled, "go outside and look for them."

"But Boss…"

Rafe expected more shots when whoever Fleming was trying to send hesitated. Because that didn't happen he figured the thugs had obeyed despite their protest.

Bracing himself for others to start up the stairs soon, he leaned a shoulder against a sturdy newel post and aimed low. He didn't have long to wait. Fleming wasn't leading the assault, as Rafe had hoped, but he got off a couple of accurate shots that found their targets and stopped the rest in their tracks.

If there had not been so many armed men milling around the wounded ones on the first floor, Rafe might have gotten off a shot at Fleming, himself.

Someone yelled, "Kill the lights," and in seconds the only illumination of the lobby came from the setting sun and headlights of the patrol cars.

"Smart," Rafe murmured, not at all happy about losing clarity. He could have shot into the shadowy group and would likely have killed or wounded some, but that wasn't the right thing to do. If he intended to fire fatal shots they needed to be aimed and purposeful. Fleming's men might be random killers but they couldn't all be as bad as their leader. Capturing the bulk of them for intense interrogation was the goal of the strike team. It wasn't enough to merely end this facet of the operation here and now. They needed to take down the worldwide network, or at least as much of it as possible.

Shadows moved. Shifted. Rafe peered down. Several armed men had formed a line along the curve of the staircase and were climbing in a crouch.

"Stop. Police," Rafe shouted. "Hands up."

Nobody obeyed. He hadn't expected them to. They did, however, back off and regroup in the lobby. That would do. Anything that delayed the gang's escape gave the multiagency strike team more time to get into position for a coordinated assault. That was enough. He wasn't hoping for more.

Excitement had caused him to breathe rapidly. Suddenly, his throat itched, then burned. He coughed. His pulse leaped and stayed accelerated far beyond normal, even for a tense situation like this standoff.

Rafe gasped. Was it…? Would he really…? The obvious answer was, *Yes*. Fleming or one of his men had lit the hotel on fire, probably by igniting the spilled gasoline in that janitor's storage room.

"There was no other way to disable those gas bombs," Rafe told himself. There were too many of them to have carried them outside to empty and, given more time, the liquid would have evaporated rendering it useless. When he'd closed the door to keep his countermeasure a secret he'd inadvertently delayed the dispersal of the volatile vapors. Now, anyone inside the hotel was poised to become a victim.

No one stayed at the base of the stairway after the first cry of "Fire" echoed. Climbing away from easy exits would be foolish and these criminals were, for the most part, clever. Fleming was the worst, of course, but he was also teetering on the edge of losing self-control so there was no telling what he might do next.

Only one goal remained for Rafe. He had to find Hannah and the others and rescue them. Without getting himself killed, he added. Acrid smoke stung his eyes, made them water. Every breath, however shallow, made him cough. Fire on the ground floor was sending smoke and sparks up the open stairway as if it were a chimney. With no way to close it off, Rafe was helpless to stop or divert it.

Starting down the nearest hallway he began banging on doors as he passed and shouting "Fire!" at the top of his lungs. The farther he got from the source of the flames the better he could breathe. Smoke was layering on the second floor now, filling the space at the ceiling first, leaving air near the floor more breathable.

If it wouldn't have slowed him down he would have dropped to his knees and crawled. As it was, he bent at the waist and tried to cover his mouth and nose with fabric from his hoodie.

Nobody responded on that floor. Elevators had been out of service all along so he opened a stairway door and ran through, slamming it behind him to slow the rise of the smoke and the spread of the fire.

Arriving on the third floor Rafe secured the stairway door the same way, adding to the fire blocking. As old as the hotel was, hopefully there was not a lot of manmade material in the furnishings because fumes from plastics, etcetera, could be deadly without being concentrated.

A roof access door stood open. He braced, aiming at the space as he passed through to check. There was nobody left up there. At least not that he could see. Which meant the kidnap victims must be already outside on the ground or trapped on the third floor. Like he was.

Rafe turned on his heel, reentered the hotel from the roof access and started down the nearest hallway, hitting doors with the butt of one of the guns and shouting. Halfway down it occurred to him that even if Hannah could hear him she might think it was a trick.

Doubling over coughing, he straightened and yelled, "It's me, Rafe. The hotel's on fire." Every new door he came to got the same message, punctuated by sneezing and coughing and gasping for breath thanks to the doses of smoke he'd taken in below.

His nose was too stuffy to accurately assess the air on that floor, but he imagined there must be enough smoke seeping through for others to smell it. To believe him. To decide to show themselves and come out of wherever they were hiding.

If they stayed hidden for too long they might lose their chance to escape. Even if the old hotel had stood next to a fire station, which it did not, he doubted any efforts would stop the fire from engulfing every floor at this point.

Tears of sorrow mixed with the effects of the smoke and trickled down Rafe's cheeks. Each step he took was harder, each room he reached seemed farther from the last.

At the far end of the hallway his body gave out. He thudded against the door, hit it with his fist, then dropped to his knees with a feeble, hoarse, "Fire, fire."

Chapter Twenty-Three

Hannah and Lucy figured out what was wrong when they saw patrol cars gathering and their headlights illuminating the smoke billowing from the first floor. Some of the young women panicked while others were nearly catatonic after their long ordeal and didn't react at all.

"What do you think, Gram?" Hannah asked. "Up or down?"

"Probably up, until we figure out where everybody else is," Lucy said. "See what you can find to use as a weapon."

"I'm way ahead of you," Hannah said. "So is Kristy. She found us a couple of fancy curtain rods with pointy ends."

"You're taking a plastic lance to a gunfight?" Lucy huffed. "I had something a little more lethal in mind."

"Such as?"

"I don't know. I'm just an old lady, past her prime."

"Never," Hannah countered. "You'll never be too old for a fight. I saw you at the church, remember?"

"I do. Seems like that was months ago, not just days. I've aged a lot since."

"We all have," Hannah said. She looked to Kristy. "Look around for something else, something dangerous?"

"A lamp? The rod holding up hangers in the closet? The only other thing is an ironing board."

"Rods are good. Shower rods may be metal. Closet ones, too. And see if you can find the iron that goes with the board. It'll be hard and pointed on one end." Hannah's gaze traveled over the obviously frightened group. "All of you. Look, please. Anything is better than nothing."

Unspoken thoughts enlarged the scenario to include a face-to-face confrontation of her basically defenseless bunch of women against guns. That kind of battle was unwinnable.

So what kind is, at this point? Hannah asked herself, refusing to consider a negative answer.

Thor began to bark at the closed door. Whiffs of smoke rose in faint, twisting columns from beneath, as if someone was out in the hallway smoking a cigarette.

Hannah approached, grabbed his harness with one hand and fisted the base of a table lamp with the other. She called to Kristy. "Open it. And be ready."

"Fast or slow?" the teen asked.

Mouthing *Fast*, Hannah poised to go on the offensive.

Kristy turned the knob. Jerked open the door.

Hannah froze as Rafe McDowell fell face-first at her feet. She dropped to her knees. It was easy to tell he was still breathing because of his gasping and coughing.

She helped him sit up. He looked awful—and wonderful at the same time. Just having him with her again gave her hope.

"We saw the smoke. How bad is it?"

"Bad," Rafe choked out.

"Can you walk?" He proved the answer by standing. One hand was on the door, one on her shoulder. "Should we head for the roof?"

Rafe nodded. "Can't go down. Too much smoke and fire."

"There are fire hoses in cabinets on the walls in hallways. Can we use those?" Hannah asked. Enough smoke was beginning to reach their floor that she sneezed. Some of the others were already coughing.

"There's no water pressure to fill them," Rafe said. "They're useless."

"Maybe…" Hannah had been planning to rip linen into strips and use that to let everyone safely down from the roof. Now, she had a different idea.

She pushed past Rafe to check the hallway. "One of those hoses is right out there. We can use it like a ladder."

Lucy showed up behind her with the clothes iron and shouted, "Stand back," as she swung it at the glass cover in front of the fire suppression system.

It shattered. She knocked loose slivers from the frame with the metal iron, then stood back as Rafe pulled on the thick canvas hose. It wasn't long enough to reach very far past the window in the room they'd been hiding in but it looked adequate for a closer one.

Hannah led the way with Thor, taking care to avoid letting him step on broken glass. The guest room next to the fire hose attachment was unlocked, as were they all. She crossed quickly to the window. It wasn't designed to open so she threw a chair at it. The window vibrated but didn't break.

"Bring the iron," she called to her grandmother. "And the rest of you get in here."

Lucy used the cord to swing, whipped the heavy iron around her head like a stone in a sling and let fly at the window. It shattered into a million pieces. Grinning, she turned to Hannah. "David and Goliath."

"Good one." Now that the window was open Hannah could see plenty of activity below. If the siege was going as well as it appeared to be, the Fleming gang had been overcome.

She turned to the kidnap victims. "We're going to drop this hose out the window. You're all young and strong so you should be able to slide down. Hook one arm around it if you don't think you can hang onto the canvas covering well enough."

"I'm scared of heights," one of the girls said.

"Me, too," another echoed.

"Everybody join hands," Hannah ordered, reaching for the closest person and finding it was Rafe. She clasped his fingers tightly and felt an immediate surge of determination and strength. "We're going to pray, then we'll do this. Understand?"

Nodding, the others followed her instructions. She bowed. "Thank You, Father, for showing us a way out. Help us to complete Your plans for our rescue. Amen."

That was all that needed to be said, she decided. The asking was one step. Following through was another.

Hannah took Thor to the window, watched as Rafe and Kristy dropped the hose its full length, then backed away. She held out a hand. "Okay. Who's first?"

It had immediately occurred to her that Thor would be unable to descend the way the humans did. She vowed to get him out of the burning building one way or another, even if it meant staying with him until a fire truck with a ladder eventually arrived. She refused to entertain the notion that that might happen too late for both her and her beloved dog.

The vibration of his cell phone caught Rafe's attention. He stepped away from the window where he, Lucy and Hannah had been helping a young women over the sill and out the window. Three of them had already reached the ground and been scooped up by troopers.

"Hello."

"Status?" his superintendent asked, shouting over the background noise.

"We're on the third floor. All the victims we knew about are present, including Kristy Fellows. We've rigged a line from a window to the ground and so far it's working."

"How many more do you have?"

Rafe did a quick count. "Looks like about eighteen, not including me, Hannah Lassiter or her grandmother."

"All right. Make it fast. Fire units are still twenty to thirty minutes out. You need to evacuate."

"Copy," Rafe said. His gaze met Hannah's and lingered. "Everybody goes out the window."

"I'm not leaving Thor."

"I figured that's what you'd say. Lucy and I can handle this. You go find something to make a sling for him and I'll take him down with me."

"That's too dangerous."

"For me or for the dog?" Rafe asked, slightly perturbed.

"For both of you," Hannah answered.

He didn't like seeing tears filling her eyes. She must not give up. Not now. Not when they were so close to their goal.

"My jacket was okay for the short drop back at your house. I don't think it's secure enough for the trip down the hose. You need to rig something that fits my shoulders and attaches to his harness."

In obvious agreement, Lucy left the window with Hannah and the dog. Rafe's fondest hope was that the older woman's arms were also strong enough to keep her from falling when she took her turn to shinny down the fire hose. If it had been filled with water it would have been about two inches in diameter. Flat, it was harder to grasp securely. Not impossible, just more difficult.

He lost count of how many victims he had assisted. Turning to welcome the next he saw only Hannah, Lucy and Thor. "Ready?"

"Gram will go next," Hannah said, displaying a ripped, knotted sheet. "We've tied these strips together with a loop on one end. She'll wear it as a safety harness, then we'll pull it back up and tie a figure eight for your shoulders and fasten Thor's harness to it."

Rafe gestured to her. "Okay. You next."

"No." Hannah was shaking her head vigorously. She coughed. "I'm last."

"Unacceptable," Rafe countered.

"I have to be here to help you rig the dog for transport. He trusts me."

"He trusts me, too."

"Enough to let you manhandle him and sling him across your back? Are you sure?" She paused for a moment. "I'm the dog expert. You need to listen to me."

As much as he disliked the idea, he knew she was right. "Okay. Lucy next, then me and the dog. But I expect to see you right behind me. Promise?"

She raised a hand, palm toward him as if taking an oath. "Promise."

Lucy slipped a loop of torn sheet over her shoulders and under her arms, wincing from the pain in her ribs, then put a leg out the window. Assisting her, Rafe felt her trembling yet she showed no more outward signs of discomfort other than gritted teeth and a deep scowl. Hannah's grandma was quite extraordinary.

That thought almost made Rafe smile. Coughing hid his temporary amusement. The smoke was getting thicker, more acrid, partly because the fire below was building and partly because they had been unable to shut the door with the hose passing through its opening.

Lucy shouted and waved once her feet touched ground. Rafe hauled the sheet back up, hand over hand. Hannah was waiting to tie more knots and form a figure eight like a backpack for him to carry Thor. She explained as she prepared to tie a portion of the sheet line to the dog's harness.

"I think that will work," Rafe said, intending to encourage her.

"It had better. Sit down on the floor so I can get him closer to your back. I'll lift him when you stand up and help you through the window."

That gave Rafe pause. "Are you sure we'll fit?" Lack of

an answer was his answer. She didn't know. Neither did he. They'd have to try it to find out.

Supporting Thor and speaking gently to calm him, Hannah finished tying the knots. "Okay, Rafe, on your feet. I'll lift Thor as much as I can before I have to let go. You're bound to be off balance so plan for it."

"Gotcha." The weight of the dog would have been more of a problem if he'd tried to walk very far carrying him. As it was, the few steps to the window were manageable. He bent at the waist, still coughing some, and sat on the sill.

"Try to hold him up while I get both legs out and around the hose," Rafe said. "I'll tell you when to let go."

"Okay."

He could see her teeth clenching, a grimace on her face as she struggled to help him balance the heavy dog. Turning, he let himself down until he was hanging on the hose, alone.

"I'll keep hold of the extra sheet for as long as I can, just like we did with Gram. It might help."

"Okay, as long as you don't stop my descent," Rafe warned. "It may be a little fast." Hannah was letting the ripped fabric slip through her fingers as he pushed off and started down.

The trip took every spare ounce of his strength. When he landed there were men waiting to relieve him of his canine burden and congratulate him on the success of the mass escape.

Rafe looked up expecting to see Hannah traveling down, herself. Instead, she was leaning out the window, watching him. He gave her a thumbs-up sign and waved. "Come on."

Suddenly, her head and shoulders disappeared. Rafe held his breath waiting for her to stick a foot out and swing around to grasp the hose.

She did not.

VALERIE HANSEN

Chapter Twenty-Four

Hannah whirled. A shadowy figure appeared in the doorway behind her. For an instant she wondered if one of the troopers or government agents had come to rescue her. Then she realized who it actually was.

She backed up as far as she could. Her hips hit the window sill and she froze.

Deuce Fleming was coughing worse than Rafe had been so it took him a few seconds to speak. "Last man standing wins."

Although Hannah wanted to match wits with him and stall the inevitable, astonishment kept her quiet. This was not supposed to end this way. The good guys were supposed to win. And they had for the most part. Only one person was left to face this evil man because the rest of his victims had escaped and there was nothing he could do about it.

Except kill me, she added, wondering if it was actually God's will that her earthly life end then and there.

"Please, no, Lord," she whispered. "I don't want to die. Not now. Not like this. I haven't even had a chance to tell Rafe how much he means to me."

A massive coughing fit doubled Fleming over and he lowered the gun.

That was all Hannah needed. She threw one leg through the open window and grabbed for the hose. It slipped out of her grasp. Her second leg bent at the knee to keep her from falling, but it also kept her within range of her worst enemy.

Trying again she looped her whole arm around the hose and let herself drop outside. Both arms and legs circled the hose, slowing her descent as the rough canvas scraped off skin. Adjusting her hold she looked up. Fleming was leaning out the window and pointing his gun down at her. There was no way to duck. No way to dodge. Even if she let go and fell she'd probably die when she hit the ground so she just hung on and kept sliding.

Ten feet from the bottom she heard and saw an explosion. A ball of fire blossomed out the third floor window and the hose went slack, dropping her into Rafe's waiting embrace.

Flabbergasted, Hannah wrapped her arms around his neck as he carried her toward a waiting ambulance. Thor galloped along at his feet, barking as if they were playing a wonderful game.

The rumble of Rafe's voice was drowned out by the pounding beats of her heart and repeated explosions within the old hotel. Hannah didn't care what had blown up or why. She was simply overcome by the timing and the way God had implemented her rescue—with the use of her favorite state trooper, of course.

Clinging tightly, Hannah closed her eyes and buried her face against his smoky shoulder, hardly able to process what had just happened. None of her efforts should have been enough, yet they were. Imagine, a powerful explosion at just the right moment and this amazing man waiting below and risking his life to stay close enough to catch her.

He didn't loosen his hold and set her on her feet until they were back behind the carriage house where several ambulances waited next to the command post van. Then, he set her away, keeping hold of her shoulders.

"What do you think?" he asked, looking worried.

"About what?"

"About what I just told you."

Befuddled, Hannah kept gazing at him and cupped one of his cheeks gently. "I can hardly hear you, even now," she said. "The explosion hurt my ears."

"You're going to make me say it again, aren't you?"

Continuing to caress his beard-stubbled cheek, she smiled up at him. "If it was something good, yes."

He leaned closer to place a kiss on her smoky forehead. "I said I love you."

Hearing her own thoughts echoed was both wonderful and terrifying. "I—I was afraid of that."

"Why?"

Honesty was clearly called for and she chose her words carefully. "The only thing you and I have in common is this terrible situation. Now that it's over, what connects us?"

"I guess we'll have to get to know each other better and find out, won't we?"

"If that's what you want."

"What do you want?" Rafe asked, pulling her so close his lips brushed her temple.

Hannah was smiling when she said, "You. Whoever you are."

Epilogue

Posing in front of a full length mirror, Hannah smiled at her grandmother's reflection behind her. "I can't believe this is happening, can you?"

"As a matter of fact, I can." Eyes twinkling Lucy smoothed the flowing skirt of her Matron of Honor dress. "What I can't believe is that you chose this smoky blue color. It matches my eyes perfectly."

"It's a good thing Gavin and I waited a couple of months after we decided to get married or you might have had circles under your eyes to match, too." Hannah embraced her. "I'm so thankful you weren't hurt worse in that crash."

"Don't hug me too tightly, okay? I'm still sore in places."

"You were amazing, Gram."

"Not half as amazing as your future husband was—and is." She chuckled under her breath. "I don't know if I'll ever get over wanting to call him Rafe."

"I know. But I like his real name, too. In a couple of hours I'll be Mrs. Gavin Arthur."

"So you will." Lucy sighed. "It takes me back, seeing you in my old wedding dress. I can't believe you wanted to wear it."

"Don't be silly. I love vintage." Running her hands over

the sleek curves of the ivory colored satin, she gave a little kick to ripple the wider, fluted hem, then picked up a crown of real flowers.

"You're a beautiful bride, Hannah. I'm just surprised you didn't want a more fashionable dress."

"A more *normal* one, you mean?" She laughed. "Gavin asked me the same thing. He even offered to pay for it."

"Really? What did you tell him?"

"I reminded him that there had never been anything very normal about me or my family and suggest he'd better get used to it."

"Did he laugh?" Lucy asked with a smile.

Hannah felt her cheeks flush and saw them reddening in the mirror. "Actually," she said, pausing briefly for a sigh, "he picked me up, swung me around and kissed me breathless."

"I knew he was a keeper," Lucy said, patting her own pink cheeks with a lace handkerchief as if perspiring.

Hannah reached for her grandmother's hands and clasped them, hanky and all. "Are you sure you won't change your mind and move in with us after we come back from our honeymoon? We have plenty of room." It touched her to see happy tears welling in the older woman's eyes and her own began to fill as well.

"I'm sure."

"But what will you do with yourself when you don't have me to look after and fuss over?"

"I'll have Thor for company while you're gone. After that, I'll adjust." Lucy stood tall with her chin jutting proudly. "I was saving this for a surprise but now is as good a time as any, I guess. I'm going back to work."

"Not as a…"

"Don't be silly. Of course not." A grin split her face and tiny lines accented the corners of her eyes before she said, "I'll be joining a senior citizens group that tours all over the world." She paused, winked and added, "What could be more innocent than a dozen or so old retired folks just hanging around touristy hot spots, listening to local gossip and taking it easy?"

"A dozen plain citizens or a dozen former spies?"

Pulling away, Lucy arched an eyebrow. "You just take care of your dog and your new husband, honey. I'll send you post-cards from all the exotic places I go."

"And you'll phone me at least once a week," Hannah added. "Promise?"

"I do," Lucy said before giggling. "Hey, that's supposed to be your line."

A sharp knock on the door caught Hannah's attention. Smiling at Gram's silly joke she opened it. Her other bridesmaid, Kristy Fellows, was acting breathless. "Are you ready?"

"Very."

"Are you sure you want Lucy to give you away? My dad said he could do that and still be the best man."

"I'm positive. Gram raised me. She should be the one to walk me down the aisle."

Accepting the larger of two bouquets from Lucy, Hannah followed Kristy into the church foyer.

Ushers opened double doors for Kristy to precede them. Lucy took Hannah's arm. They stepped forward together.

Hannah realized that if her grandmother had not been there to provide support she might have faltered the moment she laid eyes on her beloved. Gavin was waiting at the altar, just as he had waited at the end of that fire hose to save her life—a life she was now going to share with him.

Blinking, she willed away her happy tears and took the first steps into her future.

* * * * *

Hunted For The Holidays
Deena Alexander

MILLS & BOON

Deena Alexander grew up in a small town on eastern Long Island where she lived up until a few years ago and then relocated to Clermont, Florida, with her husband, three children, son-in-law and four dogs. Now she enjoys long walks in nature all year long, despite the occasional alligator or snake she sometimes encounters. Her love for writing developed after the birth of her youngest son, who had trouble sleeping through the night.

Books by Deena Alexander

Love Inspired Suspense

Crime Scene Connection
Shielding the Tiny Target
Kidnapped in the Woods
Christmas in the Crosshairs
Hunted for the Holidays

Visit the Author Profile page at LoveInspired.com.

MILLS & BOON

Seek the Lord, and his strength:
seek his face evermore.
—*Psalms* 105:4

To my agent, Dawn Dowdle, you were the first to believe in me, and I will be forever grateful.

Chapter One

Cheers erupted as Gracie Evans, Shae's five-year-old daughter, smiled at the audience, waved and did a little impromptu dance that had nothing to do with her role as a sheep in the church's annual Christmas pageant. Her long, dark ponytail swung, and the stage lights made her sapphire eyes sparkle. Some of the older actors glanced at the director, then continued with their lines as Gracie jumped and wiggled, her mischievous grin charming the cheering crowd. Shae applauded loudly with the rest of the families. "Go, Gracie!"

Seconds later, an angel corralled the little girl and guided her to her proper position, and Shae checked her phone camera to be sure it was still recording. As she looked back up, satisfied she hadn't missed any of the theatrics, her gaze landed on two men dressed in dark suits standing to the side of the auditorium, their expressions harsh as they scanned the spectators rather than watching the action on stage.

No! For just an instant, recognition flared, followed almost immediately by uncertainty. Even if one of them did look familiar, who was to say it was someone from her past? Perhaps she'd met one of these men after relocating to Boggy Meadows. Still…fear flooded her system.

Because if it was someone from before… How could they have found her? They couldn't have. It wasn't possible. At least, that was what the marshals had assured her when they'd placed her in the witness protection program six years ago. Besides, Quentin Kincaid was in prison and would be for the rest of his life, thanks in large part to Shae's testimony. Could he have escaped?

In some part of her mind, she equated the applause and jubilation surrounding her with Gracie and knew her daughter must be drawing attention again, but Shae had missed it, distracted by what could be a death sentence for them both. She refocused the camera on the stage, needing to capture what might be their last moment of normalcy before the past caught up with her. No use. She held her phone up to block her face but marked the men's progress up the side aisle.

She plastered on a smile, but her cheers caught in her throat, nearly choking her. Her mouth went dry, then her shouts turned internal. She had to get her daughter off that stage and out of there.

Sweat beaded Shae's brow. She swiped at it with the back of her wrist and glanced at the clock. Run and risk drawing attention? Or stay put until the show ended and mix with the crowd to make her escape?

Maybe the two men had just arrived late and were searching for family members, but then why were the little hairs on the back of her neck standing straight up? The goose bumps racing across her skin had nothing to do with the air-conditioning, of that she had no doubt. As she waited for the pageant to end and the actors to take their bows, Shae planned escape routes and calculated the distance to exits until the curtain was finally dragged closed.

Keeping her head down and face averted behind the bouquet she'd brought Gracie, she slung her oversize bag onto her shoulder, slid into the stream of spectators and started toward the cafeteria, where other parents had already begun to gather.

"Mommy!" Gracie ran toward her, cheeks flushed, grinning from ear to ear. "Did you see? I did a dance on the stage. It was a surprise."

"It was awesome, honey. I loved it. You were amazing." Shae reminded herself not to use Gracie's name in case the men knew it. She forced an answering smile and hugged her daughter close, then handed her the flowers, shielding her as best she could.

"Thank you. They're so pretty." Gracie stuck her nose in the bouquet and inhaled deeply.

"Just like you, sweetie." As Shae kissed her daughter's head, her gaze skipped to the exits. Only one parent per child was allowed to pick the actors up from the cafeteria, which gave her a brief reprieve. But which way should she go? "Do you have your bag?"

"Uh-huh." Gracie lifted the sparkly silver duffel bag she'd fallen in love with when she'd spotted it at the holiday fair. "Got it."

Shae pulled the white sheep costume over Gracie's head, leaving her in black leggings and a long-sleeved black T-shirt, then stuffed the costume they'd worked together on all week into the bag. "All right. Let's go."

She hugged Gracie against her leg, keeping an arm wrapped firmly around her so she could hold her close and not chance losing track of her. She watched for trouble as they inched through the doorway. With so many people milling about, actors stopping in the lobby to meet up with the rest of their families and take pictures, and a small crowd already headed toward the parking lot in anticipation of getting out ahead of the rush, Shae had lost sight of the men. But the niggle at the base of her neck told her they were still lurking, still searching.

She might not be so on edge if her handler, the woman who'd placed her in the small town of Boggy Meadows, Florida, hadn't recently been killed in a car crash nearby. According to the news reports, it had been a tragic accident, but

Shae wasn't buying that. Maria Delarosa had had no business in Boggy Meadows unless she'd been trying to reach Shae. To warn her? She had no idea. All she knew was that she had to protect Gracie at all costs, which meant she needed to be somewhere else, anywhere else, as soon as possible. No matter what was going on, their time in Boggy Meadows had come to an end.

"Awesome job, Gracie! Ice cream's on me." Reva MacMillan, the director and mom of Gracie's best friend, Katie, patted Gracie's back and gestured toward a group of kids. "We're all meeting up at Jimmie's."

"Yay!" Gracie high-fived Katie. "Can we get ice cream, Mommy?"

Shae could only offer a noncommittal grunt. She had no intention of telling anyone she wasn't going to Jimmie's with the cast. If her pursuers caught wind of the planned get-together and detoured to the ice cream parlor in search of her, it might give her a couple of extra minutes to gather a few necessities and run. She was already compiling in her head a list of things she had to pack and kicking herself for not keeping their flight bags up-to-date. Gracie had probably grown two sizes since she'd last filled the bags with clothes. Oh, well, they could buy what they needed once they got away.

"Mommy!" Gracie yanked her hand, staring at her with a frustrated exasperation that told Shae she'd already called her more than once.

"Huh? What, sweetie?" Shae scanned the parking lot as they finally stepped out into the muggy Florida night.

"I said, can Katie come in our car to get ice cream?"

With both girls staring hopefully, and no good excuse to say no, Shae faltered.

"Mo-ommy." Gracie frowned. "Did you hear me?"

"Uh, yeah. I'm sorry, I'm a little distracted." Shae braced herself for the pout. "Katie can't ride with us tonight, hon.

I'm sorry, but I need to make a stop. We'll see you later, okay, Katie?"

Katie sent Shae a confused scowl before taking Reva's hand.

The two girls had become close, despite Shae's reluctance, and often spent afternoons at the park together and weekends playing soccer and attending faith formation. If it had been up to Shae, Gracie would have remained home all the time, where she could keep an eye on her, keep her safe. But Gracie, ever the social butterfly, had other ideas, and Shae did want her to have a normal life.

With that, she urged Gracie toward the car.

"We'll see you at Jimmie's, Katie!" Shae called out loud enough to be overheard if anyone cared to listen.

A dark sedan turned into the lot, battling its way upstream against the outgoing tide of cars.

Her heart thundered. She had to get out of there without being seen or any chance of escape would be gone. And not only would these men kill her and her daughter, they wouldn't hesitate to take out the whole crowd of innocent bystanders in pursuit of that goal.

Gracie lifted a hand and opened her mouth to call out to a friend.

Shae pulled her closer. "Be quiet, Gracie, and go to the car."

Gracie's eyes went wide—Shae never snapped at her—and then she whined, "But, Mom—"

"Shh. Remember cheesemonkey?" As much as she hated to use the secret code word they'd decided upon in case of an emergency, and had hoped to get Gracie out of there without scaring her or making her react in a way that might draw attention, Shae needed her to stop asking questions and move.

Gracie's steps faltered as she frowned up at Shae. "For real or for practice?"

Tell her the truth or let her maintain a blessed sense of innocence for just a little while longer? Vigilance was more important—which she couldn't maintain if Gracie didn't cooperate. She leaned close and whispered, "Real, honey. Just do like we practiced and everything will be fine."

Gracie pressed closer against Shae's leg. "Are we still gonna go for ice cream?"

Shae searched for which parking lot exit was least used. If she got caught up in the mess of strolling families and slow-moving vehicles, she'd be an easy target. "Don't say another word. Just get to the car. Now."

The dirty look the little girl shot her could have knocked her on her duff, but at least Gracie sulked quietly as she trod beside Shae, her glittery bag thumping against her leg in a steady rhythm that matched the pounding in Shae's skull. And at least she had her head down, making it more difficult to identify her if the men stalking them had pictures. Would they recognize Gracie? Did they even know about her? Probably. But why risk coming after them at a children's Christmas pageant? Why not grab them at home, where they would be less likely to be interrupted? If they'd managed to find her at the church she attended, surely they knew her address.

Unless their house was already under surveillance by the FBI or the marshals' service, and the men pursuing her somehow knew it. Had that been what Maria was doing there? Had they left Shae and Gracie in place as bait? Anger welled.

She massaged her temples as a ruse to cover her face and look around. No. She refused to believe Maria would have agreed to that, would have had any part of it without warning Shae. But… Maria was dead. And she had been near Boggy Meadows when she was killed. What if someone with less of a moral compass was calling the shots?

Shae hit the button on her key fob to unlock the doors, then looked around and opened the back door for Gracie. Once her daughter was safely inside, Shae climbed into the driver's seat, stuck the key in the ignition and hesitated. What if they'd rigged the car with explosives? Maybe it would be safer to flee on foot.

No. She had to stop second-guessing herself. Surely if they'd already rigged the car, they wouldn't be hanging around the parking lot waiting to get blown up.

She held her breath—*God, please don't let the car explode*—and turned the key. No bomb. Well, that was a relief. But that was when she spotted the two men again, weaving between cars, peeking in windows. "Get on the floor, Gracie."

"Wh-what about my b-booster seat?" The one she'd felt so grown-up moving into.

"Don't worry about it." A quick glance in her rearview mirror showed Gracie's shocked expression. "Cheesemonkey, remember? Get on the floor, pull the blanket from the back seat over you and hide. Do it, Gracie. Now."

Either the code word or her tone must have gotten through to her daughter that this was no joke, because she slid onto the floor, still clutching her flowers, and pulled the blanket they'd used at the drive-in movie what seemed like a lifetime ago over her head. Shae inched forward into the line of cars exiting the lot.

"M-Mommy?" The shakiness in Gracie's usually confident voice beat at Shae. "I'm scared."

"I know, honey, and I'm sorry. I'll explain everything. I promise." *As soon as I lose these goons and we get on the road.*

"Are the storms coming now?"

"What st...?" Oh, right. She'd forgotten Gracie had heard the weather report this morning—possibly severe storms—which had terrified her. But that was the least of Shae's problems. Florida often had storms, though the meteorologist had said these could bring tornadoes as well, thanks to El Niño. She wouldn't have given it a second thought if not for Gracie's fear of thunder. But she didn't have time for that right now. God willing, they'd be long gone from Florida in a few hours and wouldn't have to worry about any storms. The men trolling the parking lot were a much more immediate concern. "No, baby. No storms."

"O-okay." Gracie cried softly beneath the blanket on what was supposed to be such a special night, a night that should have been so filled with joy.

The phone number Shae had committed to memory six years before and had prayed she'd never need ran through her head over and over again, like a mantra. Should she call now? No. She had to stay focused on escape first. The call could be made from home. Even if someone were nearby to help, they'd never make it to her before she got out of the parking lot. Besides, she wasn't even a hundred percent sure she'd use the number. She was supposed to contact the marshals' service any time she planned to move, but what good had witness protection done her if Kincaid's men had found her? What if this was a repeat of the first time a leak somewhere in the FBI had led Kincaid straight to her?

When she finally made her way out of the lot, she resisted the urge to slam her foot down on the gas pedal—barely—but she didn't breathe a sigh of relief until they'd rounded two corners and she'd checked her rearview mirror more than a dozen times.

At a stop sign, she twisted around and said, "You can get up now, Gracie."

The little girl peered from beneath the blanket, glanced around and sniffed.

"I'm sorry, sweetheart." Where should she start? She should have had plenty of time to talk to Gracie about her past. She'd eventually have to tell her in order to keep her safe and make sure she stayed alert when she went out alone, but she should have had years before that became a concern. How did you explain to a five-year-old that bad men were trying to kill them?

Gracie crawled into her booster seat and sulked.

And Shae took the coward's way out and said nothing. Instead, myriad questions ricocheted around her head. Was she being paranoid? Or had someone actually found her? Certainly, there could be another reason two men in suits were scanning the crowd at a children's pageant, then peering in car windows throughout the parking lot. Just because one of them might have looked familiar didn't necessarily mean they were dangerous. Even if Maria Delarosa *had* been killed. But she couldn't come up with any other explanation, except...

She'd been found, which should have been impossible. But Kincaid's men had done it before, during the trial. She'd been forced to flee the safe house they'd arranged for her when one of the FBI agents charged with protecting her had betrayed them, another had been killed and another, the one who mattered to her more than anyone else, had gone missing.

Gone rogue? Gotten killed? Turned dirty? No one she'd spoken to knew.

But he'd disappeared after a yearlong relationship and one night of passion—a night Shae couldn't bring herself to regret, despite the outcome, because it had given her Gracie, her reason for living. Clearly God had forgiven her that moment of weakness since He'd blessed her with such an amazing daughter. Now, if only He'd protect her.

Shae took the turn into her driveway too fast, hit the button to open the garage door, waited impatiently as the door lumbered open and shot inside the instant it cleared her roof level. She debated leaving the door open so she could escape quickly, then decided to close it. Better if no one saw her packing up the car. She could always back through the garage door if necessary.

"Go straight in the house, dump your bag out on the floor and stuff whatever is most important to you inside, just like we practiced, okay?" Shae swung the car door open then turned to stare at her trembling daughter. "Gracie, listen to me. Everything will be okay. I will explain everything to you, I promise, but for now, you have to trust me and do as I say, exactly as I say, immediately."

"But, Mommy, I—"

"Gracie, please!"

Gracie nodded and opened her door, then grabbed the bag from the floor.

Shae walked beside her into the house and paused to listen in the doorway. Silence. "Go, now."

She lifted the phone on her way through the kitchen and followed Gracie to her room. Everything seemed to be in order. Even though she knew she wasn't handling the situation well, she couldn't seem to get her emotions under control. For years she'd kept to herself and worked as an IT tech from home, but then Gracie had started school and wanted to play sports, make friends, sing in the church choir. Shae should have known better. And now her daughter was in danger because Shae hadn't kept a low enough profile.

She dialed the number, listened to it ring…and ring. That wasn't right. Someone was supposed to be available at all times in case of an emergency, in case she was discovered. She disconnected and tried again. Nothing. Her breath came in shallow gasps. It would be okay. She'd contemplated not calling anyway, so maybe it was for the best no one answered. Maybe God was leading her elsewhere.

She hurried to Gracie's bedroom to check on her, and her heart shattered when her daughter picked up the stuffed bunny she'd stopped sleeping with a year ago and hugged it close as she filled her bag with her most prized possessions.

Shae left her to it and went to her own room. She grabbed the two flight bags, dug through one for the handgun, took the bullets from the locked safe in her closet and loaded the weapon. Then she stuck it into the waistband of her shorts and shrugged a sweatshirt over it before dropping the bags beside the door to the garage. All of her important documents were already stashed in waterproof cases inside the waterproof bag, as well as a good amount of cash she'd saved over the years. "Gracie, let's go."

Gracie emerged from the hallway, her bag and Mr. Cuddles clutched against her chest.

"Oh, baby, I—"

A car door slammed right outside the house, cutting her off.

"Get down. Hide. Now! And remember cheesemonkey. Every single thing we practiced."

Gracie scrambled beneath the Christmas tree in the corner, trampling packages, then peered between the branches.

Shae grabbed a pen and paper from her desk, scribbled the phone number down, and shoved the paper into Gracie's hand. With no time for more than a quick reassurance, Shae backed toward the door. "If anything happens to me, you run to Katie's house. Do you understand me?"

The doorbell rang.

Gracie's gaze shot to the door and she nodded, teeth chattering, eyes wide.

"When you get there…" Three houses down with two possible killers on her heels. And now she was bringing this mess onto someone else, someone who had only ever been kind to them, who'd become a friend. "You hide until Miss Reva gets home, then tell her to call that number and tell whoever answers what happened. She should tell them who you are and that you need help. Okay?"

"Uh…huh…"

An insistent pounding rattled the front door. "Avery!"

Shae's blood ran to ice as she stared deeply into her daughter's brilliant blue eyes, then yanked the handgun from her waistband. No one should know that name. She'd shed it six years ago when she'd become Shae Evans. "Get down!"

Despite her shocked expression when she caught sight of the weapon, Gracie crouched lower.

Hand shaking wildly, Shae aimed the gun at the door just as it splintered beneath a forceful kick.

Mason Payne kicked Avery Bennett's front door again. No. Wait. No longer Avery—she was Shae now, Shae Evans. He had to remember that.

He pressed his ear against the door and listened for any sound, praying he'd made it in time to save her. Her handler had been killed close by in what was no accident, considering her brake line had been cut. He could only conclude she'd been trying to reach Shae and that her cover had been blown.

Either way, whether Shae forgave him for walking away from her six years ago or not, he was going to have to convince her to let him get her to a safe house. If she was half as stubborn as he remembered, he had a battle ahead of him. That was okay, though. He'd fight whatever battle it took to see her safe, and then he'd leave her in peace and continue his mission.

The door splintered beneath his next kick. He reached through the hole he'd made, unlocked the dead bolt and shoved the door open, weapon drawn.

And there she stood, like a warrior, every bit as beautiful and courageous as he remembered her. Long, dark hair hung in waves, framing a determined expression. Eyes the color of cocoa and wide with fear stared back at him, hands shaking as she aimed a handgun directly at his head. She took his breath away.

He stood perfectly still, removed his finger from the trigger of his own weapon and slowly lifted his hands as the six years since he'd last seen her melted away as if no time had passed. He shouldn't have left, should have at least tried to explain the guilt that had tortured him over his partner's death, the pain he'd felt that one of his own associates could have betrayed them...betrayed Shae. He should have been honest that Zac Jameson had come to him with information that Shae was still in danger, should have told her he was going to try to infiltrate the Kincaid organization in an effort to keep her safe.

But instead, Mason had gone undercover with Jameson Investigations, obsessed with getting to the truth, no matter the cost. And later, when he realized he probably wasn't going to find the answers he sought, he'd maintained his undercover identity to at least help those he could.

"Av— Uh… I mean, Shae." Nothing could have prepared him for the tidal wave of emotion the sight of her would evoke. He'd thought he'd mastered his feelings, had turned them off somewhere along the line in an effort to immerse himself in his undercover persona, but now the weight of them threatened to crush him. He inhaled and ruthlessly shoved everything aside—he had to if he was going to save her. He took a step toward her, needing to gain her trust again somehow, and quickly. No easy task, if the suspicion marring her expression was any indication. "Please, there's no time to explain. I need you to lower the weapon and come with me."

"M-Mason?" Her voice shook, the question more of a *what are you doing here* than a lack of recognition, though he'd certainly changed in the years since she'd last seen him.

Instead of the short, regulation haircut she'd remember, he now boasted a tail, tied at his nape and hanging between his shoulder blades. And where he'd always been clean-shaven, his undercover persona carefully maintained a five o'clock shadow. There had been no time to change his appearance once he'd found out she was in danger. Besides, he was going to have to go back under once he saw her to safety. "Yeah."

"What are you doing here? What happened to you? Wh-where have you been?"

"I'll explain everything, I promise, but there's no time right now. We have to get out of here." He took another step toward her, then froze when she gripped the weapon tighter and took a step back. "Shae, please."

Her gaze shifted past him, and he whirled to check for threats. And stopped short when he spotted a little girl peering back at him from behind a Christmas tree trimmed with colorful homemade ornaments. She couldn't be more than four or five…

Agony plowed into his chest. He tried to suck in a breath but couldn't. Mason had thought he couldn't feel any more than when he'd lain eyes on Shae again, but the sight of the child sent waves of pain crashing through him, along with a myriad of other emotions he couldn't even begin to comprehend, never mind name. Because that child was the spitting image of her mother, except for one telling feature—his own electric-blue eyes staring back at him.

She had to be his daughter. But she couldn't be. How could he not have known about her?

"Shae, I…" What could he say? He'd abandoned her while she'd carried his child. What kind of man would do that? But he hadn't known. He'd taken off right after the night they'd spent together, a reckless moment of celebrating life after everything had gone so horribly out of control. If he had known about the child, would he have left?

"Mason…" Tears tracked down Shae's cheeks.

Tires squealed, entirely too close, and dragged him back to reality. He peered out the door as a silver sedan rounded the corner and barreled toward them. "All right… It's all right. We have to go. Now!"

Shae was already moving. She grabbed two bags from beside the door. "Gracie, grab your bag. Hurry. Cheesemonkey."

A nickname? No, a code word. Shae was savvy as ever. The little girl sobbed softly as she hugged a bag and what looked like a stuffed rabbit against her. Recognition almost drove him to his knees. He remembered the rabbit with the big floppy ears, had picked it up in the hospital gift shop and given it to Shae the night before he'd left her, the night he'd been betrayed, the night his partner had been killed. Had he known even then that he was going to leave? Had he planned all along to go undercover in search of answers?

Shae hustled Gracie past him.

He had to get himself together. "Wait!"

She stopped dead in her tracks and stepped in front of her daughter. His daughter?

The sedan skidded to a stop in front of the house. It was

too late to make it to his vehicle parked out front. "Where's your car?"

"In the garage."

"Go." He gestured with his gun, away from the front door, then followed as she ran through the kitchen and into the garage.

She flung the car's back door open and threw her bags on the floor as Gracie climbed in, then strapped her into the booster seat and slammed the door shut behind her daughter, hopped into the passenger seat and buckled her seat belt.

Mason slid behind the wheel. "Do you have a remote in the car?"

She flipped the driver's side visor down to show him.

He shifted into Reverse and hit the button. "Get down."

Gracie hunched as low as she could in the seat, and Shae slid down in the passenger seat and peered out the side window.

He slammed on the gas the instant the garage door rose high enough to clear the car's roof.

"They're coming." Shae braced herself against the dashboard. "They have guns."

The car rocked as he barely slowed to shift into Drive, then punched it. The tires spun, then gripped and shot the car forward. "Hold on."

He'd have only seconds to lose their attackers. If they reached the vehicle before he could get out of sight, they'd be harder to shake. He didn't recognize the two men, but that didn't mean anything. Mason had infiltrated the Kincaid organization six years ago, after its leader, Quentin Kincaid, had gone to prison—thanks to Shae's testimony. She'd been Kincaid's personal assistant, at least for the legal front of his business, and when she'd realized what other business he was in, she'd used her access to uncover a treasure trove of information the feds used to bury him.

But even from prison, he was in charge, using his fairly incompetent son, Sebastian, as a puppet to continue running the family business. While Mason had managed to have many of their lower-level thugs arrested and convicted, he'd never been able to make it to the top. If these were upper-level hit men, he wouldn't know them, and Shae was in even more trouble than he'd thought. On a brighter note, if he didn't know them, they wouldn't know him, either, and his cover wouldn't be compromised.

He skidded around a corner, fishtailed and regained control.

"They're following." Shae swiped at the tears on her cheeks.

A quick glance in the rearview mirror told him they weren't going to make it out of there without a chase. So be it. He pressed down on the gas pedal, increasing his already reckless speed through the residential neighborhood's narrow streets, and took another corner practically on two wheels.

The vehicle behind them sped up and closed in.

Mason hit the brakes.

Gracie squealed.

"Hold on to something!" He hit the gas again, lurching forward as the car in pursuit slowed.

Shae shifted up higher in her seat, grabbed the handle above the door, and looked over her shoulder. "Gracie, hold on tight, baby."

"Mommy?"

"It's okay, honey. I'll explain everything once we get somewhere safe." She looked at Mason, chewed on her lower lip for a moment, then seemed to make up her mind. "This is Mason, and he'll keep us safe. If anything happens to me, you listen to him. Understand?"

"Uh…huh." The little girl started to cry, and the soft sobs tore at Mason's heart.

He wanted desperately to pull over, to reassure her he'd keep her safe, to meet the daughter he'd never known existed until moments ago. *Daughter.* The word sounded so foreign in his mind. And yet, he'd apparently been a father for years. He just couldn't wrap his head around it. Instead, he kept one eye firmly riveted to the road in front of them and the other on the rearview mirror.

Shae reached back between the seats for her daughter.

Mason refrained from admonishing her, from telling her if he had to stop short, her arm would probably snap. The child clearly needed comfort, so he'd just have to be careful not to stop short. Fat chance, with their pursuers hugging his bumper.

"Watch out for the—"

He hit a speed table full on, jolting the car so hard his teeth snapped closed on his tongue. The coppery taste of blood filled his mouth. He'd forgotten about them, and in the darkness, with the reflections of Christmas lights dotting the neighborhood, he hadn't seen it. "How many more?"

"Uh…" Shae closed her eyes and mumbled something that sounded like counting under her breath. "There's a total of four along the main road out of the development, so three more."

"Hold on." He clamped his teeth together to keep from biting his tongue again but didn't slow when he came to the next one. Instead, at the last minute, he skirted around it on someone's lawn, barely missing a blow-up reindeer and losing precious seconds. Did it matter, though? He wasn't going to lose their pursuers inside the development, nor was he going to stop and give them the opportunity to attack. Considering the situation, they were pretty much at a stalemate. Cars parked along the narrow streets and the occasional car driving in the opposite direction kept them from flanking him, so he slowed for the next two speed tables.

The driver behind him did the same.

Mason barely eased off the gas as he hooked a right turn out of the development, not because he had any clue where he was going but to keep from having to wait for traffic. He accelerated, passed two cars on the left and barely missed clipping the bumper of the car in front as he nipped back into the lane just in time to avoid a head-on collision.

Hindered by oncoming traffic, his pursuers bounced along

the shoulder as they passed the same two cars on the right then tried to inch alongside him.

He swerved, tapping their car and forcing them to back off or tumble into the swampy ditch bordering the road. "They're not going to stop chasing us, and they have no regard for civilian casualties. Is there a more isolated road around here? Somewhere with less traffic and less chance for collateral damage?"

Gracie whimpered from the back seat.

Mason pushed the sound out of his mind. He had to if he was going to think clearly. He needed an open stretch to increase his lead, then some way to ditch them.

"Make the next right. If you take that all the way to the end, it turns into a dirt road."

A dirt road was risky—too dry and he'd be more likely to lose control and spin out, too wet and he could easily get stuck in the muck. "What else?"

She looked at him, held his gaze for the instant he could take his eyes off the road and shook her head. "Any other direction and we're headed into either residential developments, some of which only have one way in and out, or commercial areas with traffic lights at every intersection."

Since their pursuers had no problem driving recklessly, he assumed they wouldn't blink twice at walking up to the car at a stoplight and shooting all three of them. That was Kincaid's style. And if they worked for Sebastian Kincaid, as he suspected, they'd never risk his wrath by returning empty-handed after a hit had been ordered. Quentin was ruthless, but his son was another matter entirely. In addition to being incompetent, the man was mercilessly cruel, seemed to enjoy hurting others in the most brutal manner he could devise. Sebastian was a weapon Quentin Kincaid aimed at anyone who crossed him. It was one of the reasons Mason had never made lieutenant— while he'd been willing to do enough to maintain his cover, he couldn't condone what would be required to move up in the organization. The dirt road began to look more appealing.

He hit the brakes, spun the wheel to the right and took the turn. He fumbled his cell phone out of his pocket and glanced at it long enough to dial the most recent number.

Zac Jameson picked up halfway through the first ring. "Did you get to her?"

"I have her, but we're in trouble."

"Where?"

With a dead calm he didn't feel, despite years of practice, Mason relayed their position and the direction they were headed.

"Sending backup." And with that, Zac disconnected.

"Who was that?" Shae stared at him, her eyes filled with a distrust that served as a reminder of how horribly he'd failed her, failed their child.

But what could he have been to either of them? A man so engrossed in his own vendetta he'd had nothing left to give? They'd probably been better off without him. Until they'd been found, of course.

"Zac Jameson. I've worked with him for years, and he's a friend."

"I hope he's a better friend than the last one you trusted."

The words struck their target like an arrow straight through his heart. "I'm sorry, Shae. I don't know what else to say, except to promise I'll keep you safe. Both of you. I'll tell you everything, but I need you to trust me right now so we can get out of this mess."

She checked the side-view mirror, glanced at Gracie trembling in her booster seat, then dropped her head back and sighed. "I'm sorry, Mason. That was uncalled-for."

"But true enough, so don't worry about it." He hit the dirt road, only sliding a little, then increased his speed.

Shae closed her eyes and surprised him by mumbling a prayer. He hadn't remembered her sharing his own faith, so strong back then, before betrayal and death had hardened him, waning the longer he'd been undercover without finding answers. Perhaps it was time to turn back to it.

Metal crunched against metal as their pursuers slammed their back end, shoving them forward.

Mason increased his speed. Marshy land and murky water bordered them on both sides, cypress trees dotted the water's edge and underbrush grew thicker as they moved deeper into the swamp. Black clouds gathered, darkening the already pitch-black night as the storms Zac had warned him of moved closer. They had some time left, but not much.

Shae braced her hands against the dashboard. "You have to slow for the bridge."

"Where?"

"About a mile from here. An old wooden bridge."

"Is there any other way around?"

"No."

Kicking himself would do no good. He'd barely had time to reach Shae after he'd found out she was in trouble, hadn't been able to scope the area in search of an escape route. Now, he'd just have to make the best of the situation and hope Zac got help to them in time.

He rounded a curve, and the bridge, if you could call it that, loomed ahead of him. The wooden structure had seen better days. The railings had long ago begun to rot, probably along with most of the other boards. Shae was right; he would have to slow down.

He checked the rearview mirror. Their pursuers still clung like glue, but they'd eased off a little, no doubt assuming he'd made a mistake heading into the swamp and they'd have time to come alongside them if and when the narrow road widened.

The joints creaked and moaned as he hit the bridge too fast, bounced, then slammed on his brakes when another vehicle skidded to a stop, blocking the far end of the bridge. Hope tried to flare, but he tamped it down quickly enough. If Zac's help had reached them, they'd have waited until after Mason crossed before blocking the bridge.

They were trapped.

He slammed the shifter into Reverse, twisted around to see behind him and hit the gas.

The other driver accelerated in a game of chicken Mason had no hope of winning.

Mason tried to maneuver around him on the narrow structure, might even have made it if their pursuer hadn't yanked the wheel at the last minute and hit them from the side.

Mason's head cracked hard against the driver's side window as they spun. Darkness encroached in his peripheral vision. The car hit the railing. With one loud groan, the rail gave way and they were airborne, plunging toward the black water below.

Chapter Two

The airbag exploded in Shae's face, and she struggled to free herself, check on Gracie and get to her weapon all at once. Their attackers would stand above them on the bridge, making it easy to pick them off as they emerged from the vehicle. "Gracie?"

"M-M-Mommy?" The whisper was soft and shaky, but at least she was alive.

Now, if she could just get her out of there without anyone getting shot. "Are you hurt, honey?"

Gracie's harsh breaths echoed in the car. She sniffed. "My heart hurts, 'cause I'm afraid."

"Okay. It's okay, baby. Listen to me…" A glance at Mason made her blood run cold. His eyes were closed, head lolling at an unnatural angle. The realization that she still felt something for him hit her like a physical blow. But she had no time to reflect on it now. "Can you open your seat belt?"

Even as she asked, she reached for her own and found it stuck. A knife? Did she have one in the car? No. Maybe in one of the flight bags—she couldn't remember. "Mason?"

"Okay, I got it off." Gracie slid forward and caught herself against the two front seats. "Now what?"

Pain pounded in Shae's head, stealing her focus, making it difficult to think straight. Her ears rang viciously, drowning out any possible sounds of pursuit. She couldn't think… needed to. If they didn't get out of there, they were as good as dead. Mason…she had to wake him, shouldn't move him. But what else could she do? She couldn't leave him there. If she could even free herself from the harness. "Gracie, in the front compartment of one of my bags, there should be a knife. It's folded up. Find it, but do not open it."

She closed her eyes and held her breath for a moment, listened past Gracie's soft whimpers and rummaging, and heard Mason's ragged breathing. A wave of dizziness overtook her, and her stomach heaved. She choked down the bile surging up her throat. "Mason, you've got to wake up. We have to get out of here."

"Here, Mommy." Gracie handed her the knife, and she opened it and cut her own seat belt free.

The pressure of the lake water against the doors would probably keep them from opening. With that in mind, she opened her window. "Gracie, we have to get out my side of the car before the windows are below the waterline. Can you slide over and open your window?"

"Oh-kay."

Shae hit the mechanism on Mason's belt, and the clasp slid free. As soon as Gracie's window opened fully, she reached across Mason and shut off the headlights and the ignition. No sense announcing their location to any sniper who might be lying in wait on the bridge.

"Are we getting out into the water?" Gracie's voice was barely more than a whisper.

"Yes."

"But it's dark out. What if there are snakes? Or gators? Or…" She sucked in frantic breaths and started to hyperventilate.

"Gracie, stop! You have to calm down." Shae held Mason

tight against the seat to keep him from falling forward and hitting his face against the dashboard, which had pushed into the passenger compartment on impact. Gracie needed something to concentrate on other than the danger they faced from the swamp and the gunmen who were likely waiting on the bridge for them. Their best hope would be to get out quietly and pray their attackers couldn't see them in the dark. "I need your help."

"Uh…huh…okay." Tremors shook her voice, and she continued to cry, but she seemed to have regained some semblance of control. "What do I have to do?"

"Help me hold Mason against the seat so I can see how badly he's hurt."

The request brought a fresh wave of tears. "Is…is…he gonna die?"

"No," Shae said firmly. She wouldn't accept that, couldn't face the fact that, in another moment, she'd have to leave him there at the mercy of the gunmen. She turned, and water sloshed around her feet. They were sinking. She staved off the panic. One problem at a time. "Mason, wake up. Now! We can't stay here. We need to move."

Next to Gracie's whimpers, his soft groan was the sweetest sound she'd ever heard.

Oh, God, please help us. Help me get Gracie and Mason out of here, and help me get them to safety. Please, please, please… She repeated the plea over and over in her head. "Mason."

He lifted his head, eyes rolling once as he struggled to focus on her.

"Mason, please, wake up. They're going to find us. We have to get out of here."

Blood flowed down the side of his face.

"Gracie, give me a shirt or something out of one of the bags."

She yanked out a tank top and handed it to Shae.

Leaving it folded, Shae pressed it against Mason's wound. "Can you hear me?"

"What?" His head fell back, and he squinted out the front windshield, where nothing but blackness was visible, then lurched upright and braced himself against the steering wheel.

"We went off the bridge into the swamp. The two men who were following us are out there, plus however many more were in the second vehicle blocking the other side of the bridge. We have to move."

Coming halfway to his senses, Mason sat up straighter and patted the holster on his hip. "Where's my gun?"

"I don't know, but I have mine."

"Okay. All right." He squeezed his eyes closed then opened them a moment later. "We have to get the windows open."

"Mine already is."

"I'm mixed up. Where is the bridge?"

"To your left. We need to go out my side."

"Okay. You go first, then I'll get Gracie out to you and follow."

She had little trust that he could manage to get himself out of the car, never mind Gracie, but there was no time to argue or delay. They'd waited too long already.

"Keep your head below the roof line."

"Okay." She tucked the weapon into her waistband, then half climbed, half slid out the window into the chilly water, careful to keep her head low and stay far enough from the car that it didn't pull her under as it slowly sank. Without a sound, she treaded water and held her arms out to Gracie, who wrapped her arms around Shae's neck and wiggled out the back window.

When she hit the water, she hissed through her teeth and squeezed tight enough to cut off Shae's supply of the reeking, thick air. It was almost a relief.

She pressed her mouth against Gracie's ear, struggling to stay afloat with her daughter in her arms. "Hold on to me, but loosen your arms a little."

She nodded, teeth chattering, no doubt more from fear than the water that held only a slight chill, and wrapped her legs around Shae's waist. Her iron grip around Shae's neck eased a little.

Mason emerged and gestured her toward the far side of the lake, into the marshy wetlands.

Gunshots split the night, followed by three muffled plops as the bullets hit the water—far too close for comfort.

Gracie gasped and opened her mouth to scream, but Mason clamped a hand over her face.

Shae turned slowly and aimed her weapon toward the men illuminated in the headlights of their vehicles atop the bridge.

Mason laid a hand over the weapon, pushing it down, and shook his head. He placed his finger against his lips to shush both Shae and Gracie and slid lower into the water.

Shae followed.

Gracie clung tighter as Shae resisted the urge to rush. The more they stirred the water, the easier they'd be to locate. Full darkness had already fallen over the swamp, not even lit by the moon or stars as thick cloud cover from the coming storms blocked their light.

A few more shots rang out but found targets closer to the bridge. Their attackers must be assuming they would try for the closest shore, but instead, they swam toward the far shore, deeper into the swamp.

She had to assume the men would figure it out and follow them. Or call in whatever expert trackers and equipment they'd need to locate Shae and Gracie in the swamp. The Kincaid organization had the funds, and they could afford to wait.

Well, that was fine. It would give her, Gracie and Mason a chance to get away.

After what felt like hours but probably wasn't more than twenty minutes, she rolled onto her back, floating for a moment with her daughter lying on top of her. Between the airbag hitting her full force and having to swim while holding Gracie, Shae's chest screamed in protest.

Mason paused, treading water and resting a reassuring hand on her shoulder. Then they pressed on. She breathed a sigh of relief when her feet hit the gross bottom and she gained her footing as it began to slope upward.

Clutching Gracie tightly, Shae staggered onto the shore. She kept low, hoping their pursuers wouldn't be able to see where they'd left the lake and entered the forest.

Mason crouched down, looking toward the bridge, then urged her forward into the thick vegetation.

Everything in Shae begged her to stay where it was relatively clear, where they could see any threats nature might throw at them as their eyes adjusted to the darkness. But she did as he indicated and crept into the dense foliage with Gracie clinging tight. Who knew? Maybe they were better off not knowing what was out there. Although Shae liked living in Florida, enjoyed the year-round warmth and sunshine after spending her whole life suffering New York's cold, gray winters, she'd never been able to rid herself of the mind-numbing fear of coming face-to-face with some of the region's more deadly creatures.

She stumbled over a thick root and went down hard on one knee, biting back a cry. Then held her breath and listened to see if she'd given their position away.

Gracie snuggled against her, getting as close as possible.

It was only then that Shae realized she was still clutching Mr. Cuddles as tightly as Shae clung to her weapon. Tears threatened.

Mason leaned over them, using his body as a shield. "Are you hurt?"

Swallowing the lump in her throat, Shae shook her head.

"We have to keep moving." He glanced over his shoulder. "We've got a head start, but as soon as they get someone with an airboat and spotlights in here, we're done."

Shae nodded and struggled to her feet.

Mason slid an arm around her and helped her up as she set Gracie down beside her. He moved so the little girl was positioned between them, then pointed in the direction he wanted her to go. As they walked, Gracie hugged her bunny and clung tightly to Shae's hand, careful to stay between Shae and Mason.

What must Mason be thinking? There was no doubt in her mind he'd realized Gracie was his daughter. She'd seen that punch of recognition, followed by the instant of shock. And then he'd shut everything down, his expression going hard, his eyes unreadable. Did he blame Shae for not letting him know about her? But how could she have? She'd had no idea where to find him. Besides, Maria Delarosa had known about Gracie, and surely they'd had some contact. How else would he have known where to find her? But he'd seemed so surprised. No, he hadn't known. Of that she was certain.

So, what was going through his mind?

"Freeze!" Mason hissed, dragging her from distractions better left for a more appropriate time— or, even better, never.

Shae stopped and listened intently for whatever had put him on alert.

"Don't move." Even as he said it, he inched in front of them.

Movement caught Shae's attention, shadows flickering in the dark all around their feet, substantial, disturbed by the intrusion through their world. "What are they—"

But before she even finished the question, she realized what they were...baby alligators. Tons of them, wriggling and squirming in their muddy nest. She fought desperately against the fear threatening to paralyze her.

Standing in front of Gracie and Shae, Mason started to guide them slowly backward, retracing their steps away from the gator nest.

A low growl came from somewhere in the dark.

Shae fought the urge to lift her child into her arms, to turn and run full speed in the opposite direction, to flee back toward their pursuers who, at the moment, seemed like the less dangerous threat.

Mason extended his arms, sidestepping farther in front of Shae and Gracie, once again shielding them, placing himself between them and danger. At least she had no doubt that no matter what he thought of the fact he had a child, he would give his life to see her safe.

Another bellow sounded as something huge crashed through the brush.

There was no time to run, no time to think, only a split second to react. Keeping the eight-foot gator sprinting toward him in his peripheral vision, Mason spun around, lifted Gracie and flung her aside, and hissed, "Go, run."

Shae backed up, slid on the mud and went down hard on her bottom.

The alligator, either sensing the easier prey or seeing Shae as more of a threat to its offspring, shifted its attention from Mason and set its sights on her. When it charged, Mason kicked it hard in the side, and it whirled on him. He jumped back toward the lake to draw the gator away and give Shae and Gracie time to run deeper into the forest. The jaws clamped shut inches from his leg, then it swung back and caught him in the shin with its massive head. He went down, rolled and surged to his feet in hip-deep water.

He'd spent enough time numbing his mind in front of the Nature Channel to know he didn't want to fight a gator in the water, where it would have the advantage. Seemed ironic—all those nights spent wallowing in guilt might now save him. He surged toward land, desperate to get there before the animal attacked. The gator charged again, and he dived over it, landed hard on his hip and shoulder, then rolled back toward the not-so-dry land and scrambled to his feet. He slid as he struggled to gain purchase in the muck.

Where were Shae and Gracie? He'd lost track of them but didn't dare take his gaze off the predator hoping to make a midnight snack of him. Returning to land had brought him closer to the nest, further agitating the creature. The blood pouring down the side of his face from where his head had hit the window probably wasn't helping matters.

The gator barreled toward him again, hissing wildly. For such a large, heavy reptile, it moved incredibly fast. But only in short bursts, if he remembered correctly.

He knew he should run, not in a zigzag pattern but a full-out sprint in a straight line, hoping the gator would tire before it could catch him. But he couldn't do that, not without knowing where Shae and Gracie had gone. He didn't dare call out. The gator wasn't the only thing stalking them in the night— might not even be the most dangerous. If they could just get away from the nest, it would probably leave them be.

He caught movement in his peripheral vision. Shae appeared in the small clearing with a long branch. She prodded the creature, dragging its attention from Mason.

The instant it turned toward Shae, Mason dived onto its back, squeezed tightly with his legs and covered its eyes with his hand, forcing its head down. Then he freed one hand and clamped it over the gator's mouth, holding it closed. While alligators could snap their mouths closed with incredible force, they couldn't open them with equal strength. That much he remembered from wildlife documentaries he'd seen, while he'd silently marveled, from the safety of his couch, why anyone would willingly wrestle such a large and dangerous creature.

The gator tried to roll, a death roll if Mason couldn't hold on, if the creature got hold of him, if it got him into the water.

Mason extended one leg, dug deep into the silt. No way could he let it turn over or he'd lose his precarious hold. When it stilled, he chanced a quick glance at Shae, still holding the stick and watching warily. He didn't dare risk more than the slightest whisper. "Where's Gracie?"

"Over there." She gestured behind her toward the deeper forest.

"Safe?"

"Yes."

The gator bucked and squirmed.

"Okay, back off. I'm going to try to get off her and get out of here."

She nodded, backed up and hefted the stick higher, as if ready to strike.

He waited again for the gator to still, then shoved off, jumping backward to his feet, and braced for attack. When it remained motionless, attention still focused on Shae, he skirted around it, waded slowly into the shallow water to keep from moving closer to the nest and turned to face it as he backed toward Shae.

"Go," he whispered to her.

The alligator watched him a few moments more, then turned and lumbered back toward her nest. Mason finally exhaled the breath he'd been holding. As he followed Shae deeper into the woods, muscles he didn't know he had screamed in protest. He used the back of his wrist to wipe the blood away from his eye. Throbbing pain in his shin, where the gator's head had connected, forced him to limp, slowing his progress.

When he caught up to her, he asked, "Are you hurt?"

"I'm okay."

"Shae." He reached for her, gripped her arm and turned her to face him, running his gaze over every inch of her. "Are you hurt?"

She shook her head. "A few bumps and bruises. Nothing serious."

"Okay. What about Gracie?" He released her and resumed walking next to her.

"She twisted her ankle. I'm not sure she can walk."

He picked up his pace, the sudden need to reach the child who was hiding alone in the swamp, no doubt terrified, too overwhelming to ignore. "Do you still have your gun?"

"Yeah."

And yet she'd come to his aid carrying a large stick instead of the deadly weapon. "Why didn't you shoot the gator?"

Her gaze flicked to him, and she frowned.

"I'm not criticizing, just curious."

She studied him another moment then shrugged. "I couldn't get a shot with you in the way."

Yet there'd been times he'd backed off. "And?"

"And I didn't want to risk those men hearing the gunshots and finding us." She averted her gaze.

"Good thinking." He would have had the same thoughts under the circumstances. But there was something more, something unspoken she obviously didn't feel comfortable sharing with him. Maybe this could be his first push toward gaining her trust, because they weren't going to survive this night if he couldn't. "What else?"

She sighed, and her shoulders slumped a bit. "I wouldn't have let it kill you, or hurt you, but you seemed to be holding your own, so..."

He waited her out, but as he thought of Gracie hiding in the woods, alone with no one to protect her, he figured he already knew.

"It was the babies. I couldn't take their mother, couldn't stand the thought of leaving them alone out here when she'd done nothing but come to their defense." She swiped her palms over her cheeks. "I'll do whatever it takes to protect my daughter, to protect you, even to survive, but I won't ever take an innocent life."

My daughter. It was the perfect opening, the perfect opportunity to ask, "Don't you mean *our* daughter," to confirm what he suspected—what he knew. Instead, he remained silent. *Coward.*

They reached Gracie, curled in a small ball beneath a rotting tree that had long ago fallen. She was hugging the stuffed rabbit.

Shae pulled the little girl into her arms. "It's okay, honey. I'm here now."

Gracie wrapped her arms and legs around her mother and clung so tight Mason feared she'd never let go. Then she buried her face into Shae's shoulder and cried.

Shae cradled and rocked her and whispered softly in her ear.

As much as he hated to intrude on the moment, they had to move. The noise they'd made fighting the gator could well have drawn the attention of their pursuers. He listened but didn't hear anything to indicate they were being followed. Still, he didn't dare waste what precious lead time they had. "We have to go."

Shae glared at him over Gracie's shoulder and rubbed circles on the girl's back.

"I'm sorry, Shae, but there's no choice. We've got to keep moving."

She held his gaze a moment longer, then sighed. "All right. I know. Gracie, honey, can you walk?"

She sniffed, wiped her face with the back of her hand and nodded.

When Shae lowered her to her feet, she took one step and cried out, then slapped a hand over her mouth. "I'm sorry."

"It's okay, honey. Shh…" Shae soothed as she lifted Gracie back into her arms. She looked at Mason. "I don't think it's broken but probably badly sprained."

He approached Gracie, not knowing what to say to her. He didn't have much—or any—experience with kids. Did she know he was her father? Had she recognized him the same way he'd recognized her? What had Shae told her about him? What could this child think of the man who'd abandoned her? "Gracie, is it all right if I take a look at your ankle?"

Keeping her head against Shae's shoulder, she turned to face him and nodded.

He couldn't see well enough in the darkness to tell if it was bruised, but there was definitely swelling. She couldn't walk, so she was going to have to be carried. No matter how petite Gracie was, no way could Shae carry her all the way through the swamp, especially at night under thick cloud cover.

Thunder rumbled, deep and loud.

"Have you ever had a piggyback ride, Gracie?" He should know that, shouldn't he? Should have been there for that.

She nodded, teeth chattering.

Before he could check the instinct, he reached out to her—couldn't help himself—and tucked her long, dark hair, now matted with dirt and muck, behind her ears. "If Mom helps you onto my back, I can carry you for a bit."

She looked at her mother. A flash of lightning illuminated the terror reflected in her eyes.

Shae wiped tears from her daughter's face. "It's okay. We have to move. You understand that, honey."

She nodded, sucked in a breath and straightened.

Mason turned so Shae could help her onto his back. She was wet and cold, and he shifted her more snugly against him.

When Gracie wrapped her thin arms tightly around his neck, a kind of fear he'd never felt before rushed through him. This child, so small, so delicate, so fragile, was his responsibility, his to protect. He hooked his arms beneath her legs and boosted her higher, then started forward. He'd faced the irate alligator with less apprehension than he did his own daughter.

Then another thought struck. What if Shae wouldn't allow him to be a part of Gracie's life? Was that even what he wanted? The idea that he'd even consider it startled him. He'd never thought about being a dad. Kincaid's trial had lasted more than a year, and while he and Shae had been together through most of that time, had even discussed him leaving the

FBI to go into witness protection with her, they'd never discussed having children.

Then, after he'd had to leave her to go undercover, he hadn't allowed himself to feel anything. He'd given up all of his hopes and dreams, given up everything but the determination to take down Kincaid's organization and save as many people as possible until he could do so.

So, what now? Did he want to take on all the responsibilities of fatherhood? Would Gracie even accept him as her father after five years without him?

And how selfish was he to want to be in her life? He was in deep over his head in a criminal organization, undercover for close to six years. What would happen when Sebastian Kincaid found out the truth? He'd send assassins after him, just as he had Shae. The kindest thing he could do for both Shae and her daughter would be to see them safe and then distance himself. Besides, he had to go back undercover as soon as they were safe, so whatever he might or might not feel or want was irrelevant anyway.

Two fat raindrops dropped onto his face, and then the sky opened up and dumped gallons all at once.

When he glanced at Shae, she looked back at him, and a smiled played at the corners of her mouth. She shook her head and laughed quietly, a sound he hadn't heard in so long. Then she sighed and lifted her face to the rain.

It struck him, in that moment, how beautiful she was, both inside and out. He'd admired that about her, the way she could find happiness in the simplest moments, be grateful for even the smallest blessings. That ability to recognize and revel in the joys life brought was a skill that had always eluded him. He could also admit he admired her courage in the face of danger, the way she could find, if not humor, then irony in any situation. That was one of the things he loved most about—

Yikes! Whoa. Hit the brakes, buddy. Everything in him went still. Love? The feeling had crept up on him, surprised him. He might once have loved Avery Bennett, but that was a long time ago, and a lot had happened since that time. Too much. He was no longer the man he'd been six years ago, could no longer feel love…or pain. He'd completely detached himself from everything he'd ever known. And Avery no longer existed. He'd lost her on that long-ago night, along with his partner and whichever friend had betrayed him and stolen his ability to trust. Shae Evans was a stranger to him, just as he must be to her.

He shook off whatever emotions had begun to creep up and blindside him, probably due to the head injury he'd sustained and the waning adrenaline rush from fighting the gator. Everyone would be better off if he could keep his head in the game, because more than one gator lurked in the swamp. Aside from the human killers on their tails, the night was filled with gators, water moccasins and other venomous snakes, bears, wild boars, and panthers—all no doubt scenting the blood flowing from his head wound. And then there was the quicksand. Even if their attackers never found them, there was a better-than-good chance they'd never make it out of the swamp alive.

Chapter Three

When the rain eased up, Shae stopped walking, bent and propped her hands on her knees. She just needed a moment to catch her breath. Once she had, she straightened, then simply stood, staring at the ground.

Mason stopped beside her and waited, diligently scanning the woods in every direction.

The slow swim from the half-submerged car had soaked them, and the rain had made things worse. Shae's clothing felt heavy, like it was dragging her down. Mud, along with a bunch of other muck she didn't dare think about, caked her sneakers and legs. Her muscles screamed in pain, her chest ached from the crash, begging her to slow down, and exhaustion beat at her. And the rain would start up again soon enough as the next storm sought them out.

Mason didn't appear to be in much better shape. Though he carried Gracie on his back without complaint, his limp had increased over the past few minutes, and his pace had slowed considerably.

Plus, they had absolutely no idea where they were headed. The thick clouds blocked the moon and stars, and no lights were visible in any direction to indicate a sign of civilization.

She rested a hand on Gracie's back, feeling each tremor that shook her little girl's delicate frame, and turned to Mason. "We have to stop."

He glanced in the direction they'd come from and tilted his head, as if listening.

"I haven't heard anyone following us." And she'd been tracking the sounds around them for the past few minutes. "We can't keep going, Mason. We all need to rest. Besides, we have no clue where we're headed. For all we know, we could have circled around and be walking straight into a trap. Or we might walk so far into the swamp we can't find our way back out. With all this rain, and more on the way, it's going to start flooding."

He nodded. "I've been thinking the same, but we need higher ground and some kind of shelter, and we can't stray too far from the lake. It's the main landmark we can use as a reference."

He didn't have to tell her that. The stretch of land they'd been walking on had turned spongier, sucking at her shoes each time she took a step.

He hefted Gracie up higher, and she lifted her head. "Can we go home now? Please?"

Shae's heart ached for her, and she reached out to cup Gracie's cheek. She was so frightened. The only life she'd ever known had been filled with joy and love and fun. She wasn't equipped to handle this kind of trauma—though she'd held up well enough so far. Maybe she was stronger than Shae realized. She hoped so, considering they had a long journey ahead of them, both out of the swamp and to a whole new life. She didn't relish having to tell Gracie they could never return to the life she'd known, that even if they could escape their stalkers, they'd have to start over somewhere new, with new identities, new names. She could only deal with one crisis at a time. "It's okay, honey. For now, though, we're going to have an adventure. Okay?"

"I don't like having an adventure." Pouting, she lowered her head against Mason.

"I know, baby. I know." She rubbed her daughter's back, trying her best to soothe her. Tears threatened, but she fought them. The last thing Gracie needed was her mother falling apart. But Shae needed quiet, needed peace and time to reflect and pray, to decide what to do and where to go from there—assuming they made it through the night.

She slid her hand to the back of Gracie's head, pressing her forehead against her daughter's. "We have no choice, Gracie. Having a camp-out will be safer than walking in the dark when we don't know where we're going."

Gracie remained quiet for a moment, seeming to think the situation over. Then she nodded against Shae's head before straightening and gripping even tighter against Mason's back.

Mason frowned and looked around, then gave Gracie a bounce. "Hey, kiddo, can you pop down and stand right here and keep an eye on your mom for a few minutes while I see if I can find us a good campsite?"

Without saying anything, the little girl slid from his back and leaned against Shae's side.

Shae wrapped an arm around her shoulders and pulled her close. She was worried about her. It wasn't like Gracie to be so quiet, even if she was hurt. Gracie was an outgoing, athletic child who liked to play all kinds of games and sports, and when you played hard and with the passion for fun Gracie had, injuries came with the territory.

Mason squatted in front of her and gripped her hands. "Why don't you just think of this as a challenge, like in a book or a movie?"

Gracie shrugged, keeping her head down.

When Mason stood, he rubbed her head and squeezed Shae's arm. "I'll be back in a few minutes. If there's any problem, you have the gun. Don't hesitate to use it."

She nodded, grateful for everything he'd done for them as she watched him melt into the shadows. No matter what was going on and how she felt about him disappearing six years ago, he'd come back now, when they needed him the most, and he…

Wait… Why had he come back? How could he have known they were in danger? Shown up at the exact same moment as their attackers? Was it possible he'd kept tabs on her—on them—all along? Could he have known about his child all this time and said nothing?

No. No way. She'd seen the shock in his eyes when he'd spotted Gracie peeking out from behind the Christmas tree.

Christmas. It had to be past midnight at this point, which meant it was the twenty-fourth. Tonight would be Christmas Eve, the holiest night of the year. She thought of the presents she'd gotten Gracie, wrapped and tucked away in Shae's closet, to be put out after they'd gone to mass and Gracie had settled in bed. Gracie would be disappointed when she awoke on Christmas morning. Instead of running to the tree filled with joy and anticipation, she'd… She'd what? Would they even make it out of the swamp by then? Shae closed her eyes and prayed for a Christmas miracle, prayed they'd all make it out of this swamp alive, prayed for the strength to do whatever was necessary to survive, because she didn't think she had it in her to last another twenty-four hours slogging through the marshes, scanning every direction, wondering where the next threat would come from.

And what about Mason? Clearly, he needed medical attention. He was injured, had to be physically and mentally exhausted. And, with that, her thoughts had come full circle. So much for the momentary distraction. Mason. What was going through his head right now? He couldn't have known about Gracie. However he'd found out they were in trouble, she couldn't believe he had anything but their best interest at heart.

But they were going to have to talk about all this. She knew that…and dreaded it. Would he want to be a part of Gracie's life now? As selfish as it might be, she'd had Gracie all to herself for five years. Would she have to share her with him now? What if he was with someone else? Or even married? Would she have to share Gracie with a stepmother and send her off for weekends and holidays with people she barely knew, people who might not watch her as closely as Shae did?

She sucked in a deep, shaky breath and blew it out slowly. Okay, that wasn't fair. Mason had already risked his life numerous times to save both her and Gracie in just a few short hours. She might not know anything about his life over the past six years, but she did know he'd keep her safe.

And this was too much for her to contemplate now. But it was better than thinking about what was really gnawing at her—she would have to tell Gracie the truth, that Mason was her father. Gracie had never asked, so Shae had never brought it up. She figured if Gracie wanted to know, she'd ask, and Shae would have to decide how much or how little to tell her, depending on how old she was at the time. What would she tell her? That she'd been born from a night of passion with a man Shae had thought she'd loved and would spend the rest of her life with? Who'd then taken off and never returned? That she'd been an accident? No, she'd tell her the truth, that she was the most beautiful, incredible blessing God had ever bestowed upon Shae. And that she was loved more than anyone else in the world. If Mason could love her like that as well, then Shae would set aside her own paranoia and be happy Gracie had more people in her life that loved her.

Thankfully, movement in the shrubs to her right ripped her from contemplating the subject any further.

Mason emerged and swiped moss from his hair. "Okay, I found a spot, a downed tree with a thick canopy above it. I cleared space underneath where you should be able to lie low and hide until it starts to get light."

"What do you mean, *you*? Aren't you staying with us?" Shae massaged the bridge of her nose between her thumb and forefinger, easing some of the pressure the storms were causing on her sinuses. At least, she tried to convince herself that was the cause of the pounding headache.

"I have to backtrack, see if I can find where I lost my cell phone. It's in a waterproof case, so if I can find it, it should still work. If I can get ahold of Zac, he'll be able to track the phone and find us."

Shae didn't trust herself to speak; she was afraid she'd start blubbering at the thought of being left alone in the middle of a pitch-black swamp filled with critters, so she simply nodded. He was right. They needed help. "Do you think you can find your way back?"

"Yeah, I was careful to note landmarks." He slid a finger beneath her chin and lifted gently until her gaze met his. "I can find my way to the spot where we emerged from the water and then back to you. I promise. But it will be easier and safer for me to go alone. I won't leave you in the swamp, Shae. That's a promise."

She didn't say anything about the promises he'd made to her in the past, promises he hadn't been able to—or hadn't cared to—keep. Instead, she nodded and stepped back from his touch. "If you can't find your phone and you can make it back to the car and it's not entirely underwater, my phone is in one of the bags on the floor in the back seat."

"Got it." When he grinned, fire ignited in those electric-blue eyes, and six years disappeared.

She turned away. She had to. She'd trusted him once, with every ounce of her being, and he'd failed her, abandoned her.

"It'll be okay, Shae. We'll make it out of this."

"I know." She pulled Gracie closer. "But then what?"

His gaze slid to Gracie, and his smile faltered. "We'll figure it out. Okay?"

She nodded. What more could she do? He didn't know any more than she did about what would come next, except the obvious, that she'd have to go on the run again, might never be able to put enough distance between herself and the Kincaid organization to be safe. Best to just deal with the here and now and worry about the rest when the time came. She was a strong proponent of "put off till tomorrow what you can't fix today." She was also a strong proponent of taking time to pray, not only to ask for what she needed, but to meditate and listen for God's answer and to thank Him for keeping them safe so far. And that was what she'd do as soon as they were at the campsite—seek answers as to what path to follow.

Once she'd settled Gracie onto Mason's back once more, she followed him as he trudged even deeper into the swamp, scanning the ground and the surrounding area the best she could in the darkness, noting where the lake was in comparison to their position. While the sounds of nocturnal creatures would have made her uncomfortable, or more likely terrified her, it was more disconcerting to hear nothing as they hiked. Hopefully the silence meant the critters were holed up waiting out the storm and not that there were predators on the hunt—human or otherwise.

Mason stopped and gestured to a thick tree trunk that had long ago fallen and caught in the vee of the tree beside it.

Thick vegetation grew all around it, but a section had been pulled aside. The branches, leaves and other natural debris had been dragged out and scattered. A few more hours beneath the rain's assault and a passerby probably would not notice anything had been disturbed. It was possibly the perfect hiding place. "Did you make sure no other critters are in there hiding from the storm?"

"Absolutely." He lowered Gracie to the ground, then slicked a hand back over his soaking-wet hair to stop the runoff from flowing into his face. The cut at his temple was still bleeding, though it seemed to have slowed.

Gracie pressed tightly against Shae, favoring her injured ankle, wrapped her arms around her waist and clung. She'd always been an independent child, curious and eager to explore the world—often to Shae's dismay. Now, Shae could only hope some of that curiosity and sense of adventure would return once this was over.

"Are you sure you're all right to go traipsing through the woods alone?" If he passed out, he'd probably be eaten by something, rain or not.

"I'll be fine." He moved closer and gripped her arms. "Promise me you'll stay put beneath the log until I get back."

She'd begun to shiver, and the two spots on her arms where his hands made contact were blessedly warm. She resisted the urge to hug Gracie even closer and curl into him. "I will."

He held her gaze a moment longer, then released her and shifted the shrubbery aside for them to enter the makeshift shelter.

Shae ducked beneath the log and into the small space. Claustrophobia assailed her immediately, and she had to fight the urge to flee back out into the open. While her vision had adjusted to the darkness outside, she had no hope of seeing anything in here. The odors of mold and rotting leaves and debris gagged her.

Gracie stuck close. She crawled inside, then sat next to Shae and seemed to relax against her. Perhaps the small, closed-in space brought her more comfort than fear.

Mason dropped to one knee and peeked his head in. "Okay?"

"We're good." But the thought of sending him out into the swamp to seek help for them didn't sit well. She pulled the gun from her waistband and held it out to him. "Take this."

He closed both hands over hers holding the weapon. "Keep it. You have to defend Gracie. If anything comes, make sure you don't hesitate."

Since she couldn't force words past the lump clogging her throat, she only nodded and hoped he understood. When he released her hand and backed out of the shelter, a chill raced through her. She told herself it came from sitting on the cold ground, soaked to the bone from the rain, and almost had herself convinced. Well, at least the shelter would block a good portion of the rain. She leaned back against a tree trunk.

"Mommy?" Gracie lay against her, tucked beneath her arm.

"Yeah, baby?"

"Who is he?"

Shae's breath caught, but she forced herself to exhale and braced herself for the coming conversation she was in no way ready to deal with. Mason had been so filled with faith when they'd met. He'd even guided her back after she'd turned away when doing the right thing had cost her so much. Then, while Shae had been pregnant, she'd found God and fully embraced His teachings, had raised Gracie with that same faith. In a way, her relationship with God had kept her feeling closer to Mason after he'd disappeared. But that didn't change the fact that her child's father had never known about her, had made Shae promises and then disappeared. "Mason is an…um…a policeman, who was once a…good friend."

She nodded and shifted to relax more comfortably against Shae, and a wave of relief poured through her when Gracie didn't ask any more questions. Cowardly or not, this was something she'd prefer to deal with after they were somewhere safe and dry and warm.

Gracie's breathing became more rhythmic, tension easing from her muscles as she dozed.

Shae let her head fall back against the tree trunk, praying for guidance. Her eyes began to drift closed, and she hovered somewhere between awareness of their surroundings and the welcome comfort of sleep. She hung there on that precipice, afraid to sleep, yet too exhausted to stay awake.

The sound of gunshots yanked her ruthlessly back to full alert.

Mason dived for cover behind a massive moss-covered oak tree.

Another shot rang out, and splinters flew from the tree on impact. He should have figured they'd wait on the bridge, probably with night-vision goggles. It made sense—it's what he'd have done. Why wander through a swamp when you could stake out the car and wait for them to emerge in the most logical place—the road where they'd entered the swamp?

He scanned the brush. Would they come in after him? Most likely. At least, if they knew it was a person hiding there and they hadn't just seen movement in the brush and randomly opened fire, hoping for the best. But what if it was an innocent bystander they'd just fired at?

He massaged his temples and admonished himself. The swamp was hardly filled with innocent civilians, wandering around in the pitch black during life-threatening thunderstorms. He could only hope it was the head injury clouding his judgment and not seeing Shae again...and Gracie. He had to get a grip, had to shake everything else off and concentrate on getting them to safety. Then, once he did get them somewhere safe, he still had a mission to accomplish, one he couldn't let go...for anyone.

He pulled his balaclava, now soaked and filthy, from his back pocket and wrung it out. Better to chance any bacteria that might be lingering than to have one of Kincaid's men see and recognize him. He was going back undercover after this was over. That was what he wanted, right? He pulled the balaclava on. He'd have to remember to remove it, though, before returning to Shae and Gracie. Shae would recognize him even with his face covered. Wouldn't she? But Gracie might be frightened.

Okay. So, now what? He hadn't been able to find his cell phone by the alligator's nest, so it was either lost in the water or still in the car, since he couldn't remember what he'd done with it after speaking to Zac. He never should have left the car without his weapon, but he'd been under fire, half-conscious and desperate to get Shae and Gracie to safety. Plus, Shae had a weapon, and he hadn't planned on splitting up.

Windswept rain beat at the trees and brush as a second storm unleashed its fury.

All right, there was no time for what-ifs. He needed a phone and he needed a weapon. The nearly submerged vehicle in front of him contained both.

If the curses amid the sounds of crashing through brush were any indication, the men currently stalking him were no expert trackers, but they were still coming after him. Apparently, they hadn't all been content to wait on the bridge.

If he was quiet enough, he might just be able to outsmart them before Kincaid could send any more backup. Because whatever experts Sebastian Kincaid sent would slip through the swamp like the nocturnal predators they were. Thankfully, Mason only had to deal with those who had no experience in such matters right now.

That meant at least four—the two who'd been pursuing them, plus at least two more in the vehicle that had blockaded the bridge. He closed his eyes and listened past the sound of the rain, which would also provide him some cover when he decided to move. Two voices. He could definitely make out two different voices. That left at least two probably still playing sniper on the bridge.

The men moved closer, making enough noise to scare off every creature within a hundred miles. One of them fired a shot far to Mason's right.

He stood, pressed his back against the tree and prayed his plan would work, surprising himself that he'd reached so easily for the faith he'd lost. When the men were almost on him, both moving about a hundred yards to his left, he sucked in a breath and held it, then started to inch around the tree. Keeping his back tight against the trunk, he slid smoothly through the rain-soaked mud around the far side. Once they passed, he ducked into the shrubbery. There wasn't much time. He had to move before the attackers found Shae and Gracie. Their hiding spot wasn't as far into the swamp as he'd thought, his judgment probably thrown off by the detour to fight the gator.

He dropped flat on the ground and belly crawled toward the lake, then slid into the water as quietly as if he were a gator himself. Careful not to make the slightest sound, he moved through the dark water, keeping his head low.

Shae had already shut the headlights off, but he could make out the shape of the submerged car.

He paused when he reached the vehicle, laid a hand against the roof and took one moment to gather himself. He breathed in deeply through the fabric covering his face, then exhaled, once, twice. With the third inhale, he sucked in as much air as he could and went under. For just an instant, he opened his eyes, but there was nothing but blackness, so he squeezed them closed, pouring his full focus into his task. With his vision hindered, his other senses would have to suffice. He felt along the edge of the back window they'd escaped through.

There was no mistaking the muffled sounds of the gunshots, nor the sting of pain along his left biceps where a bullet struck. Another foot deeper and the density of the water would have rendered the bullet harmless.

Into the car? Or back to Shae and Gracie? He only had a split second to decide. Someone obviously knew he was there, and if they trapped him inside the car, Shae and Gracie would be on their own. And he'd promised her he'd return. Remaining submerged, he used both feet to push off against the car door and change direction. He dived deeper.

Where was the shooter? Not on the bridge. The car was between him and them. They'd never have hit him. So, the shot had come from land. They must have been watching the car, maybe—probably—with night-vision goggles.

He propelled himself through the water as silently as any predator. He moved smoothly and pushed himself until he could no longer hold his breath, then pushed harder. When he couldn't stand another moment without air, when his lungs burned like fire in his chest and ached for release he didn't dare allow lest he leave a bubble trail for his stalkers to follow, he rolled over, let himself float toward the surface, until just his face emerged from the water, and exhaled slowly. He only allowed himself the briefest moment before inhaling and letting himself sink once again.

More than likely, his pursuers were searching near the car, expecting him to surface somewhere in the vicinity or continue to try to make it inside. It would be foolish to try.

He accepted the defeat. Making it into the car had been a long shot anyway, finding his weapon even less likely. He had, however, hoped to find Shae's phone, kept safe and dry inside her waterproof bag. They'd have to move to plan B.

Now, he needed to find a safe place to leave the cover the murky, black water provided so he could return to Shae and Gracie. Moving slowly, careful to avoid splashing and alerting anyone—human or otherwise—to his presence, he glided in their direction.

The fact that his pursuers had made such a foolish mistake, taking a shot without a clear target, gave him some hope they weren't Kincaid's best men. Had it been Mason, he'd have waited for his prey to emerge from the vehicle or even make it back on land. Why risk a shot into dark water? Even if he'd come out of the car shooting, they'd have had the element of surprise. A sniper with night-vision goggles would have easily picked him off from the bridge.

The next time he surfaced, he risked lifting his head all the way out of the water. He had to get onto land before he became completely lost. He currently had no idea how far he'd traveled. Far enough he could no longer see the bridge, but that wouldn't take much, considering the weather. Surely he'd put enough distance between them that it should be safe. He angled toward the shore, keeping his head low. When no one had tried to put a bullet in him by the time he reached the marshy shoreline, he figured he was safe enough. Before he stood, though, he scanned a full circle around him, searching for any hint of movement or reflection that would indicate the presence of another.

When nothing moved, he crawled out of the water and

straight into the thick vegetation lining the shore, then rolled onto his back and took a moment to orient himself, to breathe the thick, rancid air. He choked back a cough.

Clearly, there was no hope of escape or rescue tonight. With their pursuers staking out the car, and no idea which way might lead them to civilization and which way to certain death, they needed to find somewhere to hunker down. But not where he'd left Shae and Gracie. Even though the first storm had passed and the torrential downpour slowed, there was a lot more rain coming, and the entire area would flood quickly.

Zac already had his last known position, and Jameson Investigations boasted a wide network of resources, including trackers. Zac would come for them as soon as possible, and he'd deal with the men guarding the car. All Mason had to do was keep Shae and Gracie safe until then.

He turned over, lifted his head above the reeds and saw no one.

Then gunfire erupted in the distance. Only this time, a second round of shots followed on the heels of the first. Answering fire? Had Zac's people arrived to help?

As he debated whether to backtrack toward the bridge and check out the situation, a single gunshot pierced the night, followed by a sound that sent ice rushing through his veins. Despite how quickly it cut off, there was no mistaking the terror in the child's scream.

Chapter Four

Shivers tore through Shae as she held her hands out in front of her, trying to blink away the rain pouring down her face, impeding her vision. The gun weighed heavily against her back where she'd tucked it into her waistband so as not to further frighten Gracie. It didn't matter, though. She'd never reach it in time. Even if she'd been holding it in her hand, everything had happened too quickly for her to have used the weapon.

The gunman had come out of nowhere, crept up on them without Shae or Gracie hearing anything. One minute, she'd been sitting with Gracie, straining to hear past the pounding rain for any further gunshots that might indicate Mason was in trouble—or worse…which she couldn't even bear to think about—and the next, Gracie was gone, yanked out of the impromptu shelter before Shae could even react. She'd scrambled out after her, but she was too late to do anything but stand there trembling. She could only pray Mason had heard the warning shot the guy had fired, or Gracie's scream, before the gunman had slapped a hand over her mouth and cut it short. If he was even ali—

No. Don't even go there.

She didn't recognize the man holding Gracie against him,

gun pressed to her temple, one hand covering her mouth. The fact that he hadn't donned a mask to cover his sharp features and short black hair wasn't lost on her. "P-please. Don't hurt her."

Gracie's tears tracked over his hand, mixing with the rain as she struggled to breathe through her nose, squirming as she clutched his wrist in both hands.

"I'll do whatever you want." Keeping her hands where he could see them, Shae rocked back and forth, inching slowly forward. Not that she had any hope of disarming him—she just needed to be closer to her daughter. "Please, let her go."

"Tell me who you're working with."

"What?"

"The identity of whoever tipped you off that we were coming after you." He squeezed Gracie's face tighter.

"I don't know what you're talking about." Her heart stuttered. "No one told me you were coming after me. I saw Kincaid's goons at Gracie's pageant and took off."

The gunman frowned and shook his head, clearly confused. Maybe Kincaid's henchmen didn't coordinate their attacks. "There has to be a mole in the organization. We got to Delarosa before she ever made contact with you. I'm sure of that. So, who's the rat?"

She started to squeeze her eyes closed, needing to think, but she couldn't tear her gaze from Gracie, who'd gone unnaturally still.

"My orders were to kill you and bring back proof you were eliminated, but it'll be even better if I can bring the name of whoever's betrayed Kincaid back to him. I'll move up to lieutenant for sure."

She had to stall, give herself time to find a way out of this, give Mason time to reach them. "What does Quentin want from me? Why can't he just leave me alone?"

"Quentin doesn't want anything now." A vicious grin split the man's face. "He's on his deathbed, barely clinging to life while his final arrangements are seen to, including who's getting promoted. And I fully expect to be on that list before the old man croaks. In prison. Where your testimony put him."

So many emotions warred for attention. While she should be relieved to hear the news about Quentin, guilt interfered. She'd been Quentin's personal assistant at one time, had liked working for the affable older gentleman. Had even considered him a friend. And he'd always been kind to her, treated her well, offered praise and bonuses when she went above and beyond. And then she'd found out exactly what he was. A mobster. A monster who planned to bomb an entire building full of innocent people just to eliminate a rival family. "So who do you work for, then?"

"His son. And Sebastian has vowed to avenge his father's death before assuming control of the family business."

An image formed, a scrawny teenager always lurking in the shadows at the office. But six years had passed, and a lot could change in that amount of time. She tucked the information away for later...if there was a later. Some part of her knew he was spilling too much information, sharing too much to have any intention of letting her leave the swamp alive. "Let my daughter go, and I'll tell you what you want to know."

"I'm willing to trade." He yanked Gracie tighter against him, lifting her off the ground with the hand covering her face as she resumed her struggles. "*You* won't be walking out of this swamp, but I don't care about the girl. Tell me what I want to know and she'll live."

Shae struggled to think, tried to survey her surroundings in her peripheral vision without shifting her gaze from the gunman.

"Be smart about this."

Anyone who would take a child hostage would have no qualms about lying to get what he wanted. She didn't believe he'd let Gracie go. She was certainly old enough to repeat everything he'd just said to the police—thus implicating Sebastian Kincaid in Shae's murder—if he set her free.

The only thing holding her together right now was the fact that he didn't seem to know Mason was with them. He thought she'd been tipped off, that was all. Mason would already be on his way, would have started toward them the instant the man had fired his weapon. If he was still alive after the barrage of gunfire she'd heard before the gunman had taken Gracie. She shook the thought off, had to if she was going to survive this mess. Mason was fine. He'd been a trained FBI agent, had survived the past six years. And he would find his way to them. If she could stall long enough, or convince the gunman to let Gracie go, Gracie wouldn't have to find her own way out of the swamp, even if he did kill Shae. "Let my daughter go first. Let her run, and I'll tell you whatever you want to know."

She didn't shift her gaze from his, not even to look at Gracie, maybe especially so. The fear in her daughter's eyes might well send her over the edge.

"The name." He pressed the muzzle harder. "Now."

Gracie squeezed her eyes closed, starting to kick and flail harder.

"Please. I'm begging you. Just let her go, and I'll tell you." Shae made no attempt to hold back the tears or control the tremor in her voice. "She's a baby. If I don't give you the information you want, how hard could it be to catch her again?"

He studied Shae, seemed to contemplate the offer.

Movement in her peripheral vision snagged her attention. Mason? She didn't dare shift her eyes. Instead, she clung to the face of the man holding her daughter hostage. She memorized every feature. The scar running from the corner of his mouth to his right ear would make him easy to identify, as would the snake tattooed on the back of his gun hand. Of course, she'd have to live long enough to give a description.

Wind whipped the palms and brush into a frenzy, rain

pelting them relentlessly. Marble-size chunks of hail battered everything.

"I'll ask once more. Who alerted you we were coming?"

"Please." She bit the name back, couldn't answer even if she'd wanted to, knowing Gracie would be killed the instant she said anything.

"I won't ask again."

Gracie yanked her head to the side, her screams muffled behind the man's hand. She kicked wildly and slid down an inch.

A man, dressed all in black, emerged from the woods directly behind the gunman. A black watchman's cap concealed his hair, black paint covered his face except for a salt-and-pepper goatee. He lifted a very scary-looking gun.

Shae lunged toward Gracie, reaching behind herself for the weapon tucked into her waistband. Shae might go down, but she'd do so fighting to give Gracie a chance to survive and get to Mason.

The gunman lost his grip on Gracie when she bit down hard on his gloved hand, and she tumbled to the ground, then scrambled through mud and puddles toward Shae. He lifted the gun, aimed directly at Shae…

"Run, Gracie!" Shae screamed and lurched toward her daughter as she whipped her gun toward the gunman. She'd never make it. *God, help me.*

Before she could get off a shot, he dropped like a rock.

The second gunman scooped Gracie up as he ran toward Shae, then shoved her into Shae's arms. "Run! Go! Now!"

Shae clutched Gracie against her, whirled and ran, crashing through the brush in a desperate bid for escape, plunging deeper into the swamp. Wind battered everything. Palm trees bowed in submission. And still, Shae ran blindly, blood roaring like a locomotive in her ears. The sound grew louder. The storm raged, unleashing its unrelenting fury. Hail assaulted her head, her face, her hands, stung her bare legs as she ran.

Then she slid, her foot going out from under her in the slick muck. She twisted, cradling Gracie's head, as she crashed to the ground amid a tangle of roots, landing hard on her hip. Pain ripped through her.

Without warning, a strong body tackled her from behind, tumbling her and Gracie over the roots and into a ditch along-side the massive tree and coming to a stop atop them both, pinning them to the ground beneath his weight.

Overhead the storm raged, the sound deafening. Trees snapped beneath its wrath, one after another in a steady path of destruction. Time stopped beneath the endless torrent. And then…

Quiet descended, but for the steady rhythm of the rain and their harsh, ragged breathing.

Shae sucked in deep lungfuls of thick, wet air.

"Are you okay?" The weight eased off her. Two strong hands gripped her arms and helped her to sit. And then Mason trapped her with his stare, those electric blue eyes delving deep as he searched for answers. "Are you hurt? Is Gracie hurt?"

He released her and lifted Gracie into her lap, pushed her soaked hair off her face, then pressed Mr. Cuddles into her arms. "I found him by the…" He hooked a thumb toward the gunman. "Over there."

The little girl hugged the rabbit close and buried her face in his muddy fur.

And Mason pulled them both against him, wrapping them in the safety of his embrace. Too bad it was only an illusion, as she'd learned all too well. "It's okay. You're okay."

"G-G-Gracie." Shae's teeth chattered as she tried to speak.

Her daughter sobbed, rocking a mud-covered Mr. Cuddles back and forth.

Shae had to get a grip, had to pull herself together long enough to make sure Gracie wasn't hurt. "Gracie, baby, it's okay. Shh…"

"We have to go, Shae." Mason stood and surveyed the area, then held out a hand.

She reached for the lifeline he offered, and he pulled her to her feet. A twinge of pain shot from her hip straight to her ankle, almost sending her back down again, but she braced herself against it, took a deep breath, held it, then blew it out, battling the pain. After two more breaths, her focus turned to the swamp. A path of destruction cleaved through the forest. For a moment, she thought it was from her flight from the gunman. "What happened?"

"A tornado, and it won't be the last."

"Tor…" The breath she'd struggled so hard for fled her lungs in a whoosh. Just what they needed—a tornado touching down as they tried to flee Boggy Meadows for good. But where would they go next? Shae had no idea. Certainly not back to New York. Somewhere else, then. Maybe a big city this time, where they could lose themselves in the anonymity.

"Come on, Shae. We have to get you somewhere safe, get Gracie medical attention for her ankle." He rubbed a circle on Gracie's back. "Sound good, Gracie? Are you ready to get out of here?"

She nodded against Shae without lifting her head.

"Right. Yes. You're right." He'd struck the exact chord necessary to get her moving again. She shifted Gracie until she could look into her eyes, ran her hands over every inch of her, searching for any sign of injury even as she spoke. "Gracie, honey, we have to go now. It's not safe here."

Gracie nodded, the expression in her eyes blank, then laid her head back against Shae's shoulder with Mr. Cuddles between them. Her body went limp.

"Stay right with me." Mason took Shae's elbow, a pistol held out in front of him, and started to guide her back in the direction they'd come from.

Shae stopped. "We'll be walking right back into the gunmen if we go this way."

Gracie stiffened and whimpered.

He paused, looked back over his shoulder, eyes darting

in every direction. "The man who killed Kincaid's gunman and told you to run. He's my boss, Zac Jameson…and he's a friend."

Shae frowned. "The man you called earlier?"

"Yes. He's waiting for us. He has the resources to keep both you and Gracie safe until we can figure out what's going on and decide who we can trust and plan a course of action." His hold on her arm tightened as he started forward again.

But she pulled away, took a step backward. "How can you be so sure you can trust him?"

"Shae, please. He has no involvement with the Kincaid organization."

She shook her head. "You can't know that."

"Yes. I can. There's no time to explain everything. Not now." He pushed the hair back off her face, cradled her cheek with his free hand and looked her dead in the eye.

The first stirring of the love she'd once felt for him struggled to surface but was instantly smothered by distrust. Maybe he sensed the chill, or maybe he was just in a hurry. Either way, he pulled back.

She refused to acknowledge her disappointment. Mostly.

He guided her to a vehicle with an enclosed platform atop large treads instead of tires not far from where the gunman had held Gracie. The man with the salt-and-pepper goatee climbed out, exchanged a few words with Mason, offered a quick introduction to Shae, then disappeared back into the swamp. Mason helped her and Gracie inside, saying something about a safe house, then climbed into the driver's seat.

She watched the mysterious Zac Jameson retreat in the rearview mirror, issuing orders as he went. Mason was right about one thing—the man apparently had resources if he'd so quickly come up with a vehicle capable of moving through the swamp, as well as the team of agents currently hustling around the clearing. "You trust this guy?"

"Yes. Completely." He glanced in the rearview mirror then lurched forward.

"How can you?" Shae hadn't trusted anyone completely since...well... Mason.

"We can talk more about it later." He shifted his eyes toward Gracie, whose rhythmic breathing indicated she might have fallen asleep. Still, he was right. They couldn't be sure what she would overhear. "I can tell you that I had no choice but to leave when I did, Shae. Zac offered me the opportunity to go undercover in Kincaid's organization with the full resources of Jameson Investigations behind me, and I took it. I had to if I was going to keep you safe and get justice for Marty. Unfortunately, things didn't quite turn out that way."

"Why not?"

He hesitated, then offered a sad smile. "Let's get Gracie somewhere safe and settled first, then we'll talk more. But I will keep you safe, Shae. That I promise."

A promise he'd made before. And hadn't kept.

Mason glanced around the residential neighborhood as he held open the front door of the vacation home Zac had rented at the last minute—a center of operations they wouldn't be able to keep Shae and Gracie at for long—and ushered them inside. Although it would be acceptable as a temporary respite from the swamp, for the Jameson Investigations team to start a preliminary investigation while Mason, Shae and Gracie cleaned up and received medical attention, there was too much of a risk someone in the Kincaid organization would discover the last-minute rental—coincidentally attained at the exact time, in the exact area, where Shae had disappeared—and dispatch someone to look into it. No, as soon as the team doctor assessed them, they'd be back on the run. Mason would keep them on the move until Zac could procure a suitable safe house and get his team in place.

Zac's team would scout the quiet streets and secure the

house. All Mason had to worry about for the moment was Shae's and Gracie's safety. Gracie... He was going to have to think about that situation at some point, but not now. He shoved the thought aside and guided them past the living room and dining room, where about a dozen agents operated in organized chaos as they set up the portable equipment they'd need to search for answers and coordinate a response, and down a hallway, then knocked on an open bedroom door. "Doc?"

"Come in, Mason." The elderly doctor had been part of Zac's team from the beginning, a man Zac trusted from long experience, who'd saved the lives of more than one Jameson Investigations team member, including Zac himself, before he'd recruited him.

Dr. Rogers boasted a robust personality, kind blue eyes, a headful of thick, wavy white hair with a neatly trimmed beard and the ability to remain calm and see to his patients no matter the circumstances. Mason had seen him administer treatment amid a barrage of gunfire without blinking an eye. No doubt he could treat any physical injuries Gracie and Shae may have suffered, but he was also hoping he'd be able to help them cope with the trauma they'd faced in the swamp, since Zac would have already briefed him.

The doc offered a kind smile and patted a gurney that had been set up against a wall. "Why don't you put Gracie down here?"

Shae glanced at Mason. When he nodded, she inched into the room, surveying every inch of the place, including the blinds-covered window that would be their only escape route if anything went wrong.

Mason gripped the doorknob. "I'll be back in a little while."

Her gaze darted to him. "Where are you going?"

"Just into the other room to see if they've found a more permanent safe house and check if they've heard from the FBI or the marshals' service." Not that he blamed her, but the distrust and suspicion in her eyes stung. He dismissed the thought for now. Technically, the marshals' service had jurisdiction over Shae, since she was part of their witness protection program, but Mason had no intention of handing her over to them until he found out who had leaked her whereabouts. Because that was the only way Kincaid could have found her. Someone had talked. And he had every intention of making sure it didn't happen again. "Let the doctor check you and Gracie over, and then I'll be back."

He only paused for a moment to study Gracie. The little girl seemed strong and courageous, had certainly held her own in the swamp. When he'd reached the small clearing and found the gunman holding her, his heart had practically stopped. But his training had taken over, had allowed him to remove the threat posed by two other shooters concealed in the brush so Zac could go for Gracie. He already had so many reasons to be grateful to Zac, and now he had to add one more. He turned away, paused a moment in the doorway as the doc questioned Gracie about her stuffed bunny, then closed the door and walked away. There were more pressing matters at hand, even if some part of him screamed that he was nothing more than a coward.

He strode into the hustle and bustle of the command center and sought out Angela Ryan—a smart, handsome woman with sharp, angular features, rich umber skin and closely cropped black hair, who could light up a room with her thousand-watt smile. "Hey, Angela. What's going on?"

That smile was nowhere to be found when she turned her dark-as-night eyes on him. "We're still setting up, but from what we can tell, Sebastian Kincaid seems to have gone completely off the grid."

"You can't find him?" He took a monitor out of the box she'd just hauled in and set it on the desk.

"No. Nor anyone else from his inner circle." She went to work unraveling and hooking up wires between devices at lightning speed.

"I recognized one of the men in the swamp. He was a mid-level soldier at best." Not that the man with the scar running down his face wasn't deadly—he was—but he didn't have the level of Sebastian's trust that would have earned him a spot at the grown-ups' table. Of course, Mason hadn't been able to reach that point, either. Even after so many years under-cover in Kincaid's organization, he'd never made it past about the same level—his own fault, since he wasn't willing to do what would be necessary to move up. Scarface obviously had no such compunction. "Which means Kincaid is keeping his lieutenants close to home."

She nodded, lower lip caught between her teeth as she ran wires, rechecked connections and whirled the monitor around. "Which means he has something else planned—something bigger that he wants his best people for."

"That's what worries me." Somehow, they had to find out what Kincaid was up to. And Shae was probably his top prior-ity if he was on a mission to prove to his father he was worthy of taking over the family business. He had to keep Shae safe, and his best chance was to stay undercover. "You're sure he can't find out Mace Lavalle is actually Mason Payne?"

"Positive." She paused to meet his gaze. "I set up your un-dercover identity myself, and I've monitored it since all this began. There is no connection between the two, and your cover has not been compromised."

He nodded. The last thing he needed was for Kincaid's men to figure out he was the mole. But, if Angela had done it herself, there would be no mistakes. And he needed to be absolutely certain of that, because… "You realize I'm going to go back in."

Angela stopped what she was doing, leaned against the table and folded her arms. "Have you discussed it with Zac yet?"

"Not yet."

"Mason…" She sighed. "Do you realize how fortunate

you were to get out in time to protect Shae and Gracie the first time?"

"I know, Angela. Believe me." He raked a hand through his hair, searching for another solution, but he couldn't come up with one. The only way he could find out what was going on would be to infiltrate the Kincaid Organization again. As much as he hated to leave Shae and Gracie in anyone else's hands, eventually he'd have no choice.

"Do me a favor then?" She studied him, lifted a perfectly sculpted brow and waited.

"What's that?"

"Get Shae and her daughter set up at the safe house first. Give me a little time to get myself together here…" She gestured at the tangle of equipment half unpacked behind her. "Let me see what information I'm able to track down before I move to the new safe house. Besides, I sincerely doubt Zac is going to agree to you going dark under the current circumstances. And you know you have to go in with no contacts. Without being able to communicate with anyone, you'd probably just blow your cover worrying if Shae and Gracie are okay."

She was right. He couldn't risk contact with the outside world while undercover. Especially now that Sebastian had moved himself from underboss, having to do as his father ordered, to boss, with an agenda of his own. The man was nothing if not paranoid, often installing spies to monitor his own men. "We'll see."

She grunted, apparently satisfied that was all he could give her, and returned to her work. She glanced back up when he started to turn away. "And while you're at it, tough guy, go see Doc Rogers and get those wounds taken care of before you end up with an infection."

He grinned. "Yes, Mother."

She shot a rubber band at him and continued working.

Mason checked his watch as he strode down the hallway toward the bedroom the doc had commandeered as an examination room. He knocked and waited for a brusque "come in" before smiling to himself and pushing the door open. "How's it going in here, Doc?"

Dr. Rogers smiled at Gracie where she sat on the examination table while he worked on wrapping her ankle. He tapped the tip of her nose.

The fact that she smiled back at the kind, elderly man had at least a few of the knots in Mason's gut unraveling.

Shae smiled at Gracie from where she sat on a chair beside the gurney, concern etched in her too-taut features.

"Shae is all fixed up and ready for a shower, Gracie is just about done and going with her, and Mr. Cuddles is tucked in a pillowcase having his bath in the washing machine." Used to dealing with agents who didn't want to take the time to have their injuries tended, the doctor eyed Mason from head to toe. "So let's pretend we had the 'I'm fine,' 'No, you're not fine' argument, and I won, which we both know I will, and you get your derrière on the examination table."

He winked at Gracie, patted her bandaged ankle gently and lifted her off the gurney and into Shae's lap, where the little girl curled up, her gaze, filled with curiosity, riveted on Mason.

What could she be thinking? Was there any part of her that recognized him as her father? Probably not, considering how young she was and what she'd been through over the past few hours. Heaving an exaggerated sigh, he took Gracie's place so the doctor could examine him. The sooner he got this out of the way, the sooner he could get Shae and Gracie to a more secure location. "Shae, why don't you and Gracie go ahead and get cleaned up now? I'd like to be on the road as soon as possible."

She nodded and stood. She was quieter now, or maybe she just had nothing to say to him. Not that he could blame her. No matter how much he'd loved her—and he *had* loved her—he'd had no choice but to leave. He could admit now, though, that he could have hung around long enough to give her an explanation. If nothing else, he could have said goodbye.

Did he still love her? Was he even capable of feeling love anymore? He felt something for her, that he couldn't deny. No matter how hard he tried to bury the feelings, they insisted on clawing their way to the surface. Aside from the sucker punch of emotions when he'd first laid eyes on her, and the shock of recognition when he's spotted his daughter and recognized her... Huh. That was the first time the thought of being a father hadn't brought almost instant panic. As interesting as that was, it was definitely a concept better left unexamined.

Angela was right. Maybe he had no business going back undercover. His thoughts were all over the place, a jumbled mess he seemed to have no hope of untangling. He couldn't even seem to get through answering his own question—was he still in love with Shae? His heart pounded painfully, his pulse rate skyrocketed and he shoved the question away. Maybe it was better left unanswered, since the outcome would be the same no matter what he decided. He would leave her again. He had no choice.

"There are shower supplies, towels and clean clothes for both of you in the back bedroom. Zac's men also retrieved your bags from the car and left them as well."

She nodded, thanked him and the doc, and started toward the door with Gracie in her arms.

"Oh, and they found your cell phone. One of the agents is going through it now, searching for any clue as to how Kincaid's men might have found you."

"You think I did something to—"

"No. Not at all. It's just standard procedure. People use their phones for everything nowadays, and you never know what might have tipped someone off."

She nodded, gaze averted. "What can I get it back?"

"You won't be able to have it back, but there's a new one with your things."

"What?" She paused. "No. I want *my* phone."

His gaze skittered to Gracie, then back to Shae as he willed her to understand. "It would be better not to take it with us, since it could be tracked."

"But… I know it's a small thing, but didn't have a chance to back up any of the pictures and videos of Gracie's pageant. It's our last normal memory." Tears shimmered in her eyes, tipped over her lashes. She squeezed her eyes closed. Of everything they'd been through since last night, the thought of losing her memories was what ended up reducing her to tears.

"Go ahead and get cleaned up and changed. I'll make sure they get all the pictures and videos off the phone for you before they destroy it. You can't sign in to any apps or access your cloud storage on the new phone until this situation is resolved, but we'll make sure you have whatever's on your phone now."

She blew out a breath and smoothed a hand over her daughter's tangled hair. "Thank you. I don't care about anything else. I just don't want to lose any of the pictures and videos of Gracie."

She didn't add since they'd most likely never be able to return there. She didn't have to. His heart, so hardened these past six years, threatened to shatter. "Why don't you and Gracie go ahead and get cleaned up? I'll find you as soon as the doc here patches me up."

She nodded, thanked the doctor again, then stood with Gracie in her arms and headed for the door.

"Shae?" He waited for her to turn back, then held her stare. "We need to talk."

Her shoulders slumped beneath whatever weight threatened to crush her, and she shifted her gaze. "I know."

Chapter Five

Exhausted and traumatized, Gracie had fallen asleep in Shae's arms as soon as they lay down on the twin-size bed. The scent of the baby shampoo that had been provided cocooned Shae in the illusion of normalcy as she stroked Gracie's still-damp hair. A soft knock on the door intruded on the only peace she'd found in the past twelve or so hours. As much as she wished she could remain frozen in that moment forever, she couldn't. She had to get up and face whatever the day might bring. So, filled with regret, she kissed Gracie's head, then shifted her onto the pillow and climbed out of the bed. Shae tucked Mr. Cuddles, whom one of Zac's female agents had brought in fresh from the dryer, into Gracie's arms, then lifted a blanket from the foot of the bed and laid it over them both. At least her daughter might be spared any more fear. For a few moments, anyway.

"Who is it?" Though she already knew, had sensed him lingering outside the door for the past few minutes, probably trying to decide whether to face the conversation they were about to have or flee to the easier task of hunting down a killer.

"It's me. Mason. Can I come in?"

With a deep breath for courage, she wiped her sweaty palms on the leggings Zac's team had left for her. While she appreciated all they'd done, and the man did seem to command an almost endless supply of resources, she still couldn't bring herself to trust these people as much as Mason seemed to. How could she? She'd trusted the marshals' service and the FBI implicitly during Quentin's trial, and they'd not only failed her, but at least one of them had betrayed them all. How could she help but view everyone with suspicion? And yet...

Everyone at Jameson Investigations had done so much for her and Gracie already, even at risk to their own lives. Seemed there were no easy answers, so she'd have to go with her gut, which said... What? The honest truth was, she had no idea. She'd trusted Mason with her life and her heart once, more than she'd ever trusted another person, more than she'd even trusted herself, and he'd let her down, walked away without a word. She sighed and opened the door. "Come on in."

His gaze darted instantly to Gracie, earning him a point or two in Shae's book, though he'd have to earn an awful lot more before he could even begin to gain her trust again. The fact that was willing to risk his life to protect Gracie might make him a good person, a courageous man, but she'd already known that about him. It was the choices he'd made that had caused the distance between them. "Can we talk?"

She glanced at Gracie, sleeping fitfully now that Shae had left her.

"The den across the hall has been set up as a conference room. If you leave both doors open, you'll be able to keep an eye on Gracie and hear her if she stirs." He stood in the doorway, waiting.

"Sure." If she didn't watch herself, his constant awareness of her concern for Gracie, and his obvious consideration for Gracie's safety at all times, might melt her hardened heart. As she nipped past him, the familiar woodsy scent of his aftershave brought back memories better left in the past.

She crossed the hall and entered a den with a sectional, a small desk in the corner and a round table with four chairs.

Ignoring the couch, which begged for her to snuggle into a corner and pull a blanket over herself, Shae took a seat at the table. Best to keep her distance if she had any hope of escaping another broken heart. If not for Gracie, and the faith Shae had discovered over the past six years, she probably would never have managed to heal after the last time he'd left her. She'd believed him with all of her heart when he'd told her he'd enter witness protection with her, that they'd spend the rest of their lives together. When he'd disappeared, she'd gone crazy with worry. And grief. She'd never believed, not even for an instant, that he'd been the one to give up her location, the one who'd betrayed his own people and caused his partner to be killed. She couldn't believe that. But he *had* left without a word. And she'd worried for six incredibly long years that Kincaid had killed him as well.

She wouldn't go through that again. She couldn't. Clearly, she'd misjudged him, just like she'd misjudged Quentin Kincaid. If it was possible to be too trusting, Shae was. At least, she had been. Not anymore.

Seeming to understand her need for a buffer between them, Mason sat across from her—a huge concession, since she'd taken the seat with her back to the wall so she could see into the room across the hall where Gracie slept. The position Mason had always taken when she'd known him. She'd laughed then, hadn't understood the need to have a wall at your back so no one could sneak up on you, had never felt the constant need to look over her shoulder, hadn't comprehended what it meant to have your whole world turned upside down when you were blindsided.

He shifted the chair enough to see the doorway in his peripheral vision, despite the numerous agents currently working just down the hall.

A small smile tugged at her. She supposed some habits died hard.

"I don't know what to say to you." His gaze dropped to his

hands, fingers interlaced in his lap. "The words *I'm sorry*— while I am, more than you could ever know—don't seem like enough."

"When I woke up the next morning and you were gone, no note, no goodbye, nothing, I didn't know what to think." There was no need to specify which morning she meant, since he'd fled after they'd spent only one night together. "Your partner had just been shot the night before, and I didn't know what to believe, whether to rage at you or grieve."

He swallowed hard. "I know, Shae, and I am so very sorry."

She fought back a sob, her emotions raw, as if she'd been dragged back six years in the past to relive the same pain all over again. "You already said that."

"Right." His eyes closed, and he nodded.

She sighed, struggled for control. That had come out harsher than intended, but the sense of betrayal, the grief at having not known whether he was alive or dead, the fear of raising the child that had been growing within her alone weighed too heavily for her to deal with. Except...

She hadn't been alone. God had stood by her, had led her to safety and protected her and her child, had given Shae time to heal and to grow stronger. Maybe it had all been because He knew she'd need to take a stand here and now, to get her life back so she and Gracie could stop running. But could she fight again? As she had against Quentin when she'd gone to the FBI, agreed to wear a wire and then testified against him? Did she have it in her to now go up against his son? And what about Gracie? If Shae stood her ground and fought back, Gracie would be in danger. No way could she let that happen. She would have to go back into witness protection. There was no other choice.

Confusion beat in time with the steady throb at her temples. She needed to deal with one crisis at a time. "You're forgiven, Mason. It's not about that. I forgave you a long time ago. I guess I just want to understand why. How could you have left without saying anything to me?"

He finally looked up at her then, a host of expressions warring across his features before finally settling on neutral, his mouth a firm, stubborn line.

Even if she had forgiven him, she still wanted…no, deserved some kind of answers—answers he didn't seem inclined to give. "You're the one who said we had to talk. So, talk. Or stop wasting my time and let me get back to my daughter."

He winced at that, massaged the bridge of his nose.

"You know what? The why doesn't even matter." When he lowered his hand, she searched his eyes for some hint of what he was feeling. "What I really need to know is, given the same circumstances, knowing what you now know, would you make the same choice?"

He blew out a breath, paused, then finally nodded once. "Most likely. Yes."

"Okay then." She slid her chair back, started to stand.

"Wait." Misery lined every feature. "Please, try to understand. I had no choice. I'll explain, just…just give me a minute. It's not easy for me to talk about all of this, and I'm sorry for that as well. I've been undercover in the Kincaid organization for the past six years. I have lived another life, the life of a criminal. I've done things I'm not proud of, things I wish I could go back and change, but I can't. I'm not a good person now, Shae. I'm not the man you remember."

She studied him for a moment while his gaze was averted, noted the pain and suffering and guilt that weighed so heavily. "I don't believe that."

When he finally met her gaze, a small flicker of hope flared in his eyes.

"Tell me. Tell me all of it."

After a quick glance over his shoulder out the doorway, he turned to face her more fully. "That last night I came to you, I came straight from the hospital."

"I remember. You'd gone to see Marty Bowers after he'd been shot."

"Yes." He raked a hand through his already-disheveled hair. "I was a mess. I needed you, needed to escape for a little while, forget about the reality of the situation for just that one moment. But I didn't use you, Shae. I loved you. At that time, I loved you with all my heart. We'd spent more than a year together while charges were brought against Kincaid and he was finally tried and convicted, and every fiber of my being ached to be with you, to marry you, to move on and spend the rest of my life with you. I wasn't supposed to fall in love with someone under my protection, but I did. I would have followed you into witness protection just to be with you."

She strained under the pressure of keeping her expression from betraying the hurt at his use of the past tense. Not that it mattered now, but it ached just the same.

"I didn't know then that I'd have to go undercover for years." He shrugged, lifted his hands, let them fall again. "Or maybe I did. I at least suspected it. But I was in denial. For the first time in my life I'd found happiness, and I couldn't bear the thought of giving that up—giving you up."

"And yet, you walked out sometime early that morning and never looked back."

"Yeah. And yet." He shoved the chair back and lurched to his feet so he could pace. "I received a phone call after you'd fallen asleep. Marty didn't make it. He died alone at the hospital, with no family members present, because it wasn't safe. Even though we had agents at the hospital, some posted outside his room, it didn't matter. Kincaid was too powerful, his reach too far. We couldn't guarantee the safety of Marty's wife and children, and we didn't know who to trust at the FBI, so Zac took them into hiding, which is what Marty would have wanted. But my partner died alone, and they never got the chance to say goodbye. And I hadn't stayed with him. I ran. Like a coward, because I couldn't face the fact that my partner was most likely going to die, couldn't deal with the certainty that the only way Marty could have been targeted was if someone had leaked his identity. And there were only a select few who knew."

"Is that why you went undercover?" Her heart ached for him. He'd been close with Marty, was godfather to his youngest child. "To figure out who had betrayed all of us?"

"Yeah. I had to know. First of all, to keep it from happening again so you would be safe. And secondly, to find justice for Marty." He stopped and faced her, hands propped on his hips as he finally made eye contact. "Plus, Zac Jameson came to me with an offer I couldn't refuse. By the time he reached out early that morning, he already had an undercover persona set up for me and was ready to get me into the Kincaid organization. Had I known that you were... Knowing about Gracie wouldn't have changed the circumstances. Most likely, it would have made me even more determined to go undercover and keep you safe."

Shae lowered her gaze to her hands, couldn't stand to see the pain in his eyes. She'd held on to her anger toward him for a long time. Maybe because it was easier to deal with than the hurt, the sense of betrayal, the fear, the grief. It wasn't that she didn't understand what he was telling her. She just needed time to process it all. For now, though... "Did you figure out who it was? The person who betrayed us all?"

He was already shaking his head. "I spent two years undercover trying to find out who it was."

"I thought you said you were under for six years?" Had he lied? Confused the timeline?

"I was." He dropped back onto his chair, as if finally sharing what had happened had left him weary. "I couldn't move up the ranks in the Kincaid organization enough to attain results. I couldn't...do the kinds of things that would have earned me a place as a trusted lieutenant. So my mission changed."

Well, she could certainly relate to that. She didn't know

what to say to him. Not that she faulted him for the decisions he'd made; she didn't. But he could have talked to her, could have called and told her what was going on, could have left a note. Anything other than walk away without looking back. "You couldn't have gotten in touch with me? Not even once in six years? You couldn't have written a letter?"

"No, Shae. I couldn't break my cover. I didn't dare. You have to remember, you were at risk, too. With a leak in the FBI that I wasn't able to find and plug, there was always a chance someone would talk. Not to mention the possibility that Quentin or Sebastian had planted spies or surveillance equipment. I had to do a lot of things I regretted, even as I did them, and I couldn't take a chance my identity might be compromised— not for anything…or anyone. I'm sorry."

Shae ignored that, didn't want to know what he might have had to do to save her, to save Gracie. Did that make her a coward? What she did know, or was at least beginning to realize, was that he'd been just as alone as she had these past six years. He might not have gone into witness protection with her, but he'd still given up everything and everyone he'd held dear and assumed a new identity to go undercover to try to save her. He'd put himself at risk—

Everything in her went perfectly still as the scene in the swamp played out in her mind. She could still see the gun pressed to Gracie's head, still feel her own painfully rapid heartbeat, and she could replay every word the man had said to her. "Kincaid's men know there's a mole."

His eyes went as dark as the storm still raging outside, rattling the windows with its wrath. "What do you mean?"

"Did you hear any of what the guy in the swamp said to me?"

He shook his head, and a bit of a smirk played at the corner of his mouth. "I was kind of occupied."

"He wanted to know who tipped me off that they were coming."

Mason sat up straighter, scooted to the edge of his seat.

"He said he'd let Gracie go if I told him who had alerted me that they'd found me."

His leg bounced up and down, as it often did when he got jittery and ready to move on something, his mind racing so fast she could practically see the gears turning. No doubt, their conversation would be ending shortly.

"Can they figure out you were the one who infiltrated their organization?"

"No. There's no way." He yanked his phone out of his pocket, started to scroll. "Within hours of Marty's death, I had an entire new persona. I became Mace Lavalle, and Mason Payne ceased to exist until I returned to you."

He really had been in a kind of witness protection, just like her. "One more thing."

"What's that?" he answered, distracted as he scrolled and tapped.

"How *did* you find us?" Because only a handful of people would have been able to point him in the right direction, and one of them was dead. "How'd you even know we were in trouble?"

He looked up then, lowered his phone to his side. "Maria Delarosa contacted Zac, told him she suspected your identity might have been compromised. The FBI had picked up one of Kincaid's midlevel enforcers. In return for a plea deal, he offered up the information that Quentin Kincaid was near death and that he'd sent Sebastian in search of you to prove his worth. An agent she was friendly with passed on the information—she didn't receive it through official channels. She said she didn't know who to trust, and she didn't want to call in case you were under surveillance. She was on her way to grab you from wherever you were and relocate you immediately. Zac sent an agent in to retrieve me. And before you ask, no, she didn't tell him about Gracie."

Shae simply nodded. What more was there to say? "So, what happens now?"

"Now, we have to figure out how Sebastian Kincaid un-
covered your identity and where to find you." He pressed the
phone against his ear. "Because you and Gracie will never be
safe until we do."

Mason waited for Shae to return to Gracie. Then, with
one lingering look at the two of them, he closed the bedroom
door—as well as the door on the past—firmly behind him.
He couldn't undo the last six years, and it would take a long,
hard look at his choices to decide if he would even choose
differently given the opportunity. A reflection he didn't have
time for. He'd spent years beating himself up with guilt over
leaving Shae without an explanation. He'd told himself keeping her safe by taking down the organization was worth it.
But then what? If he'd accomplished his goal, would he have
sought her out, returned to her, offered an explanation and
begged for forgiveness? He had no clue, because every time
that option had even flittered through his mind, he'd immediately shut it down. As he'd do again now.

He strode into the living room command center to find out
if there were any new developments and access the new safe
house information so they could get going. And stopped short
when he discovered two of Zac's agents huddled in front of a
monitor grinning widely as Gracie danced onscreen.

Until that moment, he'd only seen a frightened, timid child,
a victim in need of protection, which he would willingly risk
everything to provide. But in that instant, as Gracie wowed
the audience at her Christmas pageant, not only with her dance
moves but with a mischievous smile that had fire dancing in
those blue eyes, some part of him shattered into a million
pieces. Reality sucker punched him in the gut, robbing him of
breath. This was the child, *his* child, whom he'd abandoned.
A child so filled with life and love that it literally shone from
her to encompass everyone around her.

"Hey, Mason." Angela gestured to the screen. "Get a load of Gracie. This kid's too much."

He simply nodded, unable to draw enough air to speak. He'd never thought of becoming a father, never had any desire to do so. And yet, knowing he'd missed five years of his daughter's life weighed heavily. *Oh, God, what have I done?*

Even if he hadn't known about Gracie, he had known Shae, had loved her. The night Marty had been shot, Mason had checked on him and then fled the hospital. Not from his injured partner or the circumstances or reality, but *to* Shae. He'd wanted nothing more than to reach her. He'd seen the stuffed bunny, sitting all alone in the gift shop window, and it had called to him, a kindred spirit perhaps. Because that was how Mason had felt—alone. And, for the first time in his life, frightened. What if he couldn't keep Shae safe? Marty was a well-trained, seasoned agent, and Kincaid had managed to get to him and leave him on death's doorstep. How could Shae ever hold her own against those people?

Would it have made a difference if he'd known she would soon carry their child? He'd walked away and betrayed Shae's trust, left her with nothing but a stuffed bunny she'd not only held on to but given to their daughter, so she would have some small piece of him. Tears threatened. He shoved them away.

They deserved better than him, deserved someone who wasn't as emotionally damaged as he'd become after so many years undercover, someone who hadn't spent so long living a lie, stealing, racketeering, collecting money for the very people who were trying to kill Shae and had succeeded in killing Marty. Which was not to say he hadn't orchestrated escape for many who owed Kincaid and couldn't pay—he had, with Zac's help. When he'd realized he wasn't going to move up high enough to find out who'd murdered Marty, since he wasn't willing to kill for the opportunity, he'd made it his mission to save as many as he could. He'd spent the majority of his time undercover smuggling out as many of Kincaid's potential victims as possible, sending them on the run with nothing more than a memorized contact number for Zac Jameson.

This trip down memory lane, while enlightening, served no purpose. After one last look at Gracie's incredible smile, he started to turn away, but his gaze caught on a guy standing on the side of the auditorium on the screen. "Wait. Pause that."

Angela shifted to business mode in less time than it took her to hit the pause button.

"Back it up." He leaned over her shoulder to study the screen as she rewound. "There. Stop it. Can you play it in slow motion?"

"Sure."

Onscreen, the drama played out at a much-reduced pace. Instead of focusing on Gracie this time, Mason watched the side door, held his breath until two men entered and looked around the room. One turned and walked out of camera range without showing his face, but she'd captured a good view of the other. "Pause it."

He tapped one of the men on the screen, a tall, beefy guy with a man bun and a goatee.

"You recognize him?" Angela swiveled her chair to a second keyboard along the ell made by the desk and a table and began tapping away.

"Yeah. He's one of Sebastian Kincaid's guys—an enforcer. Lucas Gianelli." He'd met Lucas before, had even worked with him once or twice. The thought of him coming after Shae and Gracie sent a shiver rocketing up his spine. "I didn't see him at the house or in the swamp, but he's a higher-up lieutenant, works directly for Sebastian." A plan was forming in his mind.

Angela's fingers flew over the keyboard as images of Lucas popped up on her monitor—a driver's license, mug shot, arrest record… "Do you think he's still alive? He could have been killed or captured in the swamp."

He was already nodding as he scanned the information almost as fast as Angela pulled it up. "Zac sent me pictures. I tried to ID the three guys who were killed and the one who was captured—and Gianelli wasn't among them."

"I'll let Zac know." She hit the speakerphone button even as she spoke and continued to enter commands one-handed.

"Find him, Angela." Because he was the key. If Mason found him now and was willing to work with him, gain his trust—while ensuring Shae escaped—he might be able to leapfrog up in the Kincaid ranks at last, without ever putting a bullet in an innocent person. Once his old man was gone and Sebastian assumed control, he'd begin his revenge tour and would be completely paranoid about letting any but his most trusted lackeys close to him. "Have you heard anything from Zac about the guy he turned over to the police until the FBI agents can get there to take custody?"

She left Zac a quick update via voice mail and hung up. "The guy's not talking, but Zac is still at the police station where he's being booked. Local law enforcement is cooperating."

"All right." Local police didn't always share information with private security companies, but Zac had resources he could tap when that was the case. One way or the other, he usually obtained the information he was searching for in time. Time they didn't have. "Is there a new safe house set up?"

"Yes." She waited for the printer to stop, then grabbed a stack of pages and handed it to him. "This is everything we could get on the men in the swamp, as well as the information on the safe house."

"Thanks, Angela."

She pulled a flash drive from her computer and handed it to him, along with a set of keys. "The drive contains the photos and videos from Shae's phone. The keys are to the dark gray SUV out front and the safe house listed on the last page there."

"Thanks again."

"Are you going to get some sleep before you leave?"

"No." He'd sleep better with a houseful of Zac's people to

stand guard, but something was nagging at him, begging him to keep moving, and he'd learned to trust his instincts. "I'm going to wake Shae and Gracie now and get going."

"All right. Keep in touch, and I'll let you know as soon as I hear anything. Most of the agents will remain here to work for a little while longer, but I'm going to switch to the new safe house right away, so I'll see you there shortly." She hesitated as he turned to go. "And Mason?"

He paused and turned back. "Yeah."

"Zac had to notify the FBI and the marshals' service that we have their witness in our custody. They've agreed to share the knowledge with as few people as possible, but…" She shrugged and gave him a you-know-how-it-goes look.

Which he did. With a renewed sense of urgency, Mason knocked on Shae's door, then cracked it open when she called for him to come in. "We're leaving."

She stood from the armchair beside the bed and slid on new sneakers. Since the backpack Zac's men had retrieved from the car had been soaked, even though everything inside it had been protected, someone had transferred the contents into a new one, which Shae slung over her shoulder.

Mason approached the bed. "Will Gracie stay asleep if I pick her up?"

Shae smoothed their daughter's hair, kissed her temple. "She should. She was pretty exhausted."

"All right." He handed Shae the keys, then tucked the blanket around Gracie, picked her up and cradled her against his chest. "Let the agents waiting beside the door go out first, then follow them to the gray SUV in the driveway. Don't look around. Just keep your head down, go straight to the car and follow any instructions the agents give you instantly."

She nodded, lower lip caught between her teeth, terror filling her eyes.

He strode after her, stepping out into the rain and hunching over Gracie, trying to keep her dry as they hurried to the

SUV. He made sure Shae got in as quickly as possible, then gently lowered Gracie to the booster seat and buckled her in, his gaze lingering for only a moment on the sleeping child he was charged with protecting, memorizing every feature to carry with him when he left her. Maybe Shae would give him a copy of the video from the pageant. He could always leave it with Zac or Angela for safekeeping, since he could never carry evidence of Gracie with him while Kincaid was in the picture. He climbed into the driver's seat, glanced around once more and made a right out of the driveway onto the narrow residential street.

Two of Zac's people followed in a black SUV and would accompany them to the safe house, where one would stand guard inside and one outside. The fewer people who knew their whereabouts, the safer Shae and Gracie would be. Of course, the FBI and marshals' service would eventually have to know where they were holed up. Hopefully, Zac would keep their exact location secret for as long as possible.

He crept through the quiet neighborhood, the *squeak, squeak, squeak* of the windshield wipers and the torrent of rain against the glass the only sounds. He glanced in the rearview mirror, slid a look at Gracie sleeping at an awkward angle in the seat, then looked over at Shae. "You doing okay?"

"Yeah." Shae stared out at the rain, tracing lines of water with her finger as they wiggled and squirmed along the window. "Just tired."

"Did you get any sleep at all?"

"No. You?"

"No, but I'm used to going without sleep. I'll still be okay for a while." If only there was something he could say to her that would ease some of her anxiety, lessen some of the tension coiled between them. Years ago, she'd have trusted him if he'd said everything would be okay. Now, she would recognize the attempt to alleviate her fear for what it was—a deception, even if well intended and even if he believed it at the time. "Why don't you close your eyes and try to sleep until we get to the safe house?"

She clutched the seat with a white-knuckled grip. "I left my entire life behind, sacrificed everyone and everything I knew in order to do the right thing and testify against Quentin Kincaid."

A man she'd worked more than five years for, whom she'd thought of as a kind businessman and friend. That must have been a betrayal, too, when she'd realized he wasn't a simple business owner but the leader of a major crime organization and a terrorist intent on wiping out an entire family to eliminate his competition and settle some personal grudge. When Shae had overheard a phone call from one of Kincaid's lieutenants regarding the assassination attempt, she'd dug deeper, terrified but determined to save lives. She'd presented the FBI with a plethora of evidence at great personal cost. Mason resisted the urge to reach out to her, try to soothe her. He doubted she'd appreciate the gesture, no matter how badly he wanted to ease her pain.

"Sometimes I wish I'd never overheard that conversation, never learned of his intent to eliminate the Pesci family," she said, so softly he had to strain to hear her over the rain pounding against the vehicle. "Does that make me a bad person?"

"No." He did reach for her then, gripped her hand in his and squeezed. "Absolutely not. It makes you human, Shae. You've lived in fear, not only for yourself but for Gracie, for more than six years. And you did it alone. That was a tremendous sacrifice. Does it make you a bad person for wishing it hadn't happened? No. But the fact that you came forward, testified under great threat to your own well-being and saved lives in the process makes you one of the most selfless, courageous people I know."

She squeezed his hand back, then released it to swipe away the tears tracking down her cheeks. "Thank you."

The loss of contact when he'd wanted so badly to reassure

her hurt more than he'd admit to himself. But a glance in the rearview mirror at the black SUV with darkly tinted windows barreling up on the agents behind them had him shoving aside the sense of loss. "Hold on."

Chapter Six

Instinct had Shae clutching the handle above the door as her gaze shot to the side-view mirror. "Is that Kincaid's men?"

"Most likely." He eased down on the gas pedal, increasing their speed, gaze flicking between the road ahead and the vehicle coming up fast behind them. He tapped the Bluetooth device in his ear and asked, "Did you call for backup?"

"On its way," the agent in the vehicle behind them responded smoothly over the car's speakers. "You go ahead. We'll run interference."

Mason accelerated just as the sound of gunfire erupted from behind them—not a pistol, but an automatic weapon of some sort. Shae turned to look over her shoulder, first at Gracie, who was mercifully sleeping through this, then out the rear window. A moment later, their bodyguards' vehicle lurched and rolled over twice before coming to a stop upside down. The SUV pursuing them didn't slow as it careened around the wreck.

"Mason." She gripped tighter, praying fervently for some way out of this.

"I saw." He made another call as the vehicle gained on them and relayed the situation to Zac.

Shae couldn't see any way out. On their right, an already

flooded ditch cut off any hope of escape. To the left, a patch of woods separated the road from a set of railroad tracks, where a mile-long cargo train lumbered alongside them.

Mason accelerated. "Where can I get across?"

Across?

"Two miles ahead," came Zac's response through the earpiece.

He increased their already reckless speed. For an instant, the wheels lost their grip.

Shae clamped her teeth together hard to keep from crying out as they began to hydroplane and Mason fought the wheel for control. The last thing she wanted was to wake Gracie as another dangerous situation unfolded. Shae wanted to close her eyes, wanted to let go and trust Mason, trust God would see them safe, but she didn't dare. She couldn't.

Rain poured across the windshield faster than the wipers could keep up, reducing visibility to nothing more than a blur, and still Mason raced ahead.

"Mason…"

"It'll be okay. Just hold on."

Gracie's eyes opened, and she lurched upright, gripping the armrests on her seat. "Mommy?"

"It's okay, honey."

"Where are we going?" The little girl looked around, disoriented, clearly sensing some sort of danger but not seeming to comprehend where it was coming from.

"Somewhere safe," Mason blurted before Shae could say anything. "I'm taking you and your mom to a new house, where no bad guys will be able to find you."

She glanced at Shae for confirmation, and Shae nodded.

"Why are we going so fast?"

"So the bad guys won't know where we went."

Gracie nodded, seeming to accept Mason's answers, though she still clung tightly to the armrest with one hand and Mr. Cuddles with the other.

Mason began to pull ahead of the train.

Shae's heart jumped into her throat when she instantly realized what he'd meant by *across*. "Oh, no. No way. Mason."

"It'll be fine."

She stared at the train, literally thousands of tons of metal flying down the tracks. She'd often pointed them out to Gracie when they were driving alongside one or got caught at a crossing, and they'd try to guess what its variety of cars in all different shapes and sizes might hold. But the sheer size of that hulking beast speeding toward them... "But—"

"Can you do me a favor, Gracie?" Mason asked.

"Uh-huh."

"Just relax and close your eyes, okay, honey?"

"Why?"

He blew out a breath that under other circumstances Shae might have found amusing. Now, not so much. "It's a game."

Gracie gazed warily at him in the rearview mirror, an expression Shae suddenly realized was so similar to her father's. "What kind of game?"

"You close your eyes and take a guess how many cars you think are on that train, and your mom and I will count them and see if you're right."

She offered a tentative smile and closed her eyes, hugging Mr. Cuddles close. "Okay. They're closed."

He shifted in the seat, eased toward the shoulder. "All right, Gracie. How many do you think there are?"

As they rounded a curve, the tracks still running parallel, a dirt road came into view.

"Um. I think, like...a million."

Mason forced a strained laugh as he maintained a parallel course but pulled ahead of the roaring locomotive. "I bet you're about right. I'll count."

Shae held her breath, gaze riveted on the train, fear reaching up and choking her.

"One, two, three..." He swerved onto the muddy road at

the last minute, probably taking the turn on two wheels. The long wail of the train's horn drowned out any other sound as Mason nipped across the tracks, crashing through the crossing gates, leaving them in splinters and barely making it ahead of the locomotive. Then he looked in his rearview mirror and muttered, "Please, don't try it."

The sound of the train's brakes screeching and metal being torn apart echoed through the deserted area.

Gracie screamed and clapped her hands over her ears.

Mason hissed as he let off the gas, finally slowing their forward momentum as they bounced and jostled down the dirt road that only seemed to lead farther into the endless expanse of forest. He tapped his earpiece. "We're clear."

"The vehicle in pursuit?" the agent asked.

"No. We're clear, but I need a way out of here since the train is stopping and I won't be able to go back that way." He kept his gaze on the mirror, and Shae wondered if the horror in his expression was reflected back at him.

"Why didn't they just stop?" Shae asked softly as she swallowed the lump in her throat and reached back for Gracie's hand.

"They were probably more afraid of returning to Sebastian empty-handed than they were of the train." He stopped the car and twisted to see the wreckage behind him, then used his sleeve to wipe the sweat from his brow, the only outward sign of stress he'd shown.

"What kind of monster is he?" Shae wondered out loud.

"You don't want to know." He glanced at Gracie. "You okay?"

She sniffed. "Uh-huh."

"Guess what?"

"Wh-what?"

"I think you were right." He smiled at her, then turned back around and started slowly forward. "I lost count, but it seems to me there were just about a million cars."

Her smile was tentative, but it touched her eyes. "That's what I thought."

His phone beeped with an incoming call, and he tapped his earpiece. "Payne."

"I'm worried the safe house might be compromised as well, but we've arranged for another."

Mason pulled his phone from his pocket and handed it to Shae. "Enter the address into the GPS, please. Go ahead whenever you're ready, Zac."

He gave her the address, and she programmed it in. Just about half an hour north of where they were.

"You can make a right onto the paved road at the next intersection. Just follow it around and it'll get you headed back in the right direction."

"Thanks, Zac. The agents behind us?"

"No."

He blew out a breath. His hand shook as he raked it through his hair, then pressed his fingers to his eyes. "Ah, man."

"Yeah. Let me know when you reach the safe house."

"Will do." And he disconnected, removed the Bluetooth from his ear and tossed it into the cup holder harder than necessary.

"I'm sorry about your guys." Any loss of life hit her hard, but she found it nearly unbearable that she couldn't help feeling some sense of responsibility for all of these deaths. She closed her eyes, prayed for the souls of all those who'd died protecting them, prayed God would have mercy on those who'd died pursuing them, even if they had meant to harm or kill them. She wondered what could have gone so wrong in their lives that could have turned them into killers. Or had they simply been born evil? She had a feeling there was nothing simple about any of this.

They rode in silence, the hum of the tires against the pavement lulling Gracie back to sleep. The rain had finally eased up the farther north they'd driven and was now nothing more than a steady drizzle. Shae's mind begged her to allow it to shut down, even if only for a few minutes. She needed rest, had to have some downtime to recharge. Her eyes drifted closed, and before she knew it, she was back in the swamp, Gracie held tightly against the gunman, weapon pressed against—

She jerked back awake with a gasp.

"It'll take a while." Mason's eyes held only understanding.

"I suppose." Though she doubted she'd ever be able to close her eyes again without reliving that terror. "I just hope Gracie will be okay when this is all said and done."

"Zac has counselors on his team as well." He shrugged and turned his attention back to the road. "It might be something to think about."

She nodded her appreciation. "Thank you."

"If you decide that's the route you want to go, let me know and I'll talk to Zac."

She tilted her head, studied him. "That's it?"

"What do you mean?"

"You don't have an opinion? Don't want to discuss it? You're just going to leave it up to me to decide what's best for Gracie?" As if it didn't matter to him one way or the other?

He frowned. "Why wouldn't I?"

She shook her head. "Nothing. Forget it."

He started to speak, then seemed to think better of it and let the subject drop as the computerized voice of the GPS led him through a small town that appeared as if it had been suspended somewhere in the mid-1900s.

She couldn't decide whether she should be angry or relieved that he'd leave such an important decision completely up to her. Maybe he just figured she knew what was best for Gracie, since she had the benefit of five years raising her. Or perhaps he just wasn't interested in playing a role in her life. Either way, it shouldn't bother her. She'd always raised Gracie on her own and was perfectly capable of making decisions based on what would be best for her daughter. Had even dreaded the idea of sharing her when Mason first reappeared. So what was her problem? Why did it matter that Mason didn't even want to discuss Gracie's needs?

The answer hit her like a battering ram—because he wouldn't be there to discuss anything. He was going to get them somewhere safe and then leave. Again. Which was fine, especially since it wasn't only her heart on the line this time. She'd loved him once—probably still did, if she were being honest with herself—but she wasn't alone now. If he became a part of their lives and then took off again, Gracie would be hurt, too. No one needed that. The best thing they could do was work together to put an end to the Kincaid organization and allow Shae and Gracie to move on with their lives in peace. Who knew? If things went right, maybe they could even return to Boggy Meadows and resume the life they'd just been forced to abandon. Did she dare hope for that, or was it a fool's dream? Either way, whatever the future held, it seemed it would be her and Gracie on their own navigating it. A happily-ever-after with Mason Payne wasn't meant to be.

"Mommy?"

She ignored the hole in her gut. "Yes, baby?"

"Is it almost time to go to Katie's Christmas Eve party?"

Even knowing it wasn't a possibility, Shae glanced at the dashboard clock and couldn't believe it had been only around fourteen hours since their ordeal had started. "No, sweetheart."

"But we're supposed to help set up," Gracie whined.

"I know, baby, but it's not safe to go back to Boggy Meadows right now."

"Because of the bad men?" Soft sniffles had Shae digging through the backpack for tissues.

She handed a small package back to Gracie and kept one for herself. "Yes."

"But, Mommy, I really want to go. How about church in the middle of the night?"

Midnight mass on Christmas Eve had been a tradition since

before Gracie was born, where Shae would often pray for Mason's safety and that he'd return to them. She could only laugh at the irony. This mess wasn't exactly what she'd had in mind. "We'll have to see."

Gracie kicked the back of Shae's seat, startling her. "It's not fair. You promised we could go."

"I know, honey, but there's nothing I can do about this situation. It's beyond my control, so how about we just make the best of it?" She sucked in a deep breath, searching for patience. None of this was Gracie's fault. She wasn't even old enough to understand most of what was happening.

Gracie gave up arguing and started to cry instead. Shae preferred the anger. With a sigh, she turned to look Gracie in the eye over the seatback. "Listen to me, Gracie. I promise you, once this is over, we'll have a Christmas Eve party, okay?"

She sniffed and scrubbed her hands over cheeks that were red and raw from crying. "A party at our house?"

Something Shae had never done before. While they often attended church functions or gatherings at Reva's house, Shae only rarely entertained. And when she did, it was limited to Reva and Katie. Under the circumstances, she'd never been comfortable inviting a group of people into her home, her safe space. Except now it was no longer safe. Could she ever return to that little house? Even if they did take down the Kincaids? She doubted it. "Yes, honey. We'll have a party at our house, and you can invite Katie and Miss Reva and some of your friends from school and faith formation if you want."

"Uh-huh. Okay." As she scooted up straighter in the seat, the package of tissues dropped unnoticed from her lap to the floor. "And can we have pizza and soda…"

Gracie got herself all wound up with plans for a party that would probably never happen as Mason spoke to Zac on the phone, off speaker now. Shae's thoughts turned inward, to what they'd have to do if she ever hoped to have the life she'd just outlined for Gracie. She'd always been content to stay at home with Gracie, but now she wanted more than that. She wanted to live her life to the fullest, not just survive. And in order to do that, Sebastian Kincaid had to be found and dealt with. She'd gotten through one Kincaid trial—barely—and she'd get through this one, too. Which meant getting enough evidence to put him away for good.

She saw no other choice. Mason would have to leave them to go undercover.

Mason backed into the driveway of a small stucco house on the outskirts of town. Situated in one of thousands of neighborhoods just like it that could be found across Florida, nothing about it stood out. Perfect for their needs. "Wait here."

Leaving Shae and Gracie in the running SUV in case they had to make a quick getaway, Mason climbed out and surveilled the neighborhood. He walked the perimeter of the house, separated from the houses on either side by about thirty feet and a low, tan stucco wall. Satisfied that everything seemed quiet, Mason punched the key code into a lockbox on the front porch, took out the key and opened the front door. A quick recon of the minimally furnished three-bedroom, two-bathroom house showed all was well.

Leaving the front door standing open, he jogged back to the SUV and opened the passenger-side door. "You get Gracie. I'll get the bags."

Shae nodded without saying anything. She'd been quiet since Gracie's tantrum, and Mason hadn't known how to ease any of their fears. They were right to be afraid.

Without a word, he waited at Shae's side, trying to appear casual as he slowly scanned the oak-lined street, the yards, the few people walking along the sidewalks—one guy chasing after a kid on a tricycle, a woman walking a golden retriever and an elderly couple in what looked like brand-new jogging suits speed walking like their lives depended on it.

To anyone who happened to notice, Mason, Shae and Gracie would look like a family who'd rented an Airbnb for the holidays. As soon as Shae had lifted Gracie out of the car and into her arms, Mason closed the car door behind them and hurried them inside. There would be no lingering in the yard, no strolling the sidewalks, no recording Gracie's antics. Because they weren't a family. Shae and Gracie were a family, and Mason was their bodyguard. He'd do well to remember that lest he become too attached, just like the first time he'd been charged with Shae's protection.

He stuffed the keys into his pocket and set Shae's backpack on the tiled foyer floor beside the door. "There are two bedrooms next to each other in the back of the house—one with a queen-size bed and one with bunk beds—you can take either or both. The one closest to the living room will be for the FBI agents they're send—"

"Whoa. Wait. What?" Shae froze with Gracie half lowered to the floor for a moment before straightening, her daughter still in her arms. "What FBI agents? I thought you were protecting us."

"I am." There was no need to elaborate on the fact that he was no happier about the situation than she was. It would serve no purpose but to worry her even more. "I'll sleep on the couch now and then when I need to, but the FBI agents will be here, too. Whether we like it or not, they're still in charge of the official investigation into the Kincaids."

She hugged Gracie closer, eyed the front door over her shoulder, looking about ready to turn and bolt.

"Zac will have his own people in place as well, but the FBI presence is nonnegotiable." And Zac had negotiated, insistently…and loudly. At least he'd managed to talk them down from sending marshals as well. The marshals' service would only take over if and when Shae had to go back into official witness protection. "They wouldn't budge on it, Shae, so Zac had no choice but to acquiesce if he wants them to share information. It makes more sense to cooperate and share information than to run two separate investigations."

"You'll still be here, though?"

He wouldn't lie to her, nor would he flee in the night like a coward, but he didn't want her to be any more frightened than necessary, either, so he offered her the best he could. "Until I know you're safe."

She said nothing, simply stared at him with Gracie clinging tightly to her neck, legs wrapped around Shae's waist like she might never feel safe enough to let go again.

"Look, Shae." It would be a lot easier to convince her this was necessary if he was fully onboard himself. But, while he understood the importance of interagency cooperation, appreciated the willingness of local authorities to coordinate with Zac's team, he still didn't like the idea of anyone he didn't know involved. Not when they hadn't plugged the leak after last time. "The agents they're sending were handpicked by the local field office director. They have no connection to anyone in the Kincaid organization, but I'm told they all have a background in dealing with organized crime. It's the best-case scenario under the circumstances."

The doorbell rang, and Shae and Gracie both whirled toward the sound.

Whoever was out there could wait a minute, because he refused to force her to accept any situation she was uncomfortable with. If she wouldn't agree to the FBI agents Zac had only told him about on the drive here, they'd have to figure out something else. "If we go on the run, just the three of us, it would keep me from having any active role in the investigation, which could prolong this."

"How do you plan to prove Sebastian Kincaid is trying to ki...uh..." She looked down at Gracie, rubbed circles on her back. "Even with my testimony about what the guy in the swamp said to me, it's still not evidence. How can you prove he's involved?"

"I don't know yet, but we're going to. And, hopefully, take down his entire organization with him."

"Seriously?" She lifted a brow. "We couldn't dismantle the Kincaid organization when we put their boss in prison. What makes you think you can do so now?"

"Because until now, despite being in prison, Quentin was still in charge. Sebastian Kincaid lacks his father's business sense, his discipline and his discretion. It's no surprise his father is testing him. He'll mess up, and when he does, we'll grab him."

The doorbell chimed again. This time, Shae nodded, and he opened the door to two people dressed in dark suits that screamed federal agents: a woman with soft features and blonde hair pulled back into a ponytail and a tall man with black hair going gray at the temples. One look at the equally easily identifiable sedan parked at the curb had Mason biting back a sigh.

The woman held out her hand. "I'm Agent Cassidy Monroe, and this is my partner Agent Jimmy Ronaldo."

Once introductions were made, Cassidy held up a large fast food bag and tipped it back and forth. "Who's hungry?"

Gracie glanced at Shae, who nodded. "Me."

"Do you like chicken nuggets?"

Gracie nodded, seemingly shy with the new agents. It stung that Mason had no clue if it was normal for her to be leery of strangers or if that was a new development since being attacked.

"Why don't you and I go into the kitchen and set up lunch while your mom talks to Mason and Jimmy for a few minutes? You'll be able to see your mom from the table." Cassidy leaned over conspiratorially. "And I'm pretty sure there are some chocolate chip cookies in this bag, too."

Gracie grinned and wiggled out of her mother's arms. When Cassidy reached out to take her hand, Gracie cringed away, then turned back to look at Shae twice in the short walk to the kitchen.

As soon as they were out of earshot, Jimmy updated them on the progress so far. "I don't know how much you've been told, but the three men who were killed in the swamp have all been identified, and they're all connected to the Kincaid organization. The one who survived was taken into custody and refused to answer questions without an attorney present. Since the attorney of record is on Kincaid's payroll, we have little to no hope he'll take a plea deal in return for testimony against Kincaid."

"I'm not surprised." Sebastian liked control—it kept things running his way. The attorney would no doubt report right back to him if their suspect talked, and the guy would have an accident soon after, long before he ever had a chance to testify.

That was one of the biggest reasons law enforcement could never get to Kincaid—witnesses, or lack thereof. The few who had ever been willing to talk were killed or made to disappear before they saw a courtroom. Shae was the rare exception, someone who'd stumbled onto information accidentally and had managed to get to law enforcement and be placed in protective custody before Quentin Kincaid had even realized what was happening. Because he'd not only trusted her but had underestimated her as well. And even though they'd gotten Shae to a safe house early on, it hadn't stopped Kincaid from finding her. They'd had to move her several times that year and had never found the leak. "What about Lucas Gianelli? The guy I identified from the video at Gracie's pageant. Were you able to locate him or determine the identity of his partner?"

Jimmy shook his head. "No, nothing."

These people were like shadows, hovering, then disappearing in an instant. Frustrated, Mason tried to think.

"We did, however, locate Sebastian Kincaid."

That must have just happened, since Zac hadn't informed Mason yet. "Where is he?"

"He landed in a private aircraft at a small field in central Florida sometime yesterday morning."

So he'd come to Florida to oversee the situation himself. Not surprising, considering what was at stake. "Where is he now?"

Color peaked in the agent's cheeks. "We don't know that, just that he arrived in the state. We have people working alongside Zac Jameson and local police to track his movements from the time he landed."

Mason only nodded. The fact that they'd been able to place him in Florida at all was an accomplishment. "All right. Thank you."

"Sure thing." He hesitated, his gaze flitting to Shae.

"It's okay. Speak freely." Mason had no doubt Shae would handle whatever information the agent shared, just like she'd handled everything else that had been thrown at her so far, throughout the trial and during her life afterward, including the past twenty or so hours.

He winced. "They found the leak in the marshals' office."

Rage poured through Mason. He'd known there must be a leak, but having it confirmed fueled the anger he'd suppressed. "And?"

"He's dead, killed in an 'accident'..." Jimmy rolled his eyes. "A few days after Maria Delarosa was killed."

"Before Sebastian arrived."

"Yeah. Assumption is, Sebastian waited until they'd located Shae, then had the agent eliminated and made the trip." *To see to things personally*, no one said out loud. "That's why no one answered the phone when Shae tried the emergency contact number. The mole took care of that."

"That makes sense." Attack Shae while the marshals' service was scrambling to get things in order. "They had to know someone was dirty."

"It would have taken a little time to figure out who they could trust in the position."

No one. That was the simple answer. Because, somehow,

it seemed Sebastian Kincaid had a way of getting to whomever he needed, if not through bribery or blackmail, then with intimidation. Or had it been Quentin who'd overseen the operation? "Yeah."

"So, that's it for now. I'll update you as soon as I know anything else. We've been ordered to give your boss full cooperation. That man definitely has some pull."

Mason grinned. *Pull* was a nice word for it. "That he does."

Jimmy shook Mason's hand, nodded to Shae, then joined his partner in the kitchen.

Shifting so he and Shae could both keep an eye on Gracie, who was chatting happily with Cassidy while munching on chicken nuggets and fries, Mason tried to order his thoughts. "I'm going to step outside to make a few calls. I want to confirm everything Jimmy told us with Zac."

She frowned. "You don't trust him?"

He glanced into the kitchen, where the two agents sat talking quietly. "It's not that I don't trust him specifically. I don't trust anyone."

"I can understand that." She caught her bottom lip between her teeth, hesitated only a moment. "But you do trust Zac?"

"Completely. Kincaid has a way of getting to people—he bribes them, threatens them, whatever it takes to gain cooperation—but he can't get to Zac." Of that Mason was absolutely certain.

Shae frowned, understandably leery of everyone. "How can you be so sure of that?"

"Because Marty Bowers was Zac's stepbrother."

Shae gasped.

"Yeah." And when he'd gotten the opportunity to send Mason undercover, he'd jumped at it. "He never forgave himself for not being at the hospital when Marty died, even if he had been protecting his family."

"That's awful."

"Yes. It is. That's why I trust Zac so completely. Not only

is he a close friend, but he would never help any member of the Kincaid organization for any reason. You don't spend six years trying to take someone down only to turn around and join them."

"No." She checked Gracie again then lowered her gaze. "No, I suppose not."

Mason reached out, used one finger to lift her chin until she met his gaze. "I'm not going anywhere until you're safe. I'm going to step outside to make some calls right now, but if you need me, just call my cell phone. The number is programmed into your new phone." She held his gaze, then nodded. "Lock the door behind me and go have something to eat with Gracie. Do not open the door for any reason. Zac's people will be here soon, but the FBI agents will open the door for them if I'm not back in yet."

She nodded again.

He opened the door and walked out, determined to find answers.

Chapter Seven

Gracie shook Shae's shoulder, yanking her from sleep. "Wake up, Mommy. It's Christmas."

She pulled Gracie into her arms and hugged her tight, then kissed the top of her head. "Merry Christmas, baby girl."

Gracie flipped onto her stomach in the queen-size bed they'd shared, leaving the bunk beds for Mason or any of the other agents who might need to sleep. She propped her elbows on the pillow and rested her chin in her hands, her eyes filled with hope. "Do you think Santa Claus found me here?"

"Oh, Gracie." They'd gone to bed early the night before with no Christmas Eve celebration, since all of the agents were working; no mass to attend, since Mason had said there was no way to protect them in a public setting; and no further information on a permanent placement for them. She'd thought Florida would be far enough away from New York for them to be safe, and she'd been wrong. It seemed maybe nowhere would be far enough from the Kincaids. And now, she was going to have to disappoint Gracie once more. "Honey, I think maybe—"

A knock at the door interrupted, buying her a precious moment or two before having to watch the joy drain out of her child once again.

"Who is it?"

The door opened a crack, and Cassidy poked her head in. "I thought I heard a little girl awake in here. Merry Christmas."

Gracie sat up and bounced on the bed. "Merry Christmas."

She looked over her shoulder then back at Gracie, grinned and hooked a thumb down the hallway. "I think there might be a surprise out here for you. If you're ready to get up…"

Gracie launched herself off the bed so fast Shae had to laugh. "Did Santa come?"

Cassidy winked at Shae. "I do believe he did."

Gracie's excited squeal almost brought Shae to tears. It sounded like Jameson Investigations provided everything, not only what they needed to keep them safe but even gifts for Gracie.

"Why don't you and your mom get dressed and come on out into the living room? Breakfast is just about ready, too."

"Can we, Mommy?" She clasped her hands together. "Please."

"Sure thing." They dressed quickly, Shae donning leggings and a sweatshirt from her flight bag and Gracie putting on her leggings and T-shirt from the day before, since most of what was in the bag didn't fit, including the too-small pajamas she'd worn to bed.

Gracie kept up a nonstop stream of chatter, excited about the possibility of gifts, wondering what they'd have for breakfast, asking if they could maybe have something special for dinner. As excited as Shae was to see some life return to her daughter's eyes and color to her cheeks, she had no idea what to expect when they walked out. No one had said anything to her before she'd gone to bed.

Shae laid a hand on the doorknob, turned to Gracie and smiled. "You ready?"

"Yup." She gripped Shae's hand, hers feeling so delicate, so fragile.

The fact that anyone could want to hurt this child sent a surge of anger rushing through her. She tamped it right back down. No way would she let them take this moment with Gracie from her. "Don't forget to use your manners."

"I know, I know." She bounced up and down, swinging Shae's arm. "Come on."

Shae laughed and swung the door open, and the scent of bacon frying hit her full force. Her stomach growled, and she clapped her free hand over it.

The fact that Gracie stayed beside her, her grip tight as they walked down the hallway, instead of bounding ahead told her the wounds from yesterday's trauma may have diminished, but they were far from gone. She'd have to consider Mason's suggestion and ask him about counselors later.

Shae stepped into the living room and stopped short. Her mouth fell open.

Gracie squealed again, then bolted across the room to the Christmas tree in the corner.

Cassidy nudged Shae's ribs with an elbow. "She seems happy."

"I don't understand." A small tree had been set up in the corner, draped with about a thousand multicolored lights reflecting from red, green and gold glass balls. A pile of gifts was spread beneath the tree. She closed her eyes, shook her head, opened them again. Nope, not a hallucination brought on by too much stress. It was all still there.

Then Cassidy leaned closer and whispered, "Mason didn't want her to go without getting to celebrate Christmas."

"I..." But she had no clue what to say, couldn't have forced words past the lump in her throat if she'd tried. How could he have gotten all this done so quickly? The fact that he'd even thought to do it at all filled her with warmth. She glanced into the kitchen, where three agents sat at the table and two were busy setting out platters of food. "Where is Mason?"

"He had to run out, but he'll be back any minute." She waggled her eyebrows. Wherever Mason had gone, Cassidy was obviously in on it—and highly amused.

Gracie picked up a gift from under the tree, held it close to her ear and shook it gently back and forth. "Mommy, this one's for me. It's from Santa Claus. See? I knew he would find me. Can I open it?"

"Actually," Cassidy intervened, as she checked something on her phone, then stuffed it quickly back into her pocket, "why don't you hold off for a minute?"

Shae's gut cramped. The last thing she wanted was to pull Gracie out of there and go on the run again. *Oh, please, not today. Please give us just one day to rest, to recuperate, to celebrate.*

"Okay." Gracie set the package down, ran back to Shae and threw her arms around Shae's legs.

Cassidy bent low to talk to her. "Can you do something for me?"

Gracie looked at Shae, then back at Cassidy. "Okay."

She smiled. "Close your eyes."

Gracie did as instructed.

"Keep them closed, now." She walked to the front door, checked that Gracie still had her eyes closed. "No peeking."

"I won't."

Shae was happy to see Gracie seemed to be coming out of her shell a little and thrilled she'd remembered to use her manners.

Then Cassidy swung the front door open, and Mason plunged through, a wiggling mass of golden fur on a leash at his side. He met Shae's gaze as Cassidy first shut the door behind him then discreetly disappeared into the kitchen. The look he gave her—half triumph, half apology, mostly am-I-in-trouble—nearly made Shae laugh out loud. She gave him a nod.

Then his expression turned to pure joy. "You can open your eyes now, Gracie. We have a special visitor."

He led the dog toward her as Gracie's eyes popped open.

She screeched loud enough to shatter every eardrum within half a mile. "A doggie!"

The little girl dropped to her knees and wrapped her arms around the ball of fur. The dog licked her face, and she laughed out loud. "He's so cute. What's his name?"

"Storm."

"Is he your dog?"

"Actually, he's a police dog." He reached out, ruffled her dark hair. "We don't get to keep him forever, but he will stay with you and help keep you safe until we find the bad men."

Gracie lowered her face into the dog's fur and sobbed.

Mason looked up at Shae, horrified.

She laid a hand on his shoulder. "It's okay, Mason, they're happy tears."

He glanced back at Gracie, who was still sobbing as she and hugged the dog. "Are you sure?"

"I'm sure."

Looking skeptical, Mason patted Gracie's shoulder and had just started to stand when she launched herself at him, wrapped her arms around his neck and clung tight. "Thank you, thank you, thank you. He's the best."

He hugged her back, closed his eyes and breathed in deeply the scent Shae was so familiar with.

Shae didn't bother to hold back the tears, simply let them roll down her cheeks unimpeded as father and daughter embraced each other. It might be the only chance they ever got to do so.

"I'm glad you like him, Gracie." When she stepped back, Mason took a deep breath and stood. He cleared his throat, twice. "He has a special vest to wear so he'll know when he's supposed to be working. When he's wearing the vest, you won't be able to play with him. When he's not wearing his vest, like right now, you can. You're going to have to help take really good care of him, though. He needs to be fed, and given water, and brushed."

She threw her arms around Shae. "I will. I promise."

And with that, Gracie bolted down the hallway, skidded into a U-turn and ran back toward them, all with the dog in hot pursuit.

Mason's mouth fell open as he watched them barrel through the house like it was their own personal playground. "Uh… I…uh…"

"Yup." But it didn't matter to Shae—the noise, whatever mess they might make…all that mattered to her was the pure joy radiating from her daughter. "I don't know what to say, Mason. Thank you."

"I hope it's okay. When I called Zac to try to help me put together a few things for under the tree, he said he had a K-9 dog available, newly graduated. I didn't want to wake you, but you always talked about getting a puppy, said you'd never had a pet growing up, so I just figured… Plus, I thought it might help her to have something to take care of, something that will protect her and make her feel safe… You know, with—"

"Mason." She popped up on tiptoes and kissed his cheek. "He's perfect. Thank you."

He slid an arm around her shoulders and kissed her temple. "Merry Christmas."

"Merry Christmas, Mason, and thank you for making it so special for Gracie. And for me." She leaned into his side and put her arm around his waist, enjoying the strength encircling her, then rested her head against his shoulder, letting her tension dissipate. The future might hold no hope for them, but she could at least enjoy this one moment of comfortable camaraderie.

The dog bolted full force across the living room, sprang onto the couch, hit the back cushion, twisted like an acrobat and reversed course instantly, then ran the other way, all with

Gracie tagging along behind him squealing and clapping her hands. If ever there could be a perfect moment amid the recent bedlam, this was it. Shae half wondered if he would really calm down and be a working dog when he had his vest on.

"There's something else I have to tell you," Mason said quietly.

"What's that?" Gracie and Storm were getting a little too rambunctious. She was going to have to corral them…in a minute.

"We found Lucas Gianelli—"

She stiffened. The man Mason had identified from the pageant video. That pageant seemed like a lifetime ago. "Okay."

"He's staying at a low-budget motel about twenty miles from here. I'm going to—"

"Stop." She knew exactly what was coming, and she did not want to hear it. Not now. Not today. Not ever, really, though she knew she couldn't prevent his eventual departure. "Please, Mason. Give me this one moment in time to just be happy…" *With you*, though she'd never say that part out loud. "I know it won't last, but I'm so tired, and I just need peace for a little while."

"Okay." He kissed the top of her head, then released her, the few inches now separating them seeming like a chasm the size of the Grand Canyon.

"Come on, Gracie." She forced herself to step away. He was leaving, even sooner than she'd feared. They were in danger, Gracie was in danger, and Mason was leaving. Again. The fact that he was trying to find a way to protect them, to keep Kincaid from finding them, didn't help ease the pain or the fear. Even if she didn't trust him to stay, she felt safer when he was around. "Honey, you have to stop running around now. Don't you want to open your presents?"

She skidded to a stop in front of Shae, and the dog plowed into the backs of Gracie's legs, buckled her knees and had her flopping over backward in a fit of giggles.

Shae laughed, though much of the joy that had filled her a few minutes ago had turned to dread, and helped Gracie back onto her feet. She could tell Gracie was more interested in the dog than the gifts now, so she said, "Come on, you two. Why don't we snuggle on the couch and have a story, then you can have breakfast and open the rest of your presents?"

"Okay, Mommy." She hopped onto the couch and snuggled into the corner. The dog followed, curling himself up beside her and placing his head in her lap.

Shae sat beside them as Mason lingered, arms folded, one foot crossed over the other, shoulder against the entryway wall. If possible, he seemed even more incredibly handsome than ever. She sighed and turned away. "What kind of story would you like?"

"A Christmas one."

She had to lean over the dog, who seemed very content to lie between them, to put an arm around Gracie. She began the story of baby Jesus that Gracie enjoyed so much, twisting strands of Gracie's hair between her fingers as Gracie stroked Storm's soft head. When she reached the point where Mary and Joseph arrived at the inn, Gracie interrupted.

"Mommy?"

"Yes?"

"Were there dogs at the stable when baby Jesus was born?"

She'd never thought about it before. "I think there probably were."

Her daughter looked down at Storm, wrapped her arms around him and hugged him close. "And do you think they kept baby Jesus safe so no bad people could hurt Him?"

Oh, baby. No child should have to know such fear. "I do, honey, yes."

"Will Storm keep me safe?"

Pain lanced her heart. "Yes, I think he will protect you."

She looked up at Shae, tears shimmering in her eyes, tipping over thick, dark lashes to roll down her cheeks. "And then the bad men won't be able to get us?"

"No, baby, they won't."

"Okay." Gracie crawled over Storm and lay down, lowering her head to Shae's lap. The dog rearranged himself on her other side protectively. Shae looked up to find Mason still watching them from the entryway and had no doubt he was procrastinating and should already have left to return to his undercover persona. At least this time, he'd say goodbye and take the memory of his daughter with him.

Mason pulled into the garage parking lot next to the motel where Lucas Gianelli was reportedly staying. He'd spent a tense Christmas Day with Shae, Gracie and the other agents, giving Shae the moment of rest she'd asked for, but now it was time to get back to work. He needed to resume his place in Kincaid's organization, hopefully without anyone realizing he'd disappeared for a couple of days. He usually worked dark, no contact with Zac's team for long stretches. This time, he was going in with backup. This time, he wanted to get the evidence he needed to take out the Kincaids all at once. "Testing, one, two, three."

"Gotcha, Mason," Zac responded in his earpiece. The fact that Zac had come himself meant a lot. Mason knew he was in good hands, which meant he could push Lucas harder than he might otherwise, confident Zac would know when to hang back and let things play out and when to move in if Mason got into trouble. "You're sure you're good with this, Mason?"

Was he? They'd come up with the plan in the early hours of the morning, deciding to apply pressure to Lucas in the hopes of getting enough to arrest him and then get him to flip on Sebastian. This would never work in New York, where the Kincaids had too many loyal accomplices; they could either spring Gianelli from prison or see him eliminated there. But here in Florida, there might be some small hope he'd turn against Kincaid in return for immunity or a reduced sentence. Especially if he was more loyal to Quentin than Sebastian. They could play on his fear of Sebastian, his doubt about the younger Kincaid's leadership.

So Mason had to get his head in the game. But instead of reviewing his past relationship with Lucas on the ride over, searching for weaknesses to exploit, planning ways to gain information, Mason's thoughts had been filled with Shae and Gracie, their fear like a knife in his heart as he wondered what their lives could have been like if Shae had never stumbled upon Quentin Kincaid's murder plot.

Mason shrugged off thoughts of the past. Could-haves and what-ifs would do nothing to help them now.

They said God works in mysterious ways. Mason had fallen too far from his faith while undercover, excusing the theft, the intimidation, the beatings, all in the name of trying to do the right thing. He wouldn't go that route again. If he couldn't get Kincaid without resorting to that kind of behavior, they'd have to find another way. Seeing how Shae's faith had strengthened her, had led her through what had to have been a difficult and frightening six years, made him rethink the path he'd followed, the behaviors he'd excused. It was time to return to the right path, time to fully embrace the beliefs he'd always held.

He climbed out of the clunker he'd been driving while undercover, which Zac had had shipped down from New York for him. The neighborhood seemed more industrial than commercial, with a row of warehouses lining the street across from the garage. Not ideal, considering Kincaid could have men in any of them.

Trusting Zac to take care of anything that went on outside, he entered through the roll-up garage door. While the Kincaids mainly ran their business out of New York, they owned properties all over the country to help them import and ship product as well as launder their vast fortune.

"Hey! Anyone here?" His voice echoed through the space,

empty but for an old Cadillac on one of the lifts. He already knew Lucas was somewhere on the premises. Zac's agents had had him under surveillance. He strolled through the reception area, tapped a bell sitting on the dust-covered counter, then leaned over the counter and yelled into the back storage room, "Hello?"

Lucas appeared from the back, amid shelving units filled with boxes, where Mason doubted anything legal was going on, spread his hands on the counter and rested his considerable bulk. The rusty stains beneath his nails probably had nothing to do with fixing cars. "What's up, man?"

Only years of undercover experience allowed Mason to school his features enough to keep the absolute rage from showing. He had to stuff his hands into his pockets to stop himself from pummeling this guy at the thought of him attacking Shae and Gracie. "Hey, Luke."

Lucas narrowed his gaze. Either Mason hadn't hidden his anger as well as he'd thought or something else had raised Luke's suspicions. "Where you been, dude? Kenny's been looking for you. Said you were supposed to be down here helping with the boss's priority job."

Shae.

So much for hoping his absence hadn't been noticed. Kenny was the guy Mason usually worked with, low-level but trying hard to work his way up. If he thought for one instant Mason wasn't who he claimed to be, he'd have tripped over his own feet running to tattle to Sebastian.

He flung an arm toward the lot where he'd left the car, which was conveniently pouring smoke from its engine compartment, and let a bit of anger slip. "Car took a dump on the way down here. Been filling it with water and babying it all the way. Stupid pile of junk starts shaking every time I hit sixty and needs a break every hundred miles or so."

Lucas eyed him for a moment as if weighing the honesty in his words. He must have passed the test, because Lucas rounded the counter and led Mason through the garage and out to the lot. "Let's take a look."

"Yeah, thanks." When Lucas clapped him on the back, Mason's skin crawled. He considered it a win when he resisted the urge to throw him to the ground and cuff him—barely. "Anything goin' on since you got down here?" At his lower level, Mason should only know there was an important job to do here, not any details.

Lucas yanked a greasy rag from the back pocket of his jeans, wiped his hands, then stuffed it back into his pocket. "Open the hood, Mace."

Mason did as instructed, loath to turn his back on Lucas but knowing Zac probably had the man in his sights. "Do I need to get up to speed on anything?"

"Are you kidding me? You think these storms have been bad…" Lucas gestured up toward the billowing, dark gray clouds stacked above them with a wary look. "That ain't nothin' compared to Kincaid's temper since last night."

Mason swallowed hard, his Adam's apple bobbing as if nervous, and added just the right combination of fear and respect to his tone. "What happened last night? He didn't notice I wasn't here yet, did he?"

"Nah. I doubt he even knows who you are, tough guy." Lucas leaned over the engine compartment, fiddled with a few things Mason didn't pay any attention to. He had no idea what Zac's guy had done to make it smoke like it was, but it didn't matter to him if the car got fixed or not. "Kincaid didn't say anything about you, but boy, was he ticked."

"About what? You guys only been down here, like, two or three days. What could have gone wrong in that short a time?" He held his breath, waited. He needed to get something. If Lucas didn't say anything to incriminate himself, they'd have to come up with another plan.

"Hey, Luke!" The front door banged shut behind a tall, rangy guy wearing a red baseball cap crammed down over a

brown mop of frizz. Though Mason had never seen him before, he sort of matched the description Shae had given them
of the second shooter from the pageant. The build seemed
about right, and the coloring, but she'd described his hair as
short. Could be it had been slicked back or tied in a tail she
didn't notice. "What's going on?"

"Mace here's havin' car trouble. Just tryin' to help 'im out."
Lucas pulled out the dipstick to check the oil.

"Yeah, well, Kincaid says to get back to work. He needs that
stuff set up and ready to move in an hour." He gestured toward
the garage, which seemed to have no actual automotive work
going on but for a lone car on a lift with no tools in evidence.

"Yeah, yeah." He wiped the dipstick on the rag from his
pocket, checked it and replaced it.

"Want me to help out?" Mason offered, careful not to appear too eager. "It's the least I can do, since you're fixing my
car and all."

The new guy eyed Lucas as he lifted his cap, slicked his
hair back, then fitted the cap back on.

"You ever worked with C-4?" Lucas asked.

Mason shrugged. "Sure."

"Whatever, then." He hooked a thumb toward the garage.
"Go with Ronnie, and he'll show you what to do."

"All right." Leaving Lucas to puzzle over the car, Mason
strolled into the garage with Ronnie, his mind racing. He was
sure Lucas would have told him more if Ronnie hadn't shown
up when he did. He paused when Ronnie held the storage room
door open. "Oh, man, hang on. I'll be right back."

"Where you going?"

He had to get back to Lucas—alone—see if he could push
him into confessing to having gone after Shae. Although, if
Mason wasn't successful, they might be able to get them on
the C-4, if Ronnie admitted they were using it for something
illegal. And since he could see no reason an automotive repair shop would need explosives, there was a good possibility

they could prove that. He checked to be sure Lucas was still occupied, looked around to be sure Zac's men hadn't jumped the gun and decided to move at the mention of taking Mason into a roomful of explosives. All clear. Apparently, Zac trusted Mason to signal them if needed. "I forgot to give Lucas the key."

Ronnie shrugged and went inside, letting the door fall shut behind him.

"Did you get pictures of Ronnie?" Mason swiped a hand over his mouth to hide that he was speaking and kept his voice low as he jogged toward the car, praying Lucas wouldn't look in the ignition, where Mason had left the keys hanging, then breathed a sigh of relief when he found him still bent over beneath the hood tinkering with the engine.

"Yes. We're sending it to Angela at the safe house now to see if Shae can ID him as the second gunman," Zac said.

"All right. See if you can trace the C-4." He opened the driver's side door, palmed the keys and slid them into his pocket, then grabbed an old Coke can from the cup holder.

"Already on it."

"Thanks." Knowing who'd supplied the explosives might give them another avenue to pursue. As if in a hurry, Mason yanked the keys from his pocket. "I forgot to leave the keys."

Lucas held out his hand, and Mason tossed him the key ring, then started away. After only two steps, he turned back and snapped his fingers. "Oh, you started to say something about Kincaid being angry before, but you never finished. I wouldn't mind knowing what I'm dealing with."

"Yeah, right," he said distractedly. "He was pissed that the Bennett woman got away."

"Bennett?" Wild horses thundered in his chest.

"Avery Bennett? The chick that testified against his old man? Didn't they even tell you why they needed extra muscle down here?" He rolled his eyes, then used his coverall sleeve to wipe the sweat from his brow. "You know the old man's nearly had it, right? Well, Quentin ordered Sebastian to prove himself if he wants to take control. That's why he came down here himself. He wouldn't have bothered if we were just handling the explosives shipment."

"Oh, right. I didn't recognize the name."

"Uh-huh."

"So some chick got away all by herself?"

He stopped, then straightened and propped his hands on his hips. He aimed a hard gaze at Mason. "What's with all the questions?"

Mason shrugged. "I didn't mean nothin' by it. Just curious."

"Yeah, well, don't be." He stepped forward, pointed a meaty finger at Mason's chest. "We've worked together before, and you're okay, so I'm gonna give you a piece of free advice. You wanna move up? There's room now, because Kincaid lost a few guys in the swamp the other night. Keep your head down, do as you're told and don't ask questions."

"Sure, man, thanks."

"Yup." He returned to work, unscrewed the radiator cap, then looked up at Mason and grinned. "And if you want to move up fast? Get the Bennett broad."

"Yeah?" His gut cramped. "Dead or alive?"

"Don't matter." He scratched his head. "Kincaid sent some of his guys after her yesterday, but it seemed she had help to escape. He went through the roof when he found out she'd slipped out of their grasp. Again. I don't think he cares so much if she's dead—that's the ultimate plan anyway—but don't kill her until you get out of her who came to her rescue last night. Otherwise, instead of moving up, you'll get buried. Kincaid thinks we got ourselves a mole." He yanked the rag out and wiped his hands. "Oh, and make sure you get her kid, too."

"There's a kid?"

"Yeah. He didn't care about her at first..." He laughed. "But I guess after he got shown up yesterday, he's gotta save face, ya know? 'Specially if he's gonna fill the old man's shoes once he croaks."

"Yeah. Got it. Thanks." Mason seethed, barely holding on to control as he nodded. "Were you in on it last night?"

He shot Mason a cocky grin. "I located her, so that saved me. Wasn't my fault those guys couldn't get hold of her when I practically ran her straight into their arms."

"Is that how it actually went down?"

"Doesn't really matter whether it did or it didn't. That's how I spun it to Kincaid, so it got me off the hook." He laughed at that. The fact that three of his comrades had ended up dead didn't seem to matter to him at all.

Mason took a swig of warm Coke as he turned away and started back toward the building, just as Ronnie stormed out of the garage. He caught sight of Mason, gritted his teeth and yanked a pistol from a holster on his hip.

"What'd you do, man? What did you do?" he screamed, spittle spraying from his mouth as he shoved the barrel of the gun hard enough against Mason's head to have him wincing and dropping the Coke as he lifted his hands in surrender. He shoved Mason backward with him as he forced him toward Lucas. "Get in the car!"

Lucas shot his hands in the air. "Whatcha doin'? What's wrong with you, Ronnie?"

"Guy's a mole, man." He tapped the barrel against Mason's head a couple of times, his face red with rage as his gaze shot from one spot to the next like a caged animal searching for escape.

Mason backed up in pace with Ronnie. He had to move, had to get that gun away from his head long enough for someone to get a shot.

Ronnie wasn't relenting. He cupped the side of Mason's head, pressed his nose practically against Mason's and jammed the weapon harder against his head. "Start talking."

Chapter Eight

Shae stood beside the window, off to the side so as not to make a target of herself. Not that there was much to look at, other than a patch of brittle, brownish grass surrounded by a weathered, six-foot-high stockade fence. The safe house was set against the back of the development, so beyond the fence was a sump and a brick wall. Oh, well. At least the sun had chased away enough of the clouds to uncover a patch of blue sky—for the moment.

She sighed and turned away from the window.

Gracie held a bag of training treats and commanded her new companion to sit.

He flopped down, tail wagging, and his tongue lolled out the side of his mouth.

"Good boy." Gracie popped a treat into his mouth as Mason had taught her and petted his head. When he bounced back up to lick her, she started all over again. "Good boy, Storm." She giggled. "Good boy."

Cassidy knocked on the doorjamb. "It's time for Storm's walk, Gracie."

"Can I come this time?"

Cassidy's gaze flicked to Shae, then back to Gracie. "I'm sorry, honey, but not this time."

Shae redirected her daughter's attention. "While Cassidy is walking Storm, why don't you and I go through and organize your new clothes and stuff into the bags?"

She offered a sulky shrug, head down.

Cassidy shot Shae an apologetic look as she clipped Storm's leash on and ushered him out.

"Why can't I walk him?" Gracie whined.

"We've talked about this, Gracie. It's not safe yet." Shae squatted down in front of her so they'd be eye to eye and rubbed her hands up and down Gracie's arms, which felt cold. She grabbed a sweatshirt that was hanging over the arm of a chair and held it out to her. "Here, put this on."

Gracie snatched the sweatshirt from her hand and threw it back on the chair. Then she flopped down on top of it and folded her arms across her chest in a belligerent posture Shae had no tolerance for—under normal circumstances, anyway. But these were far from normal circumstances. "I hate it here. I wanna go home."

"Gracie, please…" But what could she say to her? Shae wanted to go home, too, but Boggy Meadows was no longer home. She prayed for patience, for guidance, for some way to help her daughter cope with the reality of life on the run. But would this be her life forever? Shae had worked hard to give Gracie a happy childhood, to make her feel loved, to make her part of a community, even though the thought had frightened Shae. How long would they spend trying to outrun her past? A year? Five years? Ten?

She relaxed her shoulders, seeking to ease the tension coiled in her neck and back, concentrating on a few deep breaths so she wouldn't lose her patience and say something she'd later regret. If life on the run was the life they had, Shae would just be grateful they were alive and together and make the best of a less-than-ideal situation. She picked up the new pink sequined backpack Gracie had received for Christmas. "I'm going to get us out of here as soon as I can, Gracie, but we have to be ready to go if the opportunity presents itself. So let's pack up."

She eyed Shae, seemed to be weighing her options, then finally stood, though the defiant attitude remained. "Whatever."

Figuring it was the best she was going to get, Shae held the backpack out to her. "Put this on the bed, and we'll go through your things and pack what you'd like to keep with you."

Gracie shrugged.

Ignoring the tantrum, Shae started to unpack the flight bag. While Gracie's bag would be for special things she wanted to keep with her, there was also a new duffel bag, thanks to Mason's generosity, for Shae to pack most of her own, as well as Gracie's, new clothes into. But she still needed the emergency bag, the one that had to come with them, if she was forced to leave everything else behind. Including Mason. Ugh…she needed to get off this emotional roller coaster.

They'd talked about a future back then, a home, a puppy. Though they hadn't yet discussed having children, in the back of Shae's mind the plan had always existed. And now here she was. Mason had popped into her life just long enough to open old wounds, bring the pain she'd managed to compartmentalize back to the forefront…and save their lives. Would she ever see him again?

She checked the time on her phone. It seemed like he'd been gone for days, but in reality, it had only been a few hours. For all she knew, he hadn't even met up with his contacts yet. She twisted her fingers together, anxiety sending a wave of nausea crashing through her. He was fine. He'd be fine. He'd survived six years undercover. But would he disappear for another six years? Maybe show up when Gracie was going into her teens? If he ever came back.

She choked down the scream threatening to rip free. Mason might have no role in their future, but Shae still had to move forward. Mason was doing his part to protect their daughter, and she had to do her part, too. And that meant pulling herself together and getting ready to go on the run once again.

Gracie sorted through her gifts, trying to choose which things meant the most to her. She opened a small box and pulled out a charm bracelet and examined the three small charms hanging from it—a cross, a sheep that Mason had explained was to represent her part in the pageant and a heart, so she could always remember how loved she was. Most of her other gifts had been practical, like clothing and pajamas, or meant to keep her occupied, like the tablet and the coloring books and crayons. But that one had been special, meaningful, and she slid it onto her wrist before going back to her task.

Shae turned away and dumped the remainder of the flight bag onto the bed. The flash drive containing the pictures from Gracie's Christmas pageant dropped onto the top of the pile. She picked it up. "Hey, Gracie, want to see the pictures from the pageant?"

She perked up, though tears still glistened in her eyes. "Okay."

Shae opened the laptop Angela had provided, then plugged the drive in and sat down on the bed. "Come sit with me."

Gracie scrambled across the bed and snuggled into Shae's arm, a moment Shae wished could last forever. She pulled Gracie tighter against her and set the computer on her lap.

Just as pictures began to load, Cassidy returned and unleashed Storm. "Do you guys need anything else?"

"No, thank you. We're okay for now, but thank you for everything." She didn't know how they'd have made it through the past two days without the other woman's help. Not only had she been wonderful with Gracie and Storm, but she'd provided an ear in the wee hours of this morning after Mason had left, when Shae had needed someone to talk to. At least he'd stayed through Christmas day as Shae had asked.

"Of course." She smiled, emitting a warmth that soothed Shae's raw nerves. "If there's anything else you need, just let me know. Oh, and we're probably going to put together a lunch order in about an hour if you guys are hungry."

Storm launched himself onto the bed and curled against Gracie's side. Shae reached for a stuffed dog toy Gracie had left on the nightstand and handed it to him.

"Thanks." Shae waited for the door to close, then clicked on the first video. It showed Gracie dancing around the house in her pajamas two days before the pageant. She'd been so excited, her eyes filled with innocence, and love, and hope. Had some of that dimmed permanently? Shae hoped not.

The video ended, and Shae scrolled to the next picture. While Shae scrolled, Gracie narrated every step, as if Shae hadn't been present in the moment. Tension seeped from both of them, and when Gracie laughed out loud, Shae finally breathed easier. They'd be okay. Gracie would be okay. It might take some time, and the worst of it might not be over, but they'd get through it together, and they'd come out the other side stronger.

Shae swiped the tears that had tracked down her cheeks before Gracie could notice, then tapped the arrow button and brought up the next picture—Gracie at the dress rehearsal, cheek to cheek with her friend Katie, both grinning widely. The next showed an expanded view of the auditorium with Gracie and Katie striking poses on stage. Shae froze, hand hovering above the keyboard. Then she enlarged the photo.

A woman stood in the far corner of the shot, bathed in shadows but clearly watching the audience rather than the drama onstage. Even with the long, wavy locks of auburn hair partially covering her face, Shae recognized her. At least, she thought he did.

Gracie tapped her shoulder. "Mommy?"

Shae jumped out of the bed, taking the laptop with her. "Stay there with Storm, Gracie. I'll be right back. Don't move from this room."

Gracie's chin trembled as tears welled in her eyes.

"I'll be right back, baby. I promise. I just remembered I have to give Angela something really important."

Her daughter nodded and smiled a bit shakily.

Pulling the door shut behind her, Shae jogged down the hallway and found Angela and Cassidy both in the kitchen filling mugs with coffee.

Angela held up a mug. "Want some?"

"No. Thanks. Look at this." She slapped the computer down on the counter, and both women leaned over as she pointed to the image on the screen. "This was Gracie's dress rehearsal for the pageant. There were quite a few parents there, but I didn't notice this woman before. I think I recognize her. I can't be a hundred percent sure, because her face is shadowed and when I enlarge it, it gets too blurry to see clearly. Is there anything you can do to make the image clearer?"

"Give me the flash drive." Angela held out a hand. "Who do you think it is?"

Shae ejected the drive and handed it over. "I'd rather wait until I'm sure." It had been more than six years since she'd seen her, and she'd been only a teenager at that time. She'd filled out some, matured, but Shae was almost sure it was the same woman.

Angela strode in her no-nonsense way to the living room command center, sat and got to work trying to enhance the image. It didn't take long before she sat back. "That's the best I can do."

Shae studied the woman's features, now clear thanks to Angela's finessing. "That's fine."

"Who is it?"

"Regina Kincaid."

Cassidy frowned at Angela. "Regina?"

Shae was the one who answered. "Quentin's daughter. Sebastian's sister. She's quite a bit younger than he is, and while I knew Sebastian because he'd often spend time hanging around his father's office, I only met Regina once or twice."

Angela's fingers flew across the keyboard as screen after screen popped up. "We were aware he had a daughter, but she'd been dismissed long ago. She left her father's home, attended college—in California, actually—and never returned to New York. There's no record of her ever having visited him in prison, no phone calls between them that we can tell."

"So what would she be doing at Gracie's dress rehearsal?" Shae asked.

"Are you sure it couldn't have been a coincidence? Maybe she has a child in the pageant, or a relative, or a friend?" Cassidy studied the screens, speed reading through the info almost as fast as Angela could access it.

"She's not married, has no children…" Angela recited. "And she lives all the way across the country from Boggy Meadows."

"What are the chances she wasn't working for her brother?" Sweat pooled at the base of Shae's spine even as her insides went ice-cold.

Angela was already shaking her head. "Slim to none."

Cassidy paled. "So, she was already aware of your whereabouts…"

"Two days before the attack." That woman, or someone else in Kincaid's organization, had been watching Shae and Gracie, spying on them, for at least two days. The little hairs at the back of her neck stood at attention. Someone could have taken them out at any time, and Shae hadn't even been aware of the danger.

With Ronnie's weapon pressed tightly against his temple, Mason backed up. The instant his back hit the car, he slammed his head forward into Ronnie's nose. When Ronnie stumbled back, Mason shifted enough to grab hold of his wrist. He twisted, turned and snapped the bones, sent an elbow into Ronnie's throat even as he started to scream, then yanked the weapon from Ronnie's hand and tucked it into the back of his own waistband while Ronnie gasped for breath. He shoved Ronnie backward away from him, giving himself room to fight. "What is wrong with you?"

"There're cops out back," Ronnie wheezed. Blood sprayed from his nose as he spoke, giving him a nasal, whiny sound.

Mason held his breath to see if law enforcement would swarm the lot, even though he hadn't uttered the phrase that would let them know he was in trouble and summon help. Since Zac wasn't in charge of the operation, only an adviser, he didn't have the final say on when backup moved in. It could be any minute now. Mason could envision the dispute currently taking place as Zac pleaded his case, argued for them to hold off until they could ascertain the plan for the C-4. Question was, did they have all they were likely to get, or could Mason get more?

Cradling his wrist, Ronnie turned on Lucas. "This is your fault. You brought him in, and I'm going to make sure Kincaid knows it."

"What are you talking about? He's Kenny's guy. He's worked for Kincaid for years. I worked with him in New York. Whatever you think you know, you're wrong." Lucas leveled Mason with a look that said he'd better be right.

Before Mason could reply, the world exploded into chaos around them as Zac's men, along with the FBI and local law enforcement, moved in. He didn't blame them, even agreed they weren't likely to get anything more after Ronnie had spotted the police setting up behind the garage. Sloppy work on the part of the officers posted out back? Or had he received a warning from someone in law enforcement who was loyal to Kincaid? Either way, someone had apparently deemed the information he had been able to record enough to bring the two in for questioning. Of course, Ronnie would need a detour to the hospital for treatment first.

Zac grabbed Mason roughly by the arm and whirled him toward the car, gun steadily aimed at his head. Even if Lucas and Ronnie were going to jail, it was important to maintain his cover.

"Let go of me!" Mason yelled, yanking his arm away.

"Hands on the car!" Zac shoved him face first toward the vehicle, nudging his feet apart with his boot. "Now!"

Mason leveled a glare at Lucas. If he could cause dissension among Kincaid's men, one of them might roll more easily. "What's going on here, Luke? You some kinda rat or something?"

"What?" His eyes went wide, mouth dropping open. "Don't you try to pin this on me, dude."

Mason fought back a grin at the sheer terror written on the other man's face. Zac would have a field day with him if whoever ended up with jurisdiction allowed him to interrogate the guy. Thankfully, the FBI and local police were cooperating, had even allowed Jameson Investigations' agents access to this scene. In the meantime, Mason would just plant some seeds for Lucas to nurture for a little while. He raised his voice so Ronnie, who was being led out of the parking lot in cuffs, would be sure to hear. "When Kincaid finds out you were working with the feds, you're done, man."

Zac shoved Mason toward his waiting SUV, covered his head and wrestled him inside as Mason continued to resist. When the back door finally closed and Zac jumped into the front seat, they waited and watched as the two suspects were loaded into separate vehicles and the raid on the garage began.

"They know about the explosives?" He didn't want the cops to walk into a storage room full of C-4 with no prior knowledge.

"Yeah."

Mason used the key Zac had pressed into his hand while wrestling him into the car to unlock the cuffs behind his back. He rubbed his wrists and handed the cuffs and key over the seat to Zac. "Did Shae ID the second suspect?"

"No. Angela said she wasn't sure. She thought it might be

Ronnie but couldn't be sure from the picture. We're going to pick her up and bring her in with us, see if she can ID him in a lineup." Zac turned to face him. "They did find something else, though."

"What's that?"

"Regina Kincaid. You know her?"

"The sister? No. I've never met her." If he recalled correctly, she was much younger than Sebastian, probably only in her early to mid-twenties now, and not in the picture. He tried to think back, remember what he'd heard about her, couldn't come up with anything more. "As far as I know, she wasn't involved with the business."

"Hmm…" Zac quirked a brow at him. "So what reason would she have had to be at Gracie's dress rehearsal on Wednesday night?"

None. Mason hadn't even known about the danger then. She shouldn't have been there. The fact that she was, and hadn't managed to ding anyone's radar, disturbed him. "Where is she now?"

Zac lifted his hands, let them drop, then turned back around and started the SUV. He shifted into Reverse, then hooked his arm over the passenger seat and looked over his shoulder. "Right now, finding her is a priority."

"Hang on, Zac." Mason needed to be at the police station to at least witness Lucas's interrogation, but he didn't trust anyone else to take Shae to the hospital to see if she could ID Ronnie. "Do me a favor?"

He stepped on the brake, hesitated before shifting into Drive. "What's that?"

"You have security at the hospital?"

"Of course."

"Your own?" Mason wished he could trust the FBI and the local police, but an FBI agent had given them up six years ago and had cost Marty his life. He wasn't taking any chances with Shae. Quentin Kincaid had his hands in too many high-ranking pockets. And those who weren't on the take could be threatened, coerced or even disappeared.

Zac nodded. "In addition to other agencies, yes."

"All right. I'll go pick Shae up and bring her to the hospital. I understand we'll have to do an official lineup afterward, but it would be helpful if we knew if he was the second gunman as soon as possible. In the meantime, can you go ahead to the station? I'd like you to be there in case Lucas starts talking."

"All right. Sure." Zac double-checked that the cars carrying both suspects had left the parking lot and disappeared from sight, then shifted into Park and climbed out. "You take the SUV. I'll get a ride with one of the others."

Mason hopped out and slid into the driver's seat. "Thanks, Zac."

"You bet. And Mason? Be careful. When Sebastian finds out two more of his men have been picked up, he's going to lose his mind. And if he gets an attorney in to talk to them and finds out we raided the garage right after you showed up..."

"Yeah. I get it. It won't take him long to put two and two together. As soon as they determine I'm no longer in custody, he'll figure I'm the mole, even if he doesn't know I was in Florida when Shae went on the run. I'll be careful." As careful as he could be, anyway. But what did that mean for his undercover work? Unless he could come up with a valid excuse to explain how he'd escaped custody, his time in the Kincaid organization was over. So where did that leave him? With no future? Back at the FBI? Continuing to work with Jameson Investigations? He had no idea, and the tension was turning into a dull throb in his head. Better to think about this some other time.

While he drove, he called ahead to let Shae know he was on his way to pick her up. Angela answered and went to retrieve her. Even with guards posted at the hospital, being there would still be the most dangerous part of the excursion.

She answered breathlessly. "Mason?"

"Shae, listen, I'm almost there to pick you up. I need you to come ID someone at the hospital."

"The hospital? Are you—"

"I'm fine. The guy I put in there might be less fine. And… there's something I need to discuss with you." Something she wasn't going to like.

"Okay."

"First off, the weather is brutal. Storms are picking up again, and they've already spawned two tornadoes that I know of."

"Yeah. It was sunny here for a few minutes, but it's raining buckets again now."

"Shae, you know I'll do everything I can to keep you safe. Plus, you already proved in the swamp that you know how to handle yourself, and still…"

"If Kincaid's men show up at the hospital, there could be another shootout," she finished for him.

"Yes." And since the younger Kincaid seemed even less concerned about collateral damage than his father, he'd think nothing of sending men to kill Ronnie to keep him quiet. And if they stumbled across Shae at the hospital… But how could he suggest what he knew needed to be said? He ran it through a million ways in his head.

"You want me to leave Gracie here."

He blew out a pent-up breath. Shae didn't miss a beat. "It's your decision, but I think it would be safer for her to remain at the safe house with Angela and the FBI agents on duty."

Silence hummed over the line.

He listened to the rain pound against the SUV's steel roof.

"Angela has to go out for something," she finally said.

"When?"

"I'm not sure. Now, I think."

"I'm almost there, Shae. What do you want to do?"

She groaned, clearly warring over the decision. "All right. I'll leave Gracie here."

"Meet me at the front door in two minutes. Don't come out

until I get to the door." He'd pull the SUV onto the lawn if he had to, just to get as close as possible to the front door. "Put Angela on."

"All right. I'll be ready."

"Yeah, Mason," Angela answered a moment later.

"Shae said you're leaving?"

"Just for about an hour. I have to follow up on something."

"Who's there?"

"Ronaldo, Monroe, Jenkins, and Leroy."

"You trust them?"

"Zac's worked with Jenkins and Leroy. Jimmy Ronaldo and Cassidy Monroe are new to us, but they've been vetted."

Not ideal, but at least Gracie and Cassidy had bonded over taking care of Storm. He might as well accept the fact that he wasn't going to be comfortable leaving Gracie no matter what. But it wasn't safe to take her, and they needed that ID. They had to know if one of the gunmen was still on the loose. "All right. I'm pulling in now."

He disconnected and pulled onto the lawn with the passenger-side door lined up with the front porch. The fewer people who saw Shae, the better, plus this would protect her from the weather.

Unease sat in his gut like a lead weight as he ran to the door, then guided Shae back to the SUV, shut the door behind her and pulled out. "You doing okay?"

She hesitated. "Yes."

"Shae…"

"I'm okay. I'll just feel better once we're back here, especially if I know you have both shooters in custody." She turned to face him. Dark circles sat under her eyes. Stress lines bracketed her mouth. "I'm sure Kincaid has more gunmen. They won't take away Gracie's protection just because these two were apprehended, right?"

"You and Gracie will have protection until there's no longer a threat, and we can set you up with a new identity, somewhere far from both New York and Florida."

She turned her gaze away and nodded, but not before he noted the flash of pain in her eyes.

"I'm sorry, Shae, but it won't be safe for you to return to Boggy Meadows." And it was a shame, because it seemed Shae and Gracie had both thrived there. "You know that."

"I do." She nodded. "Yes."

"But I promise you, when it's safe to do so, I'll find a way to get anything of importance from your old life to you."

"I already have the most important things with me." Her gaze turned to him, then her eyes widened and color flared in her cheeks. "I…um… I wouldn't mind having Gracie's baby things and a box of her artwork."

"Okay. I'll take care of it." Ignoring whatever that slip might have meant, he kept his eyes on the road ahead of him as the intensity of the storm increased. Hail began to pelt them. The windshield wipers couldn't keep up, reducing visibility to almost nothing. He lifted his foot off the gas some, slowing them to a fast roll. When his phone rang, he hit the button to answer it on the car speaker. "Yeah?"

"Where are you?" Zac asked.

He sensed the anger emitting from him in waves. "On my way to the hospital. Why?"

"Lucas Gianelli escaped."

"What! How could that happen, Zac? Who was transporting him?" Because if it was the FBI agents, he was turning around and going back for Gracie. He eased off the gas even more, searched for somewhere to pull over, squinting to see through the storm. He could barely tell where the road was.

"Two officers from the local police, followed by two FBI agents. All four are dead."

"Ah, man." Though losing four officers brought a wave of grief, as least none of them had been involved with Kincaid. If they had, they would still be alive. "You have enough guards on Ronnie?"

"Yeah. They won't get to him."

A bolt of lightning hit so close he could almost feel the sizzle.

Shae squealed, startled.

"What's happening, Mason?"

"Just some really intense lightning and an almost constant rumble of thunder." The roar increased until it was nearly deafening. He pulled back out onto the narrow two-lane road.

"Where are you?"

"I'm about to pull into the hospital parking lot, but visibility is awful. I'm navigating by GPS at this point."

"All right, I'm right behind you. I'll meet you there in about five minutes."

"Sounds good." He disconnected the call. The lot had already begun to flood as he searched for a spot near the hospital entrance. Nothing, and he didn't want to block the ambulance bay or the drop-off and pickup lanes. Resigned to dashing through the storm, he grabbed a spot in the middle of the parking lot as someone else backed out. "You ready?"

She looked up at the sky, then at him, and lifted a brow. "As I'll ever be, I guess."

"Sit right there until I come around." He inhaled deeply, shook off the desire to remain right where he was in the SUV with her and listen to the storm rage, and shoved open the door. "Let's do this."

He hopped out, automatically scanning for trouble as he rounded the front of the vehicle and opened the door for Shae. After waiting for her to emerge, he slammed the door shut and took her hand. "Come on."

The windshield of the Volkswagen beside him exploded beneath a barrage of automatic weapon fire.

Chapter Nine

"Get down!" Mason shoved Shae to the ground, whipped his pistol from its holster and pressed his back against the SUV. He had to realize they couldn't stay there. They had to move. "Go around the back of the Volkswagen."

Keeping in a crouch, she did as he said, sensing him following right on her heels. Where had the shots come from? She hadn't been able to tell.

"Shae? You okay?" Mason's voice called from her left.

She took stock for a moment. Other than some nausea and a pounding headache, she seemed to be in one piece. "I think so. Are you hurt?"

"No. I'm fine."

She turned her head to face him.

Blood streamed from his temple as he tapped his earpiece, the wound he'd sustained in the swamp having reopened. "We're taking fire."

"Two minutes out."

"Got it." Mason stood, still stooped over, and glanced through the Volkswagen's back window toward the hospital. He rested a hand on her shoulder. "Stay down. Everything will be fine. We'll have help in a minute."

So why did his tone hold such urgency? What wasn't he telling her? "Is something else wrong?"

"Nothing specific. I just feel like a sitting duck here. We need to get away from the vehicle."

"Okay." He was right, especially since they couldn't see much of anything surrounding the vehicle, the position they'd taken cover in allowing no view. "Make sure you're not hurt. I don't want to start running and find out you're injured."

She did as instructed, taking inventory from head to toe. A few aches and pains, but nothing serious. She could run if they got a chance. She turned her attention to the cut on his temple. "You're bleeding a lot."

"It's fine. Nothing serious. It just grazed me." He swiped at the blood with the back of his hand as if it were a simple annoyance.

"Grazed? You mean you were shot?" Shae's voice rose to near hysterical, but she couldn't control it. Nor could she control the tremors coursing through her. Mason had been shot. In the head. A fraction of an inch over and he'd be dead. She started to hyperventilate.

"Hey. Look at me." Mason squatted in front of her, cupped her face. "Listen to me. I'm fine. It probably just reopened the stitches Doc Rogers put in." He grinned. "I'm gonna have to listen to a lecture about that later when he restitches me."

She shoved his hand away. "How can you joke about that?"

"I'm sorry, Shae. And trust me, I already said a prayer of thanks, but I'm okay." He shifted his gaze from their surroundings to stare into her eyes. "And we have to move. We can't stay here."

"Okay." She nodded, willing her heart back down from her throat, then swiped away tears and rain. "Okay. I'm sorry. I'm okay."

"You have nothing to be sorry for."

She had to get a grip. "C-c-could you tell where they were shooting from?"

His gaze lingered on her for another moment, then he returned to scrutinizing the lot. "The direction of the hospital, but I'm not sure where."

"How are we going to get out of here?"

He gripped her hand, lending her strength she was sorely lacking at the moment. "When I say go, I want you to stay low and head to the right. Stay behind the cars as much as possible, and when you come to that van at the end, crouch low and stay behind the back tire. Okay?"

"Yeah. Okay. Got it."

"Ready?"

She shifted, getting into a better position to push off. "Yeah."

Mason grabbed a half-full soda bottle someone had dropped in the parking lot, stood higher and tossed it in the opposite direction. "Go!"

Shots took out another windshield in the direction he'd thrown the bottle.

Shae held her breath, kept her head low and ran without looking back. When she reached the black van, she ducked behind the back bumper, careful to keep the tire directly in front of her.

Mason held his weapon in a two-handed grip, firing as he ran behind her. He reached her just as an SUV fishtailed into the lot and sped in the direction of the hospital. "I got one of them, but there's still at least one more. Zac and his guys are going after him now. Are you hurt?"

"No, I'm good. Just shaken up."

"Okay. We're going to sit tight until Zac gives the all clear."

She nodded, sucked in a deep breath and crouched to sit on the rain-slicked ground, then leaned her back against the van's bumper. Her legs were shaking too badly to hold her.

"It'll be okay, Shae. Zac had men already in the hospital to help comb the area."

"This is so ridiculous." She wrapped her arms around her legs and lowered her head to her knees, then started to laugh.

He frowned at her as if she'd finally crumbled beneath the pressure.

And she sighed. "Did you ever get the feeling you weren't meant to do something? It's like every step of the way, hurdles are thrown into our paths."

"When that happens, I usually sit back and reassess what I'm doing. I used to pray for guidance and direction, but I'm ashamed to admit it's been a long time since I've done so."

She turned her head so she could see him but kept her cheek resting on her knees. "Why?"

"I don't know. I guess I just kind of gave up after Marty was killed, after I had to leave you to go undercover…" He looked away, probably somewhere in the past. "It was the most difficult decision I've ever made, Shae. But it was something I had to do. I was a coward to leave without saying goodbye to you, without letting you know what was going on, without at least offering some explanation after everything that happened. I think I was afraid to see you, afraid you'd ask me to stay."

"And you couldn't." She understood now why he'd had to leave, just not why he'd done so without an explanation.

"No. That's just it." He paused midsearch. "I would have. *And* I couldn't."

"It's okay, Mason. It's in the past now, and when Gracie and I needed you most, you came back." She gripped his hand, willed him to believe what she was saying. "And that's all that matters."

"Thank you," he said softly.

"Now." She smiled. "If you can find any room in your heart for faith, a prayer right now probably wouldn't hurt."

He grinned back at her. "I'll see what I can do." Then he paused and raised a hand to his earpiece, listening. "Ten-four."

She shot him a questioning look.

"We're all clear. They've got two shooters in custody." He stood, stretched his back and held out a hand to Shae.

Grateful, Shae took his hand and let him help her up, then looked around the lot and moved closer to him.

He lay an arm across her shoulders, tilting his head so it leaned against hers, but she could sense his tension. "You okay?"

"Yes." And it was time to move. She didn't need Mason to tell her standing out there in the open was akin to painting a target on their backs. "Let's go. But, Mason?"

"Yeah." He gripped her hand.

"I'll take a look at the guy you want me to ID, and then we need to reassess our course of action." She gestured toward the shattered windshields. "Clearly this is not working. They keep finding us. I think maybe we're missing something, and we need to slow down for a minute and figure out what."

He nodded and kept her beneath his arm as they walked toward the hospital, but he didn't holster his weapon.

As she surveyed the damage to the vehicles, more than she'd realized from her crouched position, she offered a silent prayer of thanks that they'd survived and that she hadn't left Gracie alone in the world.

"Mason?"

"Yeah."

"I need you to promise me something." Because there was no one she'd trust with this more.

"What's that?"

She hesitated, waited until he stopped walking and turned to her, then squeezed his hand. "I want you to promise if anything happens to me, you'll take care of Gracie."

His breath whooshed out in one long rush. "Shae, I—"

"Please. We've been in witness protection her whole life. I left everyone who was once a part of my life behind and never trusted anyone to forge a relationship close enough that I'd trust them with my daughter's life." She squeezed his hand tighter, willed him to understand the importance of her request, the amount of trust she was placing in him. Did she hope for something more with him when all this was said and done? She had no idea, couldn't think past the here and now, but she did trust him with Gracie. Of that, she was certain. "Please, Mason. I need to know she'll be taken care of by someone who will love her and would risk his life to protect her, just like I would."

He closed his eyes, lowered his head and pressed their joined hands against his forehead, then rocked his head back and forth in a gesture she feared was refusal.

The sound of a vehicle approaching interrupted, and she figured he'd use the excuse for a reprieve. Maybe she'd overestimated his feelings for Gracie. She slid her hand out of his. "It's okay, Mason. I'm sorry. I shouldn't have asked. I didn't mean to put you on the spot."

He looked up at her then, and tears mixed with the rain dripping down his face. "Shae. I will take care of Gracie. You have my word that if anything...happens to you, I will take care of her. I will raise her to be a good, loving, faithful person, just like her mother. But nothing will happen to you, Shae, because I won't allow it. I can't."

When he cupped her cheek, she leaned into the warmth of his hand. "Thank you."

"Mason!" Zac called as he swung the door of the SUV open. "Get in."

Mason squeezed his eyes closed for a moment, then pressed his lips against Shae's forehead, held her that way for a moment, then released her.

Zac and Angela were in the front seats, so Shae and Mason climbed into the back.

"You two okay?" Zac asked.

"Yeah."

"Angela was just heading back to the safe house, but I told her to ride with me. This weather is brutal." He eyed Shae in the rearview mirror. "Did you really have to pick an El Niño winter to get found during?"

A smile tugged at her. "Sorry. I'll try to do better next time."

"See that you do." He winked at her in the mirror, then pulled up to the ambulance entrance. "Do you still want to go into the hospital?"

Mason glanced at Shae, and she nodded once. "Let's just get this done. I wasn't able to ID him from the pictures, but he looks familiar. There's something about him that I can't place, but I know I've seen him before. I'm pretty sure if I see him in person I'll recognize him."

"You don't think he's the second gunman?"

Did she? She'd recognized the picture they'd sent of Lucas Gianelli instantly. He was one of the two who had found her at the pageant. But the other guy? She knew him. She was sure of that. But from where? Granted, she'd been under a tremendous amount of pressure and stress, but then why had she recognized the first shooter so easily? At Mason's suggestion, she'd tried to envision Ronnie with his mass of frizzy hair tied or slicked back, without the baseball cap, wearing a suit. He'd advised her to close her eyes and envision him, to let her thoughts wander and see what came to her. But so far, nothing had worked.

It wasn't until they were outside the private hospital room and she peeked through the small window that recognition slammed through her. She gasped and stumbled back from the door.

"What?" Mason frowned. "You recognize him?"

"Y-yes." Bile surged up her throat, and her knees buckled.

Mason caught her before she could hit the floor. "Get a chair."

Angela dragged a chair from across the hall to them, and Mason lowered Shae into it and guided her head between her knees. Angela held a hand up to still the two confused agents standing guard on either side of the door.

Mason kept his hand on her head. "Who is he, Shae?"

"His name isn't Ronnie. At least, that's not how I knew him."

"Who is he?" Zac stood over her, phone held ready to move as soon as she made the ID.

She had to pull herself together. Slowly, she lifted her head, controlled her breathing and forced the nausea down. There was no time to fall apart. She had to get back to Gracie. "His name is Mathew Harris, and he was an assistant coach on Gracie's soccer team last year. She didn't have much interaction with him, and I didn't have reason to pay much attention to him, but I recognize him now."

Mason's eyes went ice-cold.

"Do you think Kincaid knew where Shae was even then, or do you think it was a coincidence?" Angela asked.

"No, it's no coincidence." Zac dialed and pressed the phone against his ear. "I think Sebastian Kincaid found them a long time ago, and he was just waiting for his old man to give the order before he made his move."

"But why?" Angela glanced toward the window as if the answers might be written there.

"Who knows?" Mason lay a hand on Shae's shoulder. "Maybe Quentin wouldn't sanction the hit for some reason. Or maybe Sebastian was waiting to use the hit as a power play, even before his father asked him to prove he's a strong enough leader."

Shae started for the door. "I need to get to my daughter. Now."

Mason fishtailed around the corner and sped toward the safe house with Zac and Angela right behind them. After Shae had ID'd Mathew Harris, aka Ronnie, they'd tried to contact the agents at the safe house. None of them had answered.

Shae's hands shook wildly as she tried Cassidy Monroe's number again. "Please, answer. Please, answer."

Mason didn't tell her not to bother. It was obvious something had gone wrong and no one was going to answer their calls, but having something to concentrate on beside her daughter's fate would help keep her grounded.

She dropped the phone onto her lap and scrubbed her hands over her face. "Still no answer. How could this have happened?"

Mason didn't know what to say. His only thoughts were on Gracie—his daughter—a fact that had punched through him the instant he'd realized something had gone wrong at the safe house. She was his child, his responsibility, and he had failed her repeatedly. He'd abandoned her mother, no matter the circumstances, when she'd needed him most. He'd let Sebastian's men get close days—no, at least a year—before anyone even realized they'd located Shae. He hadn't been fast enough, had left them to be terrorized for the past few days instead of getting away cleanly. He would not fail this child, *his* child, again.

He took the next turn way too fast for the slick conditions, skidding as he struggled to regain control.

Shae braced her hands against the dashboard, clenched her teeth together and said nothing.

As the safe house came into sight, he prayed fervently, begged for Gracie's well-being. Maybe the problem was with the phone service. The storms could have caused some kind of interference. Or maybe Cassidy or one of Zac's agents had managed to get Gracie to safety but didn't have their phones with them. Or maybe Gracie had managed to run or hide. They'd alerted local law enforcement, but no one had gotten back to them yet.

He surged between two patrol cars parked at awkward angles in the street, over the curb and onto the lawn.

Shae had the door open before he fully stopped.

"Shae, wait!" He shoved the car into Park, then jumped out and ran, easily overtaking her before they reached the porch. He grabbed her arm and shoved her against the wall to the side of the front door, then pressed his own back against the wall. "Stay there."

Zac leaned against the wall on the other side, Angela next to him, all of them with weapons drawn.

The sound of Storm barking frantically, scratching against something, reached them through the open front door. The dog was still alive, that was something. But one of Zac's agents lay across the entryway. A police officer lay a few feet beyond him in the foyer. "You stay right there, Shae. You'll only be in the way and could get caught in the cross fire and get Gracie hurt. You hear me?"

She nodded, lower lip trembling. She vibrated with adrenaline, but she stayed put.

Mason crouched low. With Zac covering him from behind and Angela standing guard at the door and protecting Shae, he checked both downed officers for any sign of life, then shook his head and moved forward. Jimmy Ronaldo lay half in the kitchen, half in the hallway, no weapon in sight. Knowing it was too late to help him, Mason turned into the living room where the command center had been set up and found Zac's remaining two agents. Both dead, one in the chair in front of his computer with his weapon still holstered at his side, the other lying on the floor beside the printer with papers scattered around him. Clearly, neither had seen the attack coming. Which meant they'd known their attacker. They had to have. No way could a stranger have gotten in without the guard noticing, sneaked up on two agents and killed them before they could even draw their weapons. No, this had happened quickly, *tap-tap, tap-tap* and done. A growing feeling of dread settled in his stomach.

The dog barked and howled, trying to claw and bite his way out of the bathroom where he'd been sequestered. "Gracie?" Mason called, in case she was in there, too. No answer.

Storm never would have allowed a stranger to lock him in a room. Again, he must have known the attacker. Trust them enough to let them lock him in a room without Gracie. A suspicion was growing inside him.

Mason tuned out the dog's cries. They had to clear the house before they could do anything for him, even if he knew they wouldn't find Gracie—or Agent Cassidy Monroe.

He eased around the corner into the kitchen and found another police officer down. He felt for a pulse. Nothing. He tamped down every last emotion as he and Zac moved through the house together.

"Here…"

Mason almost missed the barely audible croak. He stopped, listened, then moved into the bedroom.

A police officer lay on the floor by the bed, bleeding profusely from a gunshot wound in his gut.

Zac whipped out his radio and called for backup as Mason grabbed a stack of towels and washcloths from the bathroom and began to administer first aid. "Can you tell me what happened, Officer…?"

"Gibbons…sir," he wheezed.

"Okay, you just hold on, Gibbons. Help's coming. You hear me?"

He nodded, sucked in a deep breath and coughed. "Girl. Didn't see her."

"When you got here?" Mason folded a towel into a compress and pressed it hard against the officer's wound. "Gracie was already gone?"

He nodded, struggled for air. "Outside, guard down in back. We came in, knew it was a child in danger, didn't wait for backup…"

"There was a female FBI agent present. Cassidy Monroe. Did you find her here?"

He shook his head and wheezed deeply. His eyes fluttered closed. "Woman shooter."

"You hold on, Gibbons. You hear me?"

And then Angela was beside him. She dropped to her knees

and started chest compressions. "Ambulance is only a few minutes out. The house is clear."

"Monroe?" Rage boiled. She'd befriended Shae. And Gracie. They'd trusted her.

Angela shook her head. "I'm sorry."

He swiped a hand over his mouth, had to get to Shae. Leaving Angela to care for Officer Gibbons, he walked into the living room to find Shae sitting on the floor in the corner beside Storm, hugging the dog against her chest as she worked to soothe him.

She looked up when Mason walked in. "Gracie's not here."

"No, Shae. I'm sorry." He crouched in front of her. "We're going to find her. Do you hear me?"

Deep, racking sobs shook her as she rocked back and forth, clutching the dog. "You have to find her, Mason. You have to find my baby. Please. Oh, God, please."

He reached for her, but she yanked her arm away from him and stood.

"How could this happen?" she screamed. "How could you let this happen? I trusted you. You promised you'd keep my baby safe."

Storm stood protectively between them, eyeing Mason like he might be the villain.

"I know, Shae. I'm so sorry." No one was more furious than he was. How had he missed it? Cassidy had been so convincing, so enamored with Gracie and Storm. Of course she was. It let her lock the dog away so he didn't make a fuss while she quietly escorted the trusting child out the front door. But someone must have noticed something wrong, because she'd had to shoot her way out.

"Is she even still alive?" Shae wrapped her arms around herself and bent over. "Do you think that woman k-k—"

"No. Shae, you can't think like that." He gripped both her arms and forced her upright. "Listen to me. Gracie is alive. Do you hear me? If they were going to kill her, they'd have had no reason to remove her from the premises. She'd be here, Shae. She's alive. Okay? And we are going to do everything in our power to figure out where she is and bring her home safe."

"You find her. You find my child right now." She turned away from him then, tremors coursing through her body as she walked to the window and looked out.

Mason lowered his head to his hand, allowing the grief to flow through him for one long moment. And then he shut everything down. Just like he'd learned to do six years ago when he'd had to walk away from Shae. He shut off everything inside him, all the pain, all the anger, all the fear, even all the love, and he turned and walked out.

He found Zac standing on the front lawn watching paramedics load Gibbons into an ambulance, one phone pressed against his ear as he tapped and scrolled on another.

"Gibbons?" Mason asked.

"They said he should make it, but we won't know for sure until they get him into surgery."

Mason nodded. One more thing he couldn't do anything about right now except to pray he'd recover. "Monroe?"

"We have an APB out. Angela's inside now trying to find out more."

He left Zac to coordinate the search effort and stalked through the house to the bedroom, where he found Angela at a desk with a laptop in front of her, eyes red and puffy as she sniffled and fought for control.

"Anything?" he asked.

"You're not going to like it."

"I don't like any of this. Tell me." Fear tried to breach his barriers, but he ignored it. It would do him no good. The anger was tougher to rein in.

"Cassidy Monroe was handpicked for this assignment by a supervisor who called out sick right after assigning her." She looked up at him, sniffed. "Local police just found his body."

Mason exploded, swung and knocked a box of tissues off

the desk and across the room. "How could that have happened? Didn't anyone notice he was missing?"

Angela shook her head, unfazed by the outburst. "He called out sick, Mason. And no one had any reason to suspect Monroe. She's never been convicted of a crime, had no involvement in the Kincaid organization that I can even find after the fact. No one had any reason to look at her. She passed the background check with flying colors."

"All right. So, she's either in collusion with the Kincaids or they coerced her in some way." He huffed out a breath, raked a hand through his hair. Raging about past mistakes would do nothing to help find Gracie. "Do you have any leads?"

"Maybe." She hit a few keys, then got up and hurried to the printer. She turned and held out a page. "Her vehicle. We have it on a traffic camera getting on the turnpike heading south about fifteen minutes ago. Zac's coordinating a team."

"Thanks." Mason grabbed the page from her and took off. He'd let Shae know they had a lead, and then he'd go after Gracie himself. He strode into the living room and stopped short. She wasn't there, and a visibly agitated Storm was being leashed by a nervous agent. "Shae?"

Zac rounded the corner at a full run. "The SUV you were driving is gone."

"What?"

"One of the local officers said he saw a woman matching Shae's description take off in it about three minutes ago. He didn't know who she was, but she came from inside the house, so he had no reason to try to stop her."

"Where would she have gone?" It didn't make sense. The command center in the safe house was the first place information about Gracie would come in. It was her best chance at knowing right away if her daughter was found. "Why would she leave?"

"Unless..." Zac whirled and started for the door with Mason on his heels.

"Someone contacted her."

"Angela," Zac yelled. "Can you track Shae's cell phone?"

Mason held his breath as she accessed the information on one of the living room computers.

"It's..." She frowned and looked around the room. "It should be in here."

Mason searched in the direction she'd indicated. He found the phone stuffed beneath a chair cushion. He swiped the screen and read the text sent from Cassidy's cell phone out loud. "'We'll trade. You for Gracie. Say nothing. Leave your phone behind. Drive south on the turnpike until we intercept you.'"

Zac took the phone from him before he could throw it across the room and handed it to Angela. "Use satellites or traffic cameras, whatever you have to do, but find the vehicle Mason was driving. It left here about four minutes ago."

"Got it."

Mason had never felt so helpless as he strode toward Zac's Jeep, praying he'd find Shae and Gracie in time. His heart stopped when he found Mr. Cuddles lying beside the driveway. He bent and picked him up, pressed his face into the stuffed bunny. The tidal wave of emotions he'd so carefully suppressed broke free and inundated him.

Chapter Ten

Shae drove a steady sixty miles an hour in the right lane of the turnpike. She had no idea how Cassidy planned to intercept her, but she would make it as easy as she could. She didn't regret leaving the safe house. She had to save Gracie, and there were so few people she could trust. She did wish she'd been able to say goodbye to Mason, but he would have tried to stop her. She rubbed her chest to ease the ache there, swallowed hard to clear the lump from her throat. Was this how he'd felt when he'd left her six years ago?

It didn't matter now. Even if she wasn't about to die, there was no future for her, Gracie and Mason as a family. While she couldn't deny that she loved him with all her heart, it would never work between them. Mason was a field agent, whether he returned to the FBI or stayed with Jameson Investigations. There would always be the possibility he'd walk out again, go undercover for extended periods of time, be in danger like this on a regular basis.

So who would take care of Gracie once Shae traded herself for her daughter? She dismissed the thought—had to if she was going to make it through this. Mason might not be able to take care of Gracie himself, but Shae had no doubt he'd see to it she was cared for and loved. Zac Jameson certainly had the resources to make that happen. She shoved the thought of Gracie being raised by strangers into some deep compartment in her heart. At least her daughter would live.

An SUV pulled along Shae in the middle lane. The passenger, a guy she immediately recognized as the second gunman, gestured for her to follow.

She nodded, allowing the driver room to pull in front of her. "Mommy's coming, Gracie. This will all be over soon, and you'll be safe. I promise."

She exited the turnpike and followed the other SUV down a narrow dirt road. Trees that looked like they'd stood undisturbed for hundreds of years packed together in a thick, never-ending expanse of forest. Miles passed as her heart rate slowed. Cassidy would let Gracie go once Shae turned herself over. The woman knew Gracie, had taken care of her. She wouldn't let her die. What kind of monster would do that? Shae would convince her to drop Gracie off at a police station or a hospital or a church, somewhere she'd be safe and get help.

She prayed Gracie wasn't hurt, prayed she'd understand Shae would never leave her if there was any other choice. Surely Mason would make sure Gracie knew how much her mother had loved her. She tilted her head back and forth, easing the tension coiled in her neck. It was almost over. Once they had Shae, Gracie would no longer be in danger.

Ten miles into the woods, she entered a clearing. The lead SUV parked in front of a large cabin, probably used for hunting—or other, less legal, activities. As she looked around, she wondered how many bodies were buried in these woods and knew she'd soon join them. "God, please give me the strength to do what I need to do here. Don't let me falter."

Leaving the keys in the ignition, she got out of the SUV.

The second gunman from the pageant approached. "Face the car, hands on the roof."

She complied, let him frisk her in search of weapons or a wire, neither of which she had.

He stepped back and loosely aimed his weapon in her direction, used it to gesture toward the cabin. "Inside."

She hurried up the three steps to the front porch, registering several shadowy men there. Before she could pause, the door swung open. Cassidy Monroe ushered her inside and slammed the door behind the man who'd led her in. "Anyone follow her?"

"No. She did as you said, just ran out and drove away. No one followed."

"Good. Wait outside. Let me know immediately if anyone shows up."

He left without a word.

"How could you do this?" Shae struggled to control the anger. This woman knew her, knew Gracie, and she'd betrayed them. Confronting her would do nothing, though. She needed to get Gracie to safety first. Maybe there would be time after to say her piece. "Where's my daughter?"

Cassidy gestured toward a closed door across the large, open main room.

Ignoring her, Shae crossed the floor, then had to wait for Cassidy to unlock the door.

The instant it swung open, Shae burst through.

Her daughter lay on a cot, curled in a tight ball, shaking wildly.

"Gracie." She ran to her, scooped her into her arms and sat down on the bed when her legs gave out.

"Mommy?" She sobbed. "I knew you would come get me."

"Of course I did, baby. I'd never let anything happen to you." She only wished she could promise to stay with her always. "I love you so much, baby, more than anything in this world."

"I love you, Mommy." Gracie clung so tight Shae could barely gasp in a breath, but she just embraced her daughter, hugged her with all her might, hoping Gracie would remember this moment once Shae was gone.

"All right. Touching." Cassidy smirked. "Now, let's move."

Shae whirled on her. "You promised you'd let Gracie go if I did what you said."

"You're right." She walked across the cabin and flung the front door open, then gestured outside with the automatic weapon she held in her hand. "Get out, Gracie."

"What?" Shae lurched to her feet, Gracie clinging tightly, arms and legs wrapped around her. "You can't just throw her out in the woods."

"You want her to live?"

"Listen." Shae struggled for calm. Surely this woman could see reason. "I'll go with you without a fuss. We can drop Gracie off somewhere safe first, then I'll do whatever you want."

"Sorry, Shae, but you're not calling the shots here. And trust me…" She grinned. "You're going to do whatever I want anyway."

"She's a baby, Cassidy." They couldn't throw her out in the woods. It would be getting dark soon, and there were bears, wild boars, alligators, armed gunmen and who knew what else out there. And what if more tornadoes moved through? No way could even the most vicious woman toss a child out into the forest to survive on her own. "You can't do this. Please."

"Gracie can either walk out that front door in the next sixty seconds, or she can die here with you."

Gracie whimpered.

"I don't particularly care either way." Her grin turned feral. "Tick tock."

"You coldhearted—"

"Time's a-wasting." She glanced at her watch.

Shae lowered Gracie to the floor, crouched so she would be face-to-face with her. "Gracie, listen to me. There's a dirt road right across the clearing. I want you to follow it until you come to a paved road, then stand there and wait for a car to come by and help you. Okay?"

"No, Mommy. I can't. I'm scared. And I'm not supposed to walk on the road."

"Thirty seconds." Cassidy wagged a finger Shae was going to snap in half once her daughter was safe, even if it was the last thing she did.

"Gracie, do what I'm telling you. Right now." Shae stood and started ushering Gracie toward the door. "Cheesemonkey, okay?"

"But what about you?"

"Don't worry about me, honey. I'll be fine. I'll catch up to you as soon as I can. But you have to go now."

Gracie threw her arms around Shae's legs and sobbed. "No, Mommy. Please don't make me. I don't wanna do cheesemonkey anymore."

"Gracie." Shae held her arms. "Gracie. All you have to do is walk. Walk down the dirt road until you come to a paved road. Okay?"

"But I don't want to go out there alone."

"Ten..." Cassidy leaned a shoulder against the doorjamb and folded her arms. "Nine..."

"Hey." Shae wiped the tears from Gracie's cheeks and fought back her own. "You won't be alone, baby. God is always with you. Just pray as you walk and try to stay calm, okay?"

"Eight..."

Her little girl sucked in a deep, shaky breath. "Okay, Mommy."

"Seven..."

"Go, baby. Go now."

"Six...five..."

"I love you, baby girl, with all my heart."

"Four..."

"I love you, too, Mommy."

"Three...two..."

Gracie walked out the door. She looked back at Shae over her shoulder once, then lifted her chin and strode down the steps and started across the clearing.

Cassidy shut the door behind her. "She's a strong kid. I give her a fifty percent chance of making it. Either way, we'll be long gone before she can reach civilization and lead anyone back here."

Shae lunged and landed a solid punch to Cassidy's jaw.

Cassidy shoved her off and pointed the weapon at her. "Don't forget, my men can easily catch up with her. And if you try anything like that again, they will."

Shae clenched her fists at her sides, sucked in deep lungfuls of stale, musty air. "Why are you doing this? I don't understand."

Cassidy's mouth firmed into a tight line, her grip on the weapon tightening. "Four years ago, my husband and son were killed."

Pain stabbed Shae's heart. "I'm sorry."

"Sorry? Sorry?" She shoved Shae back with the weapon. "You know what sorry does to bring my family back? Nothing!"

"Cassidy, please. If you know what it's like to lose a child, how could—"

The slap came fast and hard, a backhand that left the coppery taste of blood filling her mouth. "Don't you dare use my grief to try to worm your way out of this."

"I didn't mean it that way, I just—"

"Do you know what happened when the FBI, the agency I devoted my life to, found their killer?"

Shae shook her head.

"They offered him immunity to testify against Antonio Pesci. The guy was one of his higher-level lieutenants, and he killed my family because I was on the team that went after Pesci for assault, money laundering and attempted murder. Of course, our witness was killed, leaving us with nothing, because the lieutenant they'd traded away my family's justice for was found dead in prison." She shoved a single tear away with the heel of her hand, and her expression hardened. Whatever bit of emotion had surfaced at the thought of the tragedy that had befallen her family disappeared in an instant, to be replaced by bitterness and anger Shae could at least understand, if not condone. "I guess bringing Pesci down was worth more than the lives of my husband and child, and they couldn't even manage to get it right."

"So, how did you get involved with Sebastian Kincaid?" Shae tried to keep her tone even, keep her talking. While her heart ached for this woman's loss, it didn't excuse her decision to work with the Kincaids and betray everyone she knew.

"Sebastian?" She laughed, a horrible, evil sound. "Honey, I have no involvement with Sebastian. As a matter of fact, by the time I finish with you and walk out of here, Sebastian will have followed his father into the grave."

Shae shook her head, trying to clear the confusion, trying to see past thoughts of Gracie wandering alone through the Florida forest so she could think. She hadn't planned anything past getting Cassidy to drop Gracie off somewhere safe. Now that she'd tossed her daughter out on her own, Shae had to try to get to her. And the only way to do that would be to go through Cassidy Monroe. She wasn't sure how yet, so she had to stall, to give herself time to come up with a plan to get past not only Cassidy, but the armed gunmen she'd stationed outside.

"Regina," Shae said, realization dawning.

"Regina," Cassidy agreed.

"But I thought she had nothing to do with the Kincaid organization."

"Of course she does. But she's smarter than her brother. She went to college, learned all she'd need to know in order to run the Kincaid empire while her brother hung around trying to follow in his daddy's footsteps like some kind of trained dog. While Sebastian racked up a criminal record, Regina got a degree. While Sebastian spent his life taking orders, Regina learned how to lead. And now that the time has come, she's making her play for the top spot."

"That's why Regina didn't move on me when she first found me. She was waiting for Quentin to die, then she was going to kill me and take over the family business instead of her brother."

"Almost. She was waiting for Quentin to be *near* death. That was the deal they made—he always promised he'd give her a chance to take over. He believed in her brains, saw more potential in her than he did Sebastian. Apparently, it's even spelled out in a document containing his final wishes and held onto by his lawyer. He'd name a target before he died, and whoever got the target won the empire. A risky power play, but a necessary one. A way to prove she commands resources Sebastian couldn't hope to wield."

For a moment, Shae remembered the man she'd worked for who'd always encouraged and praised Shae's own intelligence and creativity. She banished it from her mind. "But Sebastian was part of the organization for years. He must have contacts, loyalty—"

Cassidy spat on the floor. "Sebastian has nothing. He *is* nothing. Regina put her own lieutenant in place to undermine him every step of the way. And now she'll take over the Kincaid organization and it will become the most powerful family in the country."

Shae frowned. Something wasn't adding up. "So why am I still alive? And why did you take Gracie from the safe house when you could have grabbed me at any time?"

"We wanted you alive, needed you alive. We couldn't risk a shootout, knowing you'd sacrifice your life to save your daughter if it came down to it. It was better for me to wait, bide my time until I could slip away with Gracie. I figured she'd be easier to handle and then we could use her to lure you out, but the brat started screaming the minute she heard her stupid dog barking. I tried to get her out, but I ended up having to kill everyone."

Keep her talking, keep her talking. "That's why you took Gracie. Okay. But why do you need me alive? You already know who was protecting me, which apparently no one shared with Sebastian, so what is it you want from me?"

"The project you came across when you were working for Quentin Kincaid."

"Project?" What was she talking about? "You mean the attack he had planned on the Pesci family?"

"Exactly."

"What about it?"

"You're going to recreate it." She lifted her chin in defiance. "Regina is going to finish what her father started. And I am going to get justice, revenge, whatever, for my family. I'm going to get even with Antonio Pesci—wipe out his entire family just like he did mine."

"No." No way would Shae be complicit in a plan that would kill anyone, even a crime family. Besides, who knew how many innocent lives might be endangered in the process?

"I was afraid you'd say that." She whipped open the front door. "Go get the girl."

"No. Wait. Please." Shae had spent several terrifying weeks gathering information after she'd overheard that first awful conversation. She knew the blueprints well, the ones for the building where the Pescis' infamous New Year's Eve party always took place. The breath rushed from her lungs as she finally understood. It was the one time of year the whole family and all the highest-ranking associates gathered, and the place had better security than a prison. Regina needed the details Shae had memorized before going to the police. "New Year's Eve."

"That's right. You might have had more time with your daughter if Quentin was in better health. But since he named you as the target—just like Regina knew he would—so close to New Year's, Regina sees it as fortuitous timing. Help me now, and we don't go after the girl. And maybe you'll live to see your daughter again."

Shae only nodded. No way would she put Gracie's life in danger, but she couldn't give them the plans to kill the Pesci family, either.

"I thought you might change your mind."

Mason crept silently through the thick undergrowth parallel to the dirt road. It was perfect cover as he moved toward the cabin Zac's team had tracked Shae to. He ignored the chatter over the comms as Zac placed his agents around the perimeter and coordinated the rescue attempt. Mason had only one objective: get to Shae and Gracie, and he would see to that with single-minded determination.

The crunch of dried brush to his right had him pausing. He crouched low and turned toward the sound. Nothing. He started to turn away.

"Please, help me find help." A whisper reached through the silence, and a little voice said, "And please, save Mommy," followed by soft sobs.

His heart shattered into a million pieces as he changed direction to intercept his daughter. He found her walking on the side of the dirt road, praying through her tears. Though he hated the thought of scaring her, he couldn't take a chance she'd scream and draw attention. He waited for her to pass his position, then slid out behind her. In one smooth motion, he scooped her up and hugged her against his chest with one hand and covered her mouth with the other, then whispered urgently, "It's okay, Gracie. It's me. It's..." *Daddy*... "Mason."

Her body went limp in his arms, and she turned to face him, then wrapped her arms around his neck and hugged him.

Mason held on tight, buried his face against her shoulder and inhaled deeply the scents of baby shampoo and sweat. "It's okay, Gracie. You're okay now."

She cried so hard her entire body shook. "I want my mommy."

"I know, honey." He could have stood there forever, the weight of his daughter in his arms, the assurance she was safe, the pure love he felt for the first time in six years flowing through him unfettered. But he had to get to Shae.

With one look around to be sure he hadn't been seen, he ducked back into the woods. "Are you hurt?"

She shook her head against him, her tears soaking his neck. "Cassidy took me, and she had a gun, and she wouldn't let Mommy go."

"I know, honey. I know. I'm going to go get her. Okay?" He lowered Gracie to her feet and knelt in front of her, shifted her back so he could look her in the eye, eyes that matched his own, right down to the terror he saw reflected there. "Listen to me, Gracie, okay?"

She nodded, sniffed, her eyes so swollen from crying they were practically slits.

"I'm going to get your mommy, but I have to make sure you're safe before I can do that." He tapped the button on his communicator to summon help, then pulled Gracie into his lap and held her close. "I am so proud of you, Gracie. I know you're scared. I'm scared, too, but together we're going to get through this. I promise. I'm going to go get your mommy and bring her back to you, and then…"

And then what? He loved Shae absolutely, fiercely, with everything in him. He'd never stopped loving her, even if he'd been too stubborn to accept it, but was there a future for them? A nice little family with a small house in the suburbs, a golden retriever and a white picket fence? Even if they could get Shae and Gracie relocated somewhere they'd be safe, what then? The work Mason did…that was no life for Shae. To have her husband pop in every now and then, emotionally damaged from whatever atrocities he'd witnessed and had to turn a blind eye to in order to maintain his cover? And what about Gracie? What kind of unstable life was that for a child who'd been through so much trauma already? At one time, he'd been willing to give up his career to go into witness protection with Shae. But things had changed. He'd made it his mission to help those the Kincaids went after.

He was saved from having to search for answers when Angela emerged from the woods. Cradling Gracie in his arms, he stood, kissed her tangled hair. "Gracie, honey, I need you stay with Angela so I can go get Mommy. Okay?"

She eyed Angela with suspicion.

"You can trust her, Gracie. She's the one person I know will keep you safe." Tremors coursed through him as he handed Gracie into Angela's arms. "Please, Angela. Stay with her. Don't leave her with anyone else."

"You have my word, Mason." She hugged Gracie against her and rubbed a hand up and down her back. "I'll care for her like she's my own."

"Look who I found, Gracie." Mason reached into his pack, pulled out Mr. Cuddles and pressed him gently into Gracie's arms.

"You found him!" She hugged the stuffed bunny tight, her sobs reducing to sniffles. "Cassidy let me take him. But I dropped him on the grass when she put me in the car so Mommy would know."

"Oh, Gracie." Love poured through him. He kissed her head. "You are so smart and so brave. You're amazing, Gracie."

"Mommy says we have to stay calm and think in an emergency."

"Well, you certainly did. Your mommy is going to be so proud of you. I'm so proud of you."

She laid her head against him, her arms still wrapped around Angela's neck. Then she straightened up. "Can you go find Mommy now?"

"Yes, honey. I'm going right now." Turning away from her in that moment was one of the most difficult things he'd ever done. But Shae needed him, and he would not fail her. He resumed his trek through the woods, listening intently to catch up on where Zac's men were positioned. When he reached the clearing, he slid behind a tree and trained his binoculars on the woods surrounding the cabin. He leashed every ounce of control he possessed to keep from charging across the clearing and into that cabin. It was time to get his head in the game. "How many hostiles?"

"Six outside, one in." Zac's hushed voice in his ear brought reassurance. "Four around the perimeter, two on the front porch. Heat signatures inside show two people, one on their knees, one standing, both by the front door."

Urgency begged him not to wait any longer. "We have to move."

"Our people are about to intercept the four guarding the woods."

"Which leaves taking out the two on the porch—quietly."

"One for me, and one for you."

Mason stayed in the woods as he rounded the cabin, positioning himself slightly behind so he wouldn't be seen approaching, and waited for the signal that the four combatants in the woods had been removed. Zac's people were good. Even from Mason's position nearby, he didn't see or hear any sign of trouble. But now they had to move fast, before anyone looked for the missing guards.

Crossing the clearing would be the most dangerous part. If they were seen, he had no doubt Cassidy would kill Shae instantly. He shoved the thought aside—couldn't let it interfere.

"It's a go," Zac said.

Mason emerged from the woods and ran in a low crouch across the clearing, then placed his back against the rear wall of the cabin and took a breath. A quick glance showed Zac leaning against the wall at the far side. He signaled to Mason, and they each slipped around opposite sides of the cabin.

Mason crept forward, mindful of every step, every breath, moving as silently as any other predator roaming these woods.

When he reached the edge of the porch, he used a small mirror around the corner to check the positions of the guards. They stood on either end of the porch that ran the full width of the cabin, each cradling an automatic weapon. It was imperative he and Zac move together. They'd coordinated attacks before and could move almost as one.

"Go." Barely a whisper of sound, but all Mason needed.

He rounded the corner, vaulted the railing. The gunman must have sensed a presence, because he turned. His eyes went wide as he lifted the weapon. Mason took his shot, muffled by the silencer, then caught the guy and eased him soundlessly to the porch.

He stayed low, ducking beneath the window, held his breath. Listened. Nothing. He crept to the door while Zac attached an electronic surveillance device to the window and patched the sound through to Mason. An agent in a van at the end of the road would monitor and record the transmission for later evaluation, but in the meantime, it might provide Zac and Mason with an opening to enter and apprehend Cassidy without any further loss of life. Unfortunately, they'd had no choice but to kill the two guards on the porch, but the four in the woods had simply been rendered unconscious and would live to testify and pay for their crimes.

Shae's voice came through his earpiece, shaky but strong. "...the layout as best I can remember, but I don't recall how many devices were set or exactly where they were positioned."

Zac frowned at him.

Mason shrugged and shook his head once. He had no idea what they were talking about, but it didn't matter as long as Shae was all right. He studied the door—just one dead-bolt lock, as far as he could tell. Blinds across the front windows were closed, so he couldn't see in. But Cassidy couldn't see out, either, so he considered that a plus. Either way, they had to assume Cassidy had a weapon. But did she have it aimed at Shae?

He breathed in deeply and let it out, smooth and slow...waiting...waiting... Energy vibrated through him.

The image of Shae kneeling before Cassidy, terrified that her daughter was roaming the woods alone, in fear for her life, seared itself into his brain. "Victim is still kneeling. Suspect standing in front of her, arms at her sides."

Okay, good. That gave them the extra split second she would need to lift a weapon and aim it at Shae. A fraction of a second that would determine the rest of Shae's life, Gracie's life. His life. He didn't know how he and Shae were going to make things work between them, but he knew with every ounce of his being that he was going to try. The thought of losing her, of watching her die while he was helpless to stop it, was more than he could bear.

Okay, he could do this. As long as he put thoughts of Shae out of his mind. He'd done this many times as an FBI agent without so much as a hitch in his breathing or a spike in his heart rate. And this time, he was going through the door with Zac, his friend, a man he trusted with his life. Sweat slicked his hands, beaded at his temples.

Zac gestured two agents to move in with a battering ram.

This was it. He sucked in a breath, held it. *One...two... three—*

The door crashed open beneath the force of the ram.

Mason dived in, going low while Zac went high, and then he was in front of Shae, staring down Cassidy Monroe, his weapon held steady as he stood between Shae and danger. "Drop the weapon, Cassidy."

She froze, weapon half raised as if trying to decide if it was worth trying to escape. Her eyes flicked from side to side, taking in where Zac stood, weapon trained on her, then back to Mason.

"Don't do it, Cassidy." While anger surged through him at this woman who'd befriended Shae, her daughter, the agents she'd killed at the house—all of whom she'd betrayed—he didn't want to have to fire a fatal shot. "Lower the weapon. You can't escape. You know that, Cassidy."

He could feel Shae's presence behind him, sense her fear, but she remained perfectly still, absolutely silent.

"Drop it, Cassidy. Two of your men are already dead, and the other four are in custody. There's nowhere to go, no one to intervene. The cabin is surrounded." He had to get through to her, had to get her to give up without a fight. Had to find out what they'd been talking about. What devices? Did it have anything to do with the C-4 they'd confiscated? He lifted his weapon, firmed his stance. "Now, Cassidy. Drop it."

She must have sensed something in him, because she straightened, removed her finger from the trigger and raised her hands.

Zac moved in, cuffed her and hustled her outside.

The instant Zac had secured the suspect and no threat remained, Mason turned to Shae and held out a hand. "Are you okay?"

She grabbed his hand, surged to her feet and started toward the door. "Gracie!"

"It's okay, she's safe." He hooked her arm, turned her to face him and smoothed her hair back out of her face, cradling her cheeks between his hands. "She's safe, Shae. We have her. I found her walking down the road. She's with Angela now. Only Angela. She'll protect our daughter with her life. I promise."

"She's okay?" Tears spilled over her lashes, streamed with a mix of eye makeup down red, blotchy cheeks. And she'd never looked more beautiful. He closed his eyes, savoring the moment, pressed his forehead against hers. "She's not only fine, but an amazing, courageous, beautiful little girl."

"Mason?" Zac stood in the doorway. "I'm sorry to interrupt, but Cassidy's talking."

Chapter Eleven

Shae sat in the back of the surveillance van, listening to Zac's instructions for the third time while Mason seethed nearby. She knew he didn't want her to do this. So did everyone else in attendance, since he'd voiced his opinion quite...energetically.

"Just speak normally." Zac fiddled with some adjustment or another to make sure everything Regina Kincaid said was caught and recorded.

"Testing. One, two, three." She was going to do this. She had no choice. Well, that wasn't true. She *could* spend the rest of her life in hiding, praying every day that Gracie wouldn't be targeted again. Or she could put an end to this once and for all by confronting Regina Kincaid while wearing a wire. If she could get Regina to incriminate herself Zac's team could take her into custody. For now, they were working together with local law enforcement, but Zac had decided to leave the FBI out of the operation until they could figure out who else might be compromised and clean house.

Zac looked her in the eye, his scrutiny intense. "Are you sure, Shae?"

"Positive. I can do this." She hoped her voice held more conviction than she actually felt. Though she was determined to make this work, she wasn't all that confident in her ability to do so. She just hoped he didn't notice how badly she was shaking and terminate the operation.

He nodded and stepped back. "Okay. I'll be right back, and we'll get started."

Once Zac emerged from the van, leaving Shae and Mason alone, she turned to him. "I'm sorry, Mason. I know you don't think I'm doing the right thing, but I have to do this. I have to end this. Please try to understand."

"Ah, man, Shae." He sat on the bench across from her, gripped her hands in his. "It's not that I don't agree with you. In my head I know this is the right call, the only way to assure your and Gracie's safety. And if it was anyone else, I'd be all for it. It's my heart that's having a tough time. I just wish it wasn't you who had to go in. You know if I could, I would."

She squeezed his hands, pressed her lips against his knuckles. "I know, but I'm the only one who might be able to get a recorded confession. Cassidy's testimony might not be enough." If what Cassidy had shared was true, at least they didn't have to worry about Sebastian any longer. Apparently, Regina had had her brother killed, his body dumped in a lake, where police divers were currently searching for his remains.

"I know." He blew out a breath. "I know. But that doesn't mean I have to like it."

A smile tugged at her. She wanted so badly for this nightmare to end. She and Mason hadn't had time to talk after Cassidy gave up Regina's location, but she knew they needed to. One way or the other, they had to come to some kind of resolution, especially if he wanted to be a part of Gracie's life. *Gracie.* She lowered her gaze to their clasped hands.

The decision not to go to Gracie immediately after Mason had rescued her from the cabin had been heart-wrenching. But it wouldn't have been fair. Though Mason, Zac and his agents would make this operation run as smoothly and safely as possible, there was still an element of danger involved.

There was always the chance Regina would kill her on sight, which was, hopefully, minimized by the fact that Shae had information the wannabe crime boss needed. And there was a risk she'd discover the wire, in which case she'd kill Shae, but at least she'd be taken into custody immediately after and charged with murder, so Gracie would be safe. Either way, Shae didn't think it was fair to go to Gracie, make her think that things were over and Shae would stay with her, and then turn around and walk back out again.

She leaned her head back against the side of the van. Plus, if Gracie had begged her not to go, what would she have done? She wouldn't have been able to say no, would have stayed despite the lives her decision might cost...

Her thoughts stuttered to a stop. Weren't those the exact same reasons Mason had given for why he'd left without saying goodbye six years ago? *Ah, man...* "Mason?"

"Yeah."

"I'm so sorry."

"Sorry?" He frowned. "For what?"

"I forgave you long ago for leaving me, but until this moment, I didn't fully understand how you could have done so. And now I do."

"Shae..."

"It's okay. I don't know where things will go from here if we make it through the next few hours, but I know I want you to be a part of our lives. In whatever capacity you're able to make work. If that's what you want..."

As he opened his mouth, the door swung open. Zac stood in the doorway. "It's time, Shae."

She inhaled deeply, blew it out slowly and stood. "I'm ready."

Mason massaged her shoulders. "You remember what to do and say?"

"Yes." It wasn't like this was the first time she'd worn a wire. But still, the reminder comforted her.

"Speak clearly but not too loud, or it will alert her that you're wearing a wire." He handed her the weapon Cassidy had been holding at the cabin. "The microphone is sensitive enough to easily pick up your voice."

"Got it." She tucked the weapon into her waistband. Thankfully, Mason didn't try to stop her as she stalked across the parking lot toward the motel room Cassidy had indicated. If he had, there was a good chance she'd have backed out.

When she reached the door, she barely resisted the urge to look over her shoulder and assure herself Mason and the other agents were in place. But Mason and Zac had both drilled it into her head. *Walk straight across the lot, determined but wary. Do not look over your shoulder and give the operation away.*

She lifted a hand, fisted it and knocked on the door.

"Who is it?"

"Shae...uh, I mean, Avery Bennett." Funny, she'd only been Shae Evans for six years, yet that was the name that felt more comfortable. Was that what it was like for Mason when going undercover? "I need to talk to you. Now."

Silence. Well, at least she hadn't shot her though the door.

"Cassidy and her men are..." She looked around then as if making sure no one would overhear her, in case Regina was looking through the peephole. She injected a pleading note into her tone, letting her desperation show. "Out of the picture. I just want to talk. Please."

Regina cracked the door open, surveyed the area, then stepped back and gestured Shae in with her pistol and slammed the door behind her. "What are you talking about, out of the picture?"

"I...lost my cool when they tossed my five-year-old daughter out of the cabin in the middle of the woods by herself." She allowed her voice to rise, allowed her rage to show. It was no act. "I was willing to give you what you wanted to keep my child safe, but that witch not only betrayed me, but she didn't even give Gracie a chance. All I asked was that she drop her off somewhere safe, and I would have given you anything."

Shae sucked in a few deep breaths, struggled to contain her anger. She massaged the bridge of her nose between a thumb and forefinger, then lifted her hands in the air. "Okay. Full disclosure. I have Cassidy's weapon in my waistband. I'm not gonna lie, I thought about just coming here and shooting you after Cassidy told me where to find you—"

"There's no way Cassidy ratted me out." Regina took the weapon from Shae, placed it on a nearby table, then patted her down for more weapons and came up empty. Thankfully, she didn't notice the tiny recording device disguised as a button on her blouse.

"Yeah, well, she was mighty chatty when she thought I was going to be dead shortly. How else would I have known you'd be alone here, not surrounded by protection because you don't even trust your own people?" Shae shrugged as if it didn't matter. "Either way, all I care about is Gracie. I want my daughter safe. I don't want to spend the rest of my life looking over my shoulder, wondering where the next attack will come from."

The younger woman tilted her head, studied Shae. "So why not just kill me?"

"Because then I have to worry about retaliation from your brother."

Regina simply nodded.

When Shae's chin started to tremble, she didn't bother to firm it. She let the tears leak from her eyes, showed how vulnerable she was. "Please, Regina. All I want to do is get my daughter and go back home. I want to live in peace with her. Please. I'll do whatever it takes to make that happen."

She tilted her head, narrowed her eyes. "Even if that means helping me take out the Pescis?"

Nausea turned Shae's stomach, even though she knew that wasn't going to happen. "Sure. That's on you, not me."

"And what's to keep you from going to the police?"

"The police can't protect us. You think I haven't learned that lesson yet?"

A slow smile spread. "That's right, and don't you forget that. My reach is far and wide."

Shae nodded and lowered her head, no longer vulnerable but defeated.

"I'll accept your terms. You give me the information I want, and I give you my word you and your daughter will remain safe." Regina grinned, her eyes lighting with pure evil. "As long as my New Year's Eve plan goes off without any interference from the law."

"Fair enough. And you'll be able to keep Sebastian from coming after me as well?" If she could get her to admit to his murder, this would end right now.

"Sebastian won't be a problem."

It had been a long shot, hoping she'd boast that she'd ordered her brother's murder, but Shae was still disappointed when she didn't elaborate. "Can you pull up a blueprint of the target, or do I need to draw it out?"

"You'll draw out the diagram, mark where each of the devices should be placed for maximum carnage. If I believe you're telling me the truth, I'll pull up a blueprint and you'll show me the access points into the building and the security we need to evade."

Shae pulled out a chair and sat at the small round table. "I'll need a pen and paper."

Still keeping the weapon aimed at Shae, the younger woman dug through a briefcase and came up with a legal pad and pen, then sat across from her, weapon resting on the table, and slid them across to her.

"Can I ask you something?" Shae lifted the pen, her hand shaking so badly she was afraid she might drop it, and started to sketch an outline of the building where the Pescis hosted their annual New Year's Eve party. "Why are you doing this?

Why bother killing the Pescis when you will soon have control of the more powerful family anyway?"

She laughed out loud, tossed her hair. "I'm going to kill the Pescis because they're a threat. I've neutralized every threat I've ever faced—and that includes Sebastian."

Shae didn't hesitate when the door banged open. She simply tipped her chair and let herself fall, landing hard on her shoulder.

"Police! Freeze!"

Regina lunged to her feet, lifted her weapon toward Shae. "You—"

Mason's shot took her in the shoulder, and her weapon clattered to the floor.

A beehive of activity carried on around her, but Shae paid attention to none of it, her full focus on Mason as he helped her up.

"Are you hurt?"

"No. I'm okay." Though her shoulder would no doubt ache tomorrow, along with her chest and, well, pretty much everything.

"Shae." A small chuckle emerged, and Mason shook his head. "This is so not the time for this, and yet, somehow strangely appropriate."

She frowned, unsure what he was talking about.

He cradled her face between his hands in a gesture that had always brought comfort and that soothed now.

She tilted her cheek into his hand, let his warmth seep through her.

"I love you, Shae. With everything in me, with all my heart, and I don't want to live another minute without you." He eased her close, pressed his lips to hers, then leaned back just enough to look into her eyes. "I love you, and I love Gracie. I don't know the logistics of it all yet..."

Leave it to Mason to make starting a life together sound like a carefully planned field operation.

"But I know I want the three of us to be together."

Joy filled her, and she threw her arms around his neck. "Oh, Mason. I love you, too. I never stopped."

"She's here, Mason," Zac called from the doorway.

He wrapped an arm around Shae's shoulders, kissed her temple. "Come on. Gracie's waiting."

"She's here? You brought her here?" They were going to have to set some ground rules. One—don't take Gracie to crime scenes. But she laughed, unbelievably happy. Not only was this years-long ordeal finally over, and Gracie and Shae both finally out of danger, but Mason was back in her life—their lives—as well. A better outcome than she ever could have dreamed of.

Together, they crossed the parking lot to the diner across the street. When they rounded the back of the building, she spotted Gracie anxiously shifting back and forth beside Angela.

The instant she spotted Shae, she screamed, "Mommy," barreled across the lot and launched herself into Shae's arms.

"Oh, baby." Shae hugged Gracie tight. She might never let go. "I love you, baby. I love you so much."

Mason wrapped them both in his embrace.

Gracie lifted her head and looked back and forth between Shae and Mason. "Can we go home now?"

The realization they could return to the life they'd built in Boggy Meadows hit her. "Yes, baby. Come on. Let's go home."

Epilogue

Mason hefted the wiggling ball of golden fur into his arms and slammed the car door shut. Though he and Shae had talked about getting Gracie a puppy after Storm had gone back to his handler, the past year had been filled with one thing after another, both good and bad. They'd yet to talk much past the initial idea.

He scratched the puppy's head. "You be a good boy, now, ya hear? Don't go getting me in trouble."

The puppy wagged his whole back end, hopefully in agreement or possibly just itching to escape Mason's grasp and find some kind of trouble.

He shifted his bundle under his arm so he could dig out his key. Sometimes he still couldn't believe Shae and Gracie were a permanent part of his life. Even now, four months after he and Shae had gotten married in a small ceremony with Gracie between them, and Zac, Angela, Reva and Katie in attendance, there were plenty of nights he still woke terrified they'd be taken from him. But, over time, the nightmares would lessen. He hoped.

"Here we go, boy." He sucked in a deep breath, braced himself and pushed the front door open. "Shae? Gracie?"

Silence greeted him.

He forced back the momentary panic, tamped down the surge of terror and reminded himself there was no longer any reason to fear for their safety. As of today. He tossed his keys on the tray in the foyer. "I'm home, guys. Anyone here?"

Gracie's laughter skittered down the hallway, and he followed the sound through the small house to the backyard. They'd settled back in Boggy Meadows, with Mason working for Jameson Investigations behind the scenes rather than in the field, but they'd sold the house where Shae and Gracie had been attacked. They'd bought a new one together, a four-bedroom ranch with an office where Shae could still work from home and a big yard for Gracie to run around in.

He slid the back door open, then leaned a shoulder against the doorjamb and petted the puppy's head as he watched Gracie squeal while Shae pushed her on a swing.

The instant Gracie spotted him, she let go of the chains and swung off, landing perfectly and giving Mason a small heart attack. "Mommy, Daddy's home!"

Even after a year to get used to it, those words still had the power to drive him to his knees. He'd found his faith again, and he thanked God every night for bringing Shae and Gracie into his life.

"And he brought a puppy!" She bolted across the lawn and held her arms open. "Can I hold him?"

"Sure thing, baby girl." He handed the puppy over.

"Whose is he?" She nuzzled him against her cheek.

He glanced at Shae, who'd come up behind Gracie and stood with a huge smile on her face. He put his arm around her shoulders, pulled her close so he could kiss her temple, then whispered, "It's done."

Shae went still, and he simply smiled, then said to their daughter, "He's yours, Gracie."

"Ahh!" She set the puppy down, then flung her arms around his and Shae's legs. "Thank you, thank you, thank you."

He couldn't help but laugh. "You're welcome, honey."

And then she was off, running laps with the puppy around the fenced yard. "We talked about getting a puppy but never fully decided when…"

"He's perfect, Mason." She wrapped both arms around his waist. "Is it really over?"

"Yes. Regina was convicted today. They got her on first-degree murder in Sebastian's death and conspiracy to commit murder for the Pesci plan." Cassidy was already serving time in federal prison, a reduced but heavy sentence in exchange for her testimony against Regina.

Shae leaned into him, and he took the moment to savor having her close, watching Gracie and the puppy run and play together. Then she looked up. "I think I took the addition of the puppy very well, don't you?"

"Yes." He frowned. Not sure where she was going with this, since she'd technically already agreed to the puppy, if not the timing.

"Well, now it's your turn." A smile played at the corner of her mouth.

"What do you mean?"

"Seems a puppy won't be the only addition to our family today."

"Wha…" Everything in him went still. "Are you saying what I think you're saying?"

"Yes, Mason. You're going to be a dad again."

Emotions poured through him, and love swamped him, threatened to drown him. He pulled Shae into his arms, lifted her off the ground and swung her around, then thought better of it and lowered her gently. "I'm sorry. Was that okay?"

Her laughter filled him with joy as she flipped her long hair behind her shoulder and looked up at him from beneath her lashes. "It was fine. I'm not that fragile."

"No, you're not fragile at all. In fact, you're one of the strongest women I know. It's one of the things I love most about you. But, that said…" He guided her toward a lounge chair. "You should sit and rest."

"I don't need to rest."

He sat on the edge of the chair beside her leg and clutched her hand. "What do you need? Because I'm going to be here this time, Shae, and I am going to take care of you, and spoil you, and—"

"I don't need to be spoiled, I just need you to love me."

"I do, Shae. I love you, and Gracie, and our new baby…" The thought brought so much joy he was practically lightheaded. "With every last bit of my heart."

* * * * *

Romantic Suspense

Danger. Passion. Drama.

Available Next Month

Colton's K-9 Rescue Colleen Thompson
Alaskan Disappearance Karen Whiddon

Stranded Jennifer D. Bokal
Bodyguard Rancher Kacy Cross

LOVE INSPIRED

Christmas K-9 Guardians Lenora Worth & Katy Lee
Deadly Christmas Inheritance Jessica R. Patch

LOVE INSPIRED

Christmas Cold Case Maggie K. Black
Taken At Christmas Jodie Bailey

LOVE INSPIRED

Dangerous Christmas Investigation Virginia Vaughan
Colorado Christmas Survival Cate Nolan

Available from Big W and selected bookstores.
OR call 1300 659 500 (AU), 0800 265 546 (NZ) to order.

Visit **millsandboon.com.au**

This Christmas, could the cowboy from her past unlock the key to her future?

Don't miss this brand-new Four Corners Ranch novel from *New York Times* bestselling author

MAISEY YATES

In-store and online November 2024.

MILLS & BOON

millsandboon.com.au